# Dreamcatcher

# Dreamcatcher

## *Dead End Justice*

## Vanessa Gant

authorHOUSE®

*AuthorHouse™*
*1663 Liberty Drive*
*Bloomington, IN 47403*
*www.authorhouse.com*
*Phone: 1-800-839-8640*

*First published by AuthorHouse    08/25/2011*

*ISBN: 978-1-4567-9908-3 (sc)*
*ISBN: 978-1-4567-9909-0 (ebk)*

*Library of Congress Control Number: 2011915725*

*Printed in the United States of America*

*Any people depicted in stock imagery provided by Thinkstock are models, and such images are being used for illustrative purposes only.*
*Certain stock imagery © Thinkstock.*

*This book is printed on acid-free paper.*

Dedicated to my amazing, spectacular, sensational husband, who will always be my superhero.

I would like to say that I'm normal. I'd like to say that I had a wonderful childhood with two loving parents, a dog named Lucky, and a cute little home on a hill that resembled a dollhouse. I would like to say that I'm a normal teenager in high school doing normal teenage stuff like going to home football games or dressing up like a princess and going to a school dance with my boyfriend. Yeah, I would like to say that I am normal, but I'm not. I'm anything but normal. Shit, I wasn't normal even *before* I became a superhero.

My childhood would have been great if we weren't the weird rich people in a small town with a huge mansion (not really a "cute little home.") When you live in a small farm town three hours outside of Chicago where everyone else makes under $50,000 a year, it's always been easy for them to talk about us behind our backs. There have been many rumors such as the mob, drug dealers, assassins, and my favorite, aliens. I'd like to go into more detail of how lame the town I live in is, but this is supposed to be just an introductory page so I'll add more about my town later.

We didn't ever have a dog named Lucky, or cat for that matter, because I'm allergic to both. I couldn't have a bunny or ferret because they're too messy. No lizard or snake because they're too creepy. So, I've always had fish. My first pet ever was a goldfish named Taco (my father had had fish tacos for lunch before taking me to the pet store) who lived for three hours. I didn't know at the time that fish couldn't breathe out of water. Now Charlie takes care of the expensive fish in my aquarium.

High school, well it sucks. Do I have to say more? Okay, I apparently have to say more. School was never my cup of tea, I mean sure I got decent enough grades and everything but I went because I had to. Most rich kids get home-schooled; I wasn't that lucky. I never was social in school; not even in elementary school. I was always the weird rich girl who had issues. The teachers themselves would talk about me when they thought I wasn't listening. "Therapy Thursday," they'd whisper on days I'd have to skip recess to visit with my shrink. All of the kids made fun of me and thought it was unfair that I always had special treatment because of who I was and who my parents were. All I wanted was to be invisible, get through high school unnoticed. That didn't work out too well.

And the "loving parents" part? Well, it was true while I actually *had* parents. They died when I was four. Some guy shot them. I'm a typical Bruce Wayne charity case, without all of the cool gadgets; not that I really need the cool gadgets. My uncle took me in and raised me, although he really wasn't the best at it. He was gone a lot either at work or out of town for work, which left me alone with the maid, Cindy, and the butler, Charlie (he goes by Charles, but he lets me called him Charlie.) As I got older, I'd leave the mansion and go into town by myself. I'd go to the movies or go shopping and my uncle wouldn't even know. Not that he would care if he *did* know.

Well that's about it. You now know a brief introduction of myself. Don't worry, I'll go into a lot more detail about everything. Oh yeah, I forgot to say who I am. My name is Avery Kendall, age 15. When I'm not busy being the weird, quiet, comic book-reading, ice cream shop cashier/ sophomore at Franklin Grove High School, I kick ass and take names. I know that's not very original, but I couldn't think of anything else to say. I am a crime fighter, and inspire peace and justice. I am the avenger of my parents. I am Dreamcatcher.

# PROLOGUE

# Kings and Queens

*"The age of man is over. A darkness comes and all these lessons that we've learned here have only just begun."*

-"Kings and Queens" by 30 Seconds to Mars

The Beginning of the Beginning

Both of my parents had kept journals of their lives; personal events and work accomplishments. After they died, I found most of their journals in the locked part of their lab, a place where only I had access to. I learned of how they met and what I was like as a young child. This is their story.

Ann-Marie Circa was born in Kansas City, Missouri in 1971. She was a very outspoken Italian child with no siblings. Her parents had divorced when she was very young, her mother raised her while working three jobs. Ann-Marie lost contact with her father shortly after she started middle school when her father moved to California and remarried. She became a difficult child to raise since she was always in trouble at school for getting into fights or talking back to her teachers. Social services took her away after Ann-Marie's mother was caught with marijuana and cocaine in the house. She jumped from foster house to foster house, eventually winding up in Chicago. Once she turned eighteen, she rented her own apartment and lived on her own. She received enough scholarships to go to a decent college. She chose to attend University of Illinois although didn't know what she wanted to go for.

Meanwhile . . . .

Joseph Kendall was born in Boston, Massachusetts in the same year as Ann-Marie. His parents were very rich, and he had two siblings; an older brother named Ross and a younger sister named Beth. Beth was diagnosed with leukemia when she was seven and passed away when she was thirteen, Joseph's senior year of high school, and Ross's second year into college. Joseph had been wanting to study archeology but changed it to become a scientist. He wanted to find cures to help people like his sister. His parents of course wanted him to go to Harvard like his brother, but Joseph wanted to go somewhere new, where he'd have to make all new friends. He wanted the full college experience, not the ivy league crap his family pushed on him. So he chose University of Illinois.

Ann-Marie had finished her general education classes and received her bachelors degree, still not sure what she wanted to get her masters in. School was about to start in a couple months and she would have to have her classes set up according to her degree. But it was summer vacation and all Ann-Marie cared about was getting a tan, working as much as she could to save up some money, and spending time with her on-again-off-again boyfriend, Chase. She was on a double date with Chase and two of their friends at Navy Pier. After they got off the huge ferris wheel, they decided to play a round of miniature golf. A couple behind Ann-Marie's group was making out on the bench while they waited their turn. Ann-Marie rolled her eyes and swung the putter, making the ball roll over the two hills and land right into the hole. Ann-Marie pumped her fist in the air and then flipped her hair behind her shoulder with sass.

The couple behind her stopped kissing when Chase yelled out, "that's my girl!" The boy stood up to putt while his make-out buddy fixed her hair. Ann-Marie watched as the brown-haired, polo-wearing boy took his turn. He looked up at Ann-Marie as she quickly looked away.

"Ann," Chase touched her arm. "Come on, it's your turn."

Ann-Marie looked back at the polo guy and he was still looking at her, although he was standing behind his girl, his arms on hers, helping her swing her golf club.

"Whoa, that guy is totally eying you," Sandra whispering as Ann-Marie went to hit the ball, making her miss the ball completely.

"That counts as one," Chase laughed.

"Sorry, I know," Ann-Marie smiled at him. She quickly turned to Sandra and mouthed the words, *I know!*

Joseph was on a date with this girl named Jessica. He had met her at the coffee shop by his apartment. She was lightly dancing behind the cash register to Madonna. Even with her blonde teased hair, you still couldn't miss the huge bangle earrings. She was wearing a very short skirt with leggings and her uniform shirt was unbuttoned halfway, showing off her black bra. Joseph forgot what he wanted from the menu and cut right to the chase.

"What's your name?" he asked.

The girl pointed at her name tag. "What can I get you, sir?"

"My name is Joey. How come I've never seen you working in here? I came here every morning when school was in."

"I'm new for the summer. Now, what can I get you?"

"My usual," he smiled.

"Which is what? I told you, I'm new."

"Well, you'll have to remember what my usual is so you won't have to ask from now on."

"Look, Joey. There's a line forming behind you. Either order a drink or move so someone else can."

"My usual is a tall caramel macchiato."

"Okay, thank you. So I have one-"

"But since it is summer, I'll have a caramel frappuccino."

Jessica sighed a heavy sigh.

"Okay, thank you. I'll have your total when the drink is ready. Next!"

A red-headed lady stepped up to the cashier.

"Yes, I would just like a espresso frappuccino, please," she ordered.

"Will you go out with me this weekend?" Joe asked Jessica.

"Seriously?" She put her hand on her hip.

"Well, yeah."

"No."

"Oh, you have a boyfriend."

"No-I mean yeah. Sort of."

"You have a girlfriend then?"

The man at the counter looked from Joe to Jessica.

"No, I don't have either. But I'm not going out with you."

"Why not?" Joe asked.

"Because . . . you're not my type."

"I'm everyone's type."

Jessica scoffed and slammed his drink on the counter.

"Your total is four dollars."

"What if I give you ten? Then will you go out with me?" Joe smiled.

"You're going to pay me to go out with you?" Jessica asked.

"No, but I would like to pay for this young lady's drink since I held up the line so long."

The older lady with the red hair smiled at him.

"In fact, everyone's coffee and pastries are on me!"

After the line cleared up and Joe had stayed around to pay his $65.42 bill, he hopped up and sat on the counter.

"So, you paid for everyone's drink just to go out with me?"

"Well, I just wanted to show you how nice of a guy I am."

She looked at him a moment before smiling.

"I get off at three tomorrow. I'll meet you here."

Joe walked out of the coffee shop with a smile on his face, a smile that lasted all the way to work, which was at a clothing store.

"Thank you everyone for playing along with me, we're going on a date tomorrow night!"

Everyone working in the store clapped for him.

"You're quite welcome Joseph," said Mindy, the red-haired lady, who happened to be his boss. "But I'm not helping you out anymore until you take me on a date."

"You know I would love to take out a beauty like you but I'd rather not be killed by your husband."

Mindy giggled and went back to folding shirts.

"You all owe me back the money I spent on your damn coffee!" Joe laughed. "I am, after all, a poor college kid."

Now, on this date with a girl he had wanted so badly, all he could think about was the tan girl with the long black hair and nice butt in the cut-off shorts. She turned and faced his direction to putt and OH MY GOD, she was wearing a Billy Idol shirt! Joe loved Billy Idol. Jessica was another Madonna clone, like every other girl he knew. She wore the black lace gloves, the 50 bracelets on each arm, the big teased hair with a big bow in it, and the bright lipstick that matched her god-awful high heels. Billy Idol girl didn't have bright lipstick or 50 bracelets on. Her hair wasn't teased and wasn't wearing heels to play golf in. Joe thought he'd lose his mind if he couldn't get this girl's attention.

"Okay, so I just have to hit the ball and get it in the hole, right?" Jessica asked sweetly. Meanwhile, Billy Idol girl had just made her ball in the hole in two turns. Joe watched as Jessica violently whacked at her ball, missing or knocking it off the sides of the course.

"Here, let me show you," Joe sighed and got behind her. He wrapped his arms around her and held onto her hands, guiding the putter gently. Jessica giggled and he smiled politely, but the smile

5

faded when he looked up at Billy Idol girl and she was rolling her eyes at him.

"Okay," Joe said, patting Jessica on the shoulder. "You try."

"Ann, come on," Chase pleaded while his friend putted. "Why do you have to be so friggin' difficult?"

"*I'm* the one being difficult? I have to work in the morning, so I don't want to stay up and drink all night."

"You don't have to drink if you don't want to."

"But I'd still have to stay up late because you want me to drive you there."

The same old argument. All Chase wanted to do was drink until five in the morning and Ann-Marie had to go to work. There had been many times already that Chase had kept her up too late with partying and it had affected her at her job. When was he going to grow out of this drinking and smoking pot and acting like an idiot all the time? Maybe a drink every once in a while but every other night? It was getting to be too much for her.

"Whatever, Chase. I'm going to go get a soda from the vending machine."

"Fine, whatever."

Ann-Marie turned to walk away.

"Hey, baby," Chase said. "Will you get me one too?"

She sighed and nodded. She hated it when he called her baby, especially in public.

She walked over to the vending machine, wanting to walk past it and get in her car, leaving her boyfriend to find his own way to the party he wanted so badly to go to. She loved her car, mainly because she had bought it with the money that she had earned and saved on her own. But at the same time she loathed having a car because if she didn't have one, Chase would have to find another chauffeur which means she could have a more exciting life, besides parties. Ann-Marie put the quarters in the machine, pressed the buttons for the soda she wanted, and *ker plunk!* Two cans of soda dropped to the bottom. She bent down to pick them up and turned around.

"I love him!"

Ann-Marie jumped at the guy who was standing there. The polo guy that was with the Barbie girl.

"What?" Ann asked.

"Billy," he said, pointing to her shirt. "He's awesome."

"Yeah," she said awkwardly.

"Have you seen him in concert before? I bet he'd be great."

"Not yet," Ann looked around anxiously. "But yeah, I'm sure he'd be great. Listen, I've got to get back to my friends and my boyfriend. They're probably waiting on me."

"That guy is your boyfriend? Why?"

"Ugh, excuse me? That was kind of rude."

"I'm sorry, but I'd think a girl as pretty as you could do a lot better than that."

"Oh really? How do you know there *is* something better than that for me out there? I figure all the other guys in the world are too busy chasing girls that look like your Material Girl Barbie. You obviously did or you wouldn't be with her."

"I'm not *with* anyone. Not at the moment at least."

"Oh, I can't stand guys like you."

"Like me? You don't even know me," he smiled.

"Guys who flirt and flash money at girls to get with them so they can put another point on their score card. Just because you have money, or should I say, just because your parents have money or a big house doesn't mean you can get every girl you come across in life. It doesn't work that way for most girls."

"I have my own job, thank you. And I use money from my job to pay for school and my apartment."

"Well that's surprising. But slightly impressive for a preppy boy like you. Let me guess, you work at the Gap?"

"No, I work in the men's area at Macy's."

"Ah, fancy. Look, it was nice to meet you but I need to be going."

"My name is Joseph, or Joe if you want. Just not Joey. I can't stand when people call me that."

"Okay, well bye Joe," Ann-Marie smiled and walked off.

"Hey! What about your name?"

She stopped briefly and said, "Call me Billy."

Ann-Marie walked back to her group, who was putting up their putters and getting ready to leave. She looked back over at the course where she saw Joe smiling and walking back to his date. Ann-Marie smiled to herself and handed Chase his soda.

*Wow*, was all Joe could think. *Wow, what a cool girl. She just came right out and told me what exactly she thought of me.* He couldn't get her out of his mind nor could he put much effort into the date he was on now. Joe explained that he wasn't feeling good and would have to take Jessica back without going out for dinner. He pulled up in front of the coffee shop and smiled at her.

"Well tonight was fun."

"You're not going to walk me to my car?" She batted her eyes. "You don't want someone to get me, do you?"

*Her eyelashes are probably fake*, Joe thought. *Billy's' eyelashes were long and beautiful too but real, unlike Jessica's.*

"Uh, sure. I'll walk you to your car."

They got out and walked to the parking lot in the back of the shop where there was one car sitting by itself.

"Okay, well have a nice night," Joe said quickly.

"Wait, Joe, there's something I want to give you."

He stood there and watched as Jessica leaned in and kissed him. First she gave him a couple of small pecks that led into longer passionate ones. All Joe could think about was the other girl, and the fact that Jessica's tongue tasted like bubble gum and cigarettes. Two things he didn't like. He pulled away.

"Thank you . . . for that . . . okay, um, goodnight."

"You could come back to my place if you'd like."

*What was this girl's deal?*

"I told you, I'm really starting to feel sick," he lied, although the taste of the cigarettes had been gross enough to make him sick.

"That's okay, I'll take care of you," she said, reaching for his crotch.

*She really wasn't taking a gentle hint.*

"If you come over, I'll give you free coffee every time you come into the store."

Joe walked away, not being able to take it anymore. All he wanted was to go home, brush his teeth, and listen to Billy Idol.

The first day of school. Ann-Marie couldn't have been happier. The rest of the summer had been awful. Her car had broke down, and the cost to repair it was too much. She sold it for parts and bought a bicycle. It was more healthy for her and the environment anyways. Then, her best friend, Sandra, died of a brain aneurism in the middle of the night, which devastated Ann. Finally, she broke up with Chase after he was sent to jail for getting into a fight at a bar. The only good thing that came out of the summer was that she knew what she wanted to go to school for. She was going to become a neuroscientist and study the brain. Sandra had been the inspiration for her decision. She knew the medical courses were going to be hard and expensive, but she finally felt like she had found her calling. So now, walking into her first class of the day, she felt great.

"Billy? You have got to be shitting me!"

Polo boy from the golf course was sitting at a desk no more than three feet from where she was standing. He got up and walked over to her. Ann-Marie started fumbling around trying to get her class schedule out, dropping her books.

"Here, I'll get those for you," he said bending down.

Ann-Marie found the paper that she was looking for and read through it.

"I must be in the wrong class," she muttered looking around.

"This is Advanced Anatomy, and here are your books. I don't know if you remember me-"

"Yeah, I remember you. It's John or something, right?"

She *had* remembered Joe's name, but didn't want to seem so eager to please him.

"Close enough, it's Joe. I can't believe we go to the same school! Plus, we're even enrolled in the same class? How crazy is that?"

"Pretty crazy."

"Class," the professor interrupted. "Please find any seat and we'll get started."

Ann-Marie looked around desperately for an open seat. There was only one left. She took her seat next to Joe's and scooted her chair away from him.

"Welcome to Advanced Anatomy. Look at the person next to you. Introduce yourself to them because they're going to be your lab partner for the semester."

Joe smiled at her and held his hand out.

"My name is Joe Kendall, what's your's?" he asked.

She looked at his hand, then at his face. Without smiling or reaching her own hand out, she muttered, "Ann-Marie Circa."

The first few assignments went by with little to no talking between the two, and when someone did talk, it was always Joe. Ann-Marie would have to occasionally roll her eyes or tell him to focus on their work whenever he'd goof around to impress her. On the fourth lab assignment, however, Joe finally got Ann-Marie to talk to him. Sort of.

"I bought us drinks to get us through the work," Joe said as he slid a glass Coke bottle across the table to Ann, whose eyes were glued to her work.

"Where did you find Coke in glass bottles?"

"This little hole-in-the-wall grocery store I shop at."

"Oh," she muttered. "Thanks."

"Welcome. So, how's your boyfriend doing?" he asked.

"What boyfriend?" Ann-Marie responded, not taking her eyes off of the paper she was working on.

"Oh, I assumed that guy you were with at the golf course was your boyfriend. So, was it just a one-time date thing?"

"No, he was my boyfriend. We broke up."

"Really?"

Ann-Marie looked up to see Joe's cheesy smile.

"Yeah, thanks. And your girlfriend? How is she doing?"

"That girl was not my girlfriend, trust me. I was thinking about you the whole time I was with her."

"Ugh! You're such a pig. That poor girl-"

"Poor girl my ass! She was crazy! She tried violating me because she was so desperate! I'm a victim."

"Oh please," Ann-Marie scoffed, going back to her paper.

"I wish I would've known you were single."

"Why's that?"

"So I could've asked you out before now."

"Do you honestly think I am in any way interested in you?"

"Yes."

Ann slapped her text book shut and picked up her papers. As she stood up and grabbed her books, the now empty bottle shot onto the floor and broke. Ann-Marie bent down hurriedly to pick up the glass pieces.

"Shit," she said grabbing her hand. The palm of her left hand was cut open.

"Oh crap!" Joe got up and grabbed her hand. He took off his shirt and wrapped the wound tight.

"We should get you to a hospital," he sounded anxious and wouldn't let go of her hand.

"No, it's not that bad. I don't think I'll need stitches or anything."

"Well my apartment isn't too far from here. I have medicine."

Ann looked at him, thought about pulling her hand away from him, but nodded slowly instead.

At Joe's apartment, Ann-Marie was sitting on the couch with new bandaging and ointment on her hand and a third beer in her other hand. Joe was in a chair next to her also drinking a beer.

"Sorry I didn't have anything else to drink."

"It's okay," Ann smiled. "I'm not too shocked to see a college guy with only beer and frozen pizzas in the kitchen."

"Actually, I need to go grocery shopping. I just haven't had time with all of my school and job stuff going on. I've been eating out a lot and picking at the junk food around here. I eat pretty healthy for the most part."

"I don't know if it's the loss of blood or because I haven't drank in a while, but these beers are starting to get to me."

"You could stay here tonight if you want."

"No way, sir."

"Don't you trust me by now?"

"I don't trust anyone."

"Not even your parents?"

"What parents? I've been in and out of foster homes since I was little. I don't speak to either of my parents. Hell, I don't even know if they're still alive."

"I don't really speak much to my parents either. They wanted me to go to a better-well, I mean, a bigger school—and I didn't want to. They made fun of me when I told them I was working in a clothing store to help pay for school. My dad put $10,000 in my bank account and I haven't even touched it. My brother takes everything he can get from them without working hard for any of it. And he never appreciates what they do."

"I think it's really cool that you don't take your parents for granted like that. I respect that."

Joe reached into his back pocket and pulled out two tickets.

"I know you said you wouldn't go out with me, but I bought these hoping you would. I still want you to go, even if it's just as friends."

Ann's eyes widened as she read the tickets.

"Billy Idol!" she squealed. "You got front row tickets to see Billy Idol?"

He nodded and smiled.

"Yes! I will definitely go with you!" she wrapped her arms around him. She felt something sort of do a flip inside of her. Her heart started beating fast. Joe smelled really nice and he was warm and soft. With her arms still around his neck she looked at him briefly before kissing him. She could feel him smiling and she smiled too.

Over the next few months or so, the two of them became inseparable. They had a blast at the concert and were doing really well in their classes. Joe invited Ann-Marie to spend time with his family during Christmas vacation although she was reluctant.

"What if they don't like me?" she asked him while they were laying in Joe's bed one night.

"Are you kidding? They're going to love you, just like I do," Joe kissed her forehead.

"I don't have anything nice to wear though. All I own are like shirts and jeans."

"That's fine. I want you to wear shirts and jeans, because that's who you are. Although, I wouldn't mind you going around without a shirt and jeans."

Ann grabbed her pillow and hit Joe on the head with it.

"Sorry," he laughed.

"Good," she giggled.

"I promise, it'll be great. We'll do a lot of stuff with the family and when we have some down time we'll do stuff just us two. It will be a fun week, I promise."

"Fine. But we're not going to tell them we're engaged until right before we leave so we don't have to deal with that for a week."

"Deal with what? They'll be happy."

"Joe, we made a deal. No wedding talk until the end of the week."

"Okay, okay. But we are going to tell them still, right?"

"Yes, at the end of the week."

"Good."

Ann-Marie smiled at Joe and hit him on the head with the pillow again.

"That's it, now you're going to get it!"

Joe started tickling her and laughed as she started hysterically giggling. They settled down and turned the lights off to go to sleep. As Ann fell asleep in Joe's arms, he laid awake thinking. He had done the best he could to convince Ann that things would be fine with his family, he just needed to convince himself the same thing. He was worried to death that they weren't going to like her. She might be too simple for them. They wouldn't understand the way she made him feel. He and Ann-Marie had had a mutual discussion about getting married. He hadn't given her a ring yet or even properly proposed. He was planning on doing it in front of his family on Christmas morning. Ann might not like that idea but Joe figured his parents wouldn't cause a scene in front of other relatives and it would become more of a celebration than a disappointment.

They landed in Boston on Monday around noon and drove a rental car to his parents'. Ann looked around the neighborhood as the houses began to get bigger and bigger. She was hoping he'd stop any second before they got any bigger and when they finally turned down a long driveway that led up to one of the biggest houses on the block. Although she didn't notice herself doing it, Joe noticed her fidgeting with her hands. He grabbed one of her hands and held onto to it tight, letting go only long enough for them to get out of the car. As they walked up to the huge house, Ann noticed the five cars that were parked on the extended driveway.

"Are there other relatives here already?" she asked, pointing to the cars.

"No, those are my parents' cars. My brother isn't even here yet."

"So it's just the four of us?"

"For now, yeah," he smiled. "It's okay. They're not going to bite or anything."

The door opened before Joe could reach the bell. An older woman was standing there.

"Joseph! You're here already! I thought you said you wouldn't be in for another—oh well, I'm so happy to see you! Come in!"

They walked inside and Joe let go of Ann's hand to hug his mom. She saw his dad start to walk over and so she stuck her hand out to him.

"Hello Mr. Kendall. I'm Ann-Marie, it's very nice to meet you."

He just stared at her. She looked at Joe who started smirking.

"This would be Juan. He's our house assistant. He doesn't speak English," Joe explained. His mom was quietly laughing also. Juan took Joe's car key and walked out the door.

"Oh. Sorry," Ann blushed.

"It's alright honey," his mom said reaching a hand out. "I'm Mrs. Kendall but you can call me Barbara. Simon is on the back porch smoking a cigar. I don't allow smoking in the house. Is that going to be a problem?"

"No ma'am, I don't smoke."

"Ann-Marie, I said you can call me by my first name."

"Oh yeah, sorry. You can just call me Ann if you want."

"Alright, Ann. Let's go see what that husband of mine is up to."

Ann looked around. This place was bigger than any house or hotel she's ever been in. There were fancy paintings on the walls, exotic-looking flowers in the vases, and they had three different living room sets. They walked by the kitchen, which looked like it belonged in a five star restaurant. There were two men in the kitchen cooking and listening to music in another language.

"Here he is," Barbara said as she slid the back door open. A man was sitting on yet another couch in a closed in porch. He had a newspaper in front of his face so Ann couldn't see what he looked like. A fire pit was going so it was quite warm, even with the snowy weather surrounding them. What caught her attention was beyond the porch. There was a beautiful garden with a fountain and columns, a gazebo, a large covered swimming pool, and a tennis court powdered with snow.

"Wow, if your back yard looks like this covered in snow, I bet it's beautiful in the spring," Ann-Marie said softly to Barbara.

"Oh yes, the garden actually looks like a garden with the flowers in full bloom. The pool is opened and the tennis court is green. Oh, I hate this cold weather."

"We should have went to Florida for the winter," mumbled the man sitting on the porch. He was now watching Ann. Not looking at her, but *watching* her.

"Simon," Barbara smiled at him as he stood slowly. "This is Ann-Marie, Joseph's friend."

"She's my girlfriend actually."

Simon, still looking at her, scowled.

"Dinner should be ready," Barbara said nervously. "Why don't we head in."

As Joe started to follow his mother and Ann, his dad touched his shoulder.

"Why don't we stay out here a second and talk."

"Uh, sure."

Ann-Marie looked back at Joe as she followed his mom into the house.

"Mom?" They heard a voice call.

"Ross, is that you?" Barbara yelled back.

The two woman followed the voice to the foyer where a few people were standing.

"And look who I met on the way into the house?" said the man who had been calling for his mom. This was Ross, Joe's older brother. He was pointing at an old couple behind him.

"Mom, dad!" Barbara hugged them both. She looked a lot like her mother except for the fact she didn't have matching grey hair. She probably dyed it.

"Who is this?" Ross asked, looking at Ann.

"Ann-Marie. Joseph brought her to stay the week with us."

"Does Dad know?" he asked.

"Yes."

"Did he freak out?"

"Ross, don't be rude."

"Sorry. Where are Joe and Dad?"

"In the back, talking."

"So he did freak out."

Ann was wishing she hadn't come. Meanwhile, Joe was not happy with his dad.

"What? What's wrong with her?"

"Did I say anything?" his dad asked defensively.

"Oh come on, you've been giving her the stink eye since you saw her."

"She just seems a little . . ."

"A little what?"

" . . . Ordinary. She showed up to my house wearing sneakers."

"So what?"

"Clista never wore tennis shoes except to run and play tennis in."

"You're seriously bringing up Clista? If you like her so much why don't you try setting her up with Ross?"

"She never seemed interested in him, believe me. I tried. I've invited her to dinner tomorrow actually."

"You did not."

"Don't worry, she said she couldn't make it."

"Good. I haven't seen or heard from her in over a year."

"Shame."

"Oh Dad, let it go. I like Ann-Marie, okay? I'm in love with her. She's the most amazing person I've ever met. You know she received enough scholarships to get herself through college?"

"Her parents couldn't help?"

"She doesn't have parents."

"Did they die?"

"No, they abandoned her."

"Well that's a shame. So she doesn't have a stable up-bringing?"

"Dad!"

"I'm serious. People who grow up like that aren't mentally or emotionally stable."

"There is something really wrong with you. How can you judge someone you don't even know? Especially a sweet girl who's in love with your son."

"Is she in love with you or the money your family brings?"

At that comment, Joe walked away from his father and into the house. He walked into the dining room where Ann, along with several of his family members were already seated.

"Joseph, dear!" His grandma Nadia stood up and reached her arms out to him.

"Hey Grandma," he smiled, hugging her. He shook his grandpa's hand and hugged his aunt, uncle, and little cousin before getting to his brother, Ross. Joseph stuck his hand out to shake Ross' hand.

"Oh don't be ridiculous!" Ross laughed before wrapping his arms around Joe.

Joseph went around the large, long table and sat next to Ann-Marie, who was looking very uncomfortable.

"Hey pretty girl," Joe whispered as he scooted his seat in. "How's it going?"

"Fine," she lied through a fake smile.

"Alright, let's get started, shall we?" Simon said as he walked in the room. He sat down and smiled. "So how is everyone doing tonight? We're very happy you all could join us for Christmas these next couple of days. As you all know, my oldest son, Ross, is enrolled at Harvard. He's doing exceptionally well. My other son, Joseph, is attending a school in Chicago. He's studying to become a biomedical scientist. I couldn't be more proud of them. While Ross is busy fully focusing on his studies, Joe on the other hand, is doing a little more socializing and has brought with him a very special friend to share the holidays with us. Unfortunately, Ann-Marie doesn't have a family to be with for Christmas so Joe was kind enough to share his family with her."

Ann-Marie felt her face get warm. How embarrassing that Joe's whole family thought she didn't have anywhere to go for Christmas. Why did he have to say anything? Now they probably thought she was his charity case, or that she was only with him because of the money that was behind him. Ann looked down at her napkin that was placed in her lap. She didn't see how equally embarrassed her boyfriend beside her was. Joe, however, wasn't looking down at his lap. He wasn't taking his eyes off of his father. He never got along with him, but now he was making Ann, the girl he wanted to marry, feel like crap. And that made Joe feel more like crap.

"So, I'd like to raise a toast," continued Simon, raising his wine glass. "To wealth, health, friends, and family."

"To wealth, health, friends, and family!" everyone besides Ann and Joe replied.

Several men came out of the kitchen with plates of salad. They sat the plates in front of everyone sitting at the table.

Ann-Marie looked at her salad. There was hardly anything on it, not even dressing.

"Excuse me, Barbara?" she asked quietly.

"Yes, dear? What is it? Is there something wrong with the salad?"

"No it's fine. I was just wondering if you had some dressing? Like, ranch or something?"

"Oh yes, of course. I'm so sorry. I should have thought to have those set at the table. They're in the fridge still."

Ann-Marie stood up and all of the men dropped their forks and stood also.

"Where are you going?" Joe asked.

"To get the salad dressing."

Simon started laughing.

"Don't be silly," he chuckled. "I'll get one of the cooks to get it."

"No, really. I can get it myself, I have two legs to get up and walk just like they do."

Everyone at the table fell silent. Ann looked around nervously.

"I mean, if they stop to get the dressing, it might take away time to get the entrees. So I'll just get it myself."

Without looking at anyone, she walked through the swinging door from the dining room to the kitchen. It was uncomfortably hot in there, but Ann-Marie was more comfortable than she had just been.

"I'm sorry, can I help you?" asked one of the cooks. "Did we forget something?"

"I just wanted some salad dressing," Ann-Marie now had a lump in her throat and was fighting back tears. "I'm sorry."

"You look like you need a little break," the cook smiled. She pulled up a folding chair in front of Ann and patted it. Ann smiled back.

"Thank you."

She sat down and held her face in her hands. The holidays overwhelmed Ann anyways, but to add to it, Joe's father was not a nice person. And Joe had mentioned to him that she was an orphan, so Simon probably didn't think much of her at all now. A couple of tears fell down her cheeks and she quickly wiped them away. The nice cook handed her a tissue. Ann said thanks again and stood up. After wiping her face clean, the cook handed her a small bowl of dressing and Ann went back reluctantly to the dining room.

"*Finally.* Was there a problem?" Simon asked.

Ann-Marie shook her head and sat the bowl down on the table. Soon the cooks came out with steaming plates of prime rib, steamed green beans, and baked potatoes. Joe's little cousin had chicken fingers and fries instead. Ann and Joe both would have rather had those. There was a knock on the door frame and Juan entered while everyone was eating. He walked over to Simon and said something in Spanish. Simon nodded.

"I don't know what he's saying, I'm just nodding to pretend to know what he's saying," Simon laughed. "Ann-Marie, can you tell me what he's saying?"

Ann looked at him, then at Juan.

"I don't know Spanish," she said.

"Oh. I thought you might since you're-"

"I'm Italian," she cut him off and stood up. "Excuse me, but I'm not hungry anymore."

Ann-Marie walked out of the room. She didn't get the tour of the whole house so she wasn't quite sure where she was going. She figured the room her and Joe were staying in would be upstairs somewhere. She passed a library, a billiard room, two offices and so far, three bedrooms; but none of them had her luggage in them.

"Excuse me, miss?"

Ann turned to Ross standing about a foot away from her. She hadn't heard him come up behind her so the sudden sound of his voice made her jump.

"Sorry, I didn't mean to scare you," he half-smiled. "Joe told me you were probably looking for your room. Mom and Dad are letting you two have the guest house to yourselves. I'll show you."

Ann followed Ross down the stairs and out the side door. She could hear Joe and Simon in the dining room yelling but she couldn't tell what they were saying. She and Ross went outside to a smaller version of the main house. He opened the door and let Ann go in first.

"Mom made sure the house was cleaned and everything before you guys got here. She even had the fireplace started."

He pointed over at the stone fireplace where the flames were crackling.

"Your luggage should be in the bedroom, down the hall and it's the third door on the left."

"Thanks," Ann-Marie muttered as Ross headed towards the door. With his hand on the doorknob he turned his head back to her.

"Sorry about my dad," he said, not looking directly at her. She nodded.

Joe walked out to the guest house, half expecting Ann-Marie to be gone. He was shaking from rage and embarrassment. How could his father been so cruel? Joe remembered what it was like growing up in this house with his dad. One time in high school, Joe had asked a black girl out on a date and when his father found out, the fight ended with Joe having a black eye and having to cancel his date. His dad had always been a typical rich white man who thought he could rule the world because he helped throw all of the world's scum behind bars. Joe had always despised lawyers because of Simon, and was sad to know that Ross wanted to be just like him. He could remember a time when he and Ross had wanted to be professional skateboarders. That dream was shattered when their dad broke their skateboards and brainwashed Ross into wanting to become a lawyer like him. Simon showed Ross how much power he would have with a job like that and Ross gave into it.

Joe walked through the door of the guest house and immediately saw Ann. She was laying on the couch in front of the fireplace and had a blanket over her. She didn't look up at him, but kept looking straight ahead, her face wet from crying.

"Honey, I am so sorry. I didn't want you to get hurt like this; I only told him so he'd try to understand."

"Try to understand what?" she said, sitting up. "Try to understand why I'm so plain? Why I didn't have anywhere to go for Christmas? Why I'm not like your mother?"

"No, I meant try to understand why I love you so much."

"Why *do* you love me so much, Joe? Why do you want to marry me? Because I'm broken, is that it?"

She started sobbing, making it hard for her to yell.

"Am I some make-over project to you? Do you want to make me more acceptable by your family's standards? Sorry if I'm not boring enough for you. Sorry I'm not Clista."

Joe looked at her.

"Who told you about Clista?" he asked.

"Your brother. Thanks for telling me you were engaged to another girl before me."

"Because I didn't want to be engaged to her!" Joe's voice cracked. He was fighting back tears now. "My parents pressured me into doing it. I didn't even want to be with her anymore. That's why I wanted to go to a college far away. I couldn't deal with all the stress my family put on me. And you want to know why I want to marry you?"

Ann-Marie looked down at her lap.

"Because Clista was too boring. Nobody in their right mind would want to be with someone like her, someone like my mom. I've grown up watching how my dad treats my mom and I hate it. She's like his little puppet, making her put makeup and heels on just to go shopping. She's a step ford wife. She's always smiling and making other people feel welcome when she's so miserable. I'd hear her crying sometimes and when I'd ask what was wrong she'd always say nothing. I envy the life you've had, Ann. You've been able to do whatever you want, nobody to tell you how bad you make your family look. You've never had to wear a school uniform. You've always had to work for everything so you appreciate it more.

I hate being a rich, spoiled brat. I thought if I had you in my life, it would bring more normality to my life."

Ann stood up and hugged Joe. They both stayed there for a while just holding each other. Finally, Ann-Marie looked at Joe.

"So, what all did you say to your dad?"

"Well one thing I did do was remind him that when he met my mom, she was going to a community college majoring in art."

"Wow, really?" Ann smiled.

"Yeah, and she dropped out of school to move closer to my dad. I told him what you were going to school for, and paying your own way through it. He said he was surprised and slightly impressed."

Joe and Ann unpacked and got ready for bed.

"Let's not tell them we're getting married," Ann said, cuddling up to Joe in bed. "Please?"

Joe looked at her and nodded. He had a very difficult time falling asleep because the next day was Christmas, and he had already put Ann's engagement ring by the Christmas tree.

The next morning, Joe woke Ann up with breakfast in bed and a bouquet of purple mini-calla lilies.

"I thought we could exchange our gifts to each other now, before we get with the rest of the family," Joe said, tucking a strand of Ann's hair behind her ear.

"Okay," Ann responded, getting out of bed to get Joe's present out of one of her suitcases. Joe opened a gift bag,

"Batman #181! This is the first appearance of Poison Ivy!" Joe said excited. "Oh my god, thank you so much!"

"You're welcome, sweetie," Ann smiled. "I knew this was one you didn't have and wanted. I wanted to buy you the one that first shows The Joker but it was really expensive."

"Well yeah, duh. That's because The Joker first appeared in Batman #1. It's super expensive."

"Well maybe one day I'll be able to get it for you."

There was a knock on the door. Barbara came in and announced her presence.

"I was just popping in to let you know that everyone is awake and waiting for you to come inside to open presents."

"Thanks Mom!" Joe hollered back. The door shut and Joe got up.

"Okay, your turn," he smiled handing her a gift box.

Ann opened the box and held up a camera.

"Oh wow, I love it! Thank you so much!" She squealed.

"I'm so glad you like it. I couldn't remember which kind you said you wanted."

"This one is perfect!" Ann said, already opening the camera's box.

"Well before you start playing with that gift, why don't you get dressed so we can go open other gifts?"

"Okay sounds good."

Joe and Ann walked over to the main house after getting dressed up. Joe had on a gray cashmere sweater and black slacks. Ann was wearing the only dress she owned. It was gray and black, so it matched what Joe was wearing. Ann had worn this dress to her grandma's funeral a few years ago. It was a miracle that it even still fit. Having the dress made her sad. Not only because it reminded her of her grandma's funeral, but also it reminded her that she had felt completely alone at that funeral. Her dad hadn't shown up for his own mom's funeral and the relatives that did attend didn't even know who Ann was. She had only seen her grandma once or twice when she was little. The only reason she went to the funeral was to hopefully see her dad. He called her late one night and told her about the funeral. She drove from Chicago to Kansas City and visited some of her childhood places, including the place she grew up with her parents. After the funeral, Ann called her dad to ask why he hadn't come. He didn't answer or ever call back. She didn't bother calling back either.

"Merry Christmas!" Joe's family cheered as he and Ann walked into one of the living rooms. There was a gigantic Christmas tree covered in ornaments and tinsel. Under the tree was a mountain of wrapped gifts. In the middle was Joe's little cousin, who was almost completely covered in boxes.

"Jason already has his pile, I see," Joe laughed.

"Yeah, we told him he had to wait to start opening until you two joined us. But we already went ahead and handed him his gifts."

Barbara handed Ann two envelopes and handed Joe two envelopes and three gifts.

"Nobody was sure what to get you; I hope money is okay."

Ann nodded slowly and opened the first envelope. It was a card that very bluntly just said "Merry Christmas." The inside was signed from Joe's grandparents, aunt, and uncle. The check was for $500.

"Holy—um, thanks but this is really too much," Ann said.

"Maybe you could use it to go shopping or something," Joe's grandma smiled.

Ann was anxious to open the other envelope. This one was from Barbara and Simon, although Ann could tell that Barbara had signed both of the names.

"$1,000?" Ann shrieked looking at the check. "Oh my God!"

"It's really not that much, it's the least we could do," Barbara said. "Okay, Joe. Your turn."

In the time it took Ann to look at two envelopes, Jason had already opened all of his toys and gifts. He was opening most of them up to play with them, and the clothes he had received were thrown to the side. Joe opened his two envelopes. One had a check from his aunt for $200, and the other had a check from his parents for $1,200. Joe's three gifts were a really nice set of three polo shirts (from Ross), a new laptop (from his grandparents), and a Rolex watch (from his mom and dad.) After everyone had opened their gifts, one of the servants came in with a tray of hot chocolate and cookies.

"Hold on," Joe said all of a sudden. Everyone looked at him. "I think I see another present in the tree!"

"*In* the tree?" Ann asked.

"Yeah," Joe said, grabbing a small box from a branch. "And it has your name on it."

All of the blood drained out of Ann's face. She knew what was coming, and there was no way out of it. Joe got down on one knee, in front of his whole family and opened the box. Inside was an engagement ring with a diamond almost the size of a quarter. Ann gasped.

"Ann-Marie Circa, you are, without a doubt, the love of my life. I don't want to live if it doesn't mean spending every day for the rest of my life with you. Will you marry me?"

Ann tried not looking around at everyone watching. She closed her eyes and nodded, smiling.

"Yes I will."

There was a faint clapping as Joe placed the ring on Ann's finger, stood up, and hugged her.

"We're getting married!" Joe announced.

Ann finally focused in on everyone's reaction. They all looked happy except for Simon, who was crying.

"Dad, are you okay?" Joe asked.

"Yes, I'm more than okay. I'm sorry about how I acted before. I can see that you really do love her, so if she's perfect to you then she's alright in my mind."

Simon stood up and hugged Joe. Barbara and Ross hugged Ann.

"Well I guess this means I'll be getting a little sister," Ross laughed.

The rest of the week went by fast, filled with family activities and talk about the wedding. Joe and Ann decided to wait until after both of them graduated from school to get married. As the week came to an end and everyone was saying goodbye, Simon hugged Ann as Joe packed their luggage back into the rental car.

"Take care of him," Simon smiled.

"Will do," Ann replied.

The car slowly made its way out of the snowy driveway and Ann was happy to finally have a family. Joe and Ann made a plan to move in together after Ann's apartment lease was up in the Spring, however, she still spent practically all of her time at Joe's. The next Sunday was New Year's Eve. The two spent the evening cuddling on the couch, watching television. Joe had bought a bottle of champagne, although Ann hadn't touched her glass all night.

"What's wrong?" Joe asked.

"Nothing."

"That's a lie. I know you and I can tell when something is wrong."

"Shh, the countdown is starting." *10, 9, 8.*

"Ann, come on, just tell me. What's wrong?" *7, 6, 5.*

"I love you," Ann's eyes filled up with tears. *4, 3, 2, 1.*

"I love you too. Happy New Year."

"I'm pregnant."

## The End of the Beginning

After finding out Ann was pregnant, she and Joe changed all of the wedding plans and moved the wedding to the following autumn. The baby was due in August and they had planned to have the wedding September 2nd. Although their families were shocked to hear about the baby, they were still very excited about both the baby and the wedding.

Ann and Joe were going to have a baby boy and name him Noah. One early July night Ann woke up having very bad stomach pains. When the pains didn't stop, Joe took her to the hospital. The doctors told her that she was going into premature labor and that the baby was coming. Then Ann started bleeding and the doctors told Joe to leave the room. After a while the doctor came out to tell Joe that Ann had lost the baby and it was possible that she wouldn't be able to have children. Somehow, Ann was strong enough to push through the incident and continue with school. She and Joe still had the wedding on September 2nd and both worked really hard to finish their college degrees.

After graduating, Ann and Joe moved to a small town called Franklin Grove and started building a house there. Between the money they received from the wedding, and the money they were already making from their jobs, their house ended up being a little bigger than Joe's parents' house. About a year after they got married, Joe's parents were killed in a car crash, leaving the house in Ross' name. The death of their parents brought the two brothers closer and they visited each other often. Although the doctors were against it, eventually Ann wanted to start trying to have another baby. Joe wanted to focus mainly on their careers, which were involved with the government and highly secretive. But deep down, Joe wanted a baby as well.

Finally they both forgot about baby plans and worked hard on the assignments given to them. They were both very happy with their jobs and with each other. Life was going very well for them. So, when Joe came home one day from the lab, he was surprised to find Ann on the bathroom floor crying.

"Ann, what's wrong?" Joe asked, kneeling down next to her.

"Look in the sink," she sobbed.

Joe saw a pregnancy test laying in front of him. There was a + for positive.

"We're pregnant?" Joe gasped. She nodded.

"I'm scared Joe. What if the same thing happens again?"

"It won't," he started crying. "This time we're going to have a baby, and it's going to be perfect."

As the pregnancy went on without any complications, the couple were very excited to find out they were having a girl this time. They decided to name the baby Avery Nasia Kendall. Avery was randomly picked by Ann because she just liked how the name sounded. Joe picked the middle name, Nasia which means "miracle." Then, on August 4ᵗʰ, Avery was born weighing 6.5 pounds and being 21 inches long. She was perfectly healthy and had no complications at all.

Avery was a very smart baby and learned everything fast. Before turning one, she was already walking well, off the bottle, and starting to talk. By the age of two, she was starting to learn basic Spanish and sign language. By the age of three she began having the night terrors. It eventually got to the point where any time Avery would fall asleep, either at night or for a nap during the day, she would wake up screaming and crying, not being able to recall why. Ann and Joe took Avery to the doctor to see what the problem was but the pediatrician explained that it was just a phase and Avery would grow out of it. Although Avery wasn't in any physical harm from her nightmares, they were still affecting her emotionally. Also, Avery was not allowed to nap with the other children at daycare because she always woke them up by screaming in her sleep. Avery was always tired and never really felt like playing with her friends or toys. She mostly kept to herself and stayed in her room quietly. Ann and Joe were not going to wait and see if Avery would grow out of her nightmares, instead they took matters into their own hands.

Avery's parents started running tests, taking notes, and watching Avery to find out how they could help. Experiment after experiment was done on Avery, putting her to sleep and watching her stress levels, brain waves, etc but her parents couldn't find anything to base their prognosis on. Finally, one day while Ross was visiting, the three of them came up with something.

"Still no luck with Avery?" Ross asked.

"No," Joe sighed. "I'm running out of ideas. I don't even know where to start with all of this. And we're getting to the point where we get as much sleep as she does, if not a little less. I don't want her to suffer anymore."

"And sedatives and sleeping pills don't work?"

"No," Ann replied. "We can only give her so much since she's a child. We don't want to overdose her."

"What if you could film her dreams?" Ross asked.

Ann and Joe looked at each other. Joe then glanced over at an issue of his Superman comic that was laying on the table.

"Ann, that might actually work," Joe said, grabbing a notebook and pen. He started jotting down notes.

"And how do you suppose we do that?" she asked.

Joe didn't answer, but kept writing.

"Joe?" she asked again.

Still no answer.

"Joseph Kendall, you better answer me right now or-"

Look!" Joe finally answered, showing her the notebook.

As Ann read the notes, her eyes began to fill up with tears.

"I don't know, Joe. This could easily backfire."

"It's worth trying though, right? For our daughter?"

"Well if it *does* backfire, don't remind me that it was my idea," Ross half chuckled.

The next day, after Ross went back to Boston, Ann and Joe went back to work. They starting calling different sources, asking for machine parts, medicines, and special workers that were to help them. They rarely left the lab over the next few weeks, keeping Avery at the house with the nanny. When they were finally finished with the equipment, they used a test subject, a lab rat, to run the first set of tests. When the tests kept failing, they decided to go ahead and start using Avery. Still no luck. With their last chance at success failing, Ann and Joe were at the end of their rope. Other assignments were being pushed to the side or left behind to help Avery. However, now they were beginning to go back to their original work, putting Avery's work aside. Instead they focused on being her parents, other than her doctors.

Two months before Avery turned five, she was with her parents at a banquet dinner, honoring Ann and Joe for their work with the government. They were both going to receive awards, and the president himself was going to present the awards. Avery was dressed in a satin red gown that was the miniature version of Ann's dress. Joe wore a red tie that matched his wife and daughter with his suit. The three of them got into a limo to ride to Chicago in. As the limo finally approached the city, Ann and Joe started looking at the notes they had written down for their speeches. Avery tried taking a nap but was too excited to sleep. All she knew was that a lot of important people, including the president, would be having a big party for her parents. She was asked to be on her best behavior, not that Ann and Joe were really concerned about her behavior. Although she was a very shy little girl, Avery always answered when spoken to in the most polite-little-girl way she could. The only time Ann had to get on to Avery in the limo ride was when Avery would pull at her curled hair.

"But Momma, my hair itches," Avery pouted.

"I know, sweetie. But you told the girl at the salon that you wanted your hair to look like mine. Just leave it alone for right now."

"Okaaay," Avery folded her arms over her chest and sighed. Ann noticed that the dark circles under Avery's eyes were getting worse.

The limo pulled up to the building where the banquet was to be held. Joe, Ann, and Avery got out and cameras started flashing. Avery was used to it by now and just smiled, holding on tight to Ann's hand. The pictures didn't last long because the cool evening wind was a bit too chilly. As the three of them walked inside, they were greeted by Avery's nanny.

"Hi Avery! What a beautiful dress!" She exclaimed. Avery frowned and looked up at Ann.

"Mommy, I want to sit with you and Daddy."

"I know, I'm sorry. I wish you could sit with us but we won't be sitting at a table like everybody else. We'll be sitting at the front table with the president. But as soon as they're done giving away awards and everything, I'll come sit with you."

"Promise?" Avery asked.

"I definitely promise."

Avery smiled.

"We better go in now," Avery's nanny said, taking her hand.

"I want a kiss and hug first," Avery shook her hand loose and jumped up into Joe's arms. She gave him a tiny little peck on his cheek.

"I love you, Daddy," she giggled as Joe kissed her on her neck. That was Avery's most ticklish spot. Joe handed her to Ann.

"Love you too Mommy."

"I love you baby girl. We'll see you in a little bit."

Ann sat Avery down and watched as she took the nanny's hand.

Avery waited until her parents walked out of sight around the corner until she started to walk away.

"So, do you think they'll have any good desserts?" her nanny asked. "I hear the president has a very big sweet tooth."

Just then, two loud bangs shot out somewhere in the building. Everyone either ran out the door or got down on the ground. Avery stood where she was while her nanny ran off. The building was in a panic, security guards and policemen started to come out of nowhere. Avery ran after them around the corner. Two policemen were arresting a man with a ski mask on, a gun laid by his feet. Two bodies were laying on the floor, a man and a woman. The woman was wearing a dress exactly like Avery's.

"Mommy! Daddy!" Avery cried, running over to them. Her father's eyes were closed and there was a dark red stain on his white shirt. Ann was holding her stomach, blood seeping out between each finger.

"Avery," she said weakly. "Are you okay?"

"Yes Mommy," Avery sniffled. "Are you okay? Daddy's not moving."

"Listen to me Avery," Ann continued as tears ran down her face. "I love you with all of my heart and soul. You are the very best thing that has ever happened to me. You're my little miracle. Whatever happens in your future, however much power you have, use it for doing good things. The house, the laboratory, and everything else that was your father's and mine is now yours. Don't let anyone find out what's behind the door-"

Ann started coughing, blood coming out of her mouth and nose.

"Mommy!" Avery sobbed as Ann's head finally relaxed and she closed her eyes. Avery put her head down on Ann's chest and couldn't feel or hear anything inside. Avery closed her eyes and wiped her nose, not wanting to let go. An arm touched her back and Avery looked up to see an officer. He took his hat off and had tear-filled eyes.

"I'm sorry, but we need to take your mom and dad now."

"Are you taking them to the hospital? Are they going to fix them?"

"I'm afraid they can't be fixed, sweetheart. But we need to get you out of here in case there are more bad guys."

He started to pull Avery away, but Avery swung her hand and hit him right in the nose. It started bleeding instantly. The officer grabbed his nose and let out a loud yowl. Avery, scared of what she just did, stood up to run away. Another officer, however, came up behind Avery and grabbed her, hoisting her over his shoulder. She kicked and screamed but finally gave in and just started crying for her parents. They took her to the police station until someone could come for her.

"Please, I'm sorry!" Avery cried. "I didn't mean to hit the policeman!"

The officer she had hit had to go to the hospital because she had broke his nose. The officer that brought her to the station was smiling, pushing a cup of hot chocolate towards her.

"You're not in trouble," he said. "I'm kind of impressed though. For something so little, you can really pack a punch. You got any siblings?"

Avery shook her head, staring at the cup.

"Well, you know better now not to hit a policeman now, right? Because we're here to protect and help people."

"You didn't help my mommy and daddy," Avery muttered.

"I know, kid, and I'm real sorry to hear about your folks. But we did catch the bad guy. And he'll be brought to justice."

"What's justice?" Avery asked.

"Uh, ya know, like being fair. Since he did something bad, he'll have to go to court and jail, unless of course he has a lot of money and an outstanding lawyer. Basically, he's in a lot of trouble and now he has to pay for it."

"Like being put in time-out?" Avery asked.

"Uh, yeah like time-out. Don't you have any relatives around here?"

"Nope."

"Out of town relatives?"

"Just my uncle. But he went home yesterday."

"Where does he live?"

"I don't remember. But they have red socks there."

"Boston? You mean the Red Sox baseball team?"

"Yeah that!" Avery giggled. "Uncle Ross always says, 'those sockies will do better next time!'"

"Yeah, my wife and son like the Red Sox," the officer laughed. "I say, 'How can you live in Chicago and not be a Cubs fan,' ya know?"

"My daddy likes the Cubs," Avery frowned.

The policeman looked at Avery.

"Hey look, I'm going to go to get a burger or something, kid. Do you want anything?"

Avery shook her head.

"You sure? I know a 24-hour diner that has the best food ever. Burgers, fries, shakes, anything you could want. Come on, let's get you some food."

Avery slowly slid out of the chair.

"There we go. I'll even let you ride in the front."

"Really?" Avery asked excitedly.

"Yeah but don't tell anyone okay? I don't want to get in trouble by my boss. It'll be a secret."

"Okay, a secret," Avery repeated.

After they returned with food, Avery ate it all kind of fast and started yawning.

"You tired?" The officer asked, throwing away the food trash. Avery nodded and scratched at her hair.

"Do you want me to take some of the bobby pins out?" he asked. "It's probably not very comfortable having your hair pinned like that."

Avery walked over and stood in front of him. Every time he took a pin out, Avery would say *ow!* After he was done, Avery rubbed her head. The policeman took his jacket out of the small closet in the corner and pulled out a folded futon bed.

"It's not the most comfortable thing to sleep on but it's what I use when I have to stay here late and be here again early the next day."

"You don't go home?" Avery asked, taking her small shoes off.

"Nah, it'd be kind of a waste of a drive to go all the way home just to sleep for a few hours and drive right back here where a lot of my stuff is."

"What about your family? Does your son miss his daddy?"

He wrapped his large jacket around her and helped her onto the bed.

"I'm sure he misses me, just like I miss him."

"I miss my mommy and daddy too."

"I know. I'm sorry."

"You should go home and hug and kiss your son, even if it's far from here."

"You know something," he said as tears fell down his face. "You're a very, very smart little girl. And I might just have to go home and do that."

He patted Avery on the head and turned off the main light to the room, leaving only the small desk lamp on.

"Hey," Avery sat up. "Could you please play with my hair for a little bit? It helps me fall asleep. My mommy always does it for me."

"Okay, sure."

The officer knelt down next to the cot and ran his fingers through Avery's soft hair. She fell asleep right away, and the officer went back to working at his desk. It was the first time in months that Avery had had a full night's sleep without any bad dreams. The next morning, Avery woke up to see her uncle standing over her.

"Uncle Ross!" Avery leapt up and hugged him.

"Hi," he patted her back with one hand. "I'm here to pick you up. You're going to be coming home with me."

Ross had met with some policemen and lawyers while Avery had been sleeping. Ann and Joe had left signed papers asking Ross to take full custody of Avery and the house if something were to happen to them.

"We're going home?" Avery asked.

"We're going to my home, in Boston."

"No!" Avery started crying. "I want to go to my house!"

"I know you do, Avery. But for now, until I can get all of this mess figured out, you're going to have to come home with me for a little bit. Then I'll move into your house with you."

"You promise?"

Ross looked at her with one raised eyebrow and his lips slightly puckered out, his signature look.

"Uh yeah, I promise. Just get your shoes on so we can stop by your house before we catch the plane. I'll pack some essential things that you'll need while you stay with me."

"What's that mean?" Avery asked.

"Um, it means stuff that you really need. Like pajamas or something."

"Can I bring my stuffed animals to sleep with and play with?"

"You can bring two."

"Two!" Avery folded her arms. "What about the other ones? They'll get lonely!"

"They'll be fine for the week you'll be with me."

"Can't I bring three? Please?"

Ross sighed and nodded.

"And I'll need my tooth brush and my hair brush and my pink pony big girl panties!"

"Avery," Ross stopped her. "Just bring whatever you need to bring, you don't have to list everything."

Avery said goodbye to the officer who had taken care of her the previous night and left with Ross. She tried grabbing his hand to cross the street but he put his hand in his coat pocket when she touched him. When they arrived at Avery's house, Ross waited inside the door while Avery went up to her room to pack. She started grabbing clothes, toys, and other things she wanted to bring. She zipped everything up in her suitcase by herself and walked down the hallway. Before reaching the stairs she stopped at the door of her parents' bedroom. Avery left her suitcase in the hall and carefully went in. It looked as though everything was normal. The bed was still unmade, a glass half full of water on her father's night stand, a book halfway read on her mother's side. The remote to the television was in the middle of the messy bed. A pile of dirty clothes laid in the corner of the room. On the wall were two framed pictures; one was of Avery right after she had been born. The other was Ann and Joe's wedding picture. Avery reached up for the picture but couldn't get it down; she was too short.

"Avery where are-" Ross stopped at the door. "What are you doing??"

"I need a picture," Avery pointed at the frame. "I can't get it."

"Avery, come on. We're running behind. I'm sure I have a picture of your parents at my house."

"I want this one."

Ross looked at her.

"Please?"

"If I get the picture for you will you come on?"

Avery nodded. Ross grabbed the picture and Avery's suitcase as he went back downstairs. Avery looked around the room once more and turned off the light before walking out. Avery slowly slumped down the stairs, Ross tapping his foot on the marble floor. The taps echoed through the house as Avery reached the bottom step.

"I don't feel good," Avery grabbed her stomach.

"You're just worried. It'll be just like when you stay at my house for vacation."

"But Mommy and Daddy are always with me. I'm scared."

"I know, and I'm sorry. But I don't know what to do about it. Okay, let's go."

"It's quiet," Avery looked around as she followed Ross out the door.

They left the house for the airport, Avery had fallen asleep in the car. Ross woke her up as they arrived at the airport, and had to stop by the bathroom because Avery had to "go potty." They cut it close but barely made it onto the plane. Avery had always enjoyed riding in planes and had her nose pressed against the window the whole way to Boston while Ross worked on his paper work. When they landed in Boston, a limo was waiting for Ross and Avery.

"Hey, Charles," Ross said, handing the driver Avery's suitcase. "This, as you remember, is Avery."

"Look how big you've gotten!" Charles exclaimed. Avery smiled.

"My mom says I grow too fast."

"I think she may be right about that!"

Ross cleared his throat and shook his head at Charles. Charles nodded and continued talking to Avery.

"The last time I saw you, you were just a tiny little baby. I had to move back home with my sister because she fell ill but your uncle was kind enough to let me come back to work for him."

"Is your sister better now?" Avery asked.

"She is doing a lot better, thank you. She had pneumonia and I'm the only family she has now."

"I've had a cold before," Avery explained. "I coughed a lot and had big green boogers in my nose that wouldn't come out."

"Avery!" Ross scolded. "Not in public."

"That's alright, sir," Charles laughed. "Avery, if you need anything at all, you let me know, alright? And you may also call me Charlie if you wish."

Avery smiled at Charlie, reached out her hand, and held hands with him as they crossed the street to the limo. On the ride to Ross' house, Charlie and Avery talked, asking each other questions and telling each other stories. Ross just sat in silence. They pulled up to the giant house, and Avery instantly became homesick. She gave her teddy bear she had been holding a super tight squeeze and the car stopped.

"Well," Ross sighed. "Welcome home, I guess. At least for the next week or so. By the time I get all of my work transferred and get some of my belongings moved into the other house, you'll be used to this house. You won't be afraid anymore. And plus, some of the money I'll get for buying this house will go toward your schooling. And not home-schooling or public school either. I'll make sure you go to a great private school."

"Will I have to wear a uniform?" Avery whined.

"Of course! It'll be great. I'll make sure you get into all of the ivy league schools, clubs-"

"Clubs!" Avery got excited. "Like in a tree house? Can we build a tree house?"

"Uh, no. That's not what I meant. At all."

"Oh. Can I have sleepovers?"

"I don't know, that's a little far away. We'll talk about it more once Autumn rolls around and we get you enrolled."

Ross walked Avery through the house to show her where her room was.

"This can be your bedroom for now so you can go ahead and do whatever you want in here. And if you need anything, you can use this intercom-"

Ross pointed at the speaker system on the wall.

"You can hit any of these buttons and it will connect you to any room. But if I'm in my office don't bother me, okay?"

"Okay. Can you tuck me in? I like the blanket extra tight."

Ross pushed one of the intercom buttons.

"Yes? This is Charles," said the voice.

"Yeah, uh, could you come tuck Avery in? She's ready for bed."

"Yes, of course sir."

"Um, thanks Uncle Ross," Avery said quietly. "Good night."

"You're welcome, and good night."

"I love you."

"Yeah, thanks."

Ross walked out the door and Charles came in.

"Do you have your pajamas on already?" Charlie asked.

"Yes," Avery smiled, pointing to her pink pjs.

"Have you brushed your teeth?"

"Yes."

"Really?"

"Um, yes."

"So if I go into your bathroom and feel your toothbrush, it'll still be wet from you using it, right?"

Avery walked into the bathroom and started brushing her teeth. After she was done, she came back into the bedroom where Charlie was waiting.

"I'm sorry for lying Charlie," Avery said without looking at him.

"It's alright, but no more lying. Okay?"

"Okay."

"So, why don't you hop in bed and I'll tuck you in and read you a story."

"Oooh yeah a story!" Avery jumped onto the bed. "What about my teddy? He needs to be tucked in too."

"Alright, where is your teddy?"

Avery pointed over at where her luggage was sitting. Charles opened up Avery's suitcase and pulled out not only her teddy bear but also the picture of Avery's parents that she had brought. Charles handed her the bear and sat the picture on the nightstand by the bed. He pulled the blankets up to Avery's neck and tucked them under her nice and tight. Avery smiled and rubbed her eyes.

"Goodnight, Avery."

"Goodnight Charlie. Sweet dreams."

"You too."

The next week dragged by for Avery. She was either playing with her few toys she had brought or watching television. Ross spent most of the time in his office or away at work. When he was home and not working, he was helping Charles pack their things, getting ready to move. Avery caught bits and pieces of conversation between her uncle and other people. It was mostly talk of "buying" and "selling" and "documents" and so on. Nothing Avery was particularly interested in. As each day passed, the house grew more and more empty; boxes filled with things being put away in trucks and going off to Avery's house. The last night in Ross' house, Avery slept on a couch in one of the living rooms. Charlie was tucking her in when Avery asked, "Why doesn't Uncle Ross like me? He doesn't talked to me a lot."

"Avery," Charlie sighed. "He loves you very much. He just doesn't know how to talk to children since he doesn't have any kids of his own. He doesn't know how to play or pretend, so you'll have to show him how to do those things."

"He doesn't know how to play?" Avery asked. "That's so sad!"

"I know. But I think once you show him how, he'll become a fun uncle to be around."

"Okay. I just want to be home again."

"I know you do, Avery. You'll be back home tomorrow. Goodnight."

"Hey Charlie," Avery sat up again. "I'm glad you're moving home with me. You're my best friend."

"Well thank you Avery. You're my best friend too."

The next day, Avery woke up, got dressed in a hurry, and packed everything into her suitcase. She ran all around the big, empty house looking for anything she might have forgotten. She ran into Ross' room to see if he was awake. He too was packing a suitcase.

"Uncle Ross!" said Avery, skipping into the room. "Hurry up! I'm ready to go home! Come on, hurry!"

"Avery!" Ross yelled. "Stop shouting and running around. Go get your stuff together."

"I already have my stuff together."

"Then go stand by the door until I'm ready."

Avery hung her head low and stuck her bottom lip out. She grabbed her luggage from her room and waited patiently by the door. Finally, after another fifteen minutes had passed, Ross came out of his room and met her at the door.

"Where's Charlie?" Avery asked as Ross opened the door.

"He's already at the house, getting everything ready for us to get there."

"Yay! I can't wait to be home!"

The ride to the airport and the plane ride seemed a lot longer this time to Avery. She didn't sleep at all on the way home because she was too excited to be going back to her house. She kept her eyes glued to the car window until her house was in sight.

"We're home! We're home!" Avery started bouncing up and down. "I'm going to jump on my bed and play with all of my toys at the same time and watch all of my movies and eat some cereal!"

"Okay, calm down," Ross sighed. "Now I've got to warn you, Avery. The house is going to look a little different then before."

Avery, not really paying attention to Ross, jumped out of the car before it came to a complete stop and ran up to the front door.

"Charlie!" Avery knocked on the door. "It's Avery! Open up!"

The door opened and Avery ran into Charlie's arms to hug him.

"We made it home!" Avery giggled. "I-"

Avery stopped to look around. She almost didn't recognize her home. The furniture was different, some of it belonging to Ross' house. Some of the walls were painted different colors. There were different pictures and paintings hung up. Avery ran through the house, not liking all of the new changes. It was bad enough that she had remembered that her parents weren't ever coming home, but at least they wouldn't have to see their beautiful house turned into a cold, dull place. The family room that Ann, Joe, and Avery had spent playing board games and eating pizza was now a trophy room with swords hung up on the walls. The dining room, where there was a eight-seat table, now had a table big enough to seat twenty people. Avery's drawn pictures that were on the refrigerator were gone, along with the alphabet magnets that held up the pictures. The hallway upstairs that was covered in family pictures was now empty except for a large picture of Avery's grandpa, Ross' father. Avery ran to her parents bedroom but the door was locked shut.

"Avery," Ross was standing at the end of the hallway. "I'm sorry. I know it's a lot different, but it'll be okay. This is a brand new start for the both of us. I don't know how to act around little kids because, well, I never really got to be one myself. My father was very strict with me, set rules and goals that were almost impossible for me to reach. I strived to be the best at everything I did for him. I never really wanted to be a lawyer, I just did it because it's what my father wanted. Anyways, so yeah. I'm sorry if I don't seem fun or laid back like your folks."

"Why did you lock this door?"

"I wanted to leave their room alone, out of respect for them. I, uh, took your room since it's one of the bigger ones. And now your room is where your play room used to be. I put some of the extra toys of yours in the den downstairs."

Avery's eyes filled with tears. Ross stood there awkwardly for a moment and then turned to walk away.

"You're a mean uncle!" Avery screamed at him. "You ruined my mommy and daddy's house and you took my room away from me and you make Charlie do everything for you because you had a mean daddy!"

"Avery that is enough!" Ross yelled.

"I hate you! You'll never be my daddy because you're too mean and don't like playing!"

Avery ran off to her room and slammed the door. Avery was crying and shaking. She had never talked to a grown up like that before. She plopped down on her bed and buried her head in her pillow. She wondered how long she'd have to stay like this before someone would come find her and comfort her. Finally, there was a knock on the door.

"Avery?" Charlie's voice called. "Are you still awake?"

"Yeah," Avery answered with her face still buried in the pillow.

"Do you mind if I come in?" he asked.

"You can come in."

The door opened and Charlie was carrying a tray of cookies and chocolate milk.

"Thought you might like a snack."

"Thank you, Charlie."

"You're welcome. I left your dress for tomorrow hanging up in your closet."

"My dress? What's tomorrow?" Avery asked, shoving a cookie in her mouth.

"Your uncle didn't-?"

Charlie walked over to Avery's closet and opened it. Right away Avery saw the little black dress that was hanging up. Avery scrunched her nose.

"It's not very pretty. Can I just wear one of my pink dresses?"

"No, Avery. Um, when people pass away, we wear all black to their funerals out of respect for them. Sort of a sign that we are mourning them."

"Mourning?" Avery asked.

"Yes. It's when you show that you're sad because you have lost someone."

"I have two mournings since I lost my mommy and daddy."

"Well you can only have one mourning, but I'm sure it's a lot harder losing two people instead of one."

"Are you wearing black tomorrow?" Avery asked.

"Yes I am."

"Will Uncle Ross wear black?"

"I'm sure he will."

"I don't think he has mourning. He doesn't seem sad."

"He lost his brother. I'm sure he's very sad."

Avery woke up the next morning sad and scared of going to the funeral. She put her black dress on and asked if she could wear her shiny pink dress shoes with the dress. Charlie said yes. After running the brush through her hair, Avery sat on her bed and went through pictures of her and her parents. Charlie came upstairs to get Avery and looked at the pictures with her.

"Your mother was very pretty; you look just like her."

"My daddy said that me and her are the prettiest girls in the world."

"I agree with that," Charlie smiled.

Holding Avery's hand, Charlie stayed by her side during the funeral. Avery was too afraid to go up to the caskets where her mother and father were. There were a lot of people who attended the funeral, hardly none were family though. Most were people who worked with Ann and Joe or were old friends of theirs. Avery stayed very quiet and still as the service started. The minister stood at the front by the caskets and spoke. Avery looked at all of the flowers and pictures of her parents.

"It is a sad loss to have to say goodbye to two very outstanding citizens, who have dedicated their lives to their work and to help people in the name of science. Ann-Marie and Joseph leave behind one child, Avery Nasia Kendall. They also leave behind a legacy. The Kendalls brought light to the world; they always had a kind hand to help and a kind word to speak. They helped not only their local community but also the whole country. The crime that has happened to the Kendalls will fortunately be brought to justice because the shooter was caught on sight and sent to jail. But we do not seek revenge on the guilty as children of God. Instead, we forgive those who have wronged us and our loved ones. One should not waste their blessed life on anger and guilt. That is not the life the Kendalls would have wanted all of us to live. So, do not shed a tear for them, for they are now truly home and at peace with their Lord."

"Get a load of this guy," Ross whispered to Charlie over Avery's head. "He's kind of generic, isn't he? You think he's going to add an 'amen' at the end?"

Charlie put a finger up to his mouth to hush Ross and they continued listening to the minister.

"We should rejoice not only for the life Ann-Marie and Joe lived, but also we should rejoice for the lives we have left to live. Psalm 30:5 says, 'Weeping may remain for a night, but rejoicing comes in the morning.' Also, Psalm 34:18 says, 'The Lord is close to the brokenhearted and saves those who are crushed in spirit.' Amen!"

Ross looked at Charlie and rolled his eyes, mouthing the words, *told you*.

"Are there any family members or close friends that would like to add a few kind words?"

Everyone sort of looked around at each other. Charlie looked at Ross, who was looking straight ahead. Charlie nudged Ross.

"What?" Ross asked.

Charlie nodded his head toward the podium. Ross sighed and slowly walked up to the front. He adjusted his jacket and popped his knuckles before speaking.

"Um, hello everyone. I'm Ross, Joe's older brother. Well, I didn't prepare a speech or anything because I didn't think I'd have a chance to get up and say anything so bare with me. Although Joe was younger than me, I always sort of looked up to him. He was always doing something to help someone else, never really caring if he put everyone before himself. As a defense attorney, I used to get a lot of crap from Joe, about how I was the one keeping the bad guys out of jail and defending them. And he was right, I was helping some very bad people out. But, now that I've been so closely involved with a crime, I can't see how anyone could defend a horrendous act like murder. My brother and his wife were good people who didn't deserve what happened to them. I can remember when our sister Beth passed away. We were still very young, and didn't really understand the suffering Beth had been through. We were actually mad about her passing away; thought it was unfair to lose her so young. But as we got older, we realized how much pain she was in and how glad we were that she hadn't suffered more. Now, standing here, being the only person in my family left, I can't help but feel lucky. Sure, I'm sad to be alone, but I'm lucky to have good health. I'm lucky to have Avery, my niece. And I have wealth. Thank you."

Ross walked back to his seat and sat down, glancing over at Charlie.

"Um, maybe you should have just said a small prayer or something," Charlie whispered.

"What was wrong with that speech? I thought it was pretty good considering I was put on the spot."

"Can I go up there?" Avery asked.

"I don't know if that's such a good idea," Ross smiled awkwardly.

"She can't do any worse than what you just did," Charlie smiled.

Avery, still holding hands with Charlie stood up. Charlie led her up to the podium and removed the microphone from the stand. Avery held onto it with both hands and cleared her throat.

"Hi everyone. My name is Avery Nasia Kendall. Thank you for coming to say good bye to my mommy and daddy. Um, I just wanted to tell everyone that they gave me a dream catcher and it's supposed to make my bad dreams go away and it did so now I don't have to be scared now. But I think my mommy and daddy helped make the bad dreams go away."

Avery looked back at the caskets.

"And I think my mommy looks very pretty and my daddy looks like an angel. And I think my uncle Ross is a nice uncle and I love Charlie because he's a lot like my daddy. That's all I wanted to say."

Avery gave the microphone back to Charlie and hopped off the stairs back down to her seat and sat down. A couple people stood up to speak after Avery, but mostly talked about how dedicated her parents had become to their jobs and what good people they were. They were pretty much just repeating each other. Avery was getting bored and antsy but then finally the minister got back up to speak.

"At this time, we will form a line for anyone who wishes to walk up to the caskets and say one last goodbye before we move onto the cemetery."

Everyone stood up and starting with Ross and Avery, a line formed through the church. Ross walked up to Ann's body and looked for a couple of seconds before moving on to Joe's. He put his hand in and lightly patted Joe's chest. Avery thought she saw a few tears fall from Ross' eyes. After he walked away, Charlie walked Avery up to her mother and lifted her up. Avery leaned over and kissed Ann's forehead. Avery started sobbing as Charlie carried her away from Ann and over to Joe. Avery, still crying, leaned over and kissed Joe's forehead also. She touched his hair and moved it slightly over.

"I don't want to leave them," Avery cried looking at Charlie.

"I know you don't. But we need to get to the cemetery."

Charlie carried Avery away and she started kicking and crying out loud.

"No! I want them back! Let me go!" She screamed. Charlie noticed the weather outside quickly looking worse and worse. Dark clouds gathered and thunder started rumbling.

"I want my mommy and daddy! I want them back! I don't want to leave them!"

Lightning crashed and brightened the dark sky. Rain started pouring down and tapping on the windows. Charlie struggled to hold onto Avery.

"Please, please, please! I want them! It's not fair, they're my mommy and daddy!"

A lot of the people were stopped where they were standing and either watched Avery or the weather out the windows. The wind started blowing harder. Ross came back inside, drenched from the rain. He held his hands out to Avery.

"Come here, Avery."

Avery looked at Ross for a moment before climbing into his arms and calming down. Still sniffling, Avery held onto Ross tight as he walked her out to the car. The rain had stopped and the clouds were beginning to part. Ross and Avery sat in the back of the limo as it pulled away from the church and left for the cemetery. Avery began to drift off and fell asleep by the time they arrived at the grave sights. Ross unbuckled Avery's seat belt and let her lay down in the back of the limo while the rest of the funeral continued. After the service ended and everyone else left, Charlie stood with Ross while he watched the caskets get lowered. Avery woke up when Ross shut the car door. She cuddled up to him and silently cried on the way home. Neither said much to each other the next few days, and Avery barely ate or played with her toys.

For Avery's fifth birthday, Ross and Charlie took her to Tunnel Palace, a children's play place that Avery usually liked. However, she sat most of the time, watching the other children playing. She ate a tiny piece of cake and left two of her four birthday presents unopened. She had opened the two from Charlie and Ross but when she saw that Ross had found two from her parents that they had kept, Avery didn't want to do anymore birthday stuff. When Charlie tried opening them, Avery got mad and told him to give them to another kid who wanted them. From then on, Avery wasn't as happy as she had been. She spent most of her time in her bedroom and spoke to Ross and Charlie only when she needed something.

Ross enrolled Avery into kindergarten in the Fall. She attended a private school outside of town. Along with Avery starting school, Ross also hired a maid/nanny for the house named Cindy. She took Avery to school every morning and picked her up every afternoon. When Avery came home she'd go straight up to her room and start on her homework if she had any. After homework, Avery would go down to the kitchen and either Cindy or Charlie would fix her something to eat. Once Avery was done with dinner, she'd run herself a bath and get ready for bed. She started seeing Ross less and less because once he gained the rights to the laboratory, he was always working. He quit his job at the law firm he was at and began managing the lab by himself. Ann and Joe's lawyers had sat him and Avery down to discuss wills, the house, custody of Avery, and the laboratory. They had left everything in Avery's name but since she was too young to do anything with it all, and they had left Ross to be her guardian, it was agreed that Ross would take over everything until Avery turned eighteen and could decide on her own whether she wanted the lab or not.

As Avery grew a little older, she began getting into fights at school, not getting along with the other children. She got in trouble often and Ross made her start seeing a therapist once a week. Finally, in seventh grade, Avery was kicked out of her school and

Ross was forced to send her to the local public school. Once Avery started her freshman year at Franklin Grove High School, she was barely passing her classes and had become extremely anti-social. The only people at school she hung out with were the other outcasts like herself. Avery hadn't realized just how much of an outcast she really was.

# CHAPTER 1

# Anthem Part 2

*"Let this train wreck burn more slowly, kids are victims in this story.*
*Drown the youth with useless warnings, teenage rules they're fucked and boring."*

-"Anthem Part 2" by Blink 182

It all started while I was sitting in my history class, halfway listening to the lesson, not taking notes as usual. It was a cool Thursday in October and I was a couple months away from being halfway done with my freshman year at this stupid, crappy high school with all of these hick kids. Even though there were only 100 kids in my graduating class, I only knew about twenty of them. I liked about five of them, and hated the other fifteen, which were the preppy, popular people in my grade. Most of the popular girls dated older boys, always wore pink or skirts or high heels, planned parties while their parents were out of town, and ruled the school. They had their own tables at lunch time and if anyone dared to sit at the table, well, that kid was in for a rude awakening. There really wasn't one girl I hated more than the rest because they were all pretty bad. They made fun of me in the locker room, calling me a boy or a lesbo and didn't want to undress in front of me. I'm neither, by the way. I'm a straight girl. I like boys, I just don't talk about them or date them. Most of the guys at my high school aren't my type anyways. Farmer boys, wanna-be cowboys, and jocks are the main boy populous at Franklin Grove and if you saw me on a daily basis you'd know that those are the type of boys I'd rather beat the shit out of than date.

I had been on one date before. His name was Kevin, but he went by Sly. I don't know why he went by Sly, he just did it to be cool I guess. Anyways, we met when I went to the mall with my two best friends, Kelly and Ryan. Usually we don't hang out at the mall because that's where all the preps go when they're not partying or basking in each other's awesomeness at school. We were at the mall to buy a new video game that had just came out. Sly was working at the video game store. He told us that the game was already sold out but that if we wanted to come hang out with him after work, he'd let us play the game at his house. We were hesitant at first because we pretty much just stick with each other, but I knew Kelly was dying to get his hands on that game. Because I'm such a good friend and Ryan is such a good sister, we went ahead and said we'd hang out with Sly, for Kelly. The whole time we were hanging out with him, Sly hit on me and was creepily staring at me while Kelly and Ryan played the video game. Okay, so maybe that isn't considered a date. So, I guess I haven't actually been on a date.

By the way, I'm sure you're extremely confused about Kelly and Ryan. Their parents were high or something when they decided to name them, or they couldn't figure out who was who with their diapers on. See, Ryan and Kelly are twin brother and sister. Kelly was born first, and then Ryan was born after him. To this day, I'm still not sure why Kelly was given a girl name or why Ryan was given a boy name. Their parents had to have known how much shit they'd be given once they reached high school. And believe me, they get *a lot* of shit at school. But do you think they care? No way. They're just like me; unless someone puts their hands on me or threatens me, they don't exist. God forbid if they do put their hands on us though, because that's when it really hits the fan. I don't consider myself a bad kid, just sort of misunderstood. I'm just trying to get through high school so I can move to a better place, like California or England or New York. Anywhere would be better than here. I hate living where I lived with my parents.

Anyways, I'm getting way off topic. So there I was, sitting in my history class, thinking about anything other than the Boston Tea Party, which I already knew about anyways. There was a knock on the door and I started putting my books away into my backpack, knowing already who it was. My therapist, Julia, came through the door and smiled at me. I looked at my history teacher who nodded.

"Avery, just read the rest of the chapter and do the questions at the end. We'll have a vocabulary test tomorrow and the questions will be due when you walk in."

I nodded in agreement and picked up my backpack.

"Therapy Thursday, like always," Amanda smiled. Her gaggle of airheads giggled.

Amanda Davis was one of the elite preps at my school, probably the most elite from my grade. Her parents owned the bank, the grocery store, and one of the towns few clothing boutiques. She was disgustingly perfect in every way imaginable. She was 5'8" and probably weight 110 pounds soaking wet. She had elbow length blonde hair and emerald green eyes that pierced right through you if you were caught looking at her. She always had the best of everything and wore the trendy, fashionable clothes. Normally when she made remarks like the one she just made, I'd just keep walking or roll my eyes at her, but today I chose to make it a little interesting.

"Dumb blonde, like always," I smiled back.

"Excuse me?" Amanda whipped her head around at me.

"What, does the peroxide affect your hearing as well as your intelligence?"

Now I had the attention of the whole class. My therapist was pulling at my arm asking me to let it go and come with her. Amanda's face was turning pink.

"Just because your parents died and made you a social retard doesn't mean you should get special treatment from all of the teachers."

"That's enough, Amanda," Mr. Paige, the history teacher said. "Avery, please leave."

"And just because your parents own half of the town doesn't make you Queen Bitch of this high school," I added. I was starting to shake a little from the adrenaline rush I was having.

*If only you knew my parents, I hate them more than I hate you. I'm glad they're getting a divorce.*

"I think the whole town is glad they're getting a divorce," I replied. "They'll see how not so perfect your family is."

Everyone in the room looked at Amanda, who's face was completely red now.

"How did you know they were getting a divorce?" she asked.

"You just said it in front of the whole class, idiot!"

"I didn't say anything you freak!" She started crying. Amanda stood up and ran out the door, pushing into me on her way by, leaving all eyes on me.

"I'm sorry Avery, but you leave me no choice," Mr. Paige sighed. "I'm giving you a detention."

"Put it on my tab," I spat before slamming the door behind me.

"Avery, you can't let people get to you like that," Julia said once we were in the hall.

"Yeah, I know. But it felt good getting at Amanda like that."

"Did it fix any of your problems?"

"What?" I looked at her.

"How did it make you feel better? Because you made her cry? Because you embarrassed her like she embarrassed you? How did hurting her fix any of your problems? Sure, it makes you feel good for a moment but it ultimately doesn't change anything. Your parents are still gone."

"Well thanks for bringing that up."

"Avery, why do you think we have to meet every week?"

"I've been wondering that since I was five, although I have to say, you're a lot nicer than the last two therapists."

"Well thank you. So what have you been up to since last week?" She asked as we approached her office.

Julia was nice, but you could totally tell she was just out of school and not quite sure what she was doing. She was only about 24 years old and recently engaged. I've seen a picture of her fiancé, and I think she could do way better. He's shorter then her and really nerdy looking. I wouldn't ever say anything to her about how ugly he is because she hasn't done anything yet to make me be mean to her.

"Not much, same old crap I always do. Either at school, at home, or with my friends," I plopped into the recliner I usually sat in.

"Kelly and Ryan?" She took out a pen and her trusty little notebook marked "Kendall." I've noticed at the end of each session, she puts the notebook in a drawer that she locks before we leave her office. There are several other notebooks in the drawer and I would love to know what other kids have big enough problems to need a shrink. I never see anyone else come in here so it has to be before or after school sessions.

"Yeah," I smiled. "They're my buddies."

"Do you ever confide in them how you feel about your parents' deaths?"

"Do you mean like cry on their shoulder while I reminisce my dark childhood?"

"Something like that, yes."

"Hell no!" I laughed. "I don't want to talk about it and they don't want to hear about it."

"Are you sure about that?" Julia asked.

"Yeah, I'm sure."

"How can you be so sure? You've never even tried."

"So? I'm not going to go around saying, 'woe is me. Have pity for the girl with the dead parents.' That's not my style."

"Okay well sooner or later, you're going to have to open up to someone about it, Avery. And when you do, you'll feel a weight lifted off of your shoulders."

"Doubt it," I stared up at the ceiling.

*I wish I had someone like me to talk to about my problems.*

"What problems do you have?" I asked.

"What?" Julia looked up at me.

"You don't seem like you have anything to worry about. You're getting married, you have a really nice house and car that's all paid for by a decent job. What do you have to worry about?"

"I, uh, never said I *did* have anything to worry about, but since you asked, I'll tell you. That is of course, if you really want to hear it."

"I don't care, go ahead. What is it? You have a bunch of student loans you still have to pay off?"

"I wish that was all I had to deal with," Julia sighed. "There's a possibility that I might not even be able to get married now."

"How come?" I asked.

"Because my heart isn't really in it to marry him. I was engaged before to another guy when I was 20. I was so madly in love with him, and I really believe he was my soul mate."

Julia's voice cracked and I saw tears fill up her eyes.

"What happened?" I asked. "Did you catch him with another girl?"

"No, he died. He was serving in the military and was killed overseas one week before he was supposed to come home. It was about a month before the wedding was scheduled. I was beyond devastated, I tried killing myself three times. When I was finally able to leave the house, I met my fiancé at a meeting for people who lose loved ones in the military. We were just friends at first but then he started telling me he loved me and then proposed to me. I said yes just because, I don't know, I didn't want to hurt his feelings I guess. I don't want to get married though. I don't think I could marry anyone except the man I really truly loved. And now I don't know what to do. If I call off the wedding, I'll break his heart, but if I go through with it then I won't be truly happy."

I sat there listening to Julia, a little in shock that not only had she opened up so much to me, but the fact that she had all of this going on and I thought she had no worries. As she finished, she grabbed a Kleenex from the box and wiped her face.

"Oh Avery, I am so sorry. I don't know why I told you all of this."

"No, it's cool," I shifted in my chair. "What if you just tell him to post-pone the wedding for now and when the time is right, tell him you can't get married."

"I just don't want to hurt him. He lost his sister just like I lost my fiancé so we have that connection."

"But he doesn't know how it feels to lose a fiancé like that. You don't have to be mean about it, and you don't have to break up with him. Just take a second to think about what you really want and need in your life right now."

"Oh my god, Avery. I'm sorry, but we're here to talk about you, not me. I'm being so unprofessional right now."

"It's okay, Julia," I gave her a half smile.

"Maybe we should just end today's session and we'll pick back up with you next week."

"Okay," I said, standing up.

As I left Julia's office, on my way downstairs towards the Foreign Language hallway, I started recapping what had happened so far during the day. I had heard Amanda say that her parents were getting a divorce, but then she said she hadn't said anything. And the same thing happened in Julia's office. Either I was going crazy or I was able to . . .

*Brrring!*

The school bell rang and doors swung open, students started pouring out the classrooms. Ryan came out of her Spanish class and smiled when she saw me.

"What's up?" she put her arms through her backpack straps.

"Not much," I answered. "I've had a pretty interesting afternoon so far."

"Uh, yeah. Kelly sent me a text message saying you and Amanda got into it during History."

"How did he know?" I asked, surprised.

"We're in high school now, Avery. Word travels fast, especially when it involves a prep like Amanda. Did you really make her run out of the room crying?"

I looked at Ryan and we both started laughing.

"Wait for me!" we heard Kelly yell. We turned around to see him shuffle down the hall and catch up with us.

"You weren't going to leave without me, were you?" Kelly looked at me.

"Of course not," I said sarcastically. "What is that?"

Kelly was holding something that was a light pinkish color.

"It's my art project. We're doing sculptures."

"What the hell is it supposed to be?" Ryan asked, poking it.

"Don't touch it! I'm not sure what it is yet, I haven't decided what I'm going to make."

"Are you going to take that over to Sly's house?"

I looked at Ryan.

"You're going over to Sly's house? Since when?"

"Since he invited us over and it gives us something to do," Ryan said.

"Oh come on, Ryan. He's creepy! Or do you not remember him staring at us the whole time Kelly played that game?"

"I know, but I've been actually talking to him lately and he's kind of cool."

"Well, I can't go," Kelly said as we left the school. Although it was a drag having to walk home and to school every day, it was a lot better than riding the bus or having Charlie drive me back and forth every day. Besides, walking home gave me extra time to talk to Ryan and Kelly.

"Why can't you go?" I asked Kelly.

"I have way too much homework, and I haven't updated my blog in almost a week."

"Oh no, not your blog!" I teased him.

"Oh shut up," Kelly gave me a little shove. "I need to write regularly so I don't get rusty. Just because I already have a career picked out and you two don't, doesn't mean you can trash talk it."

"Being a writer isn't a career, it's a hobby," Ryan laughed. "And if you don't want a social life at all, that's on you."

"I have a social life, thank you."

"I don't think playing your co-op video games with twelve year olds online counts as a social life. But that's fine, Avery will go with me, right?"

My face scrunched up when Ryan looked at me.

"Come on," she pleaded. "I really want to go and I don't want to go by myself."

"How are we going to get there when neither of us drive yet?" I asked.

"He said he'd pick us up at the gas station, and that's like right past my house. We have to stop by to drop Kelly off anyways."

"I can find my own way home actually," Kelly shot Ryan a dirty look.

"Well if we're going I'll have to stop in to change my clothes. Avery, please?"

"Okay fine," I sighed. "But I don't want to stay out all night. If I fall asleep during class tomorrow and get in trouble again, I'm going to be pissed."

"Alright, I'll tell him we have a curfew and to take us home around ten or so. You can just spend the night at my house."

Once we got to Ryan and Kelly's house, Kelly said goodbye to us and disappeared into his room. I used to feel awkward going over to their house because you could fit three of their houses into mine. Ryan's bedroom was the size of my bathroom. But now, more than anything, I envy them. I've found the bigger the house, the more empty it feels. When I'd stay for dinner, we'd all cramp together around the dining room table or use tv trays and eat in the living room. Between Ryan, Kelly, me, their little sister Amber, their mom, their dad, and their grandma who lived with them, the house always seemed crowded. And I loved that about that house. I liked being able to walk into any of the rooms in the house and find someone in them. Ryan's dad turned the basement into to bedrooms for her and Kelly. Their parents were totally hippies back in the day and they still are kind of. They eat organic and are both vegetarians although none of their kids are. They also don't care if Kelly and Ryan smoke pot because they did and sometimes still do.

I've seen Kelly and Ryan do it before but very rarely. They're not straight edge kids like I am but they're not alcoholic dope heads either.

I don't like labeling myself as "straight edge" but there really isn't any other way to describe myself. I refuse to smoke anything, drink alcohol, or even eat or drink anything with a lot of caffeine in it. And if that makes me boring to some people, they can get over it. I don't need shit like that to have a good time or make myself feel better. I enjoy chilling in the background watching all the other kids get drunk and act stupid. It's cheap entertainment. I don't think I dress like a stereotypical straight edge kid. I have no tattoos or piercings, and I don't want any. I know I'm only fifteen but I'm sure there's nothing important enough to stain into my skin permanently. I don't draw x marks on my hands either. I don't promote myself as a straight edge, I just live the lifestyle. I think kids like that are kind of posers. No one cares that you don't drink or smoke, unless it's your parents or your D.A.R.E. officer from like fifth grade.

My sense of style is very simple, and affordable. I like shopping at thrift stores, although that seems a little stereotypical of me. I shop mostly online. I like a lot of vintage clothes, mostly t shirts of bands that I will never have the luxury of seeing live, like The Ramones. I don't buy pre-ripped jeans, or even rip my own jeans. I don't like being considered a punk, even though that's the best description the old people can come up with. I do like wearing makeup but I don't cake on the bronzer and mascara like the preps do. I like some eyeliner and I'll even wear some lip stick. I've never dyed my natural black hair, and I like keeping it long so I can either straighten it or wear it up in a ponytail. I've never had a perm, scrunched, or teased my hair. My hair makes me look even more like my mom, which I'm proud of. Same goes for my natural tan. I've never "fake baked" and I don't want to. I don't need to anyways because of the Italian in me.

Ryan looks a lot different than me. She has a pierced lip and short, light brown hair. She wears thick black glasses and goes for more of the "hipster chick, semi-scene" look. She's shorter than me, and also way thinner than me. I'm not fat, but I have way wider hips than her. Cindy always told me I had "child-bearing hips." I also have way bigger boobs than Ryan, which she hates. I don't mind it but it makes it impossible for us to wear each other's clothes. So when we stopped so she could change clothes, I was left with very few options. I kept my jeans on but switched to a purple low-cut top that wasn't even that revealing when Ryan wore it. Of course when I wore it though, it showed the top part of my cleavage that wasn't held down by my sports bra.

"Well, what do you think?" Ryan asked, turning slowly. She was wearing a long-sleeved, blue shirt that buttoned all the way down, a black skirt, pink leggings, and her sneakers.

"You look cute," I smiled.

"Cute as in 'that chick looks like a twelve year old' or cute as in 'oh wow, I wish I wasn't a twelve year old boy so I could get with that chick?'"

"Uh, the second one?"

"Okay good."

So there we were, standing in front of the gas station, waiting for the weasel face guy that Ryan wanted to impress and flirt with. Finally, after waiting for over half an hour, a crappy car sputtered into the parking lot. Sly was in the driver's side and a guy I didn't recognize was sitting in the passenger side. He got out of the car and pushed the seat forward.

"Great," I muttered. "I loved feeling cramped in the back of a two-seater with two guys I don't know."

"Shush!" Ryan whispered as we started walking toward the car. "You kind of know Sly."

"Hey there, pretty," Sly smiled at Ryan.

"Hey," she almost purred at him, batting her eyes.

"Hi," the other guy stuck his hand out at me and Ryan. "My name is Andrew McDermont."

"How's it going?" I walked passed him and crammed myself into the back of Sly's car. Ryan slid in next to me and Andrew got in before we sped off down the road. Sly didn't live in our town so I had no idea where we were. When we pulled in the driveway of the house, I had a gut feeling that this was not a good idea. My stomach felt like it was filled with nails and someone was shaking me. I felt uneasy and unsafe. We got out of the car and as soon as we got within reach of the door, I could smell pot. I walked through the door and saw a dozen people sitting around that looked as shady as Sly. I stood awkwardly in the corner for a few minutes before Ryan had me sit on a small couch with her.

"So what's the point of us being here?" I asked Ryan.

"To have fun and meet new people who don't go to our boring school."

"Are you having fun?"

"We just got here, Avery. Calm down."

"I'm not calm," I lowered my voice. "I'm nervous and I don't like this."

"Stop it, everything is fine."

Sly scooted in next to Ryan on the couch and wrapped his arm around her. I was already uncomfortable but now I was almost unbearably uncomfortable. Ryan and Sly started making out next to me, and my butt was almost completely off of the couch. Finally, Sly stood up and grabbed Ryan's hand, pulling her off the sofa. I stared at her as she let Sly lead the way toward the staircase. She was going to ditch me. I looked at Ryan with pleading eyes but all she gave me was a slight shrug and went up the stairs. Out of the corners of my eyes I could vaguely see movement around me. I gazed at my hands and started picking off my purple nail polish. I started spacing off and thinking about the dream I had had the night before. The first nightmare I had had since my parents died.

I was at a party, like this one, except the place was different and most of the people were different. The only people that were the same was Ryan, Sly, and Andrew. Which was really weird because I had never met Andrew before tonight, but he was definitely in my dream. It followed all of the events that had already happened today, starting with Kelly having his sculpture project to work on and couldn't go with us. We stopped by their house so Ryan could change clothes and waiting for Sly at the gas station. Everything that led up to right now was exactly what happened in the dream. The next thing was hearing Ryan's voice crying out for help, except it wasn't really her actual voice because the party was too loud to hear her yelling. I could hear her mentally yelling for me. I ran up the stairs to Sly's room and found him choking Ryan, pinning her down on the bed. I could hear Sly thinking about the gun hidden in the dresser drawer. When I ran towards the dresser, he grabbed me and threw me down on the bed next to a barely conscious Ryan. He retrieved the gun from the drawer and shot me, and that's when I woke up, sweaty and shaking.

I stood up quickly, knocking over a beer that was on the floor. I made my way toward the stairs. A hand touched my shoulder, startling me.

"Is something wrong?" Andrew asked me.

"I need to go check on Ryan," I replied.

"She went upstairs with Sly. You're not going to leave me down here with these people by myself, are you?"

"Aren't they your friends too?" I asked.

"No! I don't know anyone here. I work with Sly and he said that Ryan wanted him to bring a nice guy to the party to meet you. I barely ever talk to Sly, and I just rode with him straight from work to pick you two up."

"Oh, well I have a curfew so I need to get home soon."

Before Andrew could say anything else, I ran up the stairs and started checking all of the rooms. The living room, kitchen, and first two bedrooms were empty but I could see at the end of the hallway that a door was shut and light was coming from the cracks.

"Sly, stop it!" I could hear Ryan saying.

Without hesitation, I opened the door to Sly's room. He was on top of Ryan, both were fully dressed. He had both hands on her sides.

"That tickles!" Ryan laughed. "That-"

They both stopped and looked at me.

"Avery?" Ryan sat up. "Is something wrong?"

"Are you okay?" I asked, not answering her.

"We were just playing around," Sly said, standing up. "I wasn't hurting her or anything."

"Oh," I was embarrassed. "Okay, I was just checking."

*Sly get down here!*

"What?" I asked.

"No one said anything," Sly answered.

*Jon has a gun and he's asking for his money.*

"Who's Jon?" I asked.

"What" Sly looked surprised. "Why do you ask?"

"He's here asking for his money. And he has-"

"Oh shit!" Sly ran out of the room.

"Sly, wait!" Ryan ran after him, so of course I ran after her.

By the time I got down the stairs, Jon had grabbed Ryan and had his gun up to her head. She was crying, and Sly looked panicked. Most of the place had cleared out except for a few people watching what was going on, and Andrew. He stayed next to Sly but kept looking over at me.

"Dude, what are you doing?" Sly asked.

"You don't lose a bet to me and expect not to pay it, bro," Jon pressed the gun a little harder to Ryan's temple. "This your new girl? She's kind of cute."

"Come on man, don't do this!" Sly pleaded. "This has nothing to do with her."

"I'll let her go when you give me my money, bro. I ain't leaving here without it."

"Look, look," Andrew took a step forward, which made Jon point his gun at him. "Why don't you take me instead of her? You can just let the girls go and we can settle this."

Jon took a moment to think about it before nodding Andrew over. Once Andrew was in reach, Juan shoved Ryan at me and we backed up away from the situation a little. Jon had a firm grip on Andrew and the gun was now pointed at his head.

"Okay," Andrew sighed. "Here's what you're going to do. First, you're going to let me go. Then, you're going to walk out of this house and never come back. Next, you're going to walk until you come to the next police station. You're going to hand your gun over and turn yourself in. After you serve your jail time, you're going to live a better life and treat others, as well as yourself, better. Understand?"

I watched in shock as Jon slowly lowered the gun, turned around, and started out the door. Andrew and Sly came over to us.

"Are you okay?" Andrew looked at me and asked, although I'm sure he was asking Ryan too. We both nodded.

"We should take the girls home now," he looked at Sly. "If you and Ryan drop me and Avery off at work, I'll pick up my car and take Avery home."

"Well Avery was going to spend the night at my house," Ryan said.

"I think I'm just going to go home tonight," I replied. "Andrew can take me home."

None of us spoke in the car ride to the mall. The parking lot was empty aside from Andrew's car. I got out and hugged Ryan goodbye and got into Andrew's car. I know I didn't have a good reason to trust Andrew because I barely knew him, but something told me I could feel safe with him. And I had a few questions for him like how he persuaded Jon so easily to just walk away from the party. It was almost as if Jon was obeying Andrew's command. Andrew turned the car on and turned the radio on. He went through several different stations before picking a song.

"I love this song," he turned up the music a little.

"Can I ask you something?" I asked.

Andrew nodded and turned off the radio.

"What the hell happened back there?" I asked.

"What do you mean?"

"What do I mean? You told Jon to let you go and to turn himself in to the police? Did you have a knife or bomb on you or something?"

"No," he laughed.

"Was it a really bad prank you two tried pulling on Sly?"

"No, I told you. I didn't know any of those people. I guess I don't know Sly at all either if that's the kind of crowd he hangs with."

"So then what happened?"

"You saw what happened. I asked him to let me go and to leave and he did."

"You didn't ask him though. You *told* him."

"Maybe he got scared and backed out on his plan."

"No offense, but you're not intimidating."

"Oh really?" he raised an eyebrow.

"That guy was over six feet tall and probably weighed at least 250 pounds."

"Your point?"

"You're only like an inch taller than me and weigh, what, 180?"

"175, actually. Have you ever heard the saying, 'it's not the size of the dog in the fight, it's the size of the fight in the dog.' I could have taken him down easily, especially without the gun."

"But *he* did have a gun. And all you had were words and it worked."

"I don't know, Avery!" Andrew snapped at me. "The important thing is we're all safe and he probably won't be coming back. Now, how about we talk about your little secret?"

"What secret?"

*Oh crap. He knows.*

"The fact that you've never been on a date," He smiled.

I let out a sigh.

"Well, obviously it's not that big of a secret then, is it?" I asked.

"Regardless, I'd like to fix that. If that's okay with you."

"You're asking me out on a date?"

"You catch on quickly."

We pulled onto the road I lived on. My house was the only one on Christie Road so I was sure Andrew had spotted it by now. I was waiting for him to make some remark about how big it was.

"Why?"

"Why what?"

"Why are you asking me out?"

"Because I'm interested in you."

"No."

"No?"

"No but thanks. I don't have time for a boyfriend right now. And plus, I'm only fifteen."

"Oh, your parents won't let you date yet. Do they have strict rules about it? Maybe I could meet them and talk them into letting you go out with me."

"My parents died when I was four and my uncle could care less if I date. So, no, it's not their rules, it's mine. And I say no, I don't want to go on a date with you."

As the car slowed to a stop in front of my house, I unbuckled my seat belt and opened the car door. Andrew's hand touched my shirt and lightly tugged. I turned around to face him.

"Avery, please go on a date with me."

"Okay, fine."

"Alright, I'll pick you up at eight o'clock on Saturday night. Sound good?"

"Yeah, I'll be off from work by then."

"See you then," Andrew smiled as I got out of the car and shut the door.

"What the hell?" I asked out loud as I got inside the front door. I hadn't wanted to go on a date with Andrew, but I said yes anyways. Confused and tired, I walked into the kitchen to get a glass of water.

"Do you have any idea of what time it is?" Charlie startled me.

"Jesus Christ!" I spilled half of my glass on the floor. "Were you just chilling in the corner waiting for me to get home?"

"Well I wasn't 'chilling' but yes, I've been up waiting for you. Where have you been?"

"With Ryan and some friends."

"Ryan's mother called here about two hours ago saying Ryan hadn't come home yet and then when she came home and you didn't, I was worried sick. Who brought you home?"

*You'd think after what happened to her parents, she'd be more cautious.*

"What?" I asked.

"I asked you who brought you home?"

"Andrew did."

This mind-reading thing was starting to stress me out.

"Andrew? Who is Andrew?"

"Just some guy. I'm going to bed."

"That's a good idea since you have school in about four hours. And we'll discuss this Andrew business at a later time."

"Good night, Charlie," I said, dragging my feet up the stairs.

"Good night, Avery."

Without changing into my pajamas, I plopped onto my bed. I knew I was going to wake up in the morning with just enough time to change my shirt, put on some deodorant, and brush my teeth. I'd have to do my homework for my first class while walking to school and the rest of my homework during my first class. A million things raced through my mind as I drifted off to sleep. I thought of Amanda, Julia, Kelly, Ryan, Sly, Juan, and Andrew. More than anyone else, I thought of Andrew.

"Avery! Wake up! Avery!"

I could still feel the hands on my throat choking me as I woke up from my nightmare, Charlie was standing over me. I sat up in bed and squinted at the morning light coming in through the window.

"You were having a bad dream," Charlie explained, his hand on my shoulder.

"Yeah," I panted. "Thanks for waking me up."

My alarm clock went off and I smacked it, turning it off. I put my head in my hands and grunted.

"Come on, you don't want to be late for school again. You don't need anymore detentions than you already have."

"Well get out so I can get dressed."

"Okay, I'll see you downstairs."

I sat there for a moment and tried to remember my dream from the previous night. I was being attacked by a group of thugs that were twice my size and although they were getting a few good hits in, I was apparently stronger than them. I mean, I was like super strong, pulling the guys off of me and throwing them like rag dolls. This one guy wrapped his hands around my throat and tried choking me. When I pulled him off of me, his arms were ripped from his body and the hands were still around my neck. It was creepy.

Charlie left the room and I got up, stretched, and changed my shirt. My jeans still faintly smelled like cigarettes from the party last night but I didn't care. I checked my cell phone and noticed that I had two missed text messages. The first one was from Ryan saying that she was in trouble from last night and that her mom was dropping her off at school so I'd be walking with just Kelly. The second message was from a number I didn't recognize. It was Andrew; he had gotten my number from Sly, who got it from Ryan. The message said that it was nice meeting me last night and that he was looking forward to Saturday night. Shit. Saturday night was our date. I didn't want to go, but I didn't want to blow him off either. I finished getting ready and called Kelly to see if he was ready to go. I said bye to Charlie and Cindy and headed out the door. Once I met up with Kelly, I filled him in on everything that Ryan hadn't told him about last night.

"So are you going to go on the date?" Kelly kicked a rock on the sidewalk.

"I don't know," I sighed, kicking the same rock as I walked up to it. "I mean, he seems cool and all but I don't really want to. Can you picture me on a date? I'm sitting there in the movie theater, trying to enjoy a crappy romantic comedy that Andrew picked, when I wanted to see an action flick. My hand is resting on the arm rest. Andrew moves his hand ever so gently and tries to hold my hand and then WHAM! I rack him right in the junk and go watch the action movie by myself."

Kelly and I started laughing.

"Watch this," Kelly swung his leg back and punted the rock hard into the air. It landed about 8 feet in front of us. As we got closer to it again, I pulled back my leg and kicked it as hard as I could. The rock launched into the air like a golf ball and we watched as it landed in a front yard off in the distance. Kelly turned to me slowly.

"Holy shit!" he exclaimed. "You just kicked that rock like 150 feet!"

"I'm sure it didn't go that far," my cheeks turned red.

"Avery, my god, you could kick for a pro football team!"

"Would you please just be quiet! Maybe the wind picked it up and carried it. Or it was just a one time thing. I'm surprised I didn't miss the damn thing and fall on my ass."

"Well still, you should try out for the soccer team or something. That was awesome."

"Kelly, could we just keep this between us two?"

"Uh, sure. Are you okay, Avery?"

I looked at Kelly. Although he and Ryan were my two best friends, there was no way I could tell them. I was going to wait a week, see if my "condition" got any worse, and tell Julia next Thursday during our session.

"Yeah, I'm fine. I've just had a lot on my mind lately."

"Are you really an alien?" he asked.

"No!" I laughed.

"You sure? You don't get weak at the sight of kryptonite? Turn huge and green when you get mad?"

"Kelly, can you do me a favor?" I asked.

"Don't worry, I told you, I won't tell anyone."

"Not that. Think of a number."

"Any number?"

"Just pick a number between one and ten."

"Okay."

"Think about it really hard," I started concentrating. "Close your eyes and don't move your mouth at all."

*Seven*, I heard him think. My eyes widened.

"Three," I lied.

"Nope," he smiled. "Seven. What was that about?"

I saw another rock, and barely tapping, pretended to kick it hard. It barely moved two feet in front of us.

"See?" I said. "I'm not an alien and definitely not superhuman."

I rushed into my first class and scribbled down my homework. Luckily my science homework was a worksheet about the video we had watched yesterday and I knew all of the answers. The bell rang for class to begin as I jotted down the last few answers. None of my teachers understood me. When it came to the work I did in class, I didn't do hardly any of it. I never participated in class discussions or volunteered to read or anything. I didn't want to be a part of any of it. However, I always did my best with homework and tests. So, my grades were mediocre and I was passing, but just barely. I was a smart kid, I just didn't care enough about school to put any effort into anything I was doing. During my science class, we had to watch another stupid video so I halfway watched the video and worked on my homework for other classes. I finished everything by the time class was over so I didn't have any homework issues, but being sleep deprived was starting to kick my ass so by the time gym class came around, which was third period, I wasn't feeling up to the physical tests we were going to do. We had to run laps, do push-ups, chin-ups, sit-ups, and so on to see how good of shape we were in. Great.

"Kendall," Coach Williams called. "You're next."

We were split up into several small groups, getting our names called one at a time, and did our tests while everyone watched. It was painfully embarrassing to see the non-athletic kids go after the jocks. Steven, the golden football player, had just went in front of me and of course, did like 100 push-ups without breaking a sweat. So you could imagine how I felt walking up to my gym teacher, in front of the whole gym and got down to do mine. I knew hardly no one was watching but it felt like every eye in the gym was on me. Last time we did these tests, at the beginning of the year, I could only do three real push-ups. We weren't allowed to do the "girl push-ups" for these tests. I got down on the ground and started.

"1, 2, 3, 4, 5 . . ." Coach started counting.

I realized I was doing these a lot easier than before. I had already done two more than the first time and was still going strong.

"6, 7, 8, 9, 10! Keep it going, Kendall!"

I kept going and going, my arms not getting tired at all. Once my gym teacher reached forty and I was still feeling fine, I realized that everyone was watching me. I wasn't even out of breath or breaking a sweat. I decided to stop at fifty, although I was curious to see how many I could actually do. Several people clapped for me once I was done and my teacher patted me on the back.

"Nice work, Kendall," he chuckled. "Your improvement is pretty impressive."

The next test was the mile. Before I had just walked and jogged through the rest of the class, making my mile time at 30+ minutes. However, I breezed through this mile, my legs feeling great as my feet hit the pavement.

"Kendall, your time is 5.34! Great job, kiddo!"

I went with the chin-ups next, doing an impossible 30, a lot more than the mere two I had done the last time! Although I wasn't tired at all, I faked running out of breath and getting too tired. Needless to say, I now had an A in gym. After gym, I had a test to take in my English class. We had been reading a book for homework and now had to take a test over it. I pretty much just skimmed through the book since it wasn't real interesting so I was nervous about this test. I had looked up foot notes online and printed them out but I hadn't really read through them. I was sitting there, stuck on question #35, with a pen in my hand. I must have been concentrating harder than I thought because all of a sudden my pen snapped in two and ink splattered all over my desk, my test, and my clothes. A few people snickered and my teacher let me go to the bathroom to clean up.

I grabbed a few paper towels and pulled the faucet handle, accidentally yanking it completely off. Water sprayed everything inside the bathroom including all over me. The water was making the ink bleed into my clothes, making it more difficult for me to get all of the stains out. I was getting pissed off; I didn't want to go the rest of the day with stained clothes. This whole "super strength" thing was a little more trickier than I would have thought it'd be. I wonder if any comic book characters had this many issues. Lunch time wasn't much better. I broke four plastic forks before giving up and eating with my hands. Kelly and Ryan kept giving me weird looks.

"I'm just stressed out, guys," I explained. "I think I tanked my English test and I'm covered in blue ink."

"Yeah, that's pretty sucky," Ryan laughed, taking a bite of her food. "I didn't think the test was too bad."

"That's because you actually studied," I grunted. "This school pisses me off. I hate the classes, the teachers, the homework, and the people here."

"Except us," Kelly winked.

"Yeah."

*Oh my god,* I heard Amanda think. *Just look at her! I can't wait until history class so I can give her shit. After yesterday I'm going to give that bitch a hard time until* she *cries.*

I looked over at the table that Amanda and the preps were sitting at.

"But I wasn't talking about you guys."

*I'm going to call her a lesbian, talk about how crazy she is, and especially talk about her family. Her uncle can't even stand to live with her.*

I wanted to go over to the table and wring Amanda's neck until she turned as blue as I was. I wanted to pull out all of her hair and punch her teeth in. I hated her.

*Her parents probably killed themselves and the family's covering it up. I would too if she was my kid.*

"Avery!" Ryan exclaimed.

I looked down and saw that the can I had been drinking my apple juice out of was wadded up like a piece of paper, down to almost the size of a quarter. Without even trying to explain myself, I stood up, threw away my trash and headed straight for Amanda.

# CHAPTER 2

# No Excuses

*"It's okay, had a bad day.*
*Hands are bruised from breaking rocks all day.*
*Drained and blue, I bleed for you.*
*You think it's funny, well you're drowning in it too."*

-"No Excuses" by Alice in Chains

As I charged at Amanda, a thousand thoughts went through my mind. After the events that had happened during the day so far, with my strength, there was a possibility that I could accidentally kill Amanda. I could punch her one time, as hard as I could, and bash her tiny brain out of her skull. However, I really didn't feel like getting sent to prison, so I ended up slamming my hand down on the table. Amanda jumped, startled.

"If you ever touch me, talk to me, or talk about me or my family again, I will literally beat the shit right out of you. Do you understand me?"

Amanda stared at me for a second in terror, and then her terror turned went away and she smiled at me.

"Is that a threat?" she asked.

I would have went with the whole, "no, it's a promise" thing but as I've said before, I don't like clichés.

"Yeah, it kind of is," I replied. "Just leave me alone you spoiled bitch."

All of a sudden, Amanda was on top of me, pulling my hair, and scratching and slapping me in the face. It didn't even phase me.

"Alright then," I laughed. "Have it your way."

All it took was one hit. I didn't even hit her as hard as I could have but when she fell off of me and laid on the ground, I saw the damage. Her nose looked like it was almost pushed into her face and blood was everywhere. Her eyes were already swelling up too, so she kind of looked like a pig mutant. She was screaming and crying so teachers were already coming over to check everything out. I grabbed at my head and face where she had scratched me to make it look like she had hurt me too, although I didn't feel it.

"Oh my god," One of the teachers said, bending down to look at Amanda. "She'll need to go to the hospital. I think she has a concussion!"

Amanda did end up having a concussion, and although I got away with self defense being my reason for hitting her, I was still in some major deep shit.

"Do you realize how much pain Amanda is in right now?" Principal Matthews said. "Not to mention all of the school she'll be missing."

I was sitting in the office with the principal, the teacher who broke up the fight, my uncle, Julia, and Amanda's mother. She was insisting that I be kicked out of the school and was trying to get a restraining order put on me. She was being over-dramatic and saying that I was trying to kill Amanda. I just sat there and watched her and my uncle go at each other. My uncle was mad at me but he understood why I did it since she touched me first. It was a good thing he used to be a lawyer because he was shooting legal crap at her and she didn't have a clue what he was talking about. Meanwhile, the principal, Julia, and the other teacher were trying to calm down the situation.

"If your niece ever comes near this school again, let alone my daughter-"

"Bring it on, lady! I've dealt with criminals who have done way worse than what a fifteen year old girl can do to another fifteen old girl-"

"I will absolutely not tolerate violence and harassment in my school, no matter who started it-"

"Avery is just now starting to open up about her feelings and she's not sure how to handle it-"

"When I arrived Avery hit Amanda in the face, even though she was trying to get Amanda off of her without hurting her-"

"Why would my daughter attack her for no reason. Amanda is a good student and never-"

"Avery said that they had been arguing before Amanda attacked her-"

I was about to go insane. Everyone was yelling at once, and because my nerves were on end, I could also hear all of their thoughts at once. It was the first time I could hear multiple thoughts and it was driving me crazy. I had a headache from Hell and all I wanted to do was leave. Finally everyone started calming down and we started discussing what was going to happen. The final result: Starting in January, if Amanda and I were caught fighting on school property, both of us would be expelled and possibly removed from the school. I was going to have to either attend a behavioral boot camp starting in winter break and ending in Spring or a martial arts class and a group therapy class for the next year. My uncle and

I would have to make a decision by the next morning. Things got pretty bad once we got home from school.

"What the hell were you thinking, Avery?" Uncle Ross asked as we walked through the door.

"Don't start busting my ass, okay?" I snapped. "I don't know why you even bothered showing up to school. You never show up to defend me any other time."

"They needed your legal guardian and that would be me."

"Are you sure it's not Charlie? He's the one who's raised me in this house."

"Watch your mouth, Avery. Do not disrespect me in my own home."

"It's not your god-damn home! It's my parents' home!"

"And where are they right now?"

I stopped yelling and stared at him, taken aback from what he just said. Tears filled my eyes but I dared not let them fall.

"Avery . . ." he sighed.

"Screw you," I said as I ran up the stairs and slammed my bedroom door, making a few things fall off the wall next to it. I jumped onto my bed and started crying. I hated him. If he would have stayed in Boston as just my uncle and my parents wouldn't have died, my life would have been easier. A part of me hated them too. They had left me and I couldn't fix that. They didn't just walk out on me or give me up for adoption. They didn't leave me with the satisfaction of finding them and rubbing in their faces how awful they were for leaving me and how great I was doing in life. I thought in time, my uncle and I would grow closer but I knew it wouldn't happen. I was just something he had to deal with for another three years and then I'd go off to college or get my own place and he wouldn't ever see me again.

My phone went off and I saw that it was Andrew. He sent a message asking if we were still on for the next day. I lied and said that I had to work a double at my job so I wouldn't be able to. He asked when I'd be available again and I said I'd let him know when I found out. Sort of a "don't call us, we'll call you" type thing. I felt bad for lying to him because I did think he was cute and I did want to hang out with someone, I just didn't feel comfortable going on a date. Maybe in a year, I'd feel better about it and give it another go. I started on my homework and heard a knock on the door.

"Can I come in?" I heard my uncle say.

"That depends on who you are," I didn't take my eyes off of the paper in front of me.

"You know who it is."

"Then, no. You can't come in."

"We need to discuss what our plans are for your punishment."

"You mean the camp."

"Possibly."

"Come in," I rolled my eyes.

The door opened and as my uncle came in, I contemplated throwing my text book at him as hard as I could. He sat down on the couch I had against the wall.

"So, what do you think?" he asked.

"I think it's all bullshit," I tossed my homework aside and crossed my arms.

"Well at least Amanda's family isn't pressing charges or taking you to court."

"I don't understand why she isn't in trouble. She pulled out a chunk of my hair and scratched my face."

"That's true, she did. But you hit her back and messed her up a lot more. It's not like I don't believe it, but I don't see how just one hit did that much damage."

"You don't believe me, do you?"

"It doesn't matter, Avery. What do you want to do? I think the camp would be best for you."

"No offense, but you don't know shit about what's best for me."

"I think it'll be good for you to get out of this town for a while," he continued, ignoring my comment. "It would get you away from Kelly and Ryan."

"Why is that a good thing? They're my best friends and they're not bad kids."

"But they don't hang out with good kids. Sly? You think I don't know about him? Charlie tells me more than you think."

"I don't even like Sly! I think he's a total creep!"

"Nonetheless. So, the camp?"

"No! I'm not going to B.F.E., Kansas to some camp for angry teenagers! What teenager isn't angry about something? That's the whole point of being a teenager practically!"

"I'm just afraid you'll misuse the martial arts class and get into more trouble."

"How about this then," I said. "Let me try the martial arts class and the group therapy thing and if they don't work, I'll try the camp."

"Okay," he smiled. "But here are my guidelines. No more skipping class, no more fights with anyone at school or outside of school, your grades that need improving will be improved, you're not to go out on school nights, and you are to be home by eleven on weekends."

"What!" I jumped up. "That's not fair! Eleven on the weekends? Why, I don't have anything to do except work for the most part anyways and then I want to hang out with my friends! I'll settle for two."

"Two o'clock in the morning? No deal. Eleven."

"One o'clock then? Come on!"

"Fine, Avery. One will be your curfew."

"And I can be home by ten on school nights."

"No," my uncle refused. "How about nine?"

"Fine," I grunted.

"Okay but if you break any of these rules, you'll be packing for Kansas. Understand?"

I nodded.

"Alright. Finish your homework before Cindy is done making dinner."

My uncle left my room and I updated Kelly and Ryan on everything. They were bummed like I was but happy I didn't have to go away to the camp. My first martial arts class would start on Sunday. The classes met twice a week, the other day being Wednesdays. My group sessions were on Tuesdays. My work schedule was Friday nights and Saturday days, which left me with hardly no time with my friends. This was going to suck so much, but as I said, it was better than Kansas. After dinner, I headed up to work for a couple of hours before coming back home and going to bed.

The next day was spent at work, as usual. I worked at Mr. Williams Ice Cream, the ice cream shop in town that was owned by this old guy. And before you ask, I don't have a job for the money, it just gives me something to do and I get free ice cream for working there. Kelly and Ryan also work there, but they do it for the money. Their parents make them work to save money and to buy stuff they want. It gives us another chance to hang out but it gets kind of boring sometimes. Three of us and the owner are the only employees and most of the time the only people in the store. Mr. Williams doesn't come in on Saturdays because it's his only day off. So you can imagine the sort of fun the three of us could have. After work, we decided to go see a movie with the money we made on our paychecks.

"I made a whole $192 on my check," I laughed. "Two weeks of work and this is all I made?"

"Coming from the girl who doesn't even need a job," Kelly said with a mouth full of gummy bears. "We work our asses off to pay for stuff and you do it for fun."

"And free ice cream," I added.

"Yeah one day all of that free ice cream is going to go to your butt," Ryan smiled. "We won't always have our metabolism."

"You sound like Mom," Kelly said as the lights dimmed.

"Just think," Ryan whispered to me. "You could be on a date with Andrew right now."

"I'd rather be here with you two," I said.

The following day was Sunday, my first martial arts class. I hadn't been able to hear any thoughts or have super strength since Friday at school. I was thinking I wasn't going to be able to do it anymore. I took my time getting dressed and Charlie drove me to the class. I walked in, feeling uncomfortable in a new environment. I wanted to run out the door and keep running until my legs gave out.

"Can I help you?" a man asked me.

"I start a martial arts class today and I'm not sure where to go."

"What's your name?"

"Avery Kendall."

He walked over to the front desk, typed on the computer and walked away.

"Follow me," he said walking down the hall.

I was surprised to see that none of the people who worked here were Asian. I know that seems prejudice of me but it was what I was expecting.

"Alright," the man said. "This is your class."

I walked through the doorway and the room was filled with about fifteen people, an older man standing at the front of the room. I walked over to him.

"Hi, my name is Avery," I stuck my hand out. "I'm new to the class."

"My name is Daniel, or just Dan," he shook my hand. "I will be your teacher. Please, take off your shoes and have a seat where there's an open spot."

I walked to the back of the room, removed my shoes, and sat down next to an old lady. When I say old, I mean she was like grandma old. I was eager to see how she did in this class. Maybe she'd make me look better if I stayed next to her.

"Hello," she turned towards me. "My name is Susanne. What's your name?"

"Avery," I smiled.

"Avery, what a beautiful name! Is this your first time here?"

I nodded.

"I usually do the Saturday classes, but something told me to switch to Sundays. What brings you in?"

"I, uh, got into some trouble at school and my uncle thinks this class will help me control some of my anger issues."

"Oh my! Well I certainly hope it does help you. You're too young to be worrying about anger issues. I thought this would be a good class to take for some self-defense. In case anyone tries messing with an old girl."

The class started and Dan introduced me to everyone before we started. My uncle didn't want to put me in the beginner class with all of the little kids because he thought I could handle this class. I wasn't so sure. I was nervous to see how far behind I was compared to everyone else. First, we stretched. That part wasn't so bad. Then, we did a little bit of breathing technique practices. Next, we paired off into partners, Susanne being my partner.

"Let me know if I need to ease up on you," she smiled.

*Yeah right.*

"Begin!" Dan announced.

Susanne and I bowed to each other. All of a sudden, she had me pinned down and then let go of me.

"Whoa," I grabbed at my neck. "You were super fast on that one."

"I'm sorry, I know you're new at all of this."

"It's fine. Let's go again."

Class pretty much sucked because I got my ass kicked by a sixty year old woman. I was out of breath and sore. Susanne insisted on taking me out for dinner afterwards and although I really didn't want to, I was starving. We ate at a nearby diner and talked about each other.

"Oh yeah, I lived in New York with my husband during the late seventies to the early eighties and was really into the punk scene. I practically lived at CBGB's."

"That's so cool!" I said before taking a drink of my milk shake. It was interesting listening to her stories; she was actually a cool old lady.

"So, enough about me," Susanne said. "Let's talk about you for a bit."

"Uh," I hesitated. "There's really nothing interesting about me. I'm not that old; I don't even drive yet. I pretty much just go to school, work on the weekends, and hang out with my friends."

"There's more than just that though, isn't there?" she asked, taking a sip of her coffee.

"Let's see, my parents died when I was really young. They were shot by someone and now I live with my uncle who takes care of me because he has to."

*Kind of like Batman. Nice.*

"Yeah," I laughed. "Like Batman. Except I don't wear a cape."

I looked up at Susanne. Her jaw was dropped. Oh shit, she hadn't said anything.

"Oh, was that what you were going to say?" I asked, acting like I didn't know what was going on. Why now did my thought-reading have to come back?

"Avery, did you hear what I was thinking?"

"No! That's not even possible. What a stupid question."

I grabbed a few dollars from my wallet and threw them on the table before getting up and walking out the door. I walked away without looking back. I took out my cell phone to call Charlie so he could come pick me up. A really cold wind hit me and sent shivers down my spine. A snowflake landed on my arm. I looked up and saw that it began to snow.

"What the-?" I asked before seeing Susanne behind me.

*Avery.*

I jumped at the sound of her thought. I put my phone back into my pocket and followed her. She turned down an alley and the snow had stopped falling. As I turned down the alley, I saw Susanne sitting on the ground. Her legs were crossed and her eyes were closed. I almost said something but decided against it once things started happening. Out of nowhere, flowers started growing from the dirt and it started raining. However, this wasn't a normal cold rain, it was a warm summer rain in the middle of October.

"You see, Avery," Susanne opened her eyes. "You're not alone. And you are a very special, unique person."

I sat down in front of her as the rain began to fade and the flowers bloomed.

"Fate has brought us together," she smiled. "I help young people with different abilities. We have a group that meets on Friday nights and Saturdays during the day. I would very much like you to come the next time we meet."

"I, uh, have to work during those times."

"Oh, how unfortunate. Well, the offer is always open. This is the address we meet at."

She handed me a card that she pulled from her pocket.

"I hope you do not tell anyone about this."

"Of course not," I took the card with a shaky hand.

"Good. I really do hope you can make it on Friday."

Susanne stood up and then I did too. I looked at the flowers around us. I watched Susanne as she walked down to the street.

"I'll try to get the night off," I said as she turned the corner.

*I'll see you there*, she said.

I smiled and grabbed my phone to text Kelly and Ryan, asking if either of them could cover for me, telling Mr. Williams that I had a cold or something. They both agreed and asked why I needed the night off. I lied and said I wanted to try going on a date with Andrew but not to say anything to anyone about it. They bought it so I was free to meet up with Susanne's group then. Over the next few days, a lot of weird stuff started happening though. I couldn't read thoughts anymore, and I didn't have super strength. I had a dream on Monday night that someone was chasing after me through a brick maze and I could go through the walls to get away from whoever was chasing me. However, I had only been able to do it in real life once. I was practicing in my bedroom, running at the wall and hitting it over and over. I started getting really pissed until finally I charged at the wall and went through to my bathroom. It felt insanely weird. It felt like when you pull off dead skin from a sun burn, except all over my whole body. But that was it. I couldn't figure out how to control or activate my powers. Hopefully Susanne could help me with it.

The week at school dragged by, especially when it came to talking about what had happened on Friday with Amanda. It was nice not having to see her in class though. She came back to school on Thursday but kept her distance from me. I didn't realize how much I had jacked her face up. Both eyes were swollen, but she could finally see through them now. A huge bandage covered her nose but you didn't have to see what was underneath to know how bad it probably looked. When Julia came to take me out of class for our session, Amanda didn't even look at me.

"We certainly had a lot going on Friday, didn't we?" Julia asked me, getting out her notebook. I nodded.

"You don't seem very talkative today."

"I just have a lot on my mind right now," I answered.

"That's why I'm here. Tell me what's going on."

"I don't know, I'm just going through some changes that I don't understand. I don't want to be around anyone or do anything but be myself and do what I need to do."

"It's the hormones. This is a critical time in your life right now. You're almost sixteen and a sophomore in high school. You'll start driving and dating soon. You might make more friends or different friends that you normally wouldn't hang out with. It's a hard time for a young woman."

"Please don't give me a life lecture," I started biting my nail. "I know all about puberty and peer pressure and the joys and sorrows of being a teenager. I'm just sick of coming to school every day, going to work every weekend, going home every day and doing same shit all of the time. I'm tired of it."

"Take up a new hobby. Set some personal goals for yourself."

*Starting tomorrow night, I plan on doing just that*, I thought to myself.

"Okay," I muttered. "Can we be done now?"

"One last thing."

I sighed and slumped even further down into my char.

"Avery, have you thought about what might happen when you turn eighteen?"

"What do you mean?"

"Well, you know that, for now, everything that was your parents' is in your uncle's name. But when you turn eighteen, everything will be put into your name if you want. That means, you could have control over the house and the lab. How do you feel about that?"

"Hey, my uncle can have the stupid, run-down lab. What makes you think I want it? Or that shitty house. I plan on getting accepted to a school on the coast. I'm not exactly sure what I want to go to school for, but I definitely want to move away from the Midwest. I hate living here."

"So you don't want the lab? I thought you liked science?"

"It's alright, I guess. I mean, I'd want to work in a lab, not run it. I'm not one to boss people around, figuring out how much I have to pay people and run experiments. My uncle seems to be handling things just fine without me."

"Okay," Julia sighed. "I won't mention it again. You seem to know what you want though."

I spent the next 24 hours watching the clock. I just wanted to get to the meeting Susanne was having. I wanted to meet other people like me and I wanted answers about what made me the way I am. I knew something big was in store for me, I just never thought it'd be super powers. I was so anxious for that night that I didn't even eat lunch at school. Instead, I wondered the halls, looking for something to do. A couple of teachers stopped me to ask what I was doing, and every time I lied, saying I was going to the bathroom. I found myself in front of Julia's office. The lights were off and the door was locked. No one would be around to find me inside. While no one was around, I decided to practice my new ability. I concentrated with all of my might and pushed against the wall. Nothing. I held my breath, tensed up my body and tried again, pushing into the solid wood. I started sweating, afraid someone would find me by myself and running into a door. I took a couple of steps back and tried once more. I launched myself at the door with my eyes shut. I felt my body squeeze and then I opened my eyes. I was inside the dark room and no one had caught me!

I plopped my backpack down on the floor and looked around quietly, making sure not to leave anything out of place. I sat in Julia's desk chair and hiked my feet up, helping myself to several pieces of candy that were in a bowl on the desk. I went through the desk's drawers, finding mostly women's magazines and half used chap sticks. In one of the drawers I found a small framed photo of Julia with another guy. Her hand was placed on his chest and she was staring at the engagement ring on her hand. This ring was different than the one she had now. While she was looking at the ring, the guy she was with was looking at her. It made me sad knowing that she was so much happier with the guy in the picture than she was with her fiancé now. It was kind of like me with my uncle. I was a lot happier with my parents and I'd still rather have them back but I was happy to have my uncle just to have someone there for me. I was settling for a parent replacement just like Julia was settling for a fiancé replacement. Life was unfair that way; giving you what you need, but taking away what you want.

I put the photo back in its place and noticed a set of keys on the desk. I looked over at the cabinets where I knew she stashed the notebooks. I wanted to know what she said about me. I grabbed the keys and tried a few on the cabinets. I got lucky on the fourth key and opened the drawer. I fingered through the tabs, casually looking at the last names until I reached Kendall. I pulled out my notebooks and sat back down at the desk. A lot of the notes were just quotes of things I had said, such as, "My uncle is just a shadow of my dad."

My notes weren't that interesting. I stuck them back in the cabinet and another last name caught my eye. Kelly and Ryan both had notebooks in the drawer. I pulled them out and the lunch bell rang. I'd have to leave to get back to class without getting caught by someone. I locked the cabinet, placed the keys in the same spot, and stuffed the two notebooks into my backpack. I pushed against the door, not being able to go through. I unlocked the door, opened it and locked it before shutting it behind me. I ran down the hallway and up the stairs, making it to my next class just in time. I'd have something interesting to read during the weekend while I wasn't at my super human meeting.

As soon as I got home, I changed my clothes and packed a few things into my backpack including a pen and notebook in case I wanted to take notes. I also packed a change of clothes that I'd normally wear during gym class, in case we did any physical training of any kind. I decided to wear a pair of black jeans with a button-up white shirt. I thought it would make me look like a normal person instead of the punk kid I normally portrayed. I crammed the piece of paper with the address Susanne had given me into my pocket and ran out the door. I'd have to take a bus into the city so Charlie and my uncle wouldn't know where I was. The bus took about an hour so I read some of Kelly and Ryan's notebooks. I was surprised to see my name mentioned so much. Ryan had mentioned several times of how jealous she was of me, mostly because of my inherited money. She was struggling to keep up in school because she worked so much, however she wasn't earning a lot of money from her job to save up for college. It made me feel bad because I always talked about being irritated with all the money that was in my name. I didn't have to work a single day for the rest of my life if I didn't want, but Kelly and Ryan would have to work twice as hard to barely get by.

It got worse though. I also found out that Ryan had gotten HPV from having sex with Sly, even though she told me that she had never had sex with anyone. Along with an STD, Sly also gave Ryan some bruises. If I had pushed up Ryan's long-sleeved shirt that day, I would have found hand prints all over her arms. Julia insisted that Ryan stopped talking to Sly but Ryan was convinced that he would change.

Kelly's notebook was just as interesting. I found out that not only was he bi-curious, but he had a huge crush on me. I always thought of Kelly as a brother, never really noticing how much he flirted with me and hinted his attraction. I didn't know which was more weird; knowing Kelly also liked dudes, or knowing I was one of the girls he was interested in. Right away I knew I had made a huge mistake taking the notebooks. Now every time I hung out with them, my mind would go straight to what I had read. What would happen the next time Ryan couldn't eat out with me because she was broke? Or if Kelly put his arm around me if I mentioned being cold? Would I offer Ryan some money or move away from Kelly awkwardly? The next time Ryan mentioned Sly, would I go off on her saying how big of a dickhead I thought he was for hurting her and giving her HPV? I closed the notebooks and put them back into my bag. I pressed my head against the cold window and watched the rural scenery turn into an urban city. I could see the Sears building and other familiar landmarks. When we were in the right neighborhood, I pulled on the rope above my head to let the driver know to stop. The bus slowed down and I got off. Not sure of where I was going, I stopped into a flower shop to get help on directions. The woman inside told me where to go but looked confused.

"A girl your age shouldn't be walking around down here by herself."

"I'll be fine," I smiled, getting out my pen and notebook. "And you said it's across the street from a fire station?"

"Yes, that's right. Keep going down 54th street and if you go over the railroad tracks, you've gone too far."

"Okay, thank you."

I left the flower shop, got a taxi, and told him the address. He looked back at me.

"You sure, kid?" he asked. I nodded.

He turned back around and started driving.

"You know all that's left in that area is an old fire station."

"Yeah, so I've heard."

"What's a kid like you doing out and about on a Friday evening in the city all by yourself?"

"I'm, uh, visiting my grandma."

I checked the time on my cell phone and noticed I was already fifteen minutes late. I was going to have to ask Charlie to bring me because the bus and a cab took too long and was a waste of money. The taxi slowed down and stopped in front of the fire station that I had heard so much about and I knew why everyone seemed concerned about me being alone. Graffiti covered old buildings that were empty and had bars across the windows. The taxi sped off and I crossed the street to the building that faced the fire station. The sign in the yard read, "Annie's Animals. We serve all species." I walked up to the door and rang the door bell twice, just as Susanne had written on the paper. I heard a few different locks click and the door opened. A Japanese boy was staring at me. He had the door open just enough to see most of his face and one shoulder.

"Hey," I said, hoping I hadn't went to the wrong address. He didn't respond.

"Um, is Susanne here?"

Still no answer.

"My name is Avery. I'm here for the meeting thing."

A hand swung the door open more and the Japanese boy was pushed out of the way by a pretty girl with red hair. I noticed right away that she was wearing gloves.

"I'm sorry, don't mind him. You're Avery?"

"Yeah. Do I have the right place?"

"Yes, come on in!" she grabbed me and pulled me in. "My name is Hayley, it's nice to meet you! You must be so excited since it's your first time here."

Everything was happening so fast, I couldn't take everything in. The Japanese boy that had answered the door was huge, now that I could fully see him. He had to be at least 6'6" and was ripped, especially his pecks and arms. I also noticed that he was carrying a sword. He kept his eyes on me and stayed by the door until Hayley and I were out of sight. I noticed that Hayley was wearing a yoga outfit and had her curly, dark red hair swept back into a ponytail.

"I brought a change of clothes. I wasn't sure what we'd be doing," I said, trying to make small talk.

"Yeah, you're probably going to want to change," she replied, flipping her ponytail behind her. "Okay, so on the left here is the kitchen; you can pretty much eat anything that's in there unless it's labeled. We're not allowed to have soda, candy, or any other junk food here. Only healthy crap."

"That's fine, I don't drink pop anyways."

"On the right are the locker rooms/bathrooms. Boys are the door on the left and girls are on the right. No one really showers here except for Kitashi because he lives here. Oh by the way, that was Kitashi."

She pointed backwards, where the door was.

"He doesn't really talk much, and he doesn't like new people. He has trust issues, among many other issues," she giggled.

*Great*, I thought. *She's a gossipy snob. We'll get along great.*

"So where did you meet Susanne?" Hayley asked me before showing me the recreation room. There was a television, two small couches, and a ping pong table.

"Karate class," I answered.

"And this room here is the workout room. It's open 24 hours so obviously none of us ever go to a gym since we can use this one for free."

I was wondering why she kept asking questions if she didn't seem interested in the answers I was giving. I noticed that she was wearing makeup, including lip gloss. Why would she wear makeup to work out in?

"Okay, and finally, this is where we all get together for our Friday classes or meetings or whatever you want to call them."

"Should I change first?"

"Nah, just wait and see if we even have to do any physical training first."

We walked into the room and it wasn't really what I was expecting. The room had no lights on but the whole place was filled with lit candles. Four people were sitting on large bean bag chairs, facing Susanne who was sitting at the front of the room on her own bean bag. Everyone seemed to be meditating with their legs crossed and their eyes closed. Hayley pointed to two empty chairs next to a boy who was facing Susanne.

"We'll wait until they're done," Hayley whispered. "I don't want to interrupt them."

We stood there for a few moments until the meditating was done. Finally, Susanne opened her eyes. When she saw us, she smiled and stood up slowly. A couple of heads rose when she moved. Susanne waved her arm out and all of the candles went out, making the room very dark.

"Hayley, do you mind turning the lights on for us?" Susanne asked.

"I can do it!" a voice called out before the lights came on.

"Thank you, Barney," Susanne laughed. "But try to save the practicing for later while we train."

Hayley grabbed my arm and started walking toward the group.

"You get to meet my boyfriend, he's so cute!" she squealed.

We sat down in the empty chairs next the boy she had pointed to.

"Avery, this is-"

"Andrew?" I said, shocked. *What the hell!*

"Oh," Hayley's smile faded. "Do you know each other?"

"No, Hayley," Andrew smiled, putting his hand on her neck. "Avery can read minds. Susanne already told me."

"Andrew," she pushed his hand away. "You know I don't like that. Well anyways, this is my boyfriend and Andrew, this is the new girl."

"Nice to meet you, new girl," Andrew said. As Hayley faced the front, Andrew mouthed to me not to say anything. My face was hot and all I wanted to do was kick him in the balls. He had asked me out on a date and he had a girlfriend the whole time? What a creep; I'm glad I stood him up. I tried to momentarily take my mind off of Andrew while Susanne introduced me to everyone.

"Avery, could you come up to the front?" she asked, holding a hand out to me.

I got up in front of the group and Susanne handed me a piece of paper.

"You don't have to do it, but this is a little thing we like to do to get to know each other. Just give us a few little facts about you."

I looked down at the paper and felt like I was in school on the first day. It asked me basic questions like my likes and dislikes. I started with the easiest one.

"Hey, my name is Avery Nasia Kendall. I'm from Franklin Grove which is like a little over an hour away from here. I don't have any pets or siblings. Uh, I'm fifteen and a sophomore in high school. My favorite bands are Nirvana, Green Day, The Runaways, The Ramones, The Clash, Iggy and the Stooges, and David Bowie; but I guess I'll listen to anything pretty much. My favorite color is purple. My ability is . . ."

Everyone stared at me.

"I, um, I'm not sure. I get a new one every once in a while."

"What does that mean?" a short black girl asked me, raising her hand.

"I don't know how to explain it," I started fidgeting with the piece of paper in my hand. "I have really bad dreams but however I defeat whatever is attacking me or chasing after me or whatever, I end up having that power in real life the next day."

"You can turn fantasy into reality?" a skinny boy asked me.

"I don't know," I answered. "I suppose so."

"Okay well just finish the questions already," Hayley sighed.

I looked at Andrew and then looked back at the paper.

"Favorite movie is The Breakfast Club. And my favorite food is pizza and cheese fries. Now what do I do?"

The black girl raised her hand again. I nodded.

"My name is Maddison Green. I'm sixteen years old and I have a sonic voice thingy and I just wanted to welcome you to the group."

"Maddison," Susanne said sternly. "What have we talked about, calling our abilities 'thingies?'"

"Sorry," she mumbled.

The skinny boy raised his hand.

"Hello, my name is Barnabas Noble but everyone calls me Barney. I have telekinesis and I'm eighteen years old, making me the oldest in the group."

"Barney's also extremely smart," Andrew added. "Like beyond genius smart. He graduated from high school three years ago when he was your age. He can pretty much get accepted to any college he wants to attend, but for right now he's just working. The dude's outrageous."

"Thank you for that, Andrew," Barney adjusted his glasses. "If you need anything let me know. I'll be glad to help you."

"Thanks," I smiled.

Andrew stood up.

"My name is Andrew McDermont. I can persuade people into doing anything I tell them by touching them, but it has to be skin-on-skin contact. I also have empathy which means I can read and sometimes control people's emotions. It's kind of hard if the person is really stubborn or has very strong will power. I'm seventeen years old and I am a junior in high school."

Hayley stood up as Andrew was sitting back down.

"Hey! As I've already told you, my name is Hayley Marshall. I'm also seventeen and a junior at my school. My ability is I can heal and hurt, which is why I wear gloves. I'm not really in control of my powers yet but I know I'll get it right soon. I can heal people by touching with one hand but if I do it too much it could kill me because it drains my energy. Or I can hurt people with my other hand by draining their energy and it makes me stronger. However, I just found out that it's not just people that effect my powers. For example, if I touch a tree with one hand and a dying animal with the other, I can transfer some of the energy from the tree and make the animal live! How cool is that?"

"Very cool," I replied half-heartedly.

"Kitashi has impenetrable skin," Andrew explained to me. "If you were to try and stab him, the knife would just bend. Also, he's really good with swords."

I nodded at Kitashi, who just stared at me. I felt like he was going to run at me and slice my head off; he made me feel a little uneasy.

"So what ability do you have right now?" Hayley asked me.

"I can go through walls."

"Intangibility," Barney said. "That's what it's called."

"Oh, right. I have intangibility right now."

"Show us," Hayley smiled.

"Well, I haven't quite figured out how to make myself do it, it just randomly happens."

"Well try anyways," she said to me.

"She doesn't have to," Andrew told her. Hayley snapped her head at him.

"I want to see it, Drew. Has anyone seen her actually do any powers yet?"

"Hayley, calm down."

"Drew! Just stop talking! Avery, you don't mind trying, do you?"

I looked around the room at everyone. Susanne was smiling at me. Of course being put on the spot in front of a bunch of people I didn't know wasn't helping my nerves. I walked over to the wall and put my arms out in front of me. I stepped forward and the wall pushed against my hands. I turned around, starting to shake. What if I couldn't do it? Would they kick me out of their secret group on my first day? Or would they bump me off because they didn't want me to tell anyone? I tried again but it wasn't working. I shouldn't have used up my powers at school to sneak into Julia's office.

"I don't think I can," I told everyone. "I'm sorry."

Kitashi stood up and started walking towards me. *Well this is it,* I thought. *He's going to slice my head off with one of his swords or tear me into a bunch of little pieces and bury me in a bunch of places so no one would ever find me.*

Kitashi grabbed my shoulders and faced me towards the wall.

"You need to calm down," he said softly. His voice sounded like silk on my ears. "Slow your heart rate down; I can hear it without even touching you. You need to control your breathing and concentrate on what you're doing."

"I can't though," I whispered. "I'm too nervous."

"Why? Because of us?"

I nodded.

"Don't think about anyone here. Don't think about what you want to do; just do it. Let it happen naturally."

I put my hands up to the wall again. I paused a brief second and then pushed against the wall.

"You hesitated. Don't hesitate. Just do it."

As if his voice was a gun shot, it startled me into moving. I quickly pressed into the wall and went through. Standing outside, I felt proud of myself once more. I was getting the hang of this new ability. I pressed into the wall again and was standing in the room with everyone. Susanne, Andrew, and Kitashi were smiling but Hayley wasn't.

"Alright," Susanne walked towards me. "Great job! Now, let's get started."

Everyone moved the bean bag chairs off to the side of the room and got in a circle. I stood in between Barney and Kitashi after I received a really dirty look from Hayley. We all took turns practicing our powers. Susanne told us that the more we use them, the more control we'll have. Maddison went first. We all put on the ear muffs that Susanne had given us. They were the ones they use at speedways for car races and airplanes and stuff. Susanne also placed three glasses on a small table in the middle of the circle. We all took a step back and Maddison let out a scream that broke the glasses on the table instantly. The scream only lasted a second but that was all it took. I took my ear muffs off and had a slight ringing in my ears.

"Great job, Maddie," Barney clapped.

"Thank you!" she smiled. "Your turn, Barney."

Susanne picked up the broken glass and placed three new items on the table: a pencil, a large dictionary, and an even larger rock. Then she stood next to the table. Barney stared intensely toward the table. The pencil lifted into the air followed by the dictionary, the large rock, and finally Susanne. He lifted her about three feet above the floor. Next, while still floating in the air, Barney placed the pencil on top of the rock and then placed that on top of the book. Then, he sat everything back down on the table and put Susanne back down.

"Fantastic!" Susanne laughed. "Someone has definitely been practicing!"

Barney's face lit up.

"Show off," Hayley mumbled.

"I had some spare time on my lunch break the other day and decided to pick up some new tricks. I can now write with a pencil on paper with my ability. And I can turn on the television and change the channels."

"Wow," Hayley rolled her eyes.

"Hayley, please," Susanne said sternly. "Alright, Avery. Your turn."

Shit.

"But I already did it," I said.

"Like I said, the more you practice, the stronger you get and the more control you have. I want you to be able to run through the wall and also be able to stick parts of your body through the wall and retrieve items."

"What! I don't think I can do that."

"Sure you can."

"If she can't do it, she can't do it," Hayley smiled. "Let's move onto Kitashi."

"Let her try first," Kitashi said. I looked at him and he smiled. I tried smiling back but I'm sure it looked more like I was either constipated or in pain rather than smiling. I turned towards the wall and took a deep breath. I knew what was going to happen; I was going to charge full speed into the wall and either break my nose or knock myself out.

"Avery, don't concentrate with your mind. Concentrate with this."

I turned to Kitashi, who had his hand on his chest. I nodded. I closed my eyes and took in a deep breath and ran at the wall as fast as I could, and went straight through! The only problem was that not only had I gone through the wall of Susanne's, but I had went through into the house next door. I was standing in a living room; the lights were out, the television was on, and two people were sitting on a couch. I was frozen where I was, scared to even breath. Now that my eyes were adjusting to the dark, I could see everything a little better. It was two black men sitting together on the couch. I could also see a couple of stacks of money on the table next to a white looking block.

"Yo man, you got anything to drink in the fridge?" I heard one of the men on the couch say.

"All I got is some beer, man."

"Cool, I'm-a get me one. You want one?"

"Sure since it's my god damn beer!"

The both of them laughed and one started to stand up. Not knowing what else to do, I crouched down behind the couch and watched as the man went to the kitchen and turned on the light. I was hoping he would turn the light back off before coming back into the living room because he would easily spot me.

"So did you text Jerry? Is he on his way?" yelled the man in the kitchen.

"Yeah, he's just now on the road on his way over here."

"Good. That little bitch needs to get his shit together. He's always late and forgetting shit."

"He also needs to give me the fucking money he owes me. The bitch owes me like fifty bucks."

"For what?"

"What you think? I bought his dope for him and he's never given the money back."

The light in the kitchen went out and the man came back into the room. He popped open the can of beer and walked right past me in the dark. I wondered if the group I had been with even noticed I was still gone. They probably thought I had left and weren't worried about me.

"So how much you think Jerry sold?" asked one of the men.

"Well we each got three bricks last week to sell so hopefully he's sold it by now."

"Shit, did you sell all of yours already?"

"Hell yeah, I need my cut of the money."

"How much you keep?"

"Man I don't know, nigga! You gonna ride my ass about it too? Damn, I already hear enough about it from Dante. He's always up my ass about keeping too much and not paying for it."

"I'm just sayin' man, you better be careful. Dante's killed for lesser reasons than cutting him short on his coke."

"Nah, we cool man. He's my cousin."

"By marriage! He ain't black, he's Hispanic!"

"Whatever. Still, family is family."

Great, I was not only trespassing into a run-down, shitty house, but it was a house owned by drug dealers. I was in a mess I couldn't get out of. There was a knock on the door and I was praying to God it was someone to get me the hell out of there. Someone got off the couch and went to the door.

"Jerry! Where the hell you been man?"

"I was with my girl, I got caught up with stuff. Don't bust my balls already, I just walked through the door."

Sweat was rolling down my face and dripping onto my shirt. The lights flipped on and the two men walked down the hall toward the living room. Jerry looked Hispanic and was carrying a wad of money.

"Were you guys making out in the dark?" Jerry laughed.

"Fuck you man," the other one smiled.

"What is this?" Jerry stopped, watching me. The other guy was no longer smiling.

"Who the hell are you?" he yelled at me. I stood up quickly.

All of a sudden, three guns were in my face and they were all screaming at me.

"I-I-" was all I could get out at first.

"Bitch, you better start talking before I put a hole in your head!" yelled one of the black guys. "How did you even get inside without us knowing?"

"I'm sorry!" I started crying. "I don't know how I got in. I swear I won't tell anyone, please just let me go."

"Damn right you're not telling anyone!" A gun pressed even harder into my temple. Was I really going to die like this? No one knowing where I was and all alone? I wondered if this was how my parents felt right before they were shot.

"Maybe we should have a little fun with her first," Jerry said. "Might as well if you're going to waste her anyways."

I've never been punched in the face before, but I've got to tell you, it hurt way worse than I was expecting it to. One of the hands that was holding a gun hit me from the left side, and then from the right. I yelled out in pain and blood spewed out, but my yell was cut short with a low punch to my stomach. That knocked the wind out of me and I tried falling over, however, one of the men grabbed a handful of my hair and stood me back up. They took turns hitting me and I started pleading with them with what little breath I had left to stop. Then, Jerry grabbed my bloody shirt and ripped it off of me. I didn't bother trying to hide myself because I wasn't sure if I had the strength. He pushed me up against the wall and then there was a really loud crash. We all looked at the doorway where there was no longer a door. Someone was standing where the door used to be.

# CHAPTER 3

# Sabotage

*"I can't stand rockin' when I'm in here, 'cause your crystal ball ain't so crystal clear.*
*So, while you sit back and wonder why I got this fucking thorn in my side.*
*Oh my god, it's a mirage, I'm tellin' y'all it's sabotage."*

-"Sabotage" by the Beastie Boys

Meanwhile, my uncle had his own problems to deal with.

"Ross, we've been partners for—well, without giving away either of our ages, we'll just say a while. And I have yet to see a final product. Do you know what that means? I've been spending thousands of my hard-earned dollars every year for the past nine years so you could play with your science kit and give me what I could get for free—a big fucking pile of NOTHING!"

Ross sat at the table with Dante while Sloan paced around the room. Ross glanced over at Dante, who stared blankly at the wall. Ross was intently listening to Sloan, although he could care less what this greasy, old drug lord had to say. He had been listening to him talk for the last seventeen years, beginning with the first case Ross had worked on Sloan. He had been convicted for selling drugs and although the evidence was obvious, Ross had somehow weaseled Sloan out of jail time.

"I know we haven't seen as much progress as we'd like-" Ross started.

"*Much* progress?" Sloan's face was turning red. "THERE HASN'T BEEN *ANY* GOD DAMN PROGRESS!"

"Boss, could you please keep it down a little?" Dante asked. "My kids are downstairs trying to sleep."

"Oh I'm sorry. I missed the part where I was supposed to actually give a shit. If you don't want me to be loud, don't offer to have a meeting at your house next time. And don't tell me to be quiet; who the hell do you think you are?"

"Sorry, boss."

The door opened and Dante's wife came in.

"Jesus Christ, you know we're in the middle of a meeting! You can't even knock?" Dante asked her.

"No, this is my house too, I don't need to knock. Can you keep your voices down? I just put the kids down."

"Sorry Mrs. Martinez," Sloan said. "By the way, dinner was very good. Thank you for inviting me."

"Well, I didn't. My husband did. But you're welcome."

The door closed behind Dante's wife and Sloan smiled at him.

"You got yourself a nice little piece of ass there, Dante. I'm not fond of black women myself but she's got a little something, huh?

She looks a lot better after pushing out a couple of kids than my wife does. She's got balls talking to me like she did."

"I'm so sorry, Sloan," Dante apologized. "I'll have a talk with her about it."

"Don't worry about it. I like that about her. You know, we might have to swap wives for a night, haha! I wouldn't mind."

Dante looked at the table. Ross knew if anyone else had said that, they'd have a bullet between their eyes. But this was Sloan, so Dante just sat there and took it.

"I'm screwing with you, Dante. She may be nice looking, but I still wouldn't want that nappy hair near me. You know what I'm saying?"

Sloan bumped his elbow into Ross' shoulder a couple of times, a cloud of cigar smoke blew in his face. Ross wanted to punch him in the face and put the cigar out in his eyeball. But he couldn't imagine what Dante wanted to do to him for talking about his wife like that. Sloan's wife was no prize to be won. She was an old, loud Italian woman who was basically a female version of Sloan, except she wore ten pounds of make-up. She also had a huge mole on her chin that had three long black hairs growing out of it. Everyone secretly made fun of it, but if Sloan caught you staring at her mole, you'd find yourself at the bottom of the lake with cement shoes on.

His full name was Dominic Sloan, but everyone just called him Sloan, unless you were on really good terms with him. Then, he let you call him Dom. Right now, however, no one was on good terms with him.

"Anyways, I've already wasted too much money on your little project," Sloan continued. "I could build another house or put Caterina through college if I still had all of that money. Not that I can't do either of those things anyways, but still. So here's what it's come down to: I'm not funding this little project anymore. Between paying off the police and paying for your cute little lab, I'm sick of it! What the hell has my money gone to, besides lab coats and beakers and mice and shit? I'm not doing it anymore."

"Sloan, now wait," Dante stood up and walked towards him. "You're not the only one who's pulled money out of their own pocket for this. I have too! If you just give us-"

Sloan grabbed Dante's collar and held a gun up to his chin.

"Did you just raise your voice at me, you little border-hopping spick? Do you want your children to wake up to the sound of your brains being blown out? Do you want your nigger of a wife to clean your blood out of your crappy, cheap carpet?"

"N-n-no," Dante stuttered. "I just meant, I feel you, man. You're not the only one who's been giving to this thing. That's all I meant."

Sloan let go of Dante and pushed him back into his chair.

"I'll give you until the end of next year. If I don't see any finished project on the street by next November, I'm pulling my funds and going straight to the cops. I'm not going to be a part of your little science fair project anymore."

Sloan grabbed his coat and walked out the door. Ross looked at Dante.

"Are you crazy to get in his face like that? You could have gotten us both killed."

"I'm sorry, I'm just tired of him acting like he's running this whole thing when we're the ones doing the dirty work. And you're the one who even came up with the idea. So really this is your project."

"But we need Sloan's money," Ross explained. "Plus he brings in more customers. Look, I don't like him either. A part of me wishes I would have let him go to jail when I worked on his court cases. But we need him."

"Well we won't have him for much longer, and we'll be the ones rotting in jail. There's no way we can have a finished product by the end of next year."

"It'll be fine. I'll figure something out."

"You've been saying that for years, Ross."

"Well this time I really mean it. Don't worry.

Although Ross tried to sound confident, deep inside he knew better. He knew there was a big possibility that he and Dante would be going to jail or worse; end up dead. Ross had been planning and working on this project for years, even before he had met Dante and Sloan. Before he had moved to Chicago. Before Joe and Ann-Marie were killed.

When he met Dominic Sloan, he was working in Boston as a lawyer. Sloan was charged with selling drugs, possession of drugs, and selling to minors. It was a really tough case, probably the toughest case Ross had ever or would ever have to work on. Somehow though, Sloan got away with doing a year in jail and some community service. It wasn't until after he had first met Sloan that Ross had started working full throttle on his plan. He wanted to be remembered. He wanted to influence people. He was tired of being just another scumbag lawyer keeping the bad guys out of jail. He wanted a lot more than that. He wanted to change the world and wanted to change the way the world saw him. He planned on making a new drug that would be bigger than anything else before it. He needed money, dealers, a lab, and a name that would get him in good with all of the drug users. Dominic Sloan was the name Ross needed. When Sloan was released from jail, Ross got a hold of him and talked to him about his idea. Sloan seemed interested but also very cautious. He had just served a year in a jail and wasn't about to go right back in. So he introduced Ross to Dante Martinez, who was a new face in the game at the time. Ross met up with Dante and the two started working out the details of the plan. The drug was going to be called CP-ULTRA and it was supposed to originally come out in the early 1990s, but was stalled when Ross started running into some problems. The first major problem was that Ross didn't have a lab to work in.

"Come on little brother," Ross pleaded with Joe during one of his visits to Chicago. "Do you know how much money we'd be making if this worked out?"

"I can't believe we're even having this conversation," Joe shook his head. "I always thought it was awful that you kept bad guys free and on the streets. But now, you are one of them. You're one of the bad guys."

"Oh whatever. Because I want to do something big with my life, that makes me a bad guy?"

"Why would you want to sell illegal drugs? Let alone use my laboratory, that is government funded, to make your drug?"

"You just don't understand, Joey. You don't get anywhere in life by standing behind the curtain. The people on the stage, in the spotlight, those are the people who get the flowers thrown at them. Not the people behind the curtain."

"I think you're starting to lose it, Ross. You're worrying me. I can't have you coming into my home, with my family here, and talking like this. You need to leave."

"*I'm* your family! We're flesh and blood family, not Ann-Marie. Me and you are brothers. We're supposed to always stick together."

"Well consider me sitting out on this one," Joe put his hand on Ross' shoulder. "I will always love you no matter what, but that doesn't mean I have to support every stupid idea you come up with or every decision you make. You know what my answer to this is. Now please, leave."

A few months later Joe and his wife were killed by a gunman and the house and lab were easily handed over to Ross, putting his plan back into play. He hired a group of crooked scientists and started meeting up with Sloan and Dante every so often to talk about progress, money, buyers, etc. Ross never had to worry about anyone questioning him because Avery never bothered him or cared about what he did. And Charlie and Cindy were smart enough not ask about what he was doing. Ross spent most of his time away from the house, working on the drug. And when he was at home, he was left alone to work on the project.

Ross had tried his best at raising Avery, although she did a better job raising herself. She had always been independent which made it easy on Ross. She never asked him to braid her hair or play with her or come to any school events. He did whatever he had to take care of her but nothing more. Over the years, however, he grew more and more attached to Avery. He did love her because she was after all his only living relative. He just never knew how to properly love her. He had never been married, let alone knew how to deal with kids. The closest thing he had come to a relationship was hanging out with the strippers and hookers that Sloan had introduced him to. Ross had seen first hand how annoying and dangerous it was to have a wife when dealing with drug dealers.

Dante's wife had lost a child when she was pregnant a few years back. She was pushed down a flight of stairs as a warning to Dante. I think whoever did it meant to kill her and the baby but she was lucky. She ended up only having a broken leg but had lost the baby. She hasn't been able to have anymore children since but they already had two kids. Dante freaked out on everyone when it happened, not knowing who had done it. But when he did find out who it was, he made sure they paid for what they did. The guy was found burned alive with shards of glass in his stomach; his insides all cut up.

And as far as Sloan's wife was concerned, Ross was surprised Sloan hadn't killed her just for getting on his nerves. She was always nagging at him and giving him a hard time, and sure Sloan slapped her around but he never really hurt her bad enough for her to shut up for good.

But Ross didn't have to worry about a nagging wife, and no one hardly knew Avery even existed so he wasn't worried about her either. She was a good kid who minded her own business. Ross knew he only had a few more years with her and then she'd go off to college, which made him a little sad. He remembered when she was younger and he would wait until after she fell asleep and sit in her room. The sound of her faint breathing was relaxing and comforting. And in the mornings when she'd come down stairs in her cartoon pajamas, with her rosy cheeks, and hug him while he sipped on his coffee and read a newspaper. When she'd hug him, Ross would have to move her messy hair out of his face and he'd give one little pat on her tiny back. But as she started getting older, she stopped talking to him altogether.

Avery reminded Ross of his brother, but she was the spitting image of Ann-Marie. She even made the same faces as her. Her laugh sounded exactly like Joe's though. That always made Ross a little sad. Avery was beginning to become her own individual person, developing into who she was going to be for the rest of her life, and she had done this all on her own. Ross hadn't been much of an influence to her, so whoever she was becoming was coming from the influences of her friends. That kind of worried Ross, but he was sure Avery was a smart kid and knew better than to do anything stupid. Although the fight she had just gotten into at school surprised Ross. Avery had never had any violent outbreaks like that, especially at school.

Ross came home to an empty house. Charlie and Cindy were both out and Avery must have still been at work or spending the night at Ryan's house. Ross paced the house, thinking about the meeting he had just had with Sloan and Dante. If they didn't think up something fast, the outcome would not be good. He wondered what would happen to Avery if Ross was sent to jail or killed. Probably hopping from foster home to foster home like her mother did. Ross looked out the window and saw the lab in the dark. Ross had an idea, but knew it probably wouldn't work. He hopped in the car and drove over to the lab. Inside, there were only about four people working on stuff. Ross went down to the basement level and came to the metal door that had been eating at him since Avery was little. It was bolted shut, however, there was a touch screen off to the side of the door. Ross pressed his thumb on the pad.

"Ross Kendall," the electronic voice said, the pad lit up red. "Unauthorized to enter. Sorry."

Ross sighed and went back upstairs. He walked around, looking at what everyone was doing. One of the men who had worked here while it was still operated by the government was testing a lab mouse. He gave the mouse a drop of blue liquid and took notes.

"So, any news?" Ross asked him. He shook his head.

"We're missing something, I just don't know what," he explained, still writing. "I feel like we're on the brink of something but it's like finding a needle in a sand storm."

"Hey, you know that door downstairs?" Ross asked.

"Yeah, what about it?"

"Did Joe or Ann-Marie ever say what was in it?"

"Nope. All I know is that Avery went down there a lot with them. They'd spend hours down there, just the three of them. No one was allowed in."

"I see, and do you know who *is* allowed down there?"

"I would guess Joe and Ann-Marie only wanted them and Avery to be allowed down there."

"Yeah, Avery . . ."

"Is everything okay, Mr. Kendall?"

"Yeah. It's just our deadline has been bumped up a lot and I'm needing results sooner than I had hoped."

"What's the deadline, if you don't mind me asking?"

"We need a product on the street, getting sold and used by this time next year."

"Oh. Um, wow. I don't see that happening."

Ross looked down at the mouse, who was running at the side of the cage over and over, until finally it broke its own neck. The mouse twitched a couple of times, its breathing slowed down and then stopped moving completely. Ross glared at the scientist.

"Shut up," Ross spat before walking out of the laboratory. He sat in the car and stared at the darkness in front of him.

"GOD DAMN IT!" he yelled and hit the steering wheel. "Damn it, what am I going to do?"

Later that night, Charlie came home to find a very drunk Ross sitting on the floor and surrounded by piles of pictures. He was sitting up against a wall and had his head buried in his hands. There was an empty glass on one side of Ross and an empty bottle on the other side.

"Ross?" Charlie asked. "Are you okay?"

"Oh hey, Charles," Ross lifted his head and smiled at Charlie. "Come here, have a sit and drink with me. I was just going through some old pictures and having some whiskey."

"Yes sir, I can see that."

Charlie sat down next to Ross. He was sweaty and had his shirt unbuttoned all the way, revealing his undershirt and some white chest hair.

"Have yourself a little drink," Ross handed Charlie an empty glass.

"No thank you sir. I'd rather not have a drink right now. Thank you though."

"Oh, well then do you mind pouring me another one?"

"The bottle is empty," Charlie pointed at the whiskey bottle laying next to Ross. He looked at the bottle and then at Charles.

"Well that sucks," he said before he grabbed the bottle and chucked it across the room, making it shatter against the painting of Ross' father.

"Screw you!" Ross yelled.

"Are you speaking to the bottle you just threw or of the picture of your father?"

"Both," Ross looked at Charlie with his blood-shot eyes. "I hate them both. However, whiskey was always been there for me when I needed it. Can't say the same about my old man."

"Where's Avery?" Charlie asked.

"I don't know. I think she said something about staying with Ryan tonight."

"Well I'm glad she's not here to see you like this."

"What does it matter? The kid already hates me; she can't possibly think any less of me."

Ross picked up a picture that had been laying on the ground. It was Avery when she was seven on Halloween. She was dressed in a red plaid shirt and had fake blood on her forehead. Ross gave the picture to Charles.

"Remember, she went as a Kurt Cobain zombie. That guitar she's holding was supposed to be for her music lessons only but she insisted on taking it with her."

"And she ended up dropping it. She was so scared to tell you that she broke it. But you just kind of laughed and said you'd buy her another one."

"I should have been the one who took her trick-or-treating instead of you. But instead, I was out of town for work like always."

"She wasn't mad at you," Charlie smiled. "She was a little disappointed, but she understood."

Ross picked up another picture. This one was of him and Joe when they were little kids.

"My mom always told me he looked up to me," Ross handed the picture to Charlie. "But I think it was always more the other way around. Once Joe was born, my parents ignored me. 'Why can't you be more like Joe? He was able to find someone who would marry him. Is it really that hard for you, Ross? We want more grandbabies. Joe wins awards, Joe makes a difference in the world, Joe met the god damn president.' They were always more proud of him than me. I was just another lawyer in the family. Nothing new, nothing special."

Ross' eyes filled up with tears.

"Do you know how many times I've thought about torching this place? I hate living in my dead brother's house. I miss Boston so much. I miss everything being easier. When I didn't have a teenage girl to raise or a lab to run. My life is so hard now."

"Sir, have you been listening to that depressing teen angst music that Avery makes fun of? Because that's what you sound like right now. Instead of feeling sorry for yourself, sitting here drunk and looking at pictures, you should be proving yourself and your parents wrong. You are very capable of making a difference in the world. You have potential to do something big with your life."

Ross stared at Charlie, his nose running and eyes glistening. Then, Ross started laughing.

"Oh my god," he grabbed his stomach and kept chuckling. "This is ridiculous. What *am* I doing on the floor? Getting drunk and looking at pictures of people who either are dead, hate me, or hated me when they were alive. I'm wasting my time with this shit. I should be working or something."

"It's past midnight," Charlie raised an eyebrow.

"Yeah, I might just go to bed then."

"There you go, sir," Charlie said as he helped Ross stand up. "Good job."

"Can you do me a favor?" Ross asked.

"Anything sir."

"Can you call Cindy and tell her she's fired."

"Sir?"

Ross kicked over a pile of pictures.

"And one more thing," Ross said before walking up the stairs. "I *fucking hate* it when you call me 'sir.' I always had to call my father 'sir.' If you call me that one more time, you'll be in the same spot as Cindy."

# CHAPTER 4

# Search and Destroy

*"I'm a street-walking cheetah with a heart full of napalm."*

- "Search and Destroy" by The Stooges

"What the fuck!"

As the three men let go of me, I slumped down the wall and covered my ears as the guns started firing at whoever was coming through the door. One of the lights went out making it hard for me to see what was happening. Once the guns stopped, there was a lot of yelling and banging noises. Someone shouted out my name a couple of times before I hollered back. Susanne and Andrew ran over and pulled me up off the floor.

"Barney, get the lights," Susanne called into the dark. The lights flickered on and I saw Kitashi fighting one of the guys that had been sitting on the couch. Jerry and the other guy were knocked out and laying on the floor. Susanne wrapped my shirt over my bra and buttoned the only button that hadn't been ripped off.

"I think my nose is broken," I said weakly.

"Yeah, it's safe to say that it is," Andrew smiled. "Don't worry, Hayley will fix you up."

"Come on Kitashi," Susanne said. "Stop hitting him, he's unconscious. There's no point in fighting someone who can't defend themselves."

"Even though they didn't do that for Avery," Andrew scowled.

Susanne handed me off to Kitashi who carried me in his arms like a baby. We walked back over to the house and went inside.

"Holy crap!" Maddison put her hand over her mouth.

"Do I look that bad?" I asked. My face was starting to get stiff because all of the blood on my face was beginning to dry up. I had to breath through my mouth because my nose was too broken and bloody to breath through it.

"You look fine," Andrew laughed. "I don't think those guys back there are going to be fine though. I think Kitashi might have given them permanent brain damage."

"Okay, so how bad is it?" I heard Hayley ask. Kitashi turned around to face her.

"Oh. Wow. Uh, yeah, I don't think I can repair that much damage without hurting myself. I'll need a tree or a big animal or something."

"Please don't tell me you're going to kill an animal," Barney said.

"I wouldn't have had to if Ms. Newbie here wouldn't have almost gotten herself killed. But no, I'm not going to kill anything."

We all went into the backyard where there were several large trees.

"Hayley do as much as you can without hurting yourself, okay?" Susanne instructed. "I don't want you passing out on the way home because you over-did it again."

Kitashi laid me down on the ground and Hayley sat down next to me. She laid her right hand on my face and my nose cracked.

"Aaaahhh!" I yelled out. "Stop it, it hurts too much! Fuck, stop!"

"It'll only hurt . . . for a second," Hayley panted. "Then it'll start feeling better."

She was right. The pain stopped and the feeling I started having felt like warm sunlight coming through the window on a cold day. It felt really nice.

"I can't . . . do anymore," Hayley pulled away from me. My nose started throbbing again.

"My nose is starting to hurt again," I grabbed for it. Hayley touched the closest tree with her other hand.

"There, that's better," Hayley smiled. My nose felt a whole lot better, and healed a lot faster once Hayley touched the tree. After about three minutes of Hayley healing me, my nose was completely healed and I got up with only a couple of cuts and bruises. We looked at the tree, which was now slumped over and wilting.

"I'm sorry," Hayley hung her head.

"Don't apologize," Andrew smiled. "You helped Avery. And besides, the tree will be fine. It's nothing Susanne can't fix."

"That's right, Hayley," Susanne walked over to the tree and rested her head against it. "It just needs a little love."

I watched the tree stand up straight again and where the leaves were brown and falling off, there were now bright green new leaves. Susanne had her eyes closed and was smiling as she embraced the tree like a long lost lover. It was beautiful to watch. She seemed so in tune to everything going on around her. I looked at the time on my phone and gasped.

"Oh crap! I have to get home! My uncle is going to kill me!" I said, running back into the house. There was a boy in the room who was punching the punching bag in the corner.

"Can I help you?" I asked. He looked at me.

"Oh, are you the new girl?"

"Matt?" I heard a woman call. The little boy smiled at me as the woman came into the room. "What have I told you about waiting for your brother in the car?"

She glanced over at me and stuck her hand out.

"Hi, I'm Barney's mom. Are you new to the program?"

I shook her hand and nodded as everyone else started coming in from outside. Barney's face turned red when he saw his mom and brother. His brother then stuck his hand out at me.

"My name is Matthew Noble. But everyone just calls me Matt. My mom and brother sometimes call me Mattie but I think it's a baby name."

"How old are you?" I asked shaking his hand.

"I'm twelve years old. I'm not old enough to be in this class yet but I'll be thirteen soon so I'll be joining up with you guys in no time!"

"Do you have a-uh—an-?"

"An ability?" he asked. "Oh, you bet I do! Watch this!"

All of a sudden, Matt disappeared. I looked around for him. Then, out of nowhere, he was behind me.

"See? I can teleport!"

"Matthew James Noble!" his mom scolded. "What have we talked about? No using abilities until you start classes. You know you can't fully control your teleporting yet. Remember this past summer? What happened?"

"I thought I was landing on the roof and missed and I fell," he mumbled. He smiled at me. "I broke my arm in three different places though! I got to wear a cast and everything!"

"Can we please go now?" Barney rolled his eyes. "Before Matt annoys Avery to death?"

"Well, I'll see you around Avery!" Matt waved. "It was nice meeting you!"

"Nice meeting you too," I waved as they left.

"That kid is so freaking hyper," Hayley rolled her eyes. "You'd think having severe ADD would be a powerful enough ability to defeat a villain."

"Yeah, he better be careful with his ability," Maddison added. "Or he's going to get himself in a lot of trouble."

"Hey, Avery," Andrew walked over to me. "It's pretty late, do you need a ride home?"

"No, it's fine," I said. "I'll catch a taxi."

"A taxi is really expensive; I'm free. Come on, I have to drive through your town to get to mine anyways. I don't mind."

I looked over at Hayley who looked like she was trying to read our lips so she'd know what we were saying. I glared at Andrew.

"Fine, but just this once."

"That's okay with me."

We all said goodbye to each other and left. The car ride home was incredibly awkward and silent until Andrew spoke.

"So what do you think of our group? I mean, you kind of had a rough first night but you'll be back tomorrow, right?"

"Who do you think you are?" I asked.

"I'm sorry?"

"I said, who do you think you are? You asked me out on a date and you end up having a girlfriend? Do you think you're some kind of player or something? And you do realize the only reason I said yes to the date in the first place is because you used your little persuasion touch thing."

"Avery," he smiled. "Hayley's not really my girlfriend and I didn't directly touch you. I touched your shoulder. You said yes all on your own. And plus, I'm the one who should be mad at you. You totally blew me off. You lied and said you had to work."

"I *did* have to work!"

"Sly had talked to Ryan and she said you didn't go to work. Honestly, whether you went to work or not, I still got stood up."

"I'm sorry I stood you up. I just-"

"It's cool. I'm not surprised, I didn't think you were really interested anyways."

"I just have a lot going on right now, you know, with school and work and all of this super human crap. I don't have time for boys. You understand, right?"

"Well, I quit my job. I'd rather be training and doing stuff with Susanne and everyone than working. I think the pay-off is a lot better."

"We get paid to be superheroes?"

"No," Andrew laughed. "But we get to help people. We get to fight injustice. That's better than money. And besides, isn't that what being a hero is about? Giving without expecting anything in return?"

"Yeah I guess so," I said. "Maybe I should quit my job too. I don't need a job; I just do it to have something to do on the weekends."

"Well now you have something else to do on the weekends."

"Yeah I really enjoyed getting my ass kicked by a few thugs."

"By the way, sorry we didn't get to you sooner. I had a hard time connecting with you to figure out what was going on."

"Connecting with me?" I asked.

"I told you, I can feel people's emotions. When you went through the wall and didn't come back, I tried figuring out where you were to see if you were hurt or if you just ran away and blew me off again."

I looked at Andrew and he gave me a wink.

"Hayley and Maddison thought you ran off and Barney thought you just over shot your phasing but Kitashi and I thought something had happened to you. I walked around outside for a bit and all of a sudden I could feel you again. You were not only terrified but you were also getting hurt. As soon as I told Susanne, she and Kitashi ran over to help you. Barney of course wanted to tag along."

"But Hayley didn't want to bother with me," I smiled. "She's not very fond of me, is she?"

"If I was her, I would have a hard time liking you too."

"Why?"

"Well for one, you're the new shiny toy that everyone is interested in. Hayley was Susanne's, well not favorite, but Susanne was really fascinated with what Hayley's able to do. Until you came along with your multi-ability thing. Now all Susanne will talk about is how awesome you are. Which I agree, you're pretty damn awesome."

"How do you figure?" I asked. "What Maddison can do, *that's* awesome. Barney, he's incredible with his telekinesis. And Kitashi, well, did you see what he did to those guys? All I did was go through a couple of walls without even knowing if I could for sure."

"Yeah but Avery, you're just beginning your training. We've been doing this a little bit longer than you. You actually did really good for your first time. Barney couldn't even do his ability the first time he showed up and he's like a super genius."

"Really?"

Andrew nodded as we pulled up to my house. The sun was going to be up soon but I didn't feel that tired. I was still jittery from the night.

"So, shall we expect to see you later?"

"Um, yeah. I'll come again. Hopefully I won't cause any trouble for you guys this time."

"I'm glad you're coming back. We could really use a kick ass girl like you."

I blushed and got out of the car.

"Bye Andrew. Thanks for the ride."

"Anytime Avery."

Andrew drove off and I went inside and up to my room. I peeked into my uncle's bedroom on the way and saw that he was laying on top of his blankets with all of his work clothes still on. When I got to my room, I pulled off my clothes and got into my pajamas, and noticed that there was dried blood on my shirt. Good thing I had worn a black shirt or else the blood would have been more noticeable. Cindy would probably think it was ketchup or something. I set my alarm for noon and went to sleep.

After I had woke up from another nightmare (is it still considered a nightmare if I was asleep during the daytime?) I called to quit my job. I didn't tell Ryan or Kelly because I knew I'd see them at school on Monday anyways. And when I told my uncle Ross, he didn't seemed like he cared at all. But that's when he told me about firing Cindy the night before.

"You did what?" I yelled at my uncle. "Why did you fire Cindy?"

"Technically I didn't fire her. Charlie did."

"You couldn't even fire her yourself, you made poor Charlie do it? What was wrong with Cindy?"

"We don't need her anymore. You're old enough now that you don't need a babysitter. And between you, me, and Charlie, the house chores will get done."

"She's been with us for so long though, she's like family! Where will she go? Where will she stay? Do you even care?"

"Yes Avery, I care. But you shouldn't worry about it, she'll be fine. Now, do you want to tell me where you were last night?"

"Where do you think I was?"

"With Ryan and Kelly?"

"Yup," I lied.

"Okay well then you're staying home tonight."

"The hell I am! I'm going out tonight."

"No, you're not."

"Wanna bet?"

I walked away and took a shower to calm down before I left for the evening. I was really pissed off because not only did I like Cindy a lot but she was one of the very few adults in my life that I could count on. I hated that my uncle felt like he had the right to make a decision like that without telling me or asking me about it. It wasn't fair.

I asked Charlie if he could give me a ride into the city and asked him not to tell my uncle if I promised to help him with house chores. He agreed to both but on the way there he made me tell him where he was taking me. I told him about meeting Susanne at the karate class and that she had wanted me to attend a class on "troubled teens." He not only bought my lie but promised not to tell my uncle and would give me a ride anytime I wanted to go. Now, if I could get Andrew to give me a ride home every time, I'd be set. When Charlie dropped me off in front of Susanne's, he made me promise to call if I needed anything or if Andrew couldn't give me a ride home.

I walked up to the door and heard a voice behind me call my name. I turned around and saw Barney's brother, Matt, running up to me.

"Hey Avery! Guess what! My mom talked to Susanne and Susanne said I can come to class today! Isn't that cool? I'm so excited! Aren't you excited?"

"Uh yeah," I smiled. "Pretty cool. So where's your brother?"

"Oh, he and my mom are still in the car. I kind of teleported here because I was so excited about getting to come."

"You teleported out of a moving car?" I asked. "That probably wasn't the best idea. Won't you get in trouble for doing that?"

"Probably, but I can't help it! I'M SO EXCITED!"

"Matthew Noble!"

A car pulled up in front of the house and Barney and his mom got out. His mom stormed over to us, glaring at Matt.

"Before you freak out, I'm sorry-"

"I don't want to hear it! If I hadn't already talked to Susanne and had her get equipment and stuff for you, I'd pull you out of the class before you even start. I might just go ahead and pull you out anyways."

"No! Mom, please! I'm sorry!" Matt pleaded. Barney smiled at me and we both walked inside. Everyone else was already there and meditating. I grabbed a bean bag chair and sat down next to Kitashi.

"Hey," I smiled at him. He kept his eyes closed and didn't say anything back.

"So I'm pretty sure I already told you this but thanks for saving me last night. If you hadn't shown up I would have been a goner for sure."

Nothing.

"Too bad I couldn't have had impenetrable skin too, huh? Then, I would have been just fine."

Still nothing

I gave up finally and closed my eyes as well, trying to focus on my meditation. Susanne reminded us that meditation not only relaxed our minds and muscles but also it kept us completely focused. I sat there for what felt like forever but I glimpsed at the clock on the wall and only three minutes had gone by. Luckily there was a distraction that made everyone except Kitashi turn around.

"Hi everyone!" Matt yelled. "What are we doing today? Oh, are we meditating right now? Sweet deal. So should I just grab a chair? Can I have the blue one or is that one Barney's or does it matter?"

"Matt," Susanne sighed. "Just grab a chair and sit down."

"Okay, thanks again Miss Susanne for letting me come to classes now."

"Mattie, shut up!" Barney whispered as he walked in. "You're distracting everyone."

"Oops!" Matt giggled. "Sorry! I'll just sit and be quiet."

Although he didn't stay quiet at all. I could hear him whispering the whole meditation time. After thirty minutes of meditating, we moved on to circle practicing. Matt really enjoyed getting to show off his teleporting. Andrew practiced his persuasion on Matt and told him to calm down a little bit, and it worked. Matt wasn't nearly as hyper after that. Susanne was going to skip me after what happened the previous night but I announced that I had a new ability. That caught everyone's attention.

"Yeah I had another bad dream last night," I explained. "I actually dreamt that I was back at that house next door with those guys. One of them pulled out a gun and shot it at me but the bullets turned into bubbles. Like, you know, the kind of bubbles we used to play with as kids? And then, this morning while I was brushing my hair, I was thinking about going to the beach, just spacing off, and my brush turned into sand! So I don't know what the deal is or what exactly my power is now but-"

"Alchemy," Barney answered. "When you can turn something into something else, it's called alchemy. Or it could be considered molecular manipulation, where you change the molecule structure of one item into the molecule structure of another item."

"Oh," I was disappointed in my new ability. "How is that supposed to help me?"

"Well, like in your dream, you turned bullets into bubbles," Andrew said.

"Why don't we try it out?" Hayley suggested. "We could shoot at Kitashi and Avery could practice turning the bullets into stuff."

"No!" I shrieked. "I don't think that's a good idea at all! What if I can't do it?"

"Don't worry," Andrew laughed. "Kitashi has impenetrable skin. He can't get hurt."

I looked at Kitashi and he nodded.

"And you're okay with trying it out?" I asked him. Again, he nodded. I let out a long sigh and agreed.

Susanne got out a gun from the other room and gave it to Andrew. He stood at one end of the room while Kitashi stood at the other end, while I stood behind Andrew. My palms were sweaty but no one else in the room seemed nervous about this. Oddly, Kitashi kept his eyes on me the whole time. Andrew asked both of us if we were ready and after both of us gave him the green light he took the safety off of the gun. He held it up and I concentrated on bubbles. The shot rang out and I jumped at the sound. I saw Kitashi flinched as the bullet hit him and Andrew's body moved with the power of the gun's force. I ran over to Kitashi and asked if he was okay. There was a hole in his shirt but other than that he was perfectly okay. No bruises or cuts of any kind. We all got in position again and tried once more. Right before Andrew shot the gun, he told me to concentrate on something relaxing, something easy to focus on. I thought of butterflies but that didn't work. I thought of flowers but that didn't work. Kitashi took his shirt off because he didn't want anymore holes in it. I was getting really pissed off that my ability wasn't working and wanted to cry. I was trying really hard not to cry while we tried it again and then where the bullet should have hit his chest, there was a splash of water instead.

"What were you concentrating on?" Andrew asked.

"Uh, rain," I lied. I didn't want anyone making fun of me if I had said I was trying not to cry.

"Again?" Kitashi smiled.

This time, the bullet turned into a marshmallow. I was proud of myself, but I was still bumming. How was I supposed to practice my abilities if they kept changing? Every time I got used to one power, it would go away and I would get another one in its place. After we were done with the bullets, we all decided to work out for a while. I was really, really out of shape. After about thirty minutes of exercising, I was tired and ready to be done. Kitashi was lifting weights that looked like they could crush a rhino. I walked over to him and waited until he was done. After he sat the weights down, I asked if I could talk to him about something. He nodded.

"I was wondering if sometime, when you're not busy, you could help me out. Like a one-on-one type of thing. Maybe you could come over to my house or something. I could pay you and also pay for transportation and whatever else you need."

"Why do you want it to be just the two of us?" he asked.

"Uh, well, I feel comfortable in front of you. I know you won't give me a hard time or tease me. Right?"

"Right. But why not ask Andrew? I don't think he would tease you."

"That's true. If you don't want to, I understand. Sorry for bothering you."

"When would you like to start?" he asked.

"Oh. Um, when can you come over?"

"How about Monday nights? After you get out of school?"

"Sure. Don't you go to school?"

He shook his head and went back to lifting weights. I awkwardly walked off and started working out again. After exercising we decided on what our schedule was going to be. Susanne suggested Friday nights being practice nights, while Saturdays were our martial arts and exercise days. Which meant I was going to be very busy. I was going to have gym class five days a week at school, train on Mondays with Kitashi, work out Saturdays and karate classes on Sundays and Wednesdays. Not to mention I had my group therapy sessions on Tuesdays and my meetings with Julia on Thursdays. I had more on my plate than I could handle. Andrew agreed to taking me home every Friday and Saturday, which would work out great until I turned sixteen next August.

"Costumes!" Barney exclaimed. "We definitely need costumes!"

"I do not need latex riding up my ass," Hayley said. "It's going to be hard enough fighting crime in normal clothes."

"So we really are going to be superheroes?" I asked. "Like in the comic books?"

"Duh, why do you think we're training?" Maddison laughed.

"Who are we training to fight?"

"Anyone who brings injustice upon the innocent," Susanne replied. "I don't ever expect any of you to go looking for trouble. But I don't expect you to just stand there and watch someone get mugged or beat up. I want you all to change the world we live in. These are sad, violent, cruel times. It's bad enough seeing the way humans mistreat the earth, let alone each other. It makes me so sad, and if you could hear the way the earth cries, you'd be sad too."

"We know, Susanne," Andrew said. "That's why it's up to us to stop evil from taking over the world and all that jazz."

"We also need to save the world for future generations," Kitashi added. I looked at him as he spoke. "Our parents and ancestors kept this world beautiful and safe for us to grow up in. Now it's time we return the favor."

"Yeah, that too," said Andrew.

"Okay so all those in favor for the costumes?" Barney asked.

"Aye!" I shouted.

"Aye!" Hayley, Matt, and Andrew agreed.

We looked at Maddison and Kitashi. Maddison sighed.

"Only if it isn't ugly," she said. "And I don't want it too tight on my butt."

"I will not hide my identity," Kitashi said.

"And if criminals find out who you are?" I asked.

"Then they can face me as I am. Not as someone else."

I respected Kitashi because he was such a bad ass, but at the same time I thought he had lost his marbles. He didn't seem to be afraid of anything. I was envious of that because I was afraid of a lot of stuff. We decided on what we wanted our costumes to look like and Susanne planned to order them online. Then we moved onto a new topic.

"I know I remind you guys all the time, but there was something I wanted to talk to you about," Susanne said. "I don't want you to abuse your gifts by using them for selfish reasons. I want you to use them for the good of man. Has anyone ever been tempted or did use their gifts for a wrong reason?"

I looked around at everyone. If no one else was going to talk, I definitely wasn't going to explain taking Ryan and Kelly's notebooks. I didn't want to look like the bad guy. Andrew looked at me. I turned my head away.

"Okay if no one else will admit to it, I will," Andrew said. "I've used my persuasion ability to get what I've wanted before. And I've manipulated people's emotions for my own good. And also, Hayley and Avery are guilty of doing it too so they should open up too. I can sense it."

Both Hayley's jaw and mine dropped. I couldn't believe he tattled on me. What a douche.

"Okay, yeah," I admitted. "I did something yesterday I probably shouldn't have but now I know better and I'll fix it."

"Well I don't know what Drew is talking about," Hayley flipped her hair back. "I've never abused my powers. I'm better than that."

"Hayley," Andrew pleaded. "Come on, if Avery and I can fess up, the least you can do is be honest too."

"Whatever."

"Thanks a lot," I whispered sarcastically to Andrew.

"What? I thought you would respect my honesty," he smiled. "I didn't want you to get in trouble or anything."

Andrew drove me home after our group was done with everything. I spent most of the ride listening to the radio, enjoying the music.

"So are you not going to talk to me?" Andrew asked. "Or are you just using me for a ride home?"

"Yes, that one."

"Really?"

"I thought you would respect my honesty," I smiled. "Besides, we wouldn't want Hayley thinking it was anything more than just a ride home."

"I told you, Hayley isn't really my girlfriend. I don't care what she thinks."

"So is she a part time girlfriend then?"

"You could say that."

"God, men are such pigs. How many girlfriends do you have?"

"None."

"Okay, how many part time girlfriends do you have?"

"One part time that I'd like to replace with one full time girlfriend."

"Ew, was that you trying to hit on me?"

"Did it work?"

"Not at all."

"Why do you dislike me so much?"

"Andrew, I don't dislike you. I loath you. You expect every girl to fall at your feet just because you wear name brand clothes and have a pretty face."

Andrew had a wide smile.

"What?" I asked. "Why do you have that stupid ass grin?"

"You think my face is pretty," he smirked.

"What! No! I was just saying that because I know what most girls find attractive in guys and generally boys who look and dress like a Ken doll are a turn on to those girls. But not me. I like guys who look like men. You know, scruffy faces, dirty fingernails, shoes that *don't* have those air puff things in them?"

"I don't think those have been popular since the nineties. So what, you like guys who look like they're homeless?"

"No, I just don't like guys who look like they could be gay."

"That is so offensive on so many levels and I don't look gay!"

"I didn't say you did," I laughed. "And I respect homosexuals, thank you very much. I really just don't have time for boys or dating right now though."

"Well maybe you should free up some time."

Luckily, we pulled up in front of my house at that moment.

"Avery," Andrew smiled. I looked at him after opening the door.

"Will you please consider giving me another chance? I really like you and want to go out with you."

"I'll think about it," I said getting out of the car. "Just give me some time to think about it."

I shut the door and Andrew waved before driving off. I went inside the house and smelled something burning. I ran into the kitchen to see a pot of something bubbling over. Smoke was everywhere and I grabbed the hot pot off of the stove without an oven mitt. I turned off the stove and Charlie came into the kitchen. I looked down at my blistered hands and hid them behind my back quickly.

"Oh no! The noodles!" He walked over and looked at his watch. "I totally forgot about them. Avery, I'm so sorry. Please don't tell your uncle about this."

"Don't worry about it," I laughed. "It's just pasta. I'll help you make it if you want."

"That would be great. But only if you want to. Without Cindy around, it's going to be a little difficult for me to do everything by myself."

The doorbell rang and I told Charlie I'd be right back. I checked my hands and they looked normal again. My stomach felt fluttery because I was sure it was going to be Andrew. I opened the door with a huge smile on my face.

"What the fuck!" Ryan yelled in my face.

"Well hi to you too," I said confused. "What are you two doing here"

"Ryan wanted to stop by," Kelly answered.

"Why didn't you tell either of us you were planning on quitting?" Ryan asked. "Or were you not going to even tell us and just let us find out on our own?"

"I was going to tell you Monday at school."

"You could have at least told us on the phone or something. Why did you quit?"

"Because I wanted to and I don't need a job anyways. And plus I have a lot of shit going on right now."

"Oh like what, your karate class and homework?"

"I have a lot more going on than just that."

"Andrew?" Kelly asked.

"We're just friends," I explained. "Don't be jealous, cause I know you probably are."

Shit. That wasn't supposed to come out.

"*Jealous*?" they both said.

"Now all of a sudden you think you're hot shit and think my brother is like in love with you? Seriously, what the hell is your problem!"

Kelly just stared at me, as if I had hurt him. I felt real bad but didn't know what to say to make him feel better.

"Look, I know I've been avoiding you guys over the past few days but I don't mean to. I've met some new people I'm hanging out with now and I'm still trying to figure out how to balance everyone out. You two are still my best friends and I'd never just abandon you. And I was definitely going to tell you about quitting, I just hadn't got around to doing it yet. Forgive me?"

Ryan raised one eyebrow and gave me a half smile.

"As long as you still find time to hang out with us, I forgive you. I just don't want to lose my best friend to a boy. We promised each other we wouldn't ever do that."

"Well, like I said, he's just a friend. But we're finding out that we have a lot more in common than we thought."

My phone started vibrating and I pulled it out of my pocket.

"Speak of the devil," I laughed, reading Andrew's name. I answered.

"Avery, I'm on my way back over to pick you up," Andrew sounded scared.

"What's wrong?" I asked.

"Someone set Susanne's house on fire and no one can find her or Kitashi."

# CHAPTER 5

# Today

*"Pink ribbon scars that never forget. I've tried so hard to cleanse these regrets.*
*My angel wings were bruised and restrained."*

-"Today" by The Smashing Pumpkins

"I've got to go," I told Ryan and Kelly.

"What's wrong?" Kelly asked.

"I just have something I have to help out with."

"We can come too if you want. We'll help too."

"No!" I snapped at him. Ryan glared at me. "I mean, I appreciate the offer but it's okay. We've got it covered."

"See, this is the kind of crap I'm talking about," Ryan put her hands on her hips.

"Ryan, please. Not now. I promise I will explain everything. Just not right now."

I saw Andrew's car come up the driveway. I didn't even bother telling Charlie that I was going. Andrew pulled the car up and I jumped in.

"Avery, wait!" Ryan called to me as I shut the door.

"Hurry," I said. "Let's go."

I was surprised Andrew didn't get pulled over for speeding because he did at least twenty miles over the speed limits as we drove to Susanne's. By the time we finally got there, it was about eleven o'clock at night. The fire was already put out when we arrived but too much damage was done. Barney, Matt, and Maddison were all standing outside the burned down house. Maddison looked like she had been crying.

"What happened?" Andrew asked.

"I was going to go get dinner for me, Susanne, and Kitashi," Maddison sniffled. "When I came back the house was on fire and I called the fire department."

"There's a fire department right across the street," I pointed. "How did they not see the fire?"

"It's an old building," Andrew explained. "There's no one there now."

"The firefighters said that no one was in there when they went through, no bodies or anything," said Barney. "But no one can get a hold of them."

"Why don't we go try and find them?" Matt asked.

"Are you crazy?" Andrew looked at him. "I'm sure they're fine-"

Maddison handed him a piece of paper. He read it to himself before looking at Maddison.

"What does it say?" I asked.

"Um, it's from . . . well, here, you read it," he said, handing me the note.

*Hey freaks. If you wanna see the old bag and the chink again we'll see you at the east side boat dock. If you show up with cops or don't show up at all we'll take your friends for a late night swim. Show up by midnight and don't try to pull any weird shit like last time. Sincerely, your friendly neighbors.*

I looked at everyone.

"Well that's stupid," I smirked, trying to lighten the mood. "They called Kitashi a chink. He's Japanese, not Chinese. If they were going to insult him they could have at least used the right derogatory term."

No one laughed.

"Sorry, I was just trying to ease everyone's minds. Guess it didn't work."

"So we're going, right?" asked Matt.

"*We* are, your not," Barney said.

"Oh come on! You guys need me! We have to be there by midnight or else Susanne and Kitashi are going to die and it's already 11:30! There's no way you can get there in thirty minutes."

"He's right," I said. "He'll need to teleport us."

"He's never teleported anyone besides himself!" said Barney. "What if someone gets hurt?"

"Someone is going to get hurt if we don't try it!" I argued. "Come on, Matt. Try it with me first."

"You sure?" he asked.

"Yes. I'm sure. I trust you."

Matt grabbed my hands with both of his hands. He closed his eyes so I closed mine too. I would have been scared but there was no time for that. We had to try this to get to Susanne and Kitashi. All of a sudden, it felt like I was on a rollercoaster, going upside down and backwards. I opened my eyes and threw up into the lake.

"Yeah, it made me throw up the first couple of times too," Matt rubbed my back. "You get used to it after a while. But hey, at least we know now I can teleport other people! I'm going to get the others. You okay?"

I threw up again and nodded. My stomach felt extremely queasy. Matt disappeared and I took the time to recollect myself. Out of nowhere Matt showed up with Maddison, Andrew, and Barney. They were all holding on to each other until Maddison and Barney bent over and threw up next to me. Andrew grabbed his stomach. I turned away because my stomach was still upset.

"I'm sorry guys, I didn't mean to make you sick," Matt apologized.

"You did good, Matt," Andrew smiled. "Thank you."

"Yeah good job," I added. "Are you guys alright?"

Barney and Maddison nodded and stood up.

"Okay, so now what?" Matt asked.

"We go to the east dock and kick some ass," I grinned.

We walked over to the place we were supposed to meet whoever wrote the note. It was dark and quiet and it made me feel very unsettled. We were all jumpy and reacted to any slight movement or sound.

"So you're the kids who broke into our house," said a voice from behind us. We all turned around.

"You banged up my friends pretty bad," said the man that I recognized as Jerry from the house I accidentally got stuck in. "I've seen you guys around the neighborhood, visiting that old woman. What are you, some sort of escaped lab experiments?"

"Give us our friends back!" Matt yelled at him.

"Matt!" Barney whispered. "Shut up!"

"I don't remember ever seeing you around," Jerry laughed. "How old are you, boy?"

"I'm about to turn thirteen," Matt responded. "And don't let my age fool you. I can still kick your ass."

We all looked at Matt with wide eyes and our mouths gaped open. Jerry held out a gun to Matt's face.

"You still feel tough now, you little shit?"

Matt disappeared and all of us, including Jerry, looked around for him.

"Over here, numb nuts!" Matt called from on top of one of the nearby boats. "Now hand over our friends!"

"Or else what?" Jerry said before whistling. Out of the shadows, more men surrounded us. There were probably fifteen of them versus the five of us. Even if Susanne and Kitashi were here to fight with us, we'd still be outnumbered by double. And how was my power going to help? Sure I could turn everyone's bullets into bubbles or some stupid crap like that, but what if I couldn't do it under pressure in a real fight like this? None of us had that much training. And where the hell was Hayley?

"We can take them, right?" Maddison asked as we all stood back to back. Barney looked back at Matt, who was watching from the boat still.

"Right," Andrew said. "And if we can't, well, at least we went down trying to save our friends."

As the men grew closer, I noticed that most of them had weapons. Maybe I couldn't turn all of the bullets into useless things but I could change all of the weapons. I focused on Jerry's gun pointed at us. I concentrated really hared until I busted up laughing.

"What the hell!" Jerry said, lifting the hot dog up to his face.

Maddison, Barney, and Andrew looked at me. Matt laughed.

"Jerry, look!" One of the men said, holding up a stick of cotton candy.

Okay, so yes, I picked a carnival to concentrate on and all I could get was food. But it was the first happy thought that came to mind. I turned one guy's baseball bat into a balloon animal. I was pretty proud of myself. Now none of them were able to use weapons against us.

"Good job," Andrew beamed at me. "Okay, now remember anything and everything about hand-to-hand combat we've learned. We're going to have to take these guys down by ourselves."

"Not entirely by yourselves," we heard Hayley say behind us. Her, Kitashi, and Susanne were coming up the dock to the crowd.

"I thought you guys were kidnapped!" Barney said.

"Yeah, I did too!" Jerry yelled. "How did you two get loose?"

"I think your men underestimated my ability," Susanne smiled. "You thought it'd be smart to hold hostage a woman who can control water next to a lake? Tisk, tisk."

Jerry ran at us, yelling, followed by the rest of the men. One guy was running straight for me. I dodged out of the way right before he swung at me. I was scared about getting hit since I hadn't had as much training as the others.

Maddison screamed right in one of the men's faces and he grabbed his head, crying out in pain. She was getting better at controlling and aiming her screams; it was cool to watch her. No one could even get close enough to her to hit her.

Barney was picking up random objects with his mind and chucking them at some of the men. He picked up a huge log and flung it at three men, pinning them down underneath the log. Then, lifted one of the guys and hit another man with him, knocking them both out.

Kitashi was letting guys bounce right off of him while they tried punching him and kicking him. One man hit him right in the face and yowled as he grabbed his broken hand. Kitashi came over to me.

"I'll team up with you," he smiled as he hit a man so hard in the stomach, he flew back and bounced off of a tree.

"*You* want to team up with *me*?" I laughed as he pushed away another man. "More like you need to protect me!"

Hayley grabbed one of the men with her ungloved hand and I watched as his face shrank, like a water balloon with a hole in it. She let go of him and let him fall to the ground, gasping for breath.

Matt was all over the place, teleporting from one guy to the other, hitting them or kicking them, and then disappearing before they could hit him back. It was hard to find him because he wouldn't stay still long enough. The only way I could tell where he was, was by him making comments while he fought like, "Take that!" and "Try messing with us again, suckers!"

Susanne was using water, rocks, and air to fight. She was the most fun to watch. She hit them with so much force, it was like they were getting hit with a fire hose. She set one guy's shoes on fire and he started running off into the water screaming.

While three guys were ganging up on Kitashi, another one grabbed me by my hair and started punching me in the head. It hurt really bad. Kitashi was suddenly on top of him and punched him in the face, instantly knocking him unconscious. He helped me up and rubbed my head a little before going back to the fight.

Andrew was mostly just fighting with his fists. However, one of the men grabbed him by the neck and pinned him against a big rock. Andrew casually smiled.

"Start punching yourself," he commanded. "And don't stop until you knock yourself out."

The man automatically let go of him and started punching himself.

The next thing I knew, all of the men that had attacked us were on the ground either in pain, out of breath, unconscious, or giving up. Matt high-fived his brother and Andrew before coming over to me and Kitashi.

"That was awesome!" he squealed. "Did you see me hitting all of those guys? Every time one would swing at me, I'd teleport and come back and knock them on their asses! Oh, that was fun!"

"Very impressive," someone was clapping. We all turned to face the person walking toward us, if it even *was* a person. She walked towards us so swiftly it looked like she was moving through the air. I gagged, almost throwing up, because all of a sudden I could heavily smell sulfur. Andrew and Maddison started coughing too. Her dark red cloak with a hood covering most of her face. Her arms were covered in scars and what looked like boils. She had needle scars on both arms and a tattoo on one wrist. Her fingernails were extremely long and yellow and her skin was very pale. So pale in fact that you could see veins through her skin. Her skin was also kind of shiny, which made it look like she almost had scales. As she walked up to us, still softly clapping, a few of us took a couple steps backwards.

"Jerry said you guys wouldn't disappoint and it looks like he was right,"

"Who are you?" Susanne asked with a shaky voice. "What do you want with us?"

The figure in the cloak removed the hood from her head and I heard a couple of gasps, including mine. I could definitely tell the person in front of us was a girl because she had boobs and a small, delicate voice but without those two things, I don't think I would have been able to tell. Her head was scarred like her arms and she was completely bald; no eyebrows, eyelashes, or anything. She gave us an eerie smile that showed her jagged teeth and black eyes. I wanted to look away but I couldn't move at all.

"It's alright, I'm not offended. That's usually the reaction I get from people when they see me. Let me start by introducing myself. My name is Caterina Sloan, but I am recently known as Belladonna. I didn't always look this bad. I was born with leukemia, cancer that infected my blood. I practically lived at the hospital and spent most holidays and birthday celebrating from my uncomfortable, twin-sized bed in my cold room. The doctors told my parents that I would probably only live for five years. Desperate to find some way to cure me, my father took me to a man who performed black magic. You see, my father had a friend who had visited the same man about his dying wife. The dark man cured his wife, momentarily. She was deformed from her sickness and, although cured, she went into a deep depression and was so upset with her deformities, she killed her baby and husband before killing herself.

'Not thinking anything of the great misfortunes that had happened to his friend's family, my father still wanted to take me to the sorcerer. He offered countless deals with the man until he finally agreed to help me. He told my father that I would still be sick for a while and to continue doing my chemo treatments and such with the doctors, but I'd also have to come to him and get 'treated' with his remedies. He promised that he was able to cure me, however, there was a possibility for complications and side affects. My father, only wanting me to get better, and agreed. I lost all of my hair and a lot of weight from the chemo, and all of the children at school made fun of me so my parents decided to home school me. As my treatments with the doctors and my sessions with the sorcerer continued for several years, my parents started to notice how different I was becoming.

'At the age of nine, I was completely cancer free. I was running around, playing like a normal child. I was eating a lot more and sleeping better. I wasn't getting sick all the time. Needless to say, my parents were extremely happy that not only had I lived more than what everyone said I would but that I no longer had cancer. However, no one except me began to notice the strange things that were happening to me. Whenever I would start not feeling well or whenever I would get mad, people around me would get hurt. We found that I was able to manipulate the blood of others to my advantage. I was able to cure myself without needing anymore doctors. Unfortunately, my appearance went to hell, no pun intended. My mother accused the dark magician of possessing me with a demon. All he could say was that he had warned us. That wasn't good enough for my father so he tried to kill the man. But when my father went to pay him a visit, the sorcerer was gone. I, of course, am very hesitant to show myself in public so I'm either always stuck at home or when I do go out, I have to cover most of my face up with make up and masks.

'Funny how shit works. I'm cancer free and living a full life without any sickness, but in exchange for it I'll never go on a date or get my first kiss or get married. Unlike other twenty year old girls, I'll never plan a spring break trip with friends and show off my body in a bikini. I have to live the rest of my life as a freak. An outsider. Alone. So, imagine my surprise when some of the guys who work for me and my father tell us about a group of teenagers who have these incredible abilities. You know, my father was born with powers like you guys also. Yeah, he can randomly bust out these energy blasts and he's like super strong. So here we thought we were the only two freaks out there and then we find you bunch.

'So here it is, an offer we're giving you. A 'job opportunity' if you will. Come work for my father and live a care-free life. We could take over the world, one city at a time. With all this power, we could be unstoppable. No one will ever call you outcasts or freaks ever again. So now that you've heard my little speech, what do you think? Who's in?"

No one said a word.

"Oh and another thing," she smiled. "Whoever declines, dies."

Great. Classic villain scenario. Evil monologue, life story on why they are the way they are then given the choice to either join the villain or die. Which meant I was going to have to fight this demon chick. I wasn't too worried about anyone else in the group accepting her offer so at least I wouldn't have to fight her alone.

"Screw you," I heard Matt say. "We fight evil, not work for it."

"I was afraid you'd say that," Belladonna smirked. She raised her hand at Matt but he disappeared before she could do anything.

"Clever little boy," she looked around for Matt. Suddenly, he showed up behind her and grabbed her hood, pulling it over her face.

"You should cover that face up," he laughed. "You're going to really scare someone!"

She turned around to face Matt but he disappeared again. She screamed out in frustration.

"Face me, you little asshole!" she yelled.

"Andrew," I heard Susanne say. "Get everyone out of here while she's distracted."

We looked at Susanne.

"Kitashi and I will stay and fight her."

"No freaking way!" I said to her. "We should all stay together and fight her as a team."

"Avery, we *are* a team but I can sense how powerful she is. You kids are not ready for something like this."

"But Kitashi is?" Hayley asked.

"No she's right," Maddison said. "We should go. We haven't had the training to face her."

"I'm not going anywhere without my brother," Barney said.

"He'll be okay," Kitashi said. "Now go!"

We all ran away until we got up to a hill where we could see Susanne and Kitashi fighting Belladonna.

"Do you see Matt?" Barney asked. "I don't see him anywhere."

"Susanne probably told him to run off too," Hayley said. "It's always her and Kitashi. She never lets us do anything. It's not fair."

"There's Matt!" Maddison pointed.

I saw Belladonna suddenly grab Matt by his neck and lift him off the ground.

"No!" Barney yelled and started running back to Matt.

"Barney, come back!" Hayley called.

"No! I have to help my brother!"

I looked anxiously at everyone before running after Barney. I ran as fast as I could but somehow Andrew, Maddison, and Hayley caught up with me and we made our way back to Belladonna.

"Please, just let him go!" Susanne pleaded. "He's just a child!"

"A child who is arrogant and reckless!" Belladonna yelled. She looked at Matt who was crying. "Last chance, boy. Join me, have a long, wonderful life full of everything you've dreamed of. Or die a crying coward in front of your friends!"

"I love you Barney," Matt closed his eyes and tears ran down his face.

"Please don't do this," Barney cried.

"Why doesn't he just teleport?" Hayley asked.

"Because he knows she'll kill one of us if he does," said Kitashi. "He's sacrificing himself."

"Shut up!" Barney yelled at Kitashi. "He's not sacrificing himself and he's not going to die. He's not even thirteen! Kitashi, do something! Lady, you can't hurt him! Please!"

"I'm sorry but I need to set an example with him for the rest of you. Consider this a warning. Next time, I won't leave until everyone is either on my side or dead."

Matt's eyes widen and he let out a loud, horrible gasp that ended with a weird gurgling noise. His body went limp and fell to the ground. Belladonna ran off into the woods and Kitashi ran after her while the rest of us went to Matt's body. I saw blood coming out of his mouth, ears, and nose while his eyes stared blankly up at the night sky. I bent over, facing away from everyone and dry-heaved a little. I couldn't look at the body or at Barney crying and holding Matt. He was sobbing loudly, mostly asking why and saying no. I wish I had been the one with teleporting powers because there was nothing I wanted more than to get away from this. Susanne got on her phone and called Barney's mom after calling the police. Kitashi came back sweaty but unharmed.

"What happened?" Maddison sniffled in between sobs. She had her arm around Barney and her fingers were playing with his hair.

"I asked her if she had killed Matt and what exactly she had done to him," he wiped his forehead. "She made his heart burst."

"Burst?" Andrew asked. "As in explode?"

Barney's crying grew louder as Kitashi nodded.

"She can't hurt me though. She tried to but nothing happened. I tried fighting her but she jumped into a car and they drove off."

"Well that's great news," Barney muttered.

We all looked at him.

"Because now I know that if the rest of us die, at least Kitashi gets to live. My little brother won't ever get to go to prom or get married or have babies but at least I feel better knowing Kitashi can't ever get hurt."

"I still know pain, Barney," Kitashi said calmly. "Just because I can't feel physical pain, doesn't mean I can't feel mental or emotional pain."

"Oh well that sucks! You mean to tell me that the great and powerful, unstoppable, invincible Kitashi doesn't like getting his feelings hurt?"

"We are all at a loss. We all cared for your brother-"

"Don't!" Barney yelled as he punched Kitashi. "Don't act like you understand how I feel. My dad died of a heart attack when I was seven. Matt didn't remember it but I do. My mom struggled to raise us by herself but we always managed. We were still happy and grateful to have each other. And now, I'm without a little brother too."

"I lost my family too," Kitashi explained. "I don't know who I am or where I came from and that hurts. It hurts that I can't visit my parents' graves or know if I ever had any siblings. I live my life not fully knowing who I am."

"Half of knowing who you are is knowing where you came from," I found myself saying. I didn't want them to get into a fight.

Barney and Kitashi both looked at me.

"I was four years old when my parents were shot and killed," I continued. "It's never easy losing someone, especially when you have to witness it."

Out of the corner of my eye I saw red and blue flashing lights. I was relieved the police and ambulance showed up when they did, however, when I saw Barney's mom my relief quickly faded. She pushed past the policemen and ran over to Barney and Matt. She dropped to her knees and started screaming. I wanted to go home but Susanne said we'd have to stick around for questioning. We all stuck with the same story that we were walking through the park and Matt started complaining of chest problems and all of a sudden, he collapsed.

No damage was done to the outside of his body and Barney's mom insisted that we were all his friends and wouldn't hurt him. After the police let us go, they zipped up Matt and took him away in the ambulance. He was pronounced dead on arrival. A couple of cops offered to take some of us back to Susanne's house. We didn't want them to know her house had burned down so Susanne lied and told them to stop a block away. When the police left, we walked to our cars and what was left of the building. Susanne and Kitashi tried going through the wreckage and finding their belongings.

"Where are you going to go, Susanne?" Maddison asked.

"I might spend the night at the police station until I can figure things out."

"I'm sorry but can I say something?" Hayley asked.

Susanne nodded.

"I think we should cut Avery."

"What!" I said.

"Why?" Andrew and Kitashi both said.

"None of this would have happened if it wasn't for her."

"Hayley, how could you say that?" asked Andrew. "Avery didn't do anything to hurt anyone!"

"No, she's right," I said. "If I hadn't accidentally phased into that house next door those thugs wouldn't have told Belladonna and Susanne's house wouldn't have been burned down. And Matt would be alive."

"That's ridiculous! Avery, don't let anyone guilt you into taking the blame for any of this."

"That's right, Avery," Susanne added. "I don't blame you for this at all. Hayley, I think it'd be best if you went home."

Hayley's face turned red and she stormed away to her car. Andrew asked if I was ready to leave yet but I suddenly had an idea.

"What if we move everything to my house?" I asked Susanne.

"What?" she asked.

"We could practice and train at my house. It's definitely big enough and I have enough money to buy whatever equipment we need. And you and Kitashi could live there too!"

Kitashi turned away when I said this.

"Oh Avery, that's very nice but I couldn't impose-"

"I don't think you understand. My house has a bunch of extra space in it and my uncle wouldn't care one bit. He's almost never home."

"It's true, her house is huge," Andrew added. "Like, big enough that she could start her own hotel there."

"But no one could know about us Avery," Susanne said, picking up a half-burned sweater. "I know he's your uncle, but we can't risk it."

"There are certain places in the house and lab that only I have access to. Like, only my fingerprint and password can be used. Barney could set it up where each of you has your own password and no one else would be able to get in. My parents worked for the government so their work was pretty secretive.

"That's perfect!" Andrew smiled. "When do we start?"

"Tomorrow?" I looked at Susanne. "You guys can ride home with me tonight and we can start going over everything tomorrow. Oh crap . . ."

"What?" Susanne asked.

"I forgot I have my martial arts class I have to go to every Sunday."

"Just skip tomorrow," Andrew suggested.

"I can't," I explained. "I agreed to go to these classes so I wouldn't have to go to this behavioral, angry teen boot camp my uncle wanted to send me to. I got in trouble for fighting at school and beating up this girl."

"How lady-like of you," Andrew laughed.

"I could hear her thoughts and she was talking crap about my parents," I scowled. "She deserved it."

"What if we bring your karate class to you?" Susanne asked.

"What do you mean?" I smiled.

"I could be your teacher. I know enough to teach you some stuff. And Kitashi could help too."

Kitashi gave me a small nod.

"That would actually be perfect!" I said excitedly. "Well my home is open to you two for as long as you need it until you find a more permanent situation."

"What you say, Kitashi?" Susanne asked him. "Are you okay with staying at Avery's for a while?"

He gave another slight nod.

Andrew drove the three of us to my house and helped get what Susanne and Kitashi took from her house. By this time it was past two in the morning but I still had to figure out where the two of them would be staying. I showed Susanne to one of the guest rooms that didn't have a bunch of crap piled in it while Kitashi slept on the fold out couch in the downstairs living room. Each had access to their own bathroom and knew where the kitchen was so I made my way to bed. I was beyond exhausted and was planning on sleeping in as late as possible. However, as soon as I closed my eyes and tried falling asleep, all I could see was Matt's widen eyes, blood trickling from his face. And Belladonna. The image of her deformed, demon-like features were etched into my mind. Needless to say, I didn't get the good night's sleep I was hoping for.

# CHAPTER 6

# Waiting

*"I've been waiting for a life time
For this moment to come.
I'm destined for anything at all.
Dumbstruck, color me stupid.
Good luck, you're gonna need it
Where I'm going if I get there . . .
At all . . . ."*

-"Waiting" by Green Day

I was walking through the woods alone. It was cold enough to see my breath but I was sweating, like I had been running. I came to a clearing, where there were no trees. The cold breeze sent a shiver through me and I wrapped my arms around myself. There was something on the ground up ahead. I couldn't really tell what it was since it was so dark out so I walked to it, squinting my eyes to get a better look. I tripped over a rock sticking out of the dirt and landed hard on my hands and knees. The knees of my jeans felt wet and when I lifted my hands up, they also felt wet. I stared at the dark watery substance on my hands trying to figure out what it was until I focused on the thing lying on the ground. Matt's wide eyes were staring right at me. There was a huge tear in his chest and I could see inside his body. I tried screaming but nothing came out. There was a big puddle of blood surrounding the body and I was sitting in it. I stood up quickly and tried wiping the blood off my hands, however, it wouldn't come off. I heard breathing behind me. I was shaking so hard that my teeth were chattering. I turned to face Belladonna, who was smiling and had blood smeared all over her clothes.

"Look what you've done," she grinned and pointed at Matt.

"I didn't do it! You did, you monster!" I cried out. "You killed him!"

Belladonna slowly shook her head and kept smiling. She lifted her hand to her face, holding Matt's heart. I closed my eyes as she opened her mouth. I could still hear her biting and chewing.

"Poor Avery," I heard Belladonna say. "All alone in the world with no one to save her."

"I don't need anyone to come save me. I can save myself."

She laughed at this.

"If you're going to kill me just do it already," I said.

"Don't be stupid," I jumped at the touch of her ice cold hand on my cheek. I could feel her hot breath on my neck. "You're too valuable to kill. We need you. Which is a shame because I'm sure that little heart racing inside of you would be absolutely delicious."

"*We?*" I asked, opening my eyes. "Who's *we?*"

"You'll see soon," she smiled and showed her jagged teeth. "Big things coming your way, Avery."

"What do you mean?" I asked.

"I can't tell you, obviously. However, it *is* awfully tempting *not* to kill you right now."

Belladonna stepped towards me and I somehow made myself teleport away from her. I was right outside of the park. I could hear police sirens so I teleported once more, landing in front of Susanne's burned down house.

"Avery," I heard Belladonna's voice whisper in my ear. I turned around but no one was there.

"You can run," her distant voice said. "But you know you can't hide. Your past will eventually catch up with you."

I opened my eyes slowly and immediately saw Kitashi sitting on the floor next to me. I sat up quickly, startled to see that I was downstairs on the fold out couch.

"What happened?" I asked.

"I'm not sure," he answered. "You fell down onto my bed and woke me up. I didn't want to disrespect you so I moved to the floor and waited for you to wake up."

"Oh crap," I smiled. "I teleported in my sleep! But wait, why did I end up here?"

"I don't know," Kitashi stood up. "Since you're awake, would you like to run with me?"

"What time is it?" I asked.

"Six."

"In the freaking morning? Why am I awake this early? Why are you awake this early? Let's go back to sleep. I'll give you your bed back."

"No, it's alright. I'm usually awake around this time anyways. I'm going to go find some place to run. Let me know if you change your mind."

"There's a mile-long running trail/ bicycle trail from our house to the lab if you want to use that. My parents built it for the lab employees and themselves."

"Alright, thank you."

I got up and walked to the doorway.

"I do hope you join me," Kitashi said before I went upstairs.

I ran up to my room and found a pair of sweat pants and a hoodie. Normally I slept in these clothes so it was weird changing out of my pajamas and into what was usually other pajamas. I dug around my closet for a pair of running shoes and slipped them on. I was hoping Kitashi hadn't left yet so I was very happy to hop down the stairs and see him waiting for me by the door.

"How did you know I was coming?" I asked.

"Just a guess."

"Avery?" I heard as I reached for the door knob. I turned to face my uncle.

"You mind explaining to me why an old lady is in my guest room and an Asian kid is standing in my doorway?"

"Susanne is my karate teacher. Her house got set on fire and I offered our house for her to stay at. I figured that way I could get in my martial arts lessons whenever. Is that okay?"

"God damn it, Avery! Why can't you run things by me first before you make decisions?"

"I'm sorry," my cheeks burned with embarrassment.

"You get that from your dad, you know."

"I'm so sorry to intrude," Susanne said, coming down the stairs. "I only needed somewhere for the night. My friend is going to let me stay with her until I can get back on my feet again. The only problem is that there's no room for my Japanese koi fish."

She winked and nodded toward Kitashi behind my uncle's back.

"Oh!" I said nervously. "Well . . . I don't know what to do about your fish. Maybe he could still stay here for a while."

"Anyways," my uncle interrupted. "So what's up with Jackie Chan here?"

"Jackie Chan is Chinese," Kitashi said. "I'm Japanese. I'm a foreign exchange student."

"Uh, yeah!" I chimed in. "Remember? I talked to you about it months ago. I asked if I could sign up to host a foreign exchange student and you said it would be okay."

"I don't remember us ever talking about it."

"Well we did!" I got more intense with my lying. "You can even ask Charlie! Or Cindy, if you hadn't fired her."

"He can't stay here."

"What! I can't just send him back!"

"Avery, listen to me-"

"No! You listen to me! You're never around to ask about things and that's why I make my own decisions without you. Kitashi stays."

I walked out the door and started walking toward the trail. Kitashi caught up with me and neither of us spoke while we ran over to the lab. When the trail ended, we slowed down and I realized how out of shape I was. I was breathing really hard and fast. I bent over and put my hands on my knees until my breathing and heart rate slowed down. I looked at Kitashi.

"Race you back," I smiled.

"You're on," he smiled back.

Kitashi sped off while I took my time, barely jogging. Kitashi looked back at me and I teleported next to him. I laughed and Kitashi started running faster. I teleported next to him again.

"Not fair!" he panted as he sped up even more.

"I never said we couldn't use abilities," I giggled.

I let him get a little farther up the trail before I decided to teleport again. This time, however, Kitashi tripped me. I fell hard and scraped my knee on the concrete. Kitashi immediately stopped running and came back to me.

"Oh no! Are you okay?" he bent down. "I'm sorry! I didn't mean for you to get hurt."

"Yeah, I'm fine. Karma, eh?"

"Yeah," he chuckled. "I guess so."

"Well we're closer to the lab than the house. I'm going to see if there's any band aids or a first aid kit in there for my knee."

We walked into the lab and everyone stopped to look at me for a second before going back to what they were doing. A short bald man walked up to me smiling.

"Miss Kendall! What a pleasant surprise to see you in here!"

"Yeah, hi. Do you guys have any band aids? I scraped my knee and it's bleeding pretty bad."

"Oh yes, we have a first aid kit somewhere around here. Let me go find it for you."

"Okay, thanks-?"

"My name is Mitch," he stuck his hand out. "I worked with your parents back in the day."

I shook his hand and smiled. Once he walked away I looked at Kitashi and rolled my eyes.

"Come on, let's look around."

"Won't we get in trouble?" he asked.

"I basically own this place. I can go wherever I want."

We walked through the lab, casually checking out what everyone was doing, although I had no idea what anything was. We went downstairs to the place I remembered from my childhood.

"I remember playing down here when I was little," I said as we came up to the door. I put my thumb on the scanner.

"Avery Nasia Kendall. Welcome. Please say password now."

"Oh crap," I said. "I don't know it."

"'Oh crap' is not the correct password," the computer stated. "Please try again."

Kitashi and I laughed.

"I don't know what it is," I looked at Kitashi.

"Just try some different things."

"Avery," I said loudly.

"'Avery' is not the correct password. Please try again."

"Nasia?" I tried again.

"'Nasia' is not the correct password. Please try again."

"Miracle?"

"Access granted. Welcome."

"How did you know that?" Kitashi asked.

"I just guessed. That's what my middle name means."

"It suits you."

"Thanks."

The door unlocked and I pushed it open after giving Kitashi a wide grin. I flipped on the light switch and let out a gasp. The room was filled with stuff from when I was little. Pictures I had drawn, toys I played with, photographs of me with my parents, and other things. On one wall was a bunch of files, video tapes, and a television. I picked up the cassette tape on top and saw that it said, "Avery, Tape 1." I pushed it into the tape player and turned on the television. There were a few seconds of static before the faces of my dead parents came into view. My eyes instantly filled with tears.

"Hi Avery!" my dad smiled.

"Hey Sweetie," my mom waved. "This is a bit odd filming this for you when you're in the other room sleeping. But we need to get this done before you wake up. You're probably wondering what all of this stuff is. Most of it is stuff we've kept from when you were a baby. But we also have kept a secret from you. If you're watching this video it means we weren't around to tell you in person. Sorry about that, pumpkin. So where should we start?"

She looked at my dad.

"Well, I guess I'll just go ahead and come out with it," my dad said. "Honey, you have really-had—really bad night terrors when you were little. Nothing was helping so Mom and I took matters into our own hands. We put you through some tests and, um, experiments and came up with a solution called Project Dream Catcher. If you'll look on the desk near you, there should be a file titled that for you to look through while I explain. I'll wait while you find it."

I looked around on the desk behind me for the file. Kitashi leaned across me and grabbed the file. He handed it to me and I opened it.

"I'm assuming you have it by now," my father continued. "If not, you can just push the 'pause' button and find it. We came up with the name from the dream catcher we placed over your bed. Remember the dream catcher story? The dream catcher is hung above the bed and is used as a charm to protect sleeping children from nightmares. Only good dreams would be allowed to filter through and slide down the feathers to the sleeper. Bad dreams would stay in the net, disappearing with the light of day.

'Anyways, Project Dream Catcher not only changed you but it changed our line of work. We were doing regular experiments set up by the government but we've discovered a whole new kind of science. We were able to re-structure the way the human mind controls and *changes* the human body. I hope that by now you've noticed some things that make you unique. We re-wired the way your brain reacts to your nightmares. We figured if you could somehow control what happens in the nightmares, you wouldn't have them anymore. But we discovered that whatever happened to you in your dream, happened to you in real life the following day. We never told anyone about you because we didn't want a lot of media attention. We didn't want you being treated like a freak or a monster."

"And we were afraid that someone would take you away from us," said my mom. "We never wanted anything bad to happen. And in a way, I'm sorry for what we did to you. Maybe if we had left it alone, you really would have grown out of your night terrors. But I didn't want to risk your health anymore. You weren't eating or sleeping right. It was getting in the way of school and we just wanted a normal life for you. But I guess this isn't really considered normal either. I'm sorry for that. I'm also sorry I can't be there to see you now. I'm sure you are just as beautiful now as you were as a little girl. I love you baby girl, and always will."

"I love you too honey," my dad said. "Hopefully you won't ever have to watch this video. I hope one day, when you're old enough, we'll be there to tell you ourselves. Well, that about sums up our video. Love you kiddo. See you."

Both of my parents smiled and then the video cut out with static. I put my face in my hands and cried as I felt Kitashi place his hand on my shoulder. Suddenly the static stopped and I looked up to see my dad's face again. My mom wasn't with him this time though and he had a lot of scruff on his face.

"Hey sweetie," he said, scratching his head. "It's about a week since we recorded that last video. Your mom doesn't know I'm doing this so I had to sneak away from her for a bit. She doesn't really understand how dangerous of a situation our family is in right now. A man named Dominic Sloan has threatened our lives so we have to be very careful about who we talk to and trust. You must do so also, Avery. Be careful who you trust and talk to about what you are. Even the people you least expect to betray will do so. I am leaving something for you. When the time is right, you'll know what to do with it. Behind the back shelf in this room is a freezer with vials in it. These vials contain the substance that changed you. Make sure it doesn't fall into the wrong hands. Also there is a hidden door in this room that goes down to a secret passage way. It connects to the house, however, no one knows about it except your mother, me, and now you. You can use the space down there for whatever you want, but again, do not let anyone know. Eyes are watching you where you least expect it. I know you'll do the right thing and no matter what happens, you have made me proud. I-"

My father looked behind him briefly before shutting off the camcorder. The video went black and the tape ended. That was it. The only thing I had left of my parents. I got up and walked over the back shelf. There was a low humming coming from behind it; it had to be the freezer. I moved the shelf out of the way and squeezed behind it to get to the freezer. I lifted the lid and looked inside. There were a dozen glass tubes placed on a rack. Inside the tubes was a purple liquid. I reached for one and Kitashi cleared his throat. I looked back at him and he shook his head.

"What?" I asked. "I wasn't going to do anything."

"I don't think you should mess with them until you tell someone."

"Who am I supposed to tell? My dad made it sound like no one could be trusted. And then he got shot so apparently he was right."

"Just don't say anything to anyone for a while until we figure things out."

"Fine."

"Thank you by the way."

"For what?" I asked.

"Trusting me enough to share this all with me."

"Oh. Well, you just happened to move into my house and follow me here so whatever. No big deal."

I shut the lid and grabbed all of the stuff on the desk, including the tape I had just watched.

"My dad mentioned a name. Dominic Sloan? I've heard that name before."

"You have?" Kitashi asked.

"Yeah. My uncle was his defense lawyer a while back. My uncle has kept him and some of his people out of jail. I wonder what he has to do with my parents though."

I started looking along the walls for anything suspicious.

"What are you doing?"

"Looking for an opening to that secret passage my dad was talking about."

Kitashi looked around also. He walked over to a picture of my parents and me that was hanging on the wall. He put his face right up to the picture.

"What are you doing?" I asked.

"Your faces are buttons," he said.

"Come again?"

"If you look real close, you can see that your faces are raised on the picture. They're buttons to press to unlock the door."

"How do you know that?" I put my hands on my hips.

"Do you see anything else in here that might be a hidden door?"

"Okay, so how are we supposed to know which one to push?"

"All of them need to be pushed. I just don't know what order."

I looked at the photo closely. It was one of those family portraits you'd get done at a studio for like Christmas cards and announcements. It was Christmas themed with a fake snowman and snow-covered house as the back-drop. My dad was standing next to a Christmas tree with his hands on the back of the chair my mom was sitting on. I was in her lap holding two fake candy canes.

"Well my face gets pushed twice," I guessed. "Because I'm holding two candy canes."

"I think your dad gets pushed only once because the tree resembles a one."

"That's a far stretch but okay. We can go with that. My mom isn't holding anything though so I don't know what her number is."

"How old are you in this picture?"

"Four," I answered.

I watched Kitashi push my dad's face once, my mom's four times, and then mine twice. The wall shifted and dust shot out. A section of the wall moved and made a doorway. It looked really dark and I could feel cold air coming from the area. I got out my cell phone and pushed a button to light the screen up. It wasn't much light but enough to see where I was going. Kitashi followed me as we made our way down a flight of stairs and came to a door. I opened it and it made a terrible squeal. I saw a light switch by the door and turned it on. The lights flickered for a moment before staying on completely.

"Oh my god," I gasped. "How freaking cool!"

My parents had left me my own secret lair, filled with a few things I would need for crime fighting. On one wall was a large painting of a young woman in a super hero costume. She had dark skin and most of her face was covered by long black hair. Her costume was black and purple.

"Strange," Kitashi said.

"What?" I asked, hoping he realized what I had just realized.

"That looks exactly like you."

"I know. Weird."

There were filing cabinets on one side and I was dying to know what was in them, so I walked over to take a peek. They were all filled with comic books, dating back to the early sixties.

"What the hell?" I scrunched my face. "What are these for?"

Kitashi read a note that was taped to one of the cabinets.

"They're for inspiration."

"Huh?"

"I bet your parents thought if you read these, it'd give you more ideas for powers to make up in your dreams."

"You know, sometimes I wonder why Barney is called the genius and not you," I smiled.

Kitashi's face turned a little pink. I saw a key hanging on the wall and picked it up. It was a car key.

"No way, they left me a car too?" I said excitedly. I walked around the corner and saw my car; a black and purple 1971 Camero. It looked amazing, especially with all of the black curtains hanging on the walls around it.

"Holy shit!" I ran over to it and got in. The interior was also purple and black, and was fully equipped with a GPS and tinted windows.

"How do I drive it out of here?" I asked. "There's no way out."

Kitashi walked around and pulled back one of the curtains, revealing a long wide tunnel.

"Man, I can't wait to get my license and show up to school in this."

"I think it's meant for when you want to go out without anyone knowing who you are."

"Oh. Boring."

"We should probably head back to the house now. I don't want anyone getting suspicious about where we are."

"Good idea," I said. "And plus, I want to know where this leads to inside the house."

We left the car in its place and followed the path going the opposite way. My teeth started chattering although I tried not to let Kitashi know I was cold. The path ended and there was a doorway on the ceiling above us. Kitashi pulled the string that was hanging down and a small set of stairs pulled out. Kitashi walked up the stairs and pushed on the door.

"There might be something sitting on top of it," I said.

Kitashi pushed really hard and the door popped open. He lifted his head up and looked around.

"I don't know where we are," he said.

I pushed by him and went up into the room. I knew exactly where we were.

"This used to be the wine cellar. My parents collected wine and used some of them on special occasions like anniversaries and achievements with work."

Kitashi came up and shut the hideaway door and put the rug on the floor back over it. We walked out into the main part of the basement and headed upstairs.

"If anyone asked, we'll just say I was showing you a full tour of the house."

"Aright," he said. "If you don't want me to stay here, I don't have to. I can find somewhere else to go."

"No! I don't mind at all! In fact I want you to stay here. It would give me someone to hang out with and plus you could catch me up on my training. Unless you don't want to stay here."

"No, I do," he said. "I just don't want to be a burden."

"Don't be silly. I like having you around. You keep me . . . calm. Is that weird?"

"Not at all."

"You'll need a better room than the downstairs family room. You can have my parents' old room. It's the best room in the house."

"I wouldn't feel right staying in there."

"It's not a big deal. No one else is going to use so why not? You'll have to help me clean it a little but you'll be right on the other side of the wall from me."

"Alright, if you're sure it's okay."

"Trust me, it's fine."

We went upstairs through the house and went up to my parents' room. I hadn't set foot in there in years but it didn't really bother me. I was just happy that my uncle wasn't using that room as his. We had to move some things out of the room and into the basement, like my mother's wedding dress, their clothes from the closet, and some pictures of the family.

"It's kind of dusty, but once you get all of your stuff situated, it should be fine. What do you think?"

"It's very nice, Avery. Thank you."

"Not a problem at all. And there's a balcony out the window that connects to my room."

"Wonderful. Well I'll go down and bring my things up here."

"Sounds good. I'll be in my room. Let me know if you need anything."

I went to my room and changed into better clothes. I started cleaning my messy room up a little before I heard a knock on my door. Kitashi came in and sat in the recliner I had in the corner of the room.

"Matt's funeral is on Tuesday," Kitashi told me. "And Susanne just left. Are you going on Tuesday?"

"Um, I guess I have to, don't I?" I asked. "I haven't been to a funeral since my parents died. And I kind of feel like Matt's death was because of me."

"Why do you bother listening to Hayley?" he asked. "She's just insecure and wants to make people feel bad about themselves like she does. She's used to being the center of everyone's attention and when she doesn't get it, she throws fits and is mean. You should just learn to ignore her."

"It's hard for me to ignore people," I laughed. "When someone says something that upsets me, it's sets off something that makes me go crazy. I have a slightly short temper."

"We'll have to work on that."

"How?"

"We'll talk about it whenever you're ready to start our private training."

"I'm ready whenever you are."

"Today?" he asked. I nodded.

"Alright. You didn't answer my question."

"What question?"

"About going on Tuesday."

"Oh," I said. "Yeah I'll go."

"Good. Let's get started."

"Do I need to change back into work out clothes or anything?"

"No, just follow me."

We went into his room and he sat down on a cushion that was placed in the middle of the floor. He pointed to another cushion beside him, so I sat down also. He crossed his legs, placed his hands on his knees, and closed his eyes.

"So we're going to meditate like we did at Susanne's?" I asked. "Then what are we doing?"

Kitashi didn't reply so I followed his lead and began meditating. I closed my eyes and thought mostly about going to Matt's funeral. I didn't want to go but I knew it'd be really shitty of me if I didn't. I didn't want to see his mother in tears, saying goodbye to her baby. I didn't want to see Barney, broken down and sobbing. I especially didn't want to see Matt's body, laying abnormally still in the coffin and surrounded by flowers. His face would be painted on so he wouldn't look so pale and cold. He'd be in a suit with his hands folded across his stomach. I didn't want to see any of it.

"Why are you so tense, Avery?" I heard Kitashi ask.

I opened my eyes and looked at him, but his eyes were still closed.

"How did you know I was tense?"

"I could feel you. You need to free your mind. Focus on your chi."

"My chi? That's like my soul, right?"

"No. It is your energy flow. You need to learn to control the flow of your energy. First, sit with your bottom on the edge of the zafu."

"The what?" I asked.

"The small pillow that you are sitting on."

"Oh okay."

"Cross your legs into the Burmese position. It is the easiest and most comfortable position for beginners. Your knees should be resting gently on the ground with your back straightened. Close your mouth and breathe through your nose. Tilt your head down to where your nose is parallel to your navel. Breathe with your stomach instead of your chest and focus on your breathing. Count your breaths so you're not distracted by any other thoughts. If you find your mind wandering off, go back to counting breaths. Once you are focusing solely on counting your breaths, your awareness will increase. You'll notice things that you didn't before but had always been there. When you become nervous or are put into a stressful state, your breathing becomes fast and shallow. You must control your breathing, even in a stressful state, so that you can focus your energy on your surroundings."

"Wow," I whispered. "Okay, can we try again?"

"Yes. We will start off by meditating for thirty minutes."

"Alright, no problem."

However, thirty minutes felt like fucking forever. It was really hard just sitting there and counting my breaths. Every time my mind would wander and I'd lose count, I'd have to start over. I even almost fell asleep while we meditated. After meditation, we went down to eat something. My uncle Ross was also eating. He glanced up at us briefly before going back to whatever he was reading. I knew he wasn't happy with me about Kitashi, but I also knew he didn't want to waste time or energy getting into a fight with me. I talked to him calmly about having Kitashi teach me karate so I could stay home more often and still have time for my homework. He agreed to it but still expected to see improvement. He also still expected me to go to my therapy group on Tuesdays. I agreed reluctantly. I let him know about going to Matt's funeral but told my uncle that he was someone I had went to school with. He said I could go and skip this week's therapy session for the funeral, but I had to go to all the rest of them.

The next day at school was a blur. I hated being without Kitashi for the first time in three days. It gave me time to think more about

Matt and about Belladonna. I was jumpy and depressed at the same time. I barely talked to anyone all day. When lunch time came, I couldn't eat. Of course Kelly and Ryan were curious to hear what was wrong with me. I kind of lied and told them about the group I had ditched work for but didn't tell them anything about it being a super hero group. I made it sound like they were my therapy group I met with. I don't know if they bought my lie but I didn't really care, I just wanted to get through the day and Tuesday to get the funeral over with. I could tell Ryan and Kelly were kind of pissed with the way I was acting but they could just get over it. Finally, when the bell rang and school was out, I smiled for the first time that day. Kitashi surprised me by picking me up from school.

"How the hell did you talk my uncle into this?" I asked, hopping into the car.

"I didn't. I've been talking with Charlie all day, helping him around the house. He said it was alright with him as long as I didn't get pulled over or wreck the car."

"Figures, Charlie's really cool about stuff. He trusts me a lot more than my uncle does."

"Do you have homework?"

"A little bit. Why?"

"We have training to do."

"Alright, I'll try to hurry."

"No, take your time and work on your homework first."

"God, you sound like a parent."

"I just want you to do your best and not rush any of your work."

I smiled at him but he kept his eyes on the road. I was glad to have such a cool new friend. He was quickly becoming my new best friend. I finished my homework, trained with Kitashi for a while, and then we watched a movie together before going to bed. Kitashi was impressed with my movie collection, however, he said I was missing out on a lot of other good movies. He gave me a list of movies to watch and before I went to bed, I got online and ordered every single movie from the list.

The next day was another long, slow one at school. I didn't talk much and got a lot of my work done in class so I wouldn't have homework. Kitashi once again picked me up from school, and I insisted that he did so every day. He concurred, which made me happy. We got home and changed for the funeral. Susanne picked us up from my house since she knew where the funeral was held. We talked about what we had been doing the past couple of days and started talking about the things I'd need to order for the group to work at my house. I told her about the underground secret tunnel my parents had set up and she was very interested in seeing it and using it for all of us.

We arrived at the funeral home and met up with the rest of the group. Andrew and Hayley rode together, which kind of bothered me but I didn't say anything. We got seated and the whole time the memorial service was going on, I avoided looking around too much. I could hear people crying but I didn't look to see who it was. After the funeral we all walked over to Barney and his mom to pay our respects. Barney didn't look at any of us but when Susanne spoke, he looked up finally.

"However much time you need away from the group is fine but just letting everyone know, while we're all together, meetings will be held at Avery's house."

"Well for one, we're not *all* together," Barney said roughly. "In case you didn't realize."

"I'm sorry, Barney," Susanne apologized. "I didn't mean it like that. I'm sure you need some time before you come back."

"I'm not coming back."

"What?" we all said.

"Oh come on, man," Andrew said. "I know you're having a hard time but we need you. And you need us. Matt would have wanted you to keep doing this."

"Don't talk about my brother like you know what he would have wanted. I'm sure he wanted to be alive. I should have looked after him better."

Tears fell from Barney's eyes and his mom put her arm around him.

"I'm all my mom has left now."

"If you don't finish what you've started," Barney's mom lifted his face. "Then Matt's death happened for nothing. Do it for not only Matt, but also for yourself."

"But you'll worry about me."

"I'll worry about you no matter what happens. Matt was brave enough to die for what he believed in. I know you're brave enough to keep fighting for what *you* believe in."

When we got back out to the car, Susanne turned on her car radio while Hayley, Andrew, and Maddison stood outside the car. We were casually chatting when the disc jockey announced something on the radio.

"Breaking news! A gas station on 32$^{nd}$ Street and Rhode Avenue has been held up. The owner says he was robbed at gun point and the gunman seemed to be heavily intoxicated. The criminal took off with not only the $20,000 from the store's safe but also the watch that the owner had been wearing. He says that this was more upsetting than losing the money because the watch had belonged to his father who had passed away during The Holocaust. The car containing the robber was last seen driving down Rhode Avenue. The car is an older two-door model and is white. If you have any information please call the tips hotline. Now getting back to the music with another oldies hit-"

Susanne turned off the radio and looked around at everyone.

"Let's go," I heard Barney say from behind Andrew. We all looked at him. "I feel like we should do more than just a funeral for Matt. He would have loved to have chased down a robber."

We all squeezed into Susanne's car and sped off. We drove down the street for several miles before Barney pointed out a car that fit the description parked in a bar parking lot. We all got out and made a plan.

"If he pulls out a gun, everyone duck down," Kitashi said. "I'll charge at him and pin him down. We'll make a citizen's arrest if we have to."

"But we've got to get him to admit it's him first," Barney explained. "Because if we arrest him and can't prove it's the right guy, we'll be in big trouble."

"Well I have masks in the trunk for anyone who wants one," Susanne said. "That way our identities remain unknown."

"Good idea," Maddison said.

All of us except Kitashi put masks on and went inside. We split up and walked around the place. Maddison and I walked around the billiard table area while Barney walked around the bar counter.

Susanne and Hayley covered the karaoke room, Andrew checked the bathrooms, and Kitashi skimmed the area with the booths. I saw that Barney was talking to a man at the bar so I signaled to Maddison to join him.

"That's a nice watch," Barney pointed at the man's wrist. "What store did you by that from?"

"I didn't, my wife got it for me for a present," the man slurred. "Not that it's any of your business."

"Sorry, I wasn't meaning to be nosey. I was just admiring it."

"Hey!" the man yelled at the bartender holding up a hundred dollar bill. "Here's what I owe on my tab. And I also have money to spend on drinks now."

"I don't think you need anymore sir," the bartender said.

"Fuck you! I need to take a piss anyways. But when I come back, I want more to drink, god damn it!"

The man staggered away and the bartender sighed.

"Every year on this day, he gets rip-roaring drunk and causes a scene," he explained.

"What happened on this day?" Maddison asked.

"His wife died. She was in a bad car accident. Went into a coma, and never came out of it. Ken is a regular in here anyway, but this date is always tough on him. I had to cut him off because his tab ran up to a hundred dollars and he couldn't pay it. He left for a while, came back with the money, and that watch he's wearing. I don't know where he got it because I've been serving him for five years and I've never seen that man wear a watch."

"Sir, we have reason to believe that he's a suspect in a robbery that happened not too long ago," Barney explained.

"Oh Jesus," the bartender shook his head. "I was wondering what a bunch of kids in masks were doing in here. You be careful with him, he may have a knife on him somewhere."

"Thank you sir," Barney nodded as Ken came back out.

"Something doesn't seem right, guys," Andrew said. We all looked at him.

"What the fuck are you weirdoes looking at?"

"We're going to have to ask you to hand over the watch and money that you stole," Barney held out his hand.

"How dare you!" Ken spat. "I did not steal this watch! It was given to me by-by-"

"Your wife?" the bartender asked. Andrew looked at me and shook his head.

"No," Ken said, looking confused. "You gave it to me."

The bartender laughed.

"You did! You just came into work not too long ago and said you had found it on the ground when you went to get gas at the station."

"Freeze!" Barney yelled as the bartender ducked down. He stood back up and was holding a shotgun.

"God damn it, you stupid old drunk!" the bartender yelled. "You blew my cover! I was just about to have these twerps believe you had robbed the station and then you had to run your mouth. Well, looks like you won't be making any heroic arrests today kiddies, unless you want your splattered brains to be my new fucking wallpaper!"

Barney lifted his hand toward the bartender, making the shotgun hit him in the face. The gun went off and hit the ceiling, making pieces of foam tile fall everywhere. Then, Barney somehow made the gun twist into a knot, making it unusable. The man leaped over the counter and charged at Barney. Maddison inhaled really deep and let out a loud scream. It was soft enough that I didn't need to cover my ears but powerful enough to send the bartender head first into the beer dispensers, knocking him down.

"You little bitch!" he growled, getting back up quickly.

"Don't you talk to her like that!" I said, kicking my leg up into his crotch. He bent down to grab his balls and I punched him in the face, making him let go of his package and hold his bleeding nose. Then, I elbowed him in the throat, but not too hard to break his wind pipes. Ken, the drunk guy, grabbed a half full bottle of beer and smashed it over the bartender's head, knocking him out cold.

"Heh, heh, I've always wanted to do that," he laughed.

"I just called the police and told them what happened," Susanne said, coming into the room. "Great job, everyone."

I walked over to Ken and pointed at the watch.

"This watch belonged to someone and it was very important to them. Could I have it so it can be returned to the owner?"

"But it was a gift," he said with sad, glossy eyes.

"I know. Here, I'll make a deal with you," I said, reaching into my pocket. "I'll give you three hundred dollars for the watch. But, you have to promise me that you won't spend it on alcohol."

"Christmas is coming up soon," he said, handing me the watch. "I don't have anyone to spend it with. But with this money I could fly down to Alabama and see my daughter and granddaughter. Thank you very much."

"You're welcome. Have a good Christmas," I smiled.

"What's your name?" he asked.

"Dreamcatcher," I said.

"Nice to meet you," he stuck his hand out for me to shake.

We handcuffed the unconscious bartender to the bar railing. When we heard the sirens coming, we got back in Susanne's car and drove off. That night, the whole group got phone calls from Susanne saying to turn the television on and watch the news. Our story was covered about how a masked group arrested the robber. The gas station owner got all of his money back and cried about receiving his watch. He said he was offering a reward to whoever got it for him but we knew we weren't going to claim it. The reporter interviewed Ken who couldn't talk for long because he was catching the next flight to Alabama. I went to bed feeling like a real super hero.

# CHAPTER 7

# Fly By Night

*"Why try? Now why?*
*This feeling inside me says it's time I was gone.*
*Clear head, new life ahead.*
*It's time I was king and not just one more pawn."*

-"Fly By Night" by Rush

The following February.

The past several months had been the busiest of my life. After Matt's funeral, Susanne, Kitashi, and I worked on ordering all of the things we needed to have our secret super hero hideout. With all of the training and exercise I was doing, I was in better shape than all of the girls at my school, and in better shape than most of the boys too. Kitashi and I had become inseparable and we went everywhere together. It was like having a brother without the growing up together and fighting. I tried to get him to hang out with Kelly and Ryan a few times but he didn't like them and they definitely didn't like him. I still hung out with Ryan and Kelly but it was mostly at school and we never had anything real interesting to talk about. Kitashi helped me with my school work so my grades went up a lot. I also went to all of my group therapy sessions and graduated from it. I didn't enjoy it and I didn't make any friends from it but I was glad I did it and got it over with.

We were all meeting at my house twice a week and my uncle never asked much about it because he all of sudden became really busy with his work. We were training and practicing really hard. I had learned about martial arts, making citizen's arrests, eating healthier, and learning more powers. It had really helped that my parents had left all of the comic books for me to read because it was giving me more ideas for powers to learn. Most of us were ready to start our crime fighting, however, after what happened to Matt Susanne was wanting to really make sure we were trained more so no one else would get hurt. Everyone was improving their abilities and getting better at defending themselves.

So there we were, hanging out again in our secret hideout at my house, and it was already the second week of February. It was the day before Valentine's Day, one of my least favorite holidays ever. I was glad the next day was Sunday and I didn't have school on Valentine's Day. However, Monday would be just as bad because everyone would be all over each other, making out, and giving each other roses. See, every year the high school sells roses. You pay to have them delivery a rose to someone you like and if you want to, you can even add a note to it. It's nauseating. And speaking of nauseating, Hayley and Andrew were back together. So of course

Hayley was clinging to him for dear life and God forbid I speak to Andrew because then Hayley's claws would come out and she'd rip my eyeballs out. I was just ready for winter to finally be over because Susanne said once Spring hit, we'd start going out. We had our costumes come in and we were trying them on and trying to come up with our super hero aliases.

Susanne was going to be called "Gaia," after the Greek mythological goddess version of Mother Earth. Of course Kitashi was going to just go as Kitashi and not wear a costume. My costume was black and purple, inspired by the painting that hung on the wall. My super hero name was going to be "Dreamcatcher." I liked it better as one word instead of two because it looked better that way. Maddison was going to be called "Lil Freak," after the nickname her dad had always given her because of her powers. Andrew, very arrogantly announced that he would go as "The Negotiator." Kitashi and I looked at each other and tried hard not to laugh. His costume made it even harder not to laugh because he looked like an army ballerina. He explained that the tight-fitted clothes would help him be more flexible and aerodynamic. He also admitted that he liked how the costume showed off all of his muscles. Barney liked the name "Siege" and didn't have as bad of a costume as Andrew, or should I say "The Negotiator." Hayley's, I was sad to admit, was probably the coolest. Her name that she picked was "Necrosia" and her costume was all black and white. She wore a black glove on the hand that could hurt people and a white glove on the hand that could heal. I had to admit, I was a little jealous.

I was a little jealous of all of them, actually. I wasn't the shiny new toy in the group anymore. No one really seemed interested in what new powers I was coming up with. I was envious that they all had one ability that stuck with them. They didn't have to worry about learning a new thing all of the time. It was annoying. I wanted to do something that would get everyone's attention.

"I'm visiting the man who killed my parents tomorrow," I announced. Everyone stopped and looked at me.

"What?" Susanne asked.

"Yeah, I figured visiting him would bring a sense of closure for me. His death sentence is coming up soon so I thought I'd pay him a visit before he bites the big one."

"Do you really think that would be a good idea?" Andrew asked. "I mean, that'd be pretty upsetting to anyone who's gone through something like that."

"I wouldn't be able to do it," Barney said. "I'd have to kill that bitch who murdered my brother."

"I got it under control, Barney," I explained. "I don't even remember my parents that well so I'm not going to get my revenge or anything. I just want to meet the guy."

"I'm going with you," Kitashi said.

"You don't have to."

"I know I don't have to but I want to, and I think it would be better if I did."

"Alright, if you insist."

"I do."

So the next day, Valentine's Day, Kitashi and I drove to the prison that Adam Coleman has been locked up in for ten years. That was his name; Adam Coleman. I researched him and called ahead to ask to see him. They were reluctant at first but when I said who my parents were, they gave me the okay. A guard would have to be in the room with us, Adam would be chained to a lock on the floor, and I would have to sit on the other side of the table from him. I was really nervous, but more of an excited kind of nervous instead being sad or scared. Kitashi and I signed in on the visitors log and went inside. He was already sitting at the table, waiting for me. I sat down and Kitashi stood behind me with his hands on my shoulders.

"Hello," I managed to say. He just looked at me.

"My name is Avery. It's nice to meet you, Adam."

He blinked at the sound of my name.

"Do you know who I am?" I asked.

He nodded. It sent a shiver down my spine.

"I wanted to come meet you and talk with you."

"You look like your mother," he muttered.

"Thank you," I said awkwardly. "Do you remember my parents? I wanted to talk to you about them. Why you killed them."

"When I shot your father, there was a little squirt of blood that came out of his back. Like a water gun."

I started fidgeting with my hands. I looked up at Kitashi.

"Why did you kill my parents?" I asked.

"You know why. Someone told me to."

"Who?" I asked.

"He calls himself Acheron. The river of woes and pain," he answered. "'You will reach the lifeless river over which Charon presides.'"

"What?" I asked, shifting in my seat.

"'A lake in Hades, which the dying cross over, giving the ferryman the coin which is called a danake.'"

"I'm sorry. I still don't understand."

"'A longing grips me to die and see the dewy, lotus-covered banks of Acheron.'"

"Acheron?" I asked. "What is that?"

"In Greek mythology the Acheron river is a river that borders Hell," the guard said. "The newly deceased souls paid the ferryman, Charon, to cross the river. If they couldn't pay him, they'd have to wander the banks of Acheron for a century."

I looked at Adam again, who was smiling.

"Acheron is the name of the man who hired you to kill my parents?"

"Oh, he's no man. He is a monster. Like me. You look exactly like your mommy."

"Uh, thanks. You already-"

"You even have her titties. I remember her titties."

I felt Kitashi tense up. I grabbed his hand that had been resting on my shoulder. He had it balled up in a fist.

"Knock it off, Adam," said the guard.

"When I get out, I'll finish the job I was supposed to do. I'll come back for you, little Avery. Except I won't shoot you. I'll slit your pretty little throat and rub your blood all over your tits and my dick. Happy Valentine's Day, Avery darling."

Adam tried lunging at me but luckily, his chain was tight enough to keep him from reaching me. Then, he spat on my shirt and laughed as he tried to wriggle free. The guard came over and started trying to calm him down. I stood up and walked quickly out of the room, running for the nearest bathroom. I could still hear Adam yelling as I ran down the hall.

"Acheron will rule the world!" he screamed. "He will control the minds of thousands and kill anyone who stops him!"

I barely made it to the toilet and threw up. I started crying and sat down on the floor. This trip ended up being a lot harder than I thought it would be. I had half-expected Adam to be nice to me and tell me all of the information he knew. Instead, he ended up being some psycho who just wanted to talk about a river and my boobs. I went to the sink and ran a paper towel under the faucet. With shaky hands I dabbed at the spit mark and felt like taking the shirt home and burning it. Finally, I came out of the bathroom and Kitashi was standing in the hallway. I walked over to him and he handed me my coat. I looked at him and he wrapped his arms around me. Kitashi never hugged anyone so I was really surprised that he hugged me. I just stood there, crying quietly, and let him embrace me until he let go.

"Thank you," I smiled. "I needed that."

"Let's go home," he said handing me a tissue.

The two of us didn't talk until we got back to the house and were upstairs in my room. I was online researching while Kitashi was watching a movie. He had put in one of the Japanese movies I ordered and he was really enjoying it. It was hard for me to get into it because it was in Japanese with subtitles.

"Oh, watch this part. This is the best part," he smiled.

The main character walked into a bar and suddenly cut off a guy's head with a katana he had been hiding.

"That's gruesome," I laughed.

"He deserved it."

"What did he do?"

"He was part of that gang the killed that guy's wife and baby."

"Oh. I didn't know he had a wife and baby."

"Well yeah, Avery, didn't you watch that part? He didn't just kill them for no reason. You should pay more attention to the movie."

I took a piece of popcorn from the bowl between us and threw it at him. He caught it in his mouth and we both laughed. I watched Kitashi watch the movie and couldn't fully focus on my research.

"Do you ever think about your family?" I asked. "Like your parents?"

"I don't remember them. I don't remember anything before meeting Susanne. I woke up in the middle of the woods and just kept walking until I was so exhausted that I collapsed in the middle of the road. A truck almost hit me and when it stopped, Susanne got out of it and rescued me. If she hadn't come along, I would have been hit by a car or probably killed by some drug addict. She took me in and brought me back with her to America. Susanne is the only family I know."

"Kind of how I am with Charlie. He's not my family but I'm closer to him than my uncle. It kind of sucks."

"I'm sorry for that. If it makes you feel any better, I consider you my family."

I looked at him and nodded.

"I consider you family too."

Kitashi looked back at the movie.

"Do you want to have kids someday?" I asked.

"I don't know," he said, stretching his arms out. "I've thought about it. I don't know if I'd make a good father though. I've never had anyone to be a father to me so I don't know how a father is supposed to act. How about you?"

"I feel the same," I rubbed my eyes. "I don't think I'd be a good mom."

"I think you'll make a great mom someday."

"Thanks."

I looked back at my computer and sighed.

"I can't find anything on any criminals named Acheron," I said. "I think that Adam is so screwed up in his head that he doesn't even know what's going on."

"Maybe there is and you can't find anything on him because he hasn't committed any crimes yet."

"This is irritating. I'm obviously not the detective-type of super hero. Oh who the hell am I kidding, I'm *not* a superhero. I haven't saved anyone. No one knows who I am. I'm not even old enough to drive a car!"

"Avery, none of us have really started saving people or anything. I don't consider myself a superhero."

"I consider you one," I said.

"Well thank you," he replied. "Now can you please put the computer stuff away and watch the rest of this movie with me?"

I gave him a smirk and closed all of the windows on my computer before sitting on the floor next to Kitashi and watching the movie with him.

"Do you really hate Valentine's Day that much?" Kitashi asked me.

"Huh?" I asked.

"I heard you and Maddison talking about what your schools do for Valentine's Day and you were saying how much you hate it."

"Oh, well I mean I guess it's not too bad when you're little and everyone has to give everyone a valentine, that way no one gets left out. Or if you have someone to spend Valentine's Day with it wouldn't be too bad."

"My Valentine's Day has been good," Kitashi said.

"Oh yeah, visiting a crazy killer and seeing me upset is a great day," I laughed.

"But at least I got to spend it with you."

I kept my eyes on the movie but gave him a half smile. After the movie we were both tired and went to bed. I felt something under my pillow and pulled it out. It was a little box of candy and note in Japanese that probably said something like, "Happy Valentine's Day to my best friend" or something. I fell asleep fast and stayed asleep through the whole night, even through my bad dream that I had. I woke up the next morning, anxious to see what my new power would be like. I had dreamt that Adam Coleman had escaped from prison and was coming after me with this Acheron guy he had talked about. I was able to make a bunch of clones of myself and fight both of them.

Kitashi was driving me to school when I told him about my dream.

"Come on!" I pleaded. "I really want to try it."

"It sounds really dangerous," he said. "What if you get yourself apart and can't put yourself back together? Or what if one of you gets killed somehow?"

"Then good thing there's multiples of me, right? Come on, Kitashi. I could send one of me to school, stay home as one of the others and do more research, and go out for a fun day as me. Please?"

"You do what you want but I don't approve of any of this."

"Yes!" I cheered. "Okay pull over here so I can try it out."

The car pulled off into the gas station and I ran out quickly to the bathroom. Inside, I concentrated as hard as I could. Then, I felt myself pulling in half until there was another me standing in front of me!

"Whoa!" I said excitedly. "Can you talk?"

"Duh," Clone 1 said. "You think I'm retarded or something?"

"Sorry," I said. "Okay, I'm going to make another one real quick."

"Whatever," Clone 1 rolled her eyes.

As I split in half again, I felt a lot more weak and dizzy this time. Now a third me was standing next to us.

"Oh hello," Clone 2 said. "Well, well, how strange seeing two of me standing here."

"Hey," I waved. "Okay so we have to run to the car real quick so no one notices us."

"Sounds fantastic," Clone 2 started laughing. Her laugh was a horrible snorting sound.

"Right," Clone 1 gave Clone 2 a mean glare. "Whatever, just get me out of this bathroom."

I sent Clone 2 first, to see how Kitashi would react. Then, after she was in the car, I sent Clone 1 and finally myself. I hopped in the car and chuckled at Kitashi.

"This is great," I said, turning to the two clones in the back. "I'm going to mark you guys, so I know which one is which."

I took out a marker and drew a "1" on Clone 1's hand and a "2" on the others hand. We pulled up to the school and I ducked down.

"Okay, Avery 1," I said. "Have a good day at school. Be good. Learn a lot."

"Wait a minute!" she exclaimed. "I have to go to school? Why me? What are you two doing?"

"Clone 2 is staying at the house and researching stuff for me."

"Oh research, yay!" clapped Clone 2. "Although I'd rather go to school."

"See, there you go," said Clone 1. "Let her go to school and let me stay home."

"No because you won't get anything done," I said. "Just go to school. It's not that bad."

"You go then," she said, rolling her eyes.

"I don't have to because I have you," I smiled. "I don't want to be around all of the Valentine's Day celebrating going on at school. So you have fun with that."

Clone 1 got out of the car with a lot of attitude, she even slammed the door behind her. The car pulled away and I looked in the rearview mirror and watched her walk into the building.

"One down, one to go," I said to Kitashi.

"I still don't know about this," he said.

"Is there anything else you'd like me to do while I'm home today, Avery?" Clone 2 asked. "Like clean your room or do some of your laundry or anything else you might need."

"I mean, if you feel like cleaning up a little-"

"Not a problem at all!" she giggled. "I love cleaning! And I'll research anything you want me to."

"I'm just trying to find this guy named Acheron. He might have never been sent to jail or arrested for anything but if you find anything at all, write it down for me; will you?"

"Oh yes, of course! I'm so excited!"

We dropped Clone 2 off at the house and Kitashi hadn't spoken in a while so I asked what was wrong.

"I'm just nervous about doing this. It feels wrong."

"It will be fine," I sighed. "Quit worrying so much and just relax. Today is supposed to be a fun day."

"What are we doing on our fun day?" he asked.

"Chicago," I smiled.

The day we had together was a blast. We started with the Field Museum, which was one of my favorite places in Chicago. We looked at all of the artifacts and gross taxidermy and my favorite part, which was the gem and rock section. I loved looking at all of the different colored and shaped rocks. Kitashi really liked the animal part. I'd always thought a bunch of dead, stuffed animals was gross but Kitashi actually made it a little more enjoyable. After the museum, we hit the aquarium and planetarium. I liked the aquarium a lot more, but Kitashi enjoyed the planetarium. It was funny that we were so different but got along so well.

We ate lunch at the art museum before looking around there a bit. After all of the museums, we decided to check out the stores on Michigan Avenue before heading to Navy Pier. It was a full day but it was really fun. We rode the huge Ferris wheel and then decided to leave so we could pick up Clone 1 from school on time. We waited in front of the school for thirty minutes and were starting to get worried.

"Maybe I should go in and look for her," I said.

"No, bad idea," Kitashi said. "There can't be two of you walking around. People will get really confused and ask about it. I'll go in."

"I'm going to drive over to the house real quick then and check on the other one."

"Hurry up."

"I will," I said.

I know what you're thinking. I know I'm not technically old enough to drive a car by myself. I had a permit though and it wasn't the first time I had driven a car. I made sure I was extra cautious and did the speed limit the whole time. I pulled up to the house and ran in. Charlie was sitting on the couch, reading a magazine.

"Oh hello," he said. "Back already?"

"What?" I asked.

"You said you were going out not too long ago. Thanks again for cleaning up the whole house."

"Oh, you're welcome. Hey, about how long ago did she—I mean, I leave?"

"About an hour ago. You've been acting very strange today, Avery. Like you're not all there."

"Ha, yeah. Um, I'll see you later," I called as I ran back out the door.

Great. I should have left cell phones with them. I was illegally driving around, looking for two more of me. I grabbed a hoodie of Kitashi's from the backseat and put it on after I parked the car in the school's parking lot. I ran all through the school looking for a clone or Kitashi. I found him with a clone in the library. I looked at the clone's hand.

"2?" I asked. "What the hell? You were supposed to stay at the house!"

"I know, I'm sorry but Clone 1 came home and said I had to be at school for you. I didn't want you to get in trouble and I was already done with everything at the house. Please don't be mad at me."

"I'm not mad at you," I sighed. "Did 1 say where she was going?"

"She said she was going out to have fun like you did today."

"Okay, well we need to get you and me back together so let's find a bathroom or something."

"Aw, but I have so much to learn! I even did your homework for you that Clone 1 didn't do."

"Thanks, but right now we need to get back together so we can find 1."

Clone 2 reluctantly followed me to the bathroom and pushed back into me. I felt a little better, and actually a little smarter. As I was coming out of the bathroom, Ryan was walking down the hallway.

"Hey, Ryan," I said. "I was just getting ready to leave school. Because you know, I've been here all day."

"Oh, are you admitting that you know me now?" She asked frowning.

"What do you mean?" I asked.

"Don't play stupid with me Avery. You've changed so much since you started hanging out with him."

She glared at Kitashi, who just watched us without saying anything.

"I really don't know what you're talking about," I said, getting irritated.

"What happened this morning when he dropped you off. You know, since he drops you off every day now and you can't walk to school with your real best friends. And then you have the nerve to embarrass me in front of everyone."

"What happened?"

"Oh my god, Avery, you are something else. If you weren't my friend I'd knock you on your ass. If you even are still my friend.

Seeing as though this morning when I said hi to you, you asked if you knew me and walked off."

"I'm sorry," I said. "I just haven't been myself lately. But I really have to go, it's an emergency. We'll talk later, I promise."

Before Ryan could say anything else, I walked away. When we got in the car, Kitashi stared at me.

"Go ahead," I said, tears filling my eyes. "Tell me that you told me so and that I fucked up. Because I know I did, big time. I just thought it would be nice to have a day out with you. But I should have went to school myself. At least then Ryan wouldn't be pissed at me and I wouldn't have an angst clone of myself running around somewhere."

"I'm not going to say anything. Why would I tell you those things if you already know. You've acknowledged that you have made a mistake so I don't need to tell you. It's up to you to fix it now."

"Thank you. I appreciate the fact that you're not going to give me a hard time, but I don't know where the other would be though."

"Well if the other clone was your happier, more responsible part then the other one is the opposite."

"Oh that's great," I smacked myself in the forehead.

"Where would you go? This is still you we're talking about. What do you like to do when you're feeling reckless?"

"I don't know! I'm not usually a bad kid. I don't like getting into trouble. Except for when I got in a fight with—oh crap."

"What?" Kitashi asked. "Where are we going?"

"Amanda's house," I said. "Turn around."

We pulled up to Amanda's house just in time to see Clone 1 walking up to the door. I jumped out the car and sprinted towards her. She pushed the doorbell and I tackled her as hard as I could, pushing her back inside me. I fell into the bushes and the door opened.

"Hello?" I heard Amanda ask. She looked down at me.

"Avery?" she asked.

"Hey Amanda," I said standing up.

"What the fuck are you doing in my mother's bushes? Why are you at my house?"

"I'm not sure," I brushed the dirt off my shirt. "I guess I came by to, um, *apologize* to you."

"What?"

"Yeah. Sorry about all the shit I've given you. And not just the stuff lately, but everything that we've been through. I'm tired of fighting with you so I'm putting up my white flag and apologizing and I hope you can accept it."

Amanda just stared at me for a moment.

"Stay away from me, you freak," she flipped her hair back.

"Right," I breathed. "I'll be going then."

I walked back to the car and heard Amanda call my name. I turned around.

"See you at school tomorrow," she smiled before shutting the door.

I got into the car smiling. Kitashi drove us home and I was happy to get there.

"Well now that that's done," I flopped down on my bed. "Remind me to never leave clones of myself accountable for my responsibilities. I think it's worse than having children."

"Yes, hopefully you don't ever use that ability again. Or if you do, you use it for better purposes."

My room was spotless. Clone 2 had even dusted and vacuumed, two things that I never do. There was finished homework in my backpack, an outfit ironed and hung up for school the following day, and a stack of typed papers sitting next to the computer.

"Man," I laughed. "I'm going to miss having Clone 2 around. She cleaned and even did research for me."

"And?" Kitashi asked. "What did she find out?"

"She mostly just found stuff about Dominic Sloan. Still nothing about Acheron. I wonder if the two are connected. It was Sloan's guys we fought in the park. And his daughter too. Look at this."

I held a printed off picture of a newspaper clipping. The headline read, "Crime boss' daughter saved from illness."

"What does it say?" Kitashi sat down.

"*Caterina Sloan, daughter of known crime boss, Dominic Sloan, and family received good news when they visited Caterina's oncologist on Wednesday. Nine year old Caterina had been diagnosed with leukemia when she was born. However, doctors were shocked when her tests came back completely cancer free.*

*'We were expecting very little improvement if any,' Dr. Ashley Ward says. Ward has been working with Caterina her whole life.*

*'When little Caterina was diagnosed, we gave her about a year to live,' Ward says. 'And then when she passed a year and two and three, we were amazed then. But this, this is a miracle. Not the work of doctors, but the work of God Himself.'*

*Dr. Ward says she expects Sloan to live a normal healthy life without anymore complications."*

I finished the article and looked at Kitashi.

"The work of God," I said sarcastically. "More like the work of Satan. That chick is a monster. So, that means, she's Dominic Sloan's daughter. My uncle defended Sloan when he worked on his trial case. My dad also mentioned Sloan. You don't think Caterina knows who I am, do you?"

"I don't know," Kitashi said. "I would be extra careful if I were you."

"I know, I always have to be careful. I just want to be a normal teenager or a really cool super hero. I hate this in between thing I'm going through."

"It's okay, Avery. We'll keep training a little bit more and then we'll start fighting crime and saving the world."

"I want to start now though. I hate having school five days in a row and then only getting two days of training."

"What about the training you and I do together?"

"Kitashi, while I appreciate your time and effort, sitting for hours with my eyes closed and meditating isn't really the training I was looking for."

Kitashi flung the television remote he was holding straight at my head. I ducked just in time but still felt the air as it passed. It made a sound like *whoosh*!

"What the hell was that for!" I yelled at him. "You could have broken my nose or given me a concussion or put my eye out!"

"But I didn't because you felt it coming and dodged it."

"Well yeah, I saw you throw it."

"No, you *felt* me throw it."

"What the hell are you talking about?" I asked. "Did you teach me a sixth sense I was unaware of?"

"Stand up and close your eyes."

I groaned and stood up and closed my eyes. Kitashi grabbed my scarf and wrapped it around my eyes.

"I have my eyes closed," I said. "I think the scarf is a little excessive."

"It's fine," I heard him say. "Now meditate."

"What? Are you crazy?"

"Just start counting your breaths."

I started doing so and could hear Kitashi moving around. Judging by the sounds of the floor and his movement around objects, I guessed he was by the doorway and coming up behind me. I felt fast movement and put my arm up just in time to block his strike.

"Good," he said. "Again."

He lifted his leg up to kick me and again I blocked it. We repeated this exercise a few more times before Kitashi removed my scarf. I looked at him and he was smiling.

"Now tell me that we haven't been doing significant training."

"Alright, alright. Whatever, you win. I'm going to go take a shower."

I grabbed some clean clothes and walked out of the room. When I was done with my shower I walked passed Kitashi's room and stopped to listen in on him. I could hear him whispering in Japanese. It almost sounded like he was praying. Suddenly, he stopped speaking.

"I had fun today, Avery," I heard him say. I smiled really big at the fact that he knew it was me.

"I did too," I said before heading to my room for the night. "Thank you for the candy yesterday, by the way."

"You're welcome."

"What does the note say?"

"I'll tell you later. Goodnight, Avery."

"Goodnight," I replied.

The next day at school was a little rough because I had no idea about anything my clone had learned the previous day. I was confused in all of my classes which was hard to explain to all of my teachers because all of my homework was correct. One of the morning announcements was about the big Sweethearts Dance coming up in May. It was an "end-of-the-year" celebration dance for anyone who wasn't a senior going to prom. I thought it was pretty pointless.

"Are you going to the dance?" Kelly asked me at lunch. Ryan wasn't talking to either of us.

"Hell no!" I said. "I wouldn't be caught dead at a stupid high school dance wearing a stupid dress and acting . . . stupid. I wouldn't go if someone paid me, and anyone willing to go through all that trouble and money just for a couple hours of awkward teenage grinding and dry-humping is stupid."

"Well, then I guess I'm really stupid," Ryan said without looking at me.

"No, you're not. I just don't want to go," I explained. "I didn't think you'd want to either."

"Are you kidding?" Kelly smirked. "She's going with her boyfriend."

"Sly?" I asked. "You two are still together?"

"Not that it's any of your business, but yeah we are," Ryan stood up, dumped the rest of her lunch in the trash, and stormed out of the cafeteria.

"So I take it you two are still fighting?" Kelly asked.

"I don't know what we are anymore," I said. "So are you going to the dance?"

"No, I guess not."

"How come?"

Kelly stood up and said, "Because the person I was going to ask thinks the dance is stupid."

I watched Kelly walk off before Amanda passed my table. I gave her a little wave and she let out a little "ew" and kept walking. Apparently everyone at my school hated me. I even got in trouble by my history teacher for sending a text message to Kitashi during class. My phone was taken away and Charlie or my uncle would have to come pick it up, although it would most likely be Charlie since my uncle was away for work again. I also lost any points I might have gotten for class participation for the day. I was having a pretty shitty day.

I was still in a bad mood when Kitashi picked me up. He didn't ask what had happened and I didn't want to talk about it. I just wanted to do my homework and go to bed. Kitashi stayed in his room while I stayed in mine. That upset me too because he was ignoring me so I threw one of my shoes at the wall we both shared. He came into my room shortly after and sat down next to me on the bed. I put my face into his chest and hugged him. He hugged me back and asked what was wrong. I told him what had happened at lunch and he told me everything would be okay. I wanted to believe him but I knew better. I was becoming a total loner at school with no friends at all. And it sucked big time. If it wasn't for Kitashi, I wouldn't have any friends.

"Hey Kitashi," I asked, still holding onto him.

"Hm?" he asked.

"I had a question to ask you."

"Sure, go ahead."

"I know I'm going to sound pretty . . . stupid for asking this but, do you like to dance?"

# CHAPTER 8

# Gimme Chemicals

*"All this pressure, and all this pain, and all these sins swim through my veins.*
*If I could do it again, I'd probably do it the same.*
*But I'd try to cut back on the cigarettes, singing,*
*'Hey, gimme, gimme chemicals. Gimme the fix, gimme back control.*
*A white-hot white revival, we're gonna be saved tonight.'"*

-"Gimme Gimme Chemicals" by The Pink Spiders

Ross stood in the laboratory, smiling for the first time in a long time. He watched as the door was finally pried open in front of him. When he had found out from one of the employees that Avery had visited the lab a few months ago and was able to get into the locked room, Ross spared no expenses to get into it. Avery, of course, wasn't to find out about him breaking in but he didn't care if she did find out. What would she want with anything in the lab anyways? She made it very clear that she had no intentions of claiming the lab as her property so the way Ross saw it, whatever was behind the door was his property anyways. As the final bolt came off and the door unhinged, Ross stepped toward the room. Once inside, he looked around vigorously for anything new and exciting. He tore the room apart until he reached the freezer that was hidden behind a shelf. Little did he know that the answer to all of his problem lay in that freezer and that Avery had taken everthing out of the room that would reveal what she was.

Ross opened the freezer lid and reached in, pulling out the tray of vials. His eyes widened and he carefully carried the tray out of the room.

"I want reports on everything you can find out about this stuff," Ross demanded. "Have the reports done and to me by tomorrow."

"Yes sir," said the employees.

For the first time in a while Ross felt a sense of relief. Back at the house Ross sat in silence as Avery and Kitashi ate their dinner. Ross, having already finished his meal, watched the Asian boy from the corner of his eye. He didn't like this kid for some reason and he didn't trust him. After everyone was done with dinner, Ross went out to meet Sloan, Dante, and Sloan's daughter Caterina. Caterina was never really a part of the family business until recently when she had dropped out of college and made herself a part of her fathers work. Apparently, she had met some other kids that were different like her and Sloan, and killed one of them. Dominic Sloan didn't really seem to mind but his wife was very upset with the fact that their little girl had been so eager to join the business. Also it didn't help that her husband had turned their daughter into some sort of powerful creature.

When Ross had learned of Sloan's ability to produce energy blasts, it made Ross even more afraid of him. Sloan was able to knock over whole buildings if he wanted.

"Even if I were to get arrested," Sloan told Ross once, "they wouldn't be able to keep me locked up."

Then, when Caterina started healing and becoming what she was now, Sloan became a proud father. With her, he'd say, the Sloans could rule the world. When Sloan told Ross about her killing that kid, Sloan just laughed. Ross, however, sat in terror. How many people were out there who had abilities?

Ross slowed his car to a stop in the parking lot where he was meeting everyone. A black limo pulled up next to Ross' car and he got in, sitting next to Dante and facing Sloan and Caterina. Ross tried avoiding looking at her.

"Well?" Sloan asked. "What's the big news?"

"I found vials of unknown liquid that was hidden by my brother in his lab today," Ross explained. "I think whatever it is will help with a break through in our studies for the drug."

"You wasted our time by telling us this?" Caterina glared. "I figured you wanted to tell us that you had already found something. Not that you, once again, thought you were *about* to find something."

"Oh, I'm sorry," Ross stuttered.

"But we're close, right?" Dante asked.

"Fuck, you've been saying we're close for how long now?" Caterina spat.

"Caterina," Sloan said. "Please."

"God, dad, you are one stupid fat ass sometimes, you know that? You're wanting this drug to exist so badly, you keep giving away our money for nothing. It's imprudent."

"Caterina, I've been doing this a lot longer than you, sweetie. Let me handle this."

"Whatever, asshole."

"So here's the deal," Sloan said. "You two get back to the lab. Start running tests yourselves to speed up the process, and let me know by the end of the week what we have."

"Alright," Ross said.

Ross and Dante were driving back to the lab when they lit their cigarettes.

"Thanks for sticking up for me back there, fucker," Ross said, exhaling smoke.

"Sorry," said Dante. "That Caterina scares the shit out of me."

"Yeah, me too," Ross had a shiver sent up his spine. "Me too."

The two of them worked with the other scientists for hours and hours. Everyone was yawning and took turns making coffee runs. Ross never moved away from the equipment though. He stayed focused and worked extra hard. Mouse after mouse kept dying until Ross slammed his fist on the table.

"I'm tired of doing this. Disappointment after disappointment. We're doing a human experiment."

"Sir, it's not stable enough for a human yet."

"We don't have to let Dante know that though, do we?"

"Sir?"

"I'll pay you whatever you want if you keep your mouth shut."

The scientist looked at him, sweat falling from his face, and nodded. When Dante came back with a fresh order of more coffee, Ross happily walked over to him.

"It's ready," he smiled, walking with Dante towards the chamber.

"It is?" Dante asked.

"Yes, I've already tried it on myself and now we're just waiting for the effects to kick in. Your turn."

"I don't know, man."

"Come on, you wanted this just as bad as I did. In you go."

Ross lead Dante into the chamber and shut the door behind him. The doors locked and Dante looked panicked.

"It's alright, just stay calm, Dante," Ross assured him. "The sequence has started so just breathe slowly and stay calm."

Ross couldn't understand what Dante was freaking out about because he couldn't hear what he was yelling through the thick glass.

"Should we stop it, sir?" asked one of the scientists.

"It's too late now," Ross explained. "You can't stop it once it's already started."

"Sir!" Another scientist shouted. "Look!"

Ross looked at where the woman was pointing and everyone began to panic. Dante was holding the lighter from his pocket in his hand. He was crying and yelling, and it looked like a movie scene that had been muted. Ross yelled for everyone to evacuate the lab and move a safe distance away. Everyone ran outside and didn't stop running until they heard a loud crash. Several people said they were going to call the fire department but Ross told them not to until they saw the damage. When no fire or smoke came from the building, Ross walked toward the lab by himself. As he walked inside, he saw that a lot of things had been rattled off tables, shelves, and walls. As Ross crept closer to the chamber, he couldn't see anything but smoke. A few other scientists were inside the lab by now and helped Ross unlock the door. Smoke poured out, setting off the sprinkler system inside. Everyone put on breathing masks and helped waft the smoke out.

When it finally cleared, Ross could see Dante's body, charred and laying on the ground. Ross heard someone behind him throwing up but didn't care to check on them.

"Sir, what should we do now?" someone asked. "Sir?"

"Look!" Ross pointed at the body. "He's breathing!"

Sure enough, Dante's breathing became more noticeable and then he started stirring. He slowly sat up and looked at everyone.

"Dante?" Ross asked, moving to the outside of the chamber. "Are you okay?"

Dante nodded slowly and scratched at his head. When he did so, chunks of burnt skin crumbled off and fell next to him. He picked up the pieces and looked back at Ross through the glass.

"How come there wasn't a fire?" asked one of the female employees.

"I'm guessing since he was in an air locked the fire didn't have enough oxygen to breathe. Maybe it suffocated the fire."

Dante stood up and let out a horrific scream that sounded like a wild beast roaring out in pain. Ross moved further away from Dante as he watched Dante scrape off the burned, dead skin from his head. He cried out, pounding his fist on the ground, and then smoke started coming out of his nostrils. He looked at Ross with his dark eyes and a huge burst of fire shot out of his mouth. Several people gasped and a couple of them ran back out of the lab. Dante kept hitting the glass on the inside of the chamber and yelling, spitting out flames.

"Dante," Ross repeated softly. "Are you sure you're okay?"

Dante whipped his head towards Ross. He fell to the ground and started sobbing. He pulled at the skin on his arms and chest and legs, ripping off chunks of scorched flesh. Ross could see blood and raw skin as the burnt pieces were pulled away. Ross put his hand up to his mouth, holding back the need to purge. Dante was still crying as Ross slowly walked into the chamber with him. Steam was coming off of Dante's body Ross kneeled down next to him and put his hand up to place it on Dante's shoulder but moved it away quickly.

"Ow!" Ross grabbed his hand. "You're really hot. Like, a pot of boiling water."

"I-I-I-" Dante stammered.

"What?" Ross asked. "What's wrong?"

"I-I—c-c-can't feel a-a-anything."

"You're not in pain, are you?"

"No. I'm j-just a little c-cold."

"Oh, hold on. Let me get you a blanket."

Ross stepped away to get into the first aid kit. He grabbed the flame retardant blanket and handed it to Dante. Dante, shivering, covered up in the blanket and stood back up. Everyone who had left was starting to come back into the building and were watching Dante closely.

"It's alright, everyone," Ross announced. "He's safe to be around."

"Of course I'm safe to be around," Dante laughed. "It's not like we totally just fucked me up and turned me into some human dragon thing."

Ross started laughing also but stopped when Dante started violently coughing. Blood spurted out and Dante wiped his mouth, although Ross couldn't tell if any blood had actually got on his face.

"Oh God," Dante moaned. "This is not comfortable at all."

"You're like a walking billboard for an anti-smoking ad," Ross smiled.

"Oh I'd kill for a cigarette right now. Do you have one on you, Ross?"

"Yeah, you can have the rest of the pack if you want."

"Thanks man, I appreciate it," Dante said, taking the cigarettes from Ross and holding one in front of his mouth. "Now what do I do?"

"What do you mean?" Ross asked.

Dante opened his mouth and let out a small spout of fire to light the cigarette.

"Well, I can't go out like this. I can't go home to my wife looking the way I do. What should I do?"

"I think you should still go home and tell her what happened."

"I need to get to a hospital, man. Look at me! I'm a roasted marshmallow."

"We can't take you to a hospital. It'll cause too much suspicion and I don't want people snooping around here."

"So I'm supposed to go home and act like nothing happened?"

"I don't know, Dante," Ross said as Dante finished the cigarette he had been smoking and lit another one. "By the way, I hadn't done the test yet."

"WHAT?"

"I was given a placebo," Ross lied. "Um, I think I'm still going to try it on me."

"Even after seeing this?" Dante pointed at his face. "Good luck picking up chicks, man."

"I won't have anything in my pockets like you did. I'll wear just my under shirt and my underwear."

"That'll be a sight to see, I'm sure. I think I'm going to go home and just tell her we had an accident with the project we've been working on. I'll swing by later and check up on you. Don't do anything stupid until I come back."

"Got it," Ross gave him a thumbs up. "Here, you might want this."

Ross gave Dante a mask to put over his face. Dante wrapped up in a hoodie that was already burning off of him. He ran outside to his car and drove off. Ross went back to work in the lab and prepared himself for his test. He re-checked everything to make sure nothing went wrong for him. He also asked about the progress on the drug they had all been working on.

"With this new substance you've found, I'm sure we can make a drug that is worthy of your requests, Mr. Kendall," said one of the scientists. "We should be close to finishing it."

"Excellent," Ross smiled widely. "Get the chamber prepared for a second human test run."

"Sir?"

"Are you suddenly hard of hearing?" Ross asked. "Get it ready for a second fucking test."

"Even after what happened to Dante?"

"Yes! Now set the damn thing up!"

Ross removed his pants and shirt and any jewelry that he had on, and stepped into the chamber. He kicked out all of the dead skin that Dante had picked off himself. Ross watched as everyone around him started working on the test. One person put the vial of liquid in with the substance Ross' team had come up with and was about to put it into the vapor tubes that went into the chamber when Ross stopped him. This time, Ross decided to hook up an IV so that the liquid would go straight into his system. He also had a heart rate and blood pressure monitor hooked up so that everyone could take down notes and record how his body reacted. With one final sigh, Ross nodded and the door was shut and locked. The green button was pressed and the sequence started.

"Heart rate and blood pressure is stable," said one of the women. "And we're at 10% completion."

"Doing okay, Mr. Kendall?" asked one of the men.

Ross nodded, but was starting to sweat.

"Stable at 25% completion," said the woman.

A red light started flashing and there was a fast beeping sound.

"What's happening?" the man asked the woman.

"He's becoming unstable," she said. "The liquid is entering his body too fast!"

The computer read that the process was at 50% percent and raising quickly. Ross started going into violent convulsions and his vitals were rising. Muscles began appearing in Ross' arms and legs that weren't there before. Ross' body got about twice as big as it had been. Veins were bulging out everywhere and his mouth was foaming.

"He's going to die!" cried one of the scientists, running for the chamber. The woman stopped him before he could reach the door.

"No!" she cried. "He will surely die if you stop the sequence prematurely. Besides, look at his vitals."

The red light stopped flashing and the beeping slowed down. They were now at 80%.

"He's becoming stable again."

Ross stopped moving and his eyes slowly opened again. His thinned hair was matted down with sweat and he was blinking wildly, looking around.

"Alright in there, sir?" asked the woman. Ross gave her the okay sign.

"We're at 90%," she announced. Everyone watched as the monitor read 100% and started clapping. Several men stepped toward Ross to unlock the door. However, Ross stood up and pulled all of the wires and the IV off of him.

"Sir, you shouldn't be moving quite yet," called the woman. "You're not fully stable."

Ross moved toward the door and hit it once, shattering the glass. He walked through the doorway of the chamber and started putting his clothes back on, although his shirt wouldn't button up all the way and his pants were up past his ankles.

"How is that possible?" the woman asked. "Dante couldn't even get through that glass."

Ross walked over to her and smiled. The woman seemed frightened.

"Thank you," Ross said. "You did an excellent job. I feel . . . amazing."

"Sir," the woman's voice was shaky. "Your vitals were unstable. You almost died."

"Well, I feel fine now," Ross smiled. "In fact, this is the best I have ever felt."

Ross turned towards some of the other scientists, his smile now turning into a frown.

"You, however," he pointed at one of the men. "You tried to stop the process. You almost killed me."

"Mr. Kendall, I'm sorry," the man tried explaining. "I was afraid you would die if we kept going."

"You know I could've died if you would have stopped, you moron!" Ross snarled.

"I'm sorry! I really didn't mean any harm, I swear!"

"Shut up!" Ross swung his giant hand into the man's face, sending him back several feet into some equipment. Everyone backed away from Ross.

"What are you all standing around for? We need to finish that god damn drug! NOW GET BACK TO WORK!"

Everyone hastily moved back to their work places and began going about their business. Ross went inside his office at the back of the lab. He stood in front of the full-length mirror and examined himself. His hair had thinned out quite a bit more than it already was and his clothes that had just fit him were now at least three sizes too small. It was too obvious that he had changed so much so Ross would have to come up with a way to stay hidden for a while until he could figure out a good explanation as to why he looked the way he did.

"Avery and Charles would notice a difference," Ross said to himself. "I'll just have to stay here for a while."

Ross sat down at his desk and called the house.

"Hello? Kendall residence," Charles answered.

"Hey, it's me."

"Ross?"

"Yeah. Listen, I'm going to be gone for work for a while. You mind watching the house and everything until I get back?"

"Of course," Charles answered. "The children and I will be just fine taking care of the place ourselves. Have a safe trip, sir."

"Yeah, thanks," Ross said before hanging up. There was a knock on the door.

"Come in!" Ross called. The woman from the lab came in.

"Ah, Theresa," Ross smiled. "Please, sit down."

She sat in the chair in front of the desk and crossed her legs. Ross always had a thing for her but never had the nerve to ask her out. When she got married, Ross realized that his chance had passed and tried forgetting his feelings for her.

"So, what good news do you have for me?" Ross asked.

"Well, as it turns out, the key ingredient for the drug has been right in front of us this whole time. It seems as though your blood was all that was missing. We just needed to mutate you and add some of your new, genetically enhanced blood to the mix and that did it. Anyone who uses it, will surely get what they need from it. As will you."

"And how do you know that?"

"I volunteered to try it first."

"And?"

"I'll do anything you want. Just ask and whatever you want will be yours."

Ross smiled widely before leaning back in his desk chair.

"How's that husband of yours, Theresa?"

"What husband?" she smiled.

"Good girl. Now, do you mind ordering me some bigger clothes? I've slightly outgrown these."

"Of course, sir."

"Call me Ross, please."

"Alright, *Ross*. Anything else you need?"

"There is *one* more thing that I would like but I'm afraid it'll have to wait until after I make a few phone calls. Now, go order my clothes, please."

Theresa walked out of the office and Ross watched as her butt bounced a little as she walked away. He chuckled to himself and gave his knee a slight slap. He picked up the phone and called Dante, who didn't answer so Ross left a message. Then, Ross called Sloan, who answered right away and said he'd come up to see the final product. Everything was going perfectly for Ross. For once in his life, everything was going to go exactly how he wanted it.

Dante finally showed up to the lab after Sloan had been there an hour. Ross and Sloan had been drinking in celebration, so by the time Dante arrived, the two of them were pretty buzzed. Sloan was shocked to see the difference in Ross' appearance, but was mortified when Dante walked in.

"Holy shit!" Sloan backed away, knocking over the chair he had been sitting in and dropped his glass. "Jesus Christ! Is that Dante?"

"Yeah," Ross smiled. "We had a bit of an accident with his um, experiment."

Ross looked at Dante, who wasn't saying anything or looking at either of them.

"What is it?" Ross asked.

"I killed them," Dante whispered. "I killed all of them."

"Your-your family?" Ross asked, setting his glass down and walking toward Dante.

"No!" Dante shouted. "Don't come any closer to me! I'm a monster! They all screamed when I walked through the door. My children ran away from me in fear. My wife was terrified of me. I tried explaining that it was me but they were too scared to listen. I held my wife by her neck and tried to quiet her screaming but when she stopped screaming and I let go of her, she dropped to the floor. The kids started running and I had to catch them and tell them not to say anything about me to anyone. I set the house on fire in a state of rage. I tried getting my children out safe but they wouldn't come near me. They burned inside the house and I just stood and watched it happen. I *let* it happen."

Dante sniffled as though he was crying, however, Ross couldn't tell if he was or not.

"Fuck, Dante," Sloan gasped. "What are we going to do? The police will come looking for him."

"We'll take care of him," Ross said. "Don't worry. As far as I'm concerned, Dante has been here this whole time."

"What if someone sees him?" Sloan asked. "He looks like he was caught in that fire! He's all . . . crispy."

"Sloan!" Ross gave him a look of disgust. "We're going to help him and no one is going to catch us."

They heard a knock on the door and Theresa came in with a tray. On the tray were two pills.

"Gentlemen, may I present to you the drug of an era. The drug that will change the world. CP-Ultra."

"Why are there only two?" Dante asked. "Aren't you going to have one, Ross?"

"I already had one. I'm still not sure how many you can have in a certain time frame."

"Fuck that," Sloan waved his hand at the tray. "If the guy who made it won't take it then I'm not."

"Fine," Ross sighed. "Theresa."

Ross stared at her and she nodded, soon after bringing back a smaller tray with one pill on it. Ross nodded and Theresa left, closing the door behind her. The three of them took their pills in their hands and each had a new glass of scotch.

"Here's to a new beginning," Sloan raised his glass.

"To a new life," Dante raised his.

Ross looked at the two of them before saying, "To new choices and new decisions to be made."

They swallowed their pills and chased them down with the scotch. Then, they all sat around and waited for the effects to kick in. Ross knew that the only thing that would happen to him was that he'd trip a little, like he would on acid. Since the drug was based on Ross' blood and DNA, the other side effects would do no harm to him. Slowly, Ross watched as the room started melting. The tiles were dripping off of the ceiling, revealing the night sky. Ross could feel the cold air and reached up to grab the sky. When his hand opened, some of the sky fell through his fingers like sand. He stood up carefully and watched Dante and Sloan disappear from the room. Ross called out for Theresa a couple of times before she finally came into the room. Ross removed his clothes and watched as Theresa removed hers. Ross had waited so long for this and now he was getting everything he wanted. And then, as Theresa walked towards him, Ross began to black out.

When Ross woke up, he and Theresa were on the floor of his office, covered only by Ross' coat. He looked around and saw Dante laying on the couch and Sloan was slumped down in the desk chair with his feet propped up on the desk. Theresa woke up when Ross moved and smiled. Without saying anything, she stood up and got dressed before leaving. When the door shut behind her, Sloan and Dante woke up. They were both stretching and rubbing their heads.

"Yeah, I feel like shit too," Ross smiled. "I don't really remember much from last night. So what should we get for breakfast?"

"Whatever you want," Dante said.

Sloan nodded.

"That's right," Ross laughed. "Whatever I want."

# CHAPTER 9

# The Only Exception

*"Maybe I know somewhere deep in my soul that love never lasts.*
*And we've got to find other ways to make it alone or keep a straight*
*face.*
*And I've always lived like this keeping a comfortable, distance.*
*And up until now I swore to myself that I'm content with*
*loneliness,*
*'cause none of it was ever worth the risk.*
*But you are the only exception."*

-"The Only Exception" by Paramore

I was spending more and more time with Kitashi and now that summer was just around the corner, I'd be with him even more. I was definitely okay with that. Kitashi was my very best friend and he knew more about me than anyone else who knew me. I hadn't heard much from Kelly or Ryan lately but I didn't really mind. The dance was coming up in a week and I still hadn't bought a dress. I didn't know if Kitashi had bought anything to wear because I didn't really want to talk to him about the dance. I didn't want him thinking I was overly excited about it. I was, however, in desperate need of some help and since Ryan was out of the question, I decided to ask Maddison and Hayley. Hayley couldn't come because she had to work so it was just me and Maddison at the mall.

"What kind of dress are you looking for?" Maddison asked as we walked through the aisles of one store.

"I don't know," I shrugged.

"Well do you know what he's wearing?"

"Nope."

"Uh, okay. Then how are you guys supposed to know what colors to buy to match each other?"

"We have to match?"

"Oh my God. I'll text him and ask what he's wearing and in the mean time we'll just grab a bunch of different colors and styles to see what looks good on you."

We started out with several long gowns before I decided that I'd much rather have a short dress. I figured since the weather was getting warmer a long dress would be way too hot. Besides, I'd wait to wear a long dress for prom. Maddison finally heard back from Kitashi but wouldn't tell me what he said. Instead, she put back everything she had in her hands and started over. I still didn't know what color to get but we finally narrowed it down to two dresses. One was a dark red dress that had one strap that went from my left armpit and connected to my right shoulder blade. The other was dark blue and was lace and satin with a strapless, scalloped neckline. Around the empire waist was a satin bow that tied in the back and the dress was tiered with ruffles on the skirt part. I ended up choosing the blue one.

"If this whole crime-fighting thing doesn't work out for you, you should be a model," Maddison said. "You looked stunning in every single one of those dresses. But I'm glad you picked the blue one because your legs look great in it. Now for shoes."

We picked a pair of shoes that matched the dress perfectly, however, I wasn't sure if I was going to be able to walk in them. Let alone dance in them. The shoes were covered in lace with a little bow on top. They were exact same blue as the dress and were peep-toed pumps. I didn't even know there *were* shoes called pumps. As I put them on and walked around the store a bit, I wobbled a little and the balls of my feet started tingling. They did, however, make the muscles in my calves stick out which looked really good in the mirror, so I bought them.

The last thing we did was make my hair and makeup appointment at the mall's salon. I was starting to get really excited and nervous at the same time. Before taking me home, Maddison and I decided to get our nails done and tan. I had never done either but it was kind of fun acting all girly and getting to spend time with another girl. I had a lot of fun with Maddison and definitely wanted to hang out with her again. I never thought getting a pedicure would be so relaxing, but I literally would have fallen asleep if Maddison hadn't been there to talk to. She told me about how she had to move a year ago from her home in New Jersey because her father's company promoted him to Chicago. She was really upset to leave her friends and her boyfriend that she had. But she was glad that they had moved because she made new, better friends and found out that her boyfriend from back home had been cheating on her with her best friend.

"Just because I wouldn't have sex with him, he slept with my friend," she shook her head. "If it was that easy for him to cheat on me I'm glad I didn't lose it to him. Jerk."

She and I both laughed.

"Yeah I haven't done it yet with anyone," I admitted. "I've never had a boyfriend. Or kissed a guy."

"You've never kissed a guy before?" Maddison repeated. "As pretty as you are, I'm surprised you don't have guys dropping like flies at your feet! You're gorgeous and nice and fun to be around. I'm really surprised."

"Yeah, I'm kind of invisible at my school. No one notices me."

"Is that because no one wants to notice you or because you don't want anyone noticing you?"

"Both? I don't know" I laughed. "I'll admit, I'm kind of anti-social at school. But I think it's because no one seems like they're anyone I'd normally hang out with."

"Do I seem like someone you'd normally hang out with?" Maddison asked putting her hands on her hips. "A short black cheerleader from New Jersey who loves country music?"

"What?" I asked surprised.

"That's right, I love country music. Hip hop is okay because I like dancing to it but I hate rap music that's just a bunch of loud thumping and disrespectful lyrics. See, you shouldn't assume what people are like by their appearance. I didn't think you were some punk ass who didn't give a shit about anything or anyone. I thought you'd be a really kind and shy person and I was right. And you've opened up a lot and now look at you. Getting a pedicure after buying a dress for your school's dance. You probably hated school dances before, didn't you?"

I nodded and smiled. I was beginning to really like Maddison.

When I finally got home, Kitashi was working out down stairs and listening to what sounded like classical music on his headphones.

"What are you listening to?" I asked him. He removed the headphones.

"Bach," He smiled.

"Maddison said we should be listening to music that they're going to play at the dance so we'd be prepared. She put together a mixed CD for us to play."

"Alright, let's see what's on it."

I put the disc into the player and pressed the "start" button. Of course, a hip hop song came on that neither of us recognized. Kitashi started slightly bobbing his head and snapping his fingers to the beat. I started giggling.

"What?" he smiled. "No finger snapping?"

"No!" I chuckled. "Not unless you want to get kicked out of the dance. Let's see the what the next one is."

The next song was a slow one. Kitashi and I looked at each other for a moment.

"Who doesn't already know how to slow dance," I rolled my eyes. Kitashi held his hand out to me.

"You want to dance?" I asked. He nodded. I took his hand and he gently placed his other hand on my waist. I put my other hand on his shoulder and Kitashi started leading me around the room. I was afraid I was going to step on his feet but fortunately he was graceful enough for the both of us. Dancing with Kitashi felt like floating on a river, just letting the water move you where it wants you to go. Finally the song ended and we stopped dancing. Another loud hip hop song came on and I didn't want things to stay so serious so I started dancing goofily. I was doing a move called "the running man" and Kitashi just stood there and laughed at me. I turned the music off and we went upstairs to his room.

The bedroom looked a lot different than it had when Kitashi first moved in. We had repainted it an apple red and put in all black and white furniture. Kitashi added some Japanese art and sculptures. He even ordered a small pond to put on the balcony in between our rooms and put two Koi fish in it. His room became like a sanctuary to me, a place in the house to go when I felt like escaping. Kitashi didn't have a television in his room like I did, but he did sometimes play music. It was always either classical or some sort of Asian music. His room seemed so peaceful and relaxing, just like him.

"Okay," Kitashi said as we both sat down on the floor on our pillows. "Today I am going to tell you about the virtues of Bushido."

"What's that?" I asked as Kitashi poured me some tea he had made for us.

"They are kind of like a set of rules that samurai followed a long time ago, and still do today. Bushido means 'the way of the warrior.' Avery, I will teach you the ways of the warrior. Are you ready to learn?"

I nodded.

"The first of the seven virtues is courage. You understand what courage is, right?"

"Yeah, it's like being brave, right?" I asked. He shook his head.

"Being brave means to have great courage in the face danger or pain. Courage is the ability to face danger or pain without being overcome by fear or being deflected from the chosen course of action. To have courage, you must lose all fear."

"I can't be afraid of anything?" I asked.

"There is not enough room in one's spirit to have both fear and courage. You must choose only one."

"So wait, you're telling me that you have nothing to be afraid of," I said. "I mean, I get you have unbreakable skin and all but there's really nothing that you're scared of?"

"No."

"Bullshit."

"What?"

"I don't believe you. Everyone has fears."

"No. I learn to cancel out all fears and worries."

"So you weren't scared when we fought Belladonna and all those guys at the park?"

"No. Just because you are afraid of something, doesn't mean I have to be also."

"I wasn't scared! Nervous, maybe. But not scared."

"You are not afraid of anything?" he asked me.

"Sure, I'm scared of stuff, just like any other normal person."

"What are you afraid of?"

"I don't know, just different things. What's the next virtue?"

"Just tell me, Avery."

"Okay, let's see. I'm afraid of snakes, the dark, really big spiders, never seeing my parents again, being alone. I don't know. I'm afraid of a lot."

"Alright. Moving onto the next virtue, which is rectitude. Rectitude is having moral integrity in character or actions. For example, don't lie, steal, or cheat. You get the idea."

"Right."

"Okay, after rectitude is respect, which is consideration and admiration towards somebody or something. In order to earn respect-"

"You must also show respect," I finished.

"Correct," Kitashi smiled. "Honesty, and it's more than just telling the truth. It's also about being fair and being sincere. Next, honor, is about personal integrity. Self-respect and personal dignity that may or may not lead to glory and recognition. But that is not what honor is about anyways. Benevolence is the next one. That is your disposition to do good. Benevolence is showing kindness and goodwill. 'Do unto others as you'd wish them to do to you' sort of thing. And now, for the last one. The virtue that I think you understand more than any other. Loyalty."

"Loyalty?" I asked. "But isn't that just me not back-stabbing you? Like, you can trust me and stuff?"

"You'd be surprised on how difficult it is for some people to remain loyal. People are so easily swept away in greed and selfishness that they forget where their true loyalties lie."

"That's not going to happen to me," I said. "I'd rather die than betray you and the team."

"I'm very happy to hear that," Kitashi said. "Do you think the rest of the team feels the same?"

"Duh. You don't think anyone is going to deceive us, do you?"

"I feel like something like that may be happening soon. I just can't tell from who."

"I think you need to lighten up a little bit. No one is going to betray the group."

"I hope you're right, Avery. Okay, now for my final little lesson. Keeping the soul healthy."

"How do you do that?" I asked.

"For the soul to be healthy, it needs balance. On one side, you need honesty and courage. On the other side you need kindness and love. Love makes the heart happy. When the heart is happy, the soul is healthy. Just like honesty makes the brain happy. If you lie or deceive, the brain becomes unhappy, making you feel sad or guilty. So you must keep the brain and heart happy to make the soul healthy because the soul is the bind between the two."

"Wow," I yawned and smiled. "That was deep. I'll have to keep that in mind."

"Are you getting tired?" he asked.

"Yeah. Good news is I only have two weeks of school left. Then we're staying up late every night and eating junk food and watching movies and vegging out until we go comatose!"

"I'm just looking forward to the dance this weekend," Kitashi smiled.

I blushed.

"Uh, yeah, me too," I stammered. "I'm off to bed then since I have school in the morning. Good night."

"Good night, utsukushii."

"What's that?" I asked.

Kitashi smiled and began meditating. I went to my room and stayed there for the night. Right before I put my pajamas on, I decided to take my dress out of the bag and try it on again. I couldn't wait to see what it looked like on with my hair and makeup done. And I definitely couldn't wait to see what Kitashi would look like all dressed up. I laid in bed for several minutes wondering what Kitashi was doing or what he was thinking. I fell asleep thinking about how much fun the two of us were going to have on Friday.

I knew I was dreaming. You want to know how I knew I was dreaming? Because I was talking with my parents. You see, the whole dream started out with me and Kitashi time traveling to find out what happened the night my parents were murdered. We showed up to the very place where my parents' banquet was held in Chicago. We warned them about the shooter coming and when he did, the guards were able to tackle and arrest him. My parents ended up living and I didn't have to live with my uncle. Kitashi and I ended up together and my parents were very happy about that.

When I woke up from my dream the following morning, I didn't even bother getting dressed first. I ran into Kitashi's room still in my pajamas and told him about my dream.

"Don't you see what this means?" I asked, jumping on the bed. "I have time traveling powers! We're going to go back in time and save my parents! And we can also find out what happened to your parents!"

"No Avery," he muttered,

"We can go back and save Matthew and-"

I stopped and looked at him.

"*No?*" I asked. "What do you mean *no*?"

"I mean no, Avery," he sat up in bed. "We're not time traveling for any of those reasons. We'll do it only if we absolutely have to."

"Are you kidding me!" I was getting pissed off. "Whatever. I'm going to do it. You can just stay here then."

"What about school, Avery?"

"It's time travel. I'll be back in time to do it."

Kitashi crossed his arms as I started walking out of his room.

"You're really going to do it, aren't you?" he asked.

I nodded.

"Well then I might as well go with you and make sure you don't do anything foolish. Or get yourself into trouble."

"Yay!" I clapped. "I'm going to go get dressed. I want to make sure I look good when I meet my parents."

I ran into my room and put on my best pair of jeans and a green blouse that I had only worn once since getting it from Charlie for my last birthday. I stuck a notebook into my purse and put on some comfortable shoes. Then I straightened my hair and put some eyeliner and blush on. After I was done getting ready, I grabbed my purse and met Kitashi downstairs. He had on a pair of black jeans, a red tank top, and a blazer jacket. He looked very GQ.

"You ready?" I asked.

"Yeah, you?"

I nodded. I took Kitashi's hands, closed my eyes, and thought really hard about the night my parents were killed. I remember it was cold that night. There were a lot of people there. There was a chandelier hanging from the ceiling and-

People were talking around us. I opened my eyes. Kitashi's eyes were already open and we both looked around. A couple of people were looking at us and I realized that Kitashi and I had underdressed ourselves. I saw a security guard walking towards us. I walked over to a woman who was putting on dark lipstick.

"Hey," I smiled to her. "I'll give you fifty dollars if I can have your lipstick."

She handed me her lipstick. I looked over at the guard who was stopped by an old couple to ask him something. He was still watching me.

"Keep it, and your money," she smiled back. "I have plenty of both. Enjoy it."

"Thank you very much," I said before walking back over to Kitashi.

"Go to the bathroom. Use some water to slick your hair back, and give me your jacket."

"What?"

"Just do it and meet me right back here."

"Do not speak to anyone else, Avery," Kitashi said sternly as he handed me the blazer. "Please."

"Okay, okay."

I went into the bathroom and put on Kitashi's jacket. It smelled like him, which I liked a lot. I pushed up the sleeves and dug around my purse for my sunglasses and put them on. I pulled my hair back into a bun and put the lipstick on. A crappy disguise that I knew probably wouldn't work but I needed to at least catch a glimpse of my parents. I walked out of the bathroom and looked for Kitashi, not realizing he was standing next to me. I laughed at the sight of him with his hair pulled back. And he was also wearing a scarf that was wrapped around his neck.

"Where'd you get that?" I pointed at it.

"Some elderly man said that I wasn't dressed warmly and that I needed a coat and scarf. I told him that I had a coat already but he insisted on giving me the scarf. What do you think?"

"I think it looks great," I said, noticing another guard checking us out. "Okay, just act really serious and let me do all the talking."

We walked straight up to the guard.

"Excuse me, sir," I said, doing my best at attempting a British accent. "Do you know when the ceremony will be starting?"

"And you are?" he asked me, looking at a paper. Probably the guest list. We were screwed.

"Who am I?" I asked. "We are with a very elite fashion magazine. We're here taking notes on what everyone is wearing tonight."

"What magazine?"

"Hm?" I asked.

"What's the name of your magazine?" he repeated.

"That one," I randomly pointed at the paper.

"High Voltage?" he asked.

"Yes, High Voltage. That's the one. Well, well, must be going. Neither of us will get our jobs done if we're just standing around chatting. Cheerio!"

I walked off before the guard could ask anymore questions.

"That was a lot harder than I was expecting," I looked back at Kitashi. "I don't know how the killer-Oof!"

I wasn't paying attention to where I was going and ran into a woman.

"I'm so sorry," I said, looking at her. My jaw dropped.

"It's alright, ma'am," said my mother looking right at me. "I wasn't paying attention to what I was doing either."

"Okay," I smiled and turned to walk away.

"My name is Ann Marie Kendall," she stuck her hand out to me.

"I know," I said before slowly putting my hand up. Kitashi cleared his throat. "I mean, of course I know who you are. You and your husband are the reason for this occasion."

"Oh I'm flattered but if I had it my way, I'd be at home with my family and I'd just have them send my award in the mail."

"Don't we all," I whispered.

"The reason we are here," Kitashi butted in. "Is to ask about what everyone is wearing tonight. You see, we're from High Voltage fashion magazine."

"Oh I love that magazine!" my mother smiled. "And you want to interview me?"

I nodded.

"Honey," said a man coming up behind my mom. It was my dad. "We better get in there. It'll be starting soon."

"Okay," my mom said. She turned to me. "I'm sorry, can we finish this afterwards? I'd love to be included in the article."

I just stared at them.

"That would be fine," Kitashi answered for me.

"Alright," she grinned. "Oh, I didn't catch your name."

"I'm-"

"Excuse me, Mr. and Mrs. Kendall?"

We all turned to face Adam. My eyes widened and Kitashi pulled me away once he saw the gun in the man's hand. Kitashi and I ran away as I heard gun shots and everything around me turned blurry. A little girl in a dress ran passed us and I wanted to go back and save her from seeing her dying parents.

"Get us out of here," Kitashi stopped us. "Now, Avery."

"Why didn't you let me save them?" I started crying.

"We don't have time for this," he looked at me. "Please, get us out of here."

"Start thinking about something then!" I said to him. "Think of a memory!"

Everyone was running around us. Kitashi grabbed my hands and closed his eyes. I was still looking around when the scene surrounding us melted away. Right before it disappeared, I noticed a familiar-looking man standing by a wall. I closed my eyes because they started burning, like I had been sticking my head out of the car window for a long time. When the chaotic sound of people running and screaming stopped, I could hear birds chirping and water running. I felt wind and sunshine on my face. I opened my eyes slowly and saw that Kitashi had tears running down his face. We were outside by a river and a bunch of cherry blossom trees.

"Where are we?" I asked looking around.

"Japan," Kitashi answered.

"Wow," I gasped. "What year is it? What memory did you pick?"

"The first time I met Susanne. When she found me. Come on, follow me."

I followed Kitashi through the trees, while the wind blew the scent of the blossoms past me. There was a huge mountain nearby that towered over the land. Everything around us seemed so peaceful and ancient.

"This place is beautiful," I said. "Why don't you ever visit?"

"I don't remember anything about this place. There's probably a good reason why I don't remember. Something bad probably happened to me."

"Kitashi, if you want to go-"

"No, it's fine. Look over there."

I looked to where he was pointing and saw a small body laying on the ground ahead. I took a step towards the body but Kitashi put his hand up in front of me. I looked at him and he told me to be quiet.

"Come over here," he whispered. We hid behind a boulder and watched as a truck drove up on the dirt road that divided us from the body. I watched as the little boy stood up slowly and wobbled towards the road. His face was dirty and scratched, and his clothes were badly ripped. He was holding his head and squinting, not seeing the truck coming from ahead. The truck driver must not have been paying attention because it was about to hit the little boy.

"Look out!" I yelled. Kitashi put his hand over my mouth.

The little boy looked up in my direction and then saw the truck. The truck screeched to a halt and the boy fell backwards to move out of the road. Kitashi glared at me.

"I'm sorry!" I whispered. "I didn't want him to get hit!"

"*I* wasn't going to get hit," he said softly. "It's *my* past so I know what happened. Don't try and change anything."

"Okay, I'm sorry! Sorry I tried saving your life. From now on I'll just let you die if you're in trouble. So do you want to get out of here?"

"Wait," he whispered.

We watched the truck stop and a man get out of the driver's side.

"Are you okay?" he asked the little boy.

"Is he alright?" asked a woman getting out of the truck. "He's not hurt is he?"

"I don't think so, but he's not saying anything."

"Is that Susanne?" I asked.

Kitashi nodded.

"And her husband?"

"No, he had just passed away. She came here with her friend and friend's husband. They were taking Susanne on a trip to get out of the house and see the world. And she found me. She rescued me. Just like I rescued her."

I watched as the little boy version of Kitashi got into the truck with Susanne and they drove off.

"What happened when you left here?" I asked.

"They took me to the hospital to see if I was injured and to find out where I came from. They couldn't figure it out and I couldn't remember anything. It took a while to get everything situated but Susanne was able to adopt me legally. They had to make sure no one would come claim me or that I wouldn't all of a sudden remember what had happened."

"Where did your name come from then?" I asked.

"When Susanne found me, I had a necklace in my hand that read, 'Kitashi Kendo.' But I don't know if that was really my name. No one actually uses that as their name."

"Why not?" I asked. "What does it mean?"

"Kitashi means firm or hard, I guess like my skin. And Kendo literally translates to the way of the sword. Susanne was convinced that I had been some sort of child warrior or something but I wouldn't be able to tell you if that was true or not."

"Well why don't we try it?" I asked.

"What do you mean?"

"Try finding out where you came from. It's still a memory of yours, isn't it? You were there when it happened."

"But I don't remember it," he said. "I don't think it would work."

"We can try. Give me your hands."

Kitashi placed his hands in mine once more.

"Concentrate real hard," I said. "On where you grew up. Where you were born. Concentrate on your family."

Kitashi shut his eyes tight and I closed mine. I could feel the scene around us changing. We were at a farm and a man was standing in the field wiping sweat from his forehead. We hid behind some trees as a little boy ran over to him and spoke in Japanese.

"What's he saying?" I looked at Kitashi.

"He's saying that he's done with his chores and is asking if he can go play now. The father said yes but to be home in time for dinner. The boy's name is Atsuo. My name is Atsuo. He's going inside to get his ball."

We watched the little boy run into the house and a woman holding a baby was coming outside and speaking to the father. The little boy stopped in the doorway and listened.

"The mother, who's name is Matsuyo says that the baby, Shiomi, is sick but they do not have the money to get her medicine," Kitashi explained. "The father, who is Keizo, says that he will sell some of his belongings to get the medicine and work extra hard for the family. They are about to lose their farm."

The little boy went back inside and came out holding a jar. He held it up to give to his parents.

"He says they can have the money for his baby sister," Kitashi told me. "That he doesn't need the money."

His parents started crying and his mother spoke.

"But his mothers is telling him not to give up his money and that they will be fine. His parents let him keep a part of the money he earns from working to buy himself nice things like clothes and shoes. But the little boy says that he cannot live with that on his conscious."

The little boy dropped the jar and ran off, down the dirt road. We ran after him and caught up to see the little boy being picked on by some older children. There were a bunch of children standing around by a large waterfall.

"They told him to jump off the highest part of the waterfall if he wants them to be his friends."

"Oh my God!" I gasped. "That's so high up though!"

"I know. I don't think he'll survive the fall."

I looked at Kitashi and he smiled. We watched the boy climb all the way to the very top and all the other children were watching him also. He jumped off but right before the boy landed in the water, I grabbed Kitashi's hands and concentrated really hard on getting us back to the morning I was about to go to school. We were in Kitashi's room, sitting on his bed.

"Why did you do that?" Kitashi asked.

"I didn't want to see you get hurt. At least we know your real name."

"I'll still go by Kitashi though. That's who I am."

"Did you want to see what happened to your parents?"

"No. I've seen enough. I'm sorry I didn't let you save your parents. You understand why though, right?"

"Yeah," I sighed. "It just really sucked not being able to help them. You want to know something weird though? I could have sworn I saw my uncle there. But that's impossible because I remember he had to fly from Boston."

"I'm sure it wasn't him then, Avery."

"Yeah."

"Oh no! What time is it?" he asked. I looked at the clock.

Only three minutes had passed in present time, which meant no one would notice we were gone. It also meant that I was running late for school.

"I'm just not going to go today," I said.

"No, you only have two weeks left," Kitashi responded. "You really need to go."

"Fine," I sighed. "But I'm still going to get in a little trouble for being late."

The rest of the week went by slowly and was spent mostly doing my homework and hanging out with Kitashi. I also spent a lot of time thinking about the dance but didn't let anyone know I was thinking so much about it. I hadn't seen my uncle in a while but didn't miss having to avoid him when I ran into him at the house. Finally, it was Friday. As soon as school let out, I was going with Maddison to the mall to get my hair and makeup done. Then I had to rush home and get changed into my dress. Kitashi was supposed to meet me at the house around seven. Friday dragged by and I had trouble focusing in all my classes. I wasn't even that interested in the new power I had come up with. Apparently, I had learned the power of clairvoyance. I was able to see things that were happening to people who weren't around me. Like in my science class, I started thinking about Ryan and Kelly and suddenly I could see Ryan sitting in her geography class. Then I started seeing Kelly in his computer class.

When the last bell of the day rang out, everyone practically ran out of the building so they could hurry home to get ready for the dance. Maddison picked me up right on time and we headed for the mall. We got my hair done first because Maddison said that my makeup should be fresh. My hair was pulled and tugged until the stylist got it the way she wanted it to go. Maddison had picked a cute up-do with a few curly pieces hanging down. With the makeup, Maddison didn't want it to be too drastic since I hardly ever wore makeup. She did, however, pick a dark grayish-blue eye shadow that I was nervous to have put on. We hurried home so I could get dressed and Charlie surprised me with a boutonniere to give to Kitashi. It was a simple, single white rose. I said thank you and went up to my room to get my dress on. As I slipped my new blue pumps on, the door bell rang, which I thought was cute since Kitashi lived here now. But I knew he was doing it to be respectful.

"I'm going to go down and see what he looks like!" Maddison giggled and walked out with her camera. "I'll call you when you can come down. Don't forget to bring down his flower!"

"I'm going to look stupid giving him that!" I said. "He probably didn't get me a corsage."

"I'll see you downstairs."

Maddison walked out and I stood in front of my mirror, admiring myself for a moment. I looked even more like my mother with my hair and makeup done. I was twirling in my dress and smiling when I heard Maddison call my name. I grabbed Kitashi's flower and my small clutch purse Maddison picked out and went downstairs. As I made my way down the staircase, I could already see several camera flashes. I was met by Charlie, who was crying, Maddison, Susanne, Barney, Andrew, and Hayley. Everyone gasped and awed at me. And then, Kitashi stood up from the couch and met me at the bottom of the stairs. He was holding a corsage for me, which was a set of two calla lilies, one was white and one was dark blue. They were tied together by a lacey blue ribbon. It was gorgeous.

I had always found Kitashi appealing to look at. He had silky, straight black hair and flawless light skin. I loved the way his eyes became even smaller when he smiled big or laughed. He had perfectly straight teeth except for one tooth that was slightly crooked. I called it his "rebel tooth." But honestly, I had never seen Kitashi look as good as he did when I walked down those stairs. He had on a black suit, including a black shirt, and a dark blue tie that matched my dress so perfectly, it looked like he had cut a piece straight from my dress and made his tie from it. His hair had been trimmed and he was clean shaven. His crazy, messy hair had been combed through and laid straight by his ears. I wanted to just stand there and stare at him forever until Charlie cleared his throat. I looked at him, surprised to see that he was crying.

"Sorry," Charlie wiped his eyes. "You just look so beautiful, Avery. You're not a little girl anymore."

"Thank you," I smiled.

"You look stunning," Kitashi said. "Truly my utsukushii."

"Are you going to tell me what that means?" I asked.

"It means beautiful woman."

For the first time in my life, I felt like jumping into a boy's arms and kissing him. However, I held myself together and just smiled.

"You look amazing," I said to him. He blushed.

"Okay," Susanne said. "Stand by the fireplace so we can take some pictures."

Kitashi and I walked over to the fireplace and everyone who had cameras pulled them out and flashed in our eyes as we posed. He put my corsage on and I put his boutonniere on. We took a few pictures with him standing behind me and his hands placed on my waist. I literally felt like I was going to melt into him. It felt really nice. After pictures, we left for the dance. We didn't really talk much except for the random compliments we kept giving each other. As we walked into the school's gymnasium, a few glances came our way. I noticed that Amanda looked at me and I saw Ryan had come with Sly although she barely looked at me. I didn't see Kelly anywhere so I had figured he decided not to ask anyone else. Kitashi and I danced the whole night so I ended up having to take my shoes off and leaving them at the coat check. During one of the slow dances, Kitashi decided to dance a little differently. Instead of dancing with one hand on my waist and the other hand holding mine, both hands were placed on my waist and he held me closer. I put both of my arms around his neck and looked into his eyes. My heart was going a million miles a minute. He leaned in towards my face and I closed my eyes. I was about to get my first kiss.

"Help!" I heard Andrew's voice call out. I opened my eyes and stopped dancing.

"What is it, Avery?" Kitashi asked. "What's wrong?"

I grabbed my head and closed my eyes so I could get a better idea of what was happening. I could see Andrew, Hayley, Maddison, Barney, and Susanne fighting Belladonna and another creature that looked like a really bad burn victim and was shooting out fire. There were also a bunch of thugs fighting the team. They were in danger and we had to help them. I was so disappointed. My perfect night was suddenly coming to a halt. I looked up at Kitashi with apologetic eyes.

"We have to go," I said. "Now."

# CHAPTER 10

# Familiar Realm

*"Invaded by a swarm of confliction,*
*Been penciled in but never begun.*
*Potential risks are beyond control.*
*If nothing's left to say, you've entered a familiar realm."*

-"Familiar Realm" by CKY

"So where are we going?" Kitashi asked as we walked out to the car. The school's parking lot was filled with students' cars and I was envious that everyone else was able to stay and have a good time. I didn't want to leave, but I knew I had to help the team.

"I don't know yet," I said. "I just keep having flashes of what's going on. There's a lot more this time. And there's something there that can shoot fire."

"Well good thing I always have this with me," Kitashi said as he opened the trunk of the car. He pulled out my costume and my face lit up.

"Awesome!" I laughed. "I was not looking forward to kicking some ass in a dress. I didn't want it to get torn. I get to wear this out for the first time! Uh, you mind keeping a lookout while I put it on?"

I made Kitashi turn around so I could get dressed real quick. We hopped into the car and another vision came into view. I could see Susanne fighting the fire-breathing thing she was absorbing the fire it was spewing at her and hitting it with huge burst of wind and Hayley was trying her best fighting off Belladonna.

"Well I know they're not around water this time," I rubbed my head.

"How do you know?"

"Susanne is fighting the fire thing with air, not water. She'd use water if she had it around, so they're obviously not anywhere around water."

"Well that narrows it down," Kitashi said sarcastically.

"I'm trying!" I snapped.

Kitashi kept his eyes on the road in silence.

"Sorry," I murmured. "It's just this ability is giving me a migraine. And I'm incredibly bummed that we couldn't stay for the whole dance."

"I know, I'm disappointed too."

Another painful flash caught my attention and I could see that Susanne was trying to tie Belladonna with vines up against a wall. I could see a sign on the wall above them that said, "Red's Comic Book Shop."

"How appropriate," I laughed.

"What?" Kitashi asked. "Where are we going?"

"Red's Comic Book Shop, I suppose. I don't know where it's at though."

"Good thing we've got a GPS to help. Type in the store's name for me so we know what direction to go."

"What if we don't make it in time?" I asked. "And why would they go out without us?"

"Unless they were attacked unexpectedly," Kitashi said. "And we'll make it in time."

The GPS loaded the location of the store and said it was fifteen minutes away if we stuck to the speed limit. Kitashi pushed a little harder on the gas. Luckily, there was no traffic and no police out so we arrived way under fifteen minutes. The building was run down and empty but a partial sign above the door still said "Red's" so I knew we were at the right place. We got out of the car but didn't see or hear anything at first. Kitashi opened the trunk of the car once more and pulled out three long swords. Kitashi had explained to me that they were called katanas, and that he had been practicing with them for a while. He put on a belt and a strap that went around his back. He placed two swords on his back and one on the belt.

"Ready?" he asked.

"Not as ready as you obviously," I pointed to the swords.

"At least your outfit is bulletproof," he smiled.

"So is your body!" I laughed.

When we went inside the building we could hear banging and yelling coming from the floor above us. We ran up the stairs and saw everyone fighting. One of the gangsters ran at us with a crowbar and I ducked out of the way just in time, however, he hit Kitashi in the shoulder. Kitashi let out a grunt and punched the guy in the face, knocking him out.

"Did that hurt you?" I asked, concerned.

"Nah, I'm fine. Come on, let's help the others."

Everyone seemed to have everything almost completely under control. All that was left was Belladonna and the other thing. Belladonna was struggling, trying to free herself while Hayley was trying to keep her black glove over Belladonna's eyes. I didn't understand how neither of them were dying from the other one.

"Who do we have here?" the burnt thing asked.

"They're with them, Inferno!" Belladonna yelled. "Kill all of them and get me loose!"

Every time Belladonna finally freed herself from a vine, Susanne would make another couple wrap around Belladonna's body. Inferno leaped at us and opened his mouth. Kitashi and I both ducked out of the way as a blaze of fire rolled in between us. Susanne pushed the fire back at Inferno, making him yowl in pain.

"That got in my eyes, you stupid bitch!" he yelled.

He rolled up a ball of fire with his hands and flung it at Susanne, who blew it back at him again. This time, however, Inferno was expecting her to do that so he pushed it right back at her. I dove at her and pushed her down to avoid the fire ball. Kitashi ran up behind Inferno and punched him in the back of the head. Kitashi moved his hand away quickly as if Inferno was too hot to touch. Pieces of Inferno's skin flaked off, revealing his skull.

"OW!" he screamed and grabbed at his head and fell to his knees. Kitashi kicked him in the face as hard as he could and Inferno fell back on the ground.

"Thanks Avery," Susanne said before standing up. I saw her bone sticking out of her wrist.

"Oh crap!" I gasped. "I'm sorry! I broke your wrist."

"It's alright, Hayley will fix it."

"We've got to get you out of here."

"Oh sure, make the old lady miss out on the fun," she smiled. "I'm fine, really."

"You guys should get out of here," Kitashi said. "I can get them. It's okay."

"By yourself?" I asked.

"Yeah, I got this. Go!"

"Come on," Andrew pulled on my arm. "These guys are too strong for us. Kitashi can handle it."

"No!" I pulled my arm away. "I'm not leaving him by himself! What if he gets hurt?"

"It's Kitashi, he'll be fine."

"Come on, Avery," Maddison said. "We could get hurt. Kitashi can't."

"I'll stay with him," Barney said. "The rest of you go."

It began thundering outside. I looked at Kitashi. He nodded. I had this really bad feeling in my stomach, like someone was squeezing and pulling at my insides. I knew there wasn't anything I could do to help them and that I might just get in the way but I was worried about Kitashi. I was really pissed off that I had such a lame power this time. If I had got something like water powers or super speed or strength, I could've stayed to help. Instead, I was forced to leave with the rest and hope for the best. Maddison took me home since I knew Kitashi would need his car to get back home.

"So how did you guys end up there in the first place?" I asked Maddison in the car.

"Well, Susanne and Hayley kind of got into it because Hayley wanted the group to go out and fight after she overheard on the news about some guy getting all of the criminals in the city to follow him and be his little minions. Some new guy who calls himself Acheron, and he calls his followers Acheronians. Hayley had Barney track down one of their hiding spots, which was at the closed comic book store."

"What?" I asked.

"Yeah, pretty ironic, right? So anyways-"

"You said Acheron? I've heard of him."

"Really? Where?"

"I think the guy who killed my parents worked for him. He mentioned that name when I visited him a while back."

"Huh, that's weird. Yeah, Hayley's been all over every story they've covered on this guy. I think she's trying to impress Susanne and get position of team leader."

"Well isn't Susanne the team leader?" I asked.

"Nah, she's more of just a teacher. Once we learn everything we're supposed to, Susanne will probably move onto another group of kids to teach and leave us on our own."

"Oh," I muttered. "Well that would suck for me if Hayley became the leader."

"Yeah, she's not a huge fan of yours. Which I don't get because I think you're awesome. But Hayley makes it very clear that she doesn't like you much. Anyways, Hayley got word on where all of these 'Acheronian' guys are hanging out and tells the team that we should take them out before they take us out. We didn't know that Belladonna was associated with Acheron so we got a nice little surprise when we stumbled across their little nest. What we figure is Belladonna and that Inferno guy are in charge of the thugs and Acheron is the big cheese. Like a pyramid. Lots of little guys on the bottom, a few people over them, and then one guy who's over all of them."

"I bet it's Dominic Sloan," I said.

"Who?" Maddison asked.

"I'll bet Acheron is Dominic Sloan. That would make sense. My uncle used to be his lawyer. Sloan probably found out who my parents were through my uncle and tried to make a deal with them that has something to do with the lab. When my parents refused, Sloan took them out and is probably using my poor uncle. Sloan is head guy over everyone."

"Okay, we'll let Susanne know first thing in the morning. Good job, Avery."

"Thanks," I said as we pulled up to my house.

"Sorry about ruining your dance."

"It's okay. Glad we could come help you guys. Although I wasn't very much help."

"Hey, if it hadn't been for you seeing what was happening, Kitashi wouldn't have come help us so you did real well tonight by leading him to us. Let me know when he gets home so I know he's alright."

"Alright, I'll see you later."

"Bye, Avery."

I watched Maddison drive away and I looked down in panic. I still had my costume on and my dress was in Kitashi's car. I was going to have to sneak in and get to my room without anyone seeing me. I quietly unlocked the front door and walked silently through the house. No one was around so I quickly tip-toed up to my room and shut the door. I changed into comfortable clothes and hid my costume in my closet. A sudden flash occurred and I could see Kitashi. Susanne and he were still fighting Belladonna and Inferno. I could tell that Susanne was concentrating super hard and using all of the rain around her and blasting it at Inferno. Meanwhile, Kitashi and Belladonna were doing hand-to-hand combat. Once in a while, Kitashi would swing at her with one of his swords but she kept dodging the swings. Inferno seemed to finally be out of steam (no pun intended) because he couldn't shoot out anymore fire. Then, the vision disappeared.

I could hear thunder and could see lightning outside my window. I was kind of scared so I decided to go to Kitashi's room and wait for him there. At first, I tried meditating to calm down but I kept getting distracted with the weather and the thought of Kitashi or Susanne getting hurt so I got in his bed and snuggled up underneath the covers. The lights were starting to hurt my eyes so I turned them off, I tried to stay awake for as long as I could but eventually I drifted off to sleep and had another vision. Belladonna and Kitashi were still fighting except now Belladonna had one of his swords and they were both fighting with them. It was storming outside and rain was coming into the building, soaking both of them. Kitashi swung at Belladonna but she ducked just in time and the sword got lodged into one of the book shelves. As soon as this happened, Belladonna dug her blade into Kitashi's side.

I jolted awake in a state of panic. I sent Susanne and Kitashi a text message on their cell phones and called both of them twice. Finally, Susanne answered.

"Hello?" she said, sounding tired.

"Are you still with Kitashi?" I asked.

"No, I left when Inferno ran off. Kitashi was still fighting Belladonna when I left. But that was like two hours ago."

"I just had another vision while I was sort of drifting to sleep and Kitashi got hurt."

"What? That's impossible. He can't get hurt."

"Well he did in my vision and so far none of my other visions have been wrong. I'm going to keep trying to get a hold of him."

"Let me know when you hear from him."

"Okay, bye."

I tried calling Kitashi's phone a couple more times and he still wasn't answering. I was really starting to get worried. I looked out Kitashi's window and could see a shadow on the balcony. Worried that Inferno or Belladonna had found me somehow, I grabbed a sword that was hanging on one of the walls. I used the sword to pull back the edge of the curtain to look outside. I dropped the sword and swung open the door to the balcony and ran to Kitashi.

He was sitting up against the railing and holding onto his side. He was soaked and I could see blood on the ground next to him. I used every bit of strength to pull him up and walk him into his room. After turning back on the light, I laid him on the bed and tried to get him to talk to see if he was conscious.

"Kitashi?" I cried. "Are you okay? Can you talk?"

He nodded.

"Please say something."

"I'm sorry," he whispered.

"Sorry? Don't be sorry. This isn't your fault."

"There's something I need to tell you that no one else knows."

"There's something I need to tell you too," I said as warm tears fell down my cool face. "But I need to go get Charlie so he can help you."

"No, I'll be fine. He can't know about anything."

"It's fine. He won't ask any questions and even if he does, I'll just say that you were practicing with your swords and had an accident."

"Alright, but I need to tell you something first."

"No, it can wait. We need to fix you up."

I really wanted to tell Kitashi how I felt about him but I needed to get him taken care of first. I left the room and found Charlie in his bedroom, asleep. I told him that Kitashi was badly hurt and that he needed help. Charlie got up right away and followed me carrying his first aid kit. When we got back to Kitashi's room, I could see a big dark red spot on his bed and Kitashi looked a lot paler. Charlie lifted Kitashi's shirt and I could see a gash in his side, right under his ribs, and blood was still coming out. I started freaking out and was really scared. I knew that Charlie knew how to sew up stitches because he had done it before for both me and my uncle. I think I remember Charlie telling me at some point that he had been a doctor in the military and knew a lot about healing injuries. I was desperately hoping that was true.

"Avery," Charlie looked at me. "You might want to leave us for a bit. It's not going to do anyone any good with you standing there worried. It'll just make me more nervous. Can you please go to your room?"

I nodded and walked out. Once I was in my room, I collapsed on my bed and cried myself to sleep. When I woke up again, it was daytime and the sun was pouring into my room. I went to Kitashi's room and Charlie was slumped over, sleeping in a chair next to the bed. I saw that Kitashi was asleep also so I tried leaving quietly but Charlie had been woken up.

"How is he?" I whispered.

"He's fine now," Charlie whispered back, smiling. "He was hurting a lot so I gave him some pills to ease the pain. He'll have to rest in bed for a while and he won't be able to do any heavy activity for a bit. Don't want his stitches ripping, do we? I went in to tell you when I was done but you had fallen asleep."

"Yeah sorry about that," I said. "I was really tired."

"I bet. You had a big night last night, didn't you?"

"What do you mean?" I asked.

"The dance. Didn't you go?"

"Oh yeah. Sorry, I forgot all about it since this happened. Yeah, we had a great time."

"Did you get your first kiss?" he asked.

"No. I don't think that's going to happen."

"Why not?"

"Because I don't think he-"

Charlie gave me a look like what I was saying was ridiculous. Kitashi started moving a bit and groaning. Charlie stood up and walked out of the room, closing the door behind him. I scooted the chair closer to the bed and sat down as Kitashi's eyes opened. He looked over at me and smiled.

"It's nice waking up and seeing your face," he said, still sounding groggy. "Sorry if I scared you last night."

"How are you feeling?" I asked.

"Better now that I'm sewn up and you're here with me."

I smiled. Here was my opportunity to talk to him. I opened my mouth to speak but Kitashi started to talk.

"Oh, sorry," he said. "You go first."

"No, you go ahead," I said. "It can wait."

"You sure?"

"Yes, definitely. Go ahead."

"Okay. I have to tell you something important. And I'm not telling you this to make you feel any different about me. I don't want this to come between us as friends and if you get upset by it, I'll understand. But I need to tell someone and it might as well be you."

I sat there, getting more nervous about what I wanted to tell him. Was he going to beat me to it? Did he feel the same about me?

"I'm not completely indestructible. I have my weaknesses just like anyone else."

"What?" I asked.

"My skin is impenetrable until I start having strong emotions. Usually I can control my anger and sadness, but there's one emotion that I've found to have trouble with recently. It seems that the more vulnerable my heart is, the more vulnerable my skin is. So here I am, making myself more vulnerable by telling you that I am in love with you. And I know we're both really young and the idea of love is still far-fetched but I think we both are very grown up for our ages. I think we're mature enough to handle it. The only problem is that I wouldn't be able to fight with the team anymore because I wouldn't have anything to offer them. I'd just be some kid punching and swinging swords, and you need more than just that to beat villains like Belladonna and Inferno. But I would easily give up all my hard work to be able to say that you're mine and that I love you."

I could feel my eyes weld up with tears. I was so upset. I was the reason that Kitashi had got hurt because he had feelings for me. I wanted so badly to tell him that I felt the same. Instead, I lied to save him.

"Wow," I said. "I was not expecting that at all. Um, although I'm really flattered, I only like you as a friend. I'm sorry."

I stood up and ran downstairs to the bathroom in the basement and cried. It was incredibly unfair. If Kitashi let himself love me, it would take away his powers. But if I broke his heart and lied, it would make him invincible again. It would be selfish of me to let him give up what he loved doing, and what he was really good at. For the rest of the day, I tried to keep my distance from Kitashi because it would make me too upset. The team met up the next day for practice without Kitashi, although everyone came up to check on him while I stayed in the hallway. After our practice was over, Andrew came up to me.

"How was the dance?" he asked. "Well the part that you actually got to be at."

"It was fine," I said, putting away the equipment after everyone left.

"So are you two boyfriend and girlfriend now?"

I looked at him.

"Sorry," he blushed.

"What does it matter to you anyways?" I asked. "You have a girlfriend yourself so quit butting into other people's love lives, or lack there of."

"Hayley and I aren't together anymore."

"For real? When did that happen?"

"You didn't notice us completely ignoring each other during practice? She only wanted to get back with me because she knew I was interested in you and it made her jealous. Once she thought you were more interested in Kitashi, she dumped me for someone else. He's a freshman in college. So there you have it. Now you can give me a hard time about it."

"Do you still want to go on that date?" I asked.

"What? Really?"

"Yeah. Really."

"So you and Kitashi-"

"Are just friends," I finished. "This is my last week of school and then I go on summer vacation so I'll be free whenever."

"Same here," he smiled. "Alright well then I guess I'll give you a call sometime this week."

"Okay, sounds good," I gave a half-hearted smiled. "Talk to you later then."

After Andrew left, I sat for a while trying to meditate. But it didn't work. For once, I was glad to be going to school on Monday. When I got to school that morning, several people complimented me on how I looked at the dance and I couple of girls said that my date was hot. I explained that we were just friends. Also, our teacher passed out yearbooks. Monday, Tuesday, and Wednesday were our finals but Thursday and Friday were kind of just blow off days. The last two days were for signing yearbooks and for our teachers to grade our finals and give them back to us. Thanks to all of the studying Kitashi had made me do, I felt like I had done decently in all of my finals. I breezed through them and was happy when they were all finally over with. I noticed that Ryan hadn't been at school at all during the week so on Thursday I went up to Kelly to talk to him about it.

"Hey," I said. "I know you probably don't want to, but will you sign my yearbook?"

Kelly wrote just his name and nothing else.

"Wait, you don't want me to sign yours?"

"I'm only letting my friends sign mine," he said.

"Oh okay. I understand."

Kelly opened his yearbook and had marked a page, "Do not write on."

"I saved this page for you," he smiled. "Give me back yours so I can write more."

I smiled and handed my yearbook back to him before taking his.

"So how did you think you did on your finals?" Kelly asked as he wrote.

"Eh, no telling for sure but I felt pretty good about them."

"Even the science final?" he asked. "I thought it was pretty hard."

"It wasn't as bad as I thought it'd be. But I studied so that probably helped."

"You?" he asked. "Studied?"

"Yeah, so what?" I laughed.

"Well aren't you becoming little Miss Academic. By the way, you looked really pretty at the dance."

"How do you know? Were you there?"

"Yeah, I found a last minute date to bring."

"Who?" I asked.

"Chelsea Rave."

"Really? She's like, super pretty! Good job!"

"Oh, it's not like that. We're just friends. She did look good with me though," he giggled. "Hey, can I talk to you about something?"

"Anything," I said, finishing up my note I had written.

"It's about Ryan."

"Is she okay? I noticed she hasn't been at school this week."

"She's been out with Sly. She hasn't even come home except to get a fresh change of clothes and even that has been her sneaking in and out without seeing our parents. I'm worried about her. We've always been super close but she won't talk to me. I have no way of knowing if she's in trouble or doing anything bad because she won't talk to me. It hurts really bad. I've felt so alone lately. I'm glad to be talking to you again though."

"Maybe I should try talking to her," I said. "I'll text her here in a bit."

"No! That would piss Sly off. He keeps her phone and screens all of her calls and messages."

"Well how can anyone get a hold of her?" I asked.

"You can't. Unless Sly allows you to talk to her."

"What! That's bullshit! He can't do that to her! We need to do something."

"What do you think we should do, Avery? Go rescue her like a damsel in distress?"

That was exactly what I was thinking.

I had my last session of the year with Julia in her office. She had a huge surprise for me when I arrived.

"So, are you sad that this is our last session together?" she asked me.

"Nah, I'll see you next year so it's not a big deal."

"No, I mean it's our very last session together. Permanently. I'm graduating you from the program."

"Really?" I jumped up and hugged her. "Thank you so much! Oh thank God! No offense or anything but that's a huge relief! Glad to know Therapy Thursdays are done and over with."

"Yes, well I talked to your uncle and told him how much you've improved this semester and asked if it was okay to pass you and he didn't seem to mind. Congratulations, Avery."

"Thank you," I said, my smile fading.

"Avery, what's wrong? I thought you'd be happy."

"I am, trust me. I'm extremely happy. After years of seeing therapists I'm definitely ready to be done. It's just that I'm really going to miss you. You were the first therapist, the first person really, who truly believed in me and thought I would be able to get better. Thanks, Jules."

Julia got up from her chair and hugged me. I had her sign my yearbook and she gave me my certificate for completing my therapy. For the rest of the day, our teachers let us watch movies and sign yearbooks. It was pretty laid back. The next day at school was just as laid back. We were made to clean our lockers, which was weird because I had stopped even using my locker after winter break. I started just carrying my backpack with all of my books to every class. It was heavy at first but I got used to it and plus it gave me more time to get to my classes. While I was cleaning, I found old notes from my classes, notes from Ryan she had left in my locker, candy bar wrappers, and broken pencils. I took a plastic bag that my teacher had given me and dumped everything into the bag. I shoved the bag of crap into my backpack and closed my locker. The last thing I had to do was turn in all of my text books. After that, it was time for school to let out. It was weird not being a freshman anymore.

I walked home with Kelly, like we used to, and went upstairs to my room. I flung my backpack on the bed and checked my phone for messages. I had one from Andrew. He wanted to go out the following evening on a date. I said that I would and that I was excited, but I wasn't. I had barely spoken to Kitashi during the week and I hated it. We went from being extremely close and hanging out all the time to not hardly talking to each other. And all because I had found out about his weakness. I heard a knock on my door and I said to come in. Kitashi, leaning over a little and holding onto his side, walked in. I was on my computer and tried finding stuff to keep me from looking toward him.

"Hi," he said.

"Hey," I muttered, my eyes glued to the computer screen.

"So today was your last day of school, huh?"

"Yeah."

"Did you get anyone else to sign your yearbook?"

"Yeah."

"Are you happy you're done?"

"Yeah."

Kitashi sat down on my bed and lifted a paper out of my backpack.

"You're finished with your therapy? That's great! Good job, I'm proud of you."

"Thanks."

"Avery."

"What?"

"Look at me, please."

I took my eyes off of the computer and looked at him. He looked hurt, as in emotionally hurt.

"I'm sorry I told you how I felt. I never wanted it to come between us. I miss how we used to be. This week you've been acting so differently and I know it's all my fault. I know there's no way to go back and change what I said, but I'm hoping we can both just forget about it and put it in the past."

"Okay."

"Okay? That's all you want to say?"

*No*, I thought. *That isn't all I want to say. I want to tell you how much you mean to me and how hard this week has been on me. I want to grab your face and kiss you. I want to wrap my arms around you and never let go because the closer I am to you, the safer I feel.*

"No," I said. "I'm sorry for the way I've been acting, I've just had a lot going on."

"I know. But can we go back to how things were?"

"Yes, we can," I smiled.

"So what's new with you?" Kitashi asked.

"I'm going on a date with Andrew tomorrow night."

"Oh," Kitashi muttered. "Well, have fun."

"Thanks," I said awkwardly. "Sorry. I hope it doesn't make tonight's team meeting uncomfortable for you."

"It's fine. I'll be fine."

"Alright, well I'll see you down there in a little bit," I smiled.

"Okay," he said before walking out of my room. I let out a big sigh.

I got ready for the group meeting by straightening my hair, putting on some makeup, and wearing a pair of tight shorts. I knew Andrew would like all of these things, and Kitashi would hate it. I needed to figure out something to get Kitashi back to the invincible guy he used to be. I just hated upsetting him like this.

I dug around in my backpack for a pen and a notebook that I would need for notes. I took out the bag of trash from my locker and put it aside. Something caught my attention though. It was an unopened note from Ryan from a couple of weeks ago. It said that her and Sly hadn't been getting along too well and that she tried leaving him but he got really rough with her and threatened her. She couldn't leave him because she was too afraid to. After I was finished reading the note, I dug through the plastic sack finding three other notes from her. They talked about how Sly was developing a drug problem and made her stay with him all the time. He also started beating her and took her phone away. The notes were all asking me for help; pleading for my help. I needed to do something, but I would need some assistance.

Everyone arrived down in our "secret hideout" and started talking about new plans. Now that everyone was done with school for the year, it was time for us to really start hitting the Acheronians hard. Maddison brought up what I had told her about Acheron possibly being Dominic Sloan since Belladonna was his daughter. We were going to have to find Sloan, the mastermind behind all of it. Barney volunteered to find out everything he could about Sloan while the rest of us searched for more rat nests hiding Sloan's minions. Barney also presented us with more information on "Acheron's" plot.

"He's apparently created this super meth called CP-Ultra. It's huge on the streets and it's already made a ton of money. It's mostly being sold here in the Chicago and local area but more and more people are starting to hear about it. And Belladonna mentioned something peculiar the other night when we were fighting her and Inferno. She said that whoever took the drug would have to listen to Acheron and do whatever he says. I've been researching the possible ideas on what CP-Ultra is all about. C.P. could possible be abbreviated for coercive persuasion."

"What does that mean?" Hayley asked.

"Mind control," Barney answered. "He's setting up an army to take down anyone who tries to stop him. No telling how many pawns he has protecting him. But the good thing about mind control is the faster we get to the source, the quicker we can cut off the source. We need to stop him before he figures out a way to get the masses to take his drug."

"I'm sure there's a lot of people who aren't going to want to try an illegal mind-controlling drug," Hayley rolled her eyes. "Or is he planning on poisoning the water hole?"

"Water is too filtered now to be tainted," Barney explained.

"I was being sarcastic," Hayley scoffed.

"What else is new?" said Andrew.

"Prescription drugs," I said. "Maybe he could taint over-the-counter drugs or something like that. Like if you have a headache, you take a pill, and then your brain goes to mush and is controlled by some drug lord. Just an idea."

"That's a possibility, Avery," Barney said. "I don't know, but whatever it is, we need to stop him before this gets out of hand. No telling if someone outside this state has had any of the drug yet. He might already have sellers in other states. We need to get to Dominic Sloan and put a stop to his mind control drugs."

"I have a little announcement to make," I said loudly.

"You mean besides the fact that we're going on a date tomorrow night?" Andrew laughed. Hayley's eyes widened at him and then glared at me.

"Um, anyways," I said. "My friend Ryan is in danger. Her boyfriend has her kind of locked away. She's been missing school and he took her phone away so she can't get a hold of anyone. I know where this guy lives but he could have some friends there with him. I'd rather not go alone but I understand if no one wants to help."

"No thanks," Hayley said right away. "Why don't you and Andrew do that for your little date?"

"Why do you have to be rude to me all the time?" I asked. "Seriously, it gets kind of obnoxious. Like your voice."

"It's not my fault you can only get high school boys. Which is sad because college boys are so much better."

"So now Andrew's not good enough for you again? Why, because like an idiot he went back to you?"

I looked at him.

"No offense," I smiled.

"None taken," he smiled back.

"And because he got back with you and you got what you wanted, you dumped him for someone else? Well, I hope you don't think just because someone else is interested in him you can try and win him back, because it's not happening."

"You are such a bitch!" she yelled at me.

"Hayley!" Susanne scolded.

"No! It's not fair that she comes into our group, our family, and because she has a new ability every day and she has this huge house for us to use, she acts like she can do whatever she wants! It's not fair."

"Because your ex-boyfriend would rather go out with me than you?" I asked. "You're such a brat."

Hayley stormed off and left. Andrew was still smiling at me.

"If you want, we could go help Ryan and then go on our date. Since I know where Sly lives too."

"You don't have to," I sighed. "I'll go by myself."

I grabbed my costume that was hanging up, walked out on everyone, hopped in my car, and drove off. I was pissed. I hated Hayley, I hated Andrew, and right now I was definitely hating Ryan's boyfriend, Sly. I was about to walk into a house full of hood rats to save my friend who didn't want to have anything to do with me. I parked my car down the street a bit from Sly's house. I could hear music blaring as soon as I got out of the car. I made my way toward the house and I felt a hand on my shoulder. Startled, I whipped around to face Andrew.

"So since we're doing this now, what do you want to do tomorrow for our date?"

"What the hell are you doing here?" I asked. "I told you I wanted to come alone."

"And I can read girls better than that. By saying that you actually meant that you really wanted me to come with you."

"That's actually not what I meant at all but whatever, you're already here. So how are we going to go about this?"

"I figured we could just casually walk in there like we were invited. We've been invited here before."

"Doesn't mean we're still invited. Did you bring your costume?" I asked.

"Duh, I always have it with me," he laughed. "I wear it under my clothes most of the time."

"Really?"

"Um, yeah. Don't you?"

"No. I'm going to change in my car real quick. Keep a lookout in case someone walks by."

"Alright, let me know if you need help getting your outfit on."

I glared at him and he just smiled. I got back in my car long enough to change and then got out. We snuck up to the house and peeked through the window. We could see a group of guys sitting around playing a video game and drinking beers. Some of them were also smoking joints and doing lines of coke. The video game they were playing was really violent, men were running around shooting random civilians. I looked at Andrew.

"We can take them," he said.

"I suppose so."

"By the way, what's your new ability?"

"You'll see."

"Oh, okay. Have you already tried it out?"

"Yeah, this one is kind of fun."

We kept watching the group and then I gasped.

"There's Ryan!" I whispered. "She looks awful!"

Ryan had lost a lot of weight since I saw her last. Her hair was really messy and she had a bad black eye. She looked absolutely miserable, and I had to get her out of there.

"Enjoying the show?" we heard a voice say behind us. We both turned around and were face to face with a bigger guy who had a baseball bat.

"Oh shit," Andrew breathed.

"Yeah," the guy laughed. "I'd be saying 'oh shit' if I was you too. You two are coming with me.

As the man's arm reached out for me, I used one of my new powers and turned completely invisible.

"What the fuck!" the man jumped back. Andrew laughed.

I moved out of the way and watched Andrew get grabbed by the man.

"You really didn't want to touch me," Andrew looked at him.

"What did you just say to me, faggot?"

"I said, you're not going to hurt me. First, you're going to drop your baseball bat. Then, you're going to calmly walk me into the house and act like I'm not a threat at all. Can you be a good boy and do that for me?"

"Uh huh," the guy said.

"Good. Let's go. You still here, Avery?"

"I'll be right behind you," I said.

"Alright, let's do this then."

I followed the two of them into the house and Andrew waited to shut the door behind me. The guy that Andrew had touched was looking around with a stupid grin on his face. A couple of the other guys looked at Andrew. He was trying to act cool, like he belonged there, although I could tell he was nervous. I could see Sly with his arm around Ryan while he was talking to some other guy. Ryan tried saying something but Sly smacked her mouth and told her to shut up. I was ready to pounce on this guy but I didn't want to do anything to put Andrew in danger.

"So what are you all playing?" Andrew said grabbing an unopened can of beer and walking over to the group playing the video game.

"Who are you?" one of them asked.

"Folks call me The Negotiator."

"Why are you dressed up like a queer?"

"To conceal my identity, of course. Now I'm here to take a friend of mine home. Her friends and family have been worried about her so if you don't mind, I'm just going to take Ryan home now."

"Who invited this fairy?" Sly laughed. The rest of the group started laughing, and Andrew joined in with the laughter. That's when the laughing stopped. Andrew touched the man sitting next to where he was standing on the shoulder.

"Don't fucking touch me, man!" the man jerked Andrew's hand away.

"You're not taking my girl anywhere," Sly said. "So you're going to have to just leave without her. That is if you make it out of here alive."

A few of the guys were standing up, closing in on Andrew. This was my cue. I had grabbed the baseball bat from outside and brought it in with me. I hit one of the guys going for Andrew and knocked him down to the floor. For some reason, everyone thought Andrew had done something to him so they all were standing now and running at him. Not being able to see what I was grabbing off of my utility belt, I was randomly feeling around for whatever I could get to easily. I ended up grabbing my taser gun and stunning one of the guys unconscious. I dropped the gun and just started randomly hitting guys in the face. The other men were freaked out and confused. They started swinging at the air, making it easy for me to dodge them because they couldn't see me at all. I was having fun beating up on these guys since there was only me and Andrew against like ten bigger dudes. We were doing good until Sly got involved. He grabbed one of the trays of cocaine off the table and threw it at me, covering me in powder. Luckily, none of it got in my eyes or mouth but I was now slightly visible. Sly pulled out a gun from under his shirt. Andrew ducked behind the couch, however, I didn't have enough time to move.

# CHAPTER 11

# Someone Saved My Life Tonight

*"I never realized the passing hours of evening showers.*
*A slip noose hanging in my darkest dreams.*
*I'm strangled by your haunted social scene.*
*Just a pawn out-played by a dominating queen.*
*It's four o'clock in the morning.*
*Damn it listen to me good.*
*I'm sleeping with myself tonight.*
*Saved in time."*

-"Someone Saved My Life Tonight" by Elton John

I was hit in the stomach three times, and it knocked me backwards, making me smack the back of my head on the concrete. I had heard how loud a gun shot was before but it had been outside in a wide, open area. Susanne was teaching us about guns and bullets. I recognized the type of gun Sly was using and knew that it had anywhere from 7 to 20 bullets in it. I was hoping for 7. The back of my head hit the floor and I couldn't breathe. I just laid there, motionless, while I heard four more shots to ring out. Only four more were shot and then I heard the empty clicking sound that came from the gun. I could hear Andrew yelling and running and then the two of them were moving around for a bit. I swore I could hear sirens somewhere in the distance getting louder. I tried talking but couldn't. Then, I felt something pulling on me. I wanted to say that it hurt but again, it hurt too much to talk so I kept my eyes closed and my mouth shut up.

When I heard a car door shut right next to me, I opened my eyes and saw that I was in the back of my black and purple car. Ryan was sitting in the passenger seat and Andrew was driving. I was completely visible again but it was too dark for Ryan to tell it was me. I was going to need a mask at some point, but for now I just wanted the pain to stop. Ryan looked back at me.

"Hey, your friend is starting to move around back there," I heard her say.

"You okay, Dreamcatcher?" Andrew said with a shaky voice.

"I'm fine," I gasped. "Even with a bulletproof vest, that fucking hurt! It knocked the wind out of me but at least I'm not bleeding."

"As long as you're okay though."

"Everything's fine, Negotiator. How's Ryan?"

"A little freaked out but she's good."

"How do you know my name?" Ryan asked. "Who are you two?"

"Just a couple of friends who came to rescue you?"

"Rescue me? Who said I needed rescuing? Did my brother put you up to this?"

"No," I said. "Kelly doesn't know anything about it."

"But you know me and Kelly? Who the hell are you? And what's going to happen to Sly?"

"You don't have to worry about Sly anymore," Andrew explained. "The cops probably already arrested him by now. You won't have to worry about seeing him anymore."

"I wasn't worried about him, he was my boyfriend!"

"Yeah, some boyfriend," I muttered.

"Oh what would you know about it?" she asked.

"I know that he made you miss school and that he's kept your phone away from you. He's hurt you, both emotionally and physically. People have been worried sick about you; people who love you. So how about you stay away from him and any other guy who's like him and get your shit together. If not for your family and friends, then for you. Because I know you're not happy but you deserve to be."

Ryan faced the front of the car the whole time and didn't say anything but I hoped I had gotten through to her. We dropped her off at her house and then Andrew dropped me and my car off at my house. His car was sitting in the driveway.

"If your car is here, how were you able to get to Sly's?" I asked.

"Kitashi dropped me off."

"Oh. Well that was nice of him," I said. "Well, I better get inside and get this stupid thing off."

I still had the three bullets lodged into my chest plate and I knew I was going to see some wicked bruises when I removed the plate. Andrew called Kitashi on his phone to meet us underground so I could get through the house unseen. Andrew, for some unknown reason, let Kitashi know that I had been shot. I couldn't make out what Kitashi was saying but I could hear how hard he was yelling. I glared at Andrew but I knew he was just looking out for me. It still hurt a lot to move around so Andrew walked with me to meet Kitashi inside. Kitashi came running towards us and when he saw me, he ran up and hugged me.

"Ow!" I winced.

"Sorry! Are you okay? I'm sorry."

"It's okay, I'm just bruised, that's all. I wish he would have spread the shots out a little more because they all got me in the same spot. It hurts like hell."

"I'll get you upstairs and put a hot pack on it. I'll take care of her."

"Thanks Kitashi," Andrew smiled. "I know you'll look after our girl."

"Are you hungry?" Kitashi asked, ignoring Andrew. "I could make you some soup or something."

"No, I'm just tired. I just want to go to sleep."

"Okay, I'll get you to bed," Kitashi said, reaching for me.

"Can I say goodnight to her first?" Andrew asked.

"Sure," Kitashi put his hand down and nodded.

"I'm sorry tonight didn't go as well as you wanted it to," Andrew said to me. "But I thought you were very brave to do that for Ryan. She'll learn to appreciate it, I'm sure."

"Yeah, I doubt that. Sorry about getting shot," I laughed. "Looks like we're going to have to cancel that date."

"Well, if you don't mind, I could just come over here tomorrow night and we could watch a movie or something."

"Um, yeah, that's alright with me I guess," I looked at Kitashi. "Do you mind?"

"Not at all. Whatever makes you happy."

"See? He doesn't mind!" Andrew said. "Okay, I'll come over around seven. Does that work for you? I probably won't stay long for our group meeting because I'll have to go home and get ready for our date first."

"Oh, alright. I probably won't do much since we're just going to be sitting around and watching a movie."

"That's fine! You don't have to get all dolled up just for little old me. What movie do you want to watch?"

"I'm not sure yet. We can decide tomorrow when you come over. I'll see you later."

"Okay, Avery. Goodnight. Later, Kitashi."

"Yeah," Kitashi muttered. "Have a swell evening."

Kitashi and I waited until Andrew left and went up to my room. I laid down on the bed and bent over to remove my shoes. Kitashi could see that I was in pain and he bent down on one knee and took my shoes off.

"Better?" Kitashi asked.

"Yeah, much better," I sighed. "Can you help me get my outfit off now?"

"Um, I don't think that would be appropriate, Avery."

"Oh come on, it hurts too bad for me to do it by myself. Besides, you know what a girl body looks like already, don't you? I have underwear and a bra on."

"Okay, but we can't tell anyone about this."

"That's fine," I said. "I just want this off of me. Just unzip it and pull it off."

Kitashi slowly unzipped the back for me. Since it was all one piece, I had to carefully pull my arms out of the sleeves first and then pull the pants part off. Kitashi was really gentle and tried not to look at any part of unclothed body. I thought it was really cute. I had three golf ball-sized bruises on my chest right under my boobs. I knew as much as I was hurting, I was going to hurt a lot more the next day. Kitashi brought me over one of my over-sized shirts and slipped it over my head. A piece of hair had fallen in front of my eyes and Kitashi moved it aside. I looked at him and smiled. We both just stared at each other for a bit and then he leaned in to kiss me and I let him. It felt so incredible and if I hadn't been sitting, my knees would have buckled. He pulled away fast and his cheeks were red.

"I'm so sorry," he apologized. "That was so disrespectful of me. Please forgive me, that was incredibly inappropriate."

"It's okay, Kitashi," I said, getting into bed. "No harm done."

"Just don't tell Andrew. I don't want there to be any conflicts in the group."

"I will *not* tell him, trust me. I don't want to hear him bitch about it, even though he's not my boyfriend or anything. Can you do me a favor though?"

"Sure."

"Stay close by in case our date is a total dud. Maybe you could help me escape if it turns into a disaster."

"Okay," Kitashi chuckled. "I'd be glad to help."

"Thanks," I yawned, pulling the blanket up over me. "And Kitashi?"

"Yeah?" he asked.

"One more thing, if you don't mind."

"Anything."

"Could you stay with me until I fall asleep? I don't know why but getting shot tonight kind of really freaked me out. I know it sounds stupid and you don't have to if you don't want to."

"Of course, I'll stay with you until you fall asleep. And if you need anything during the night, just let me know."

"Alright. Thank you."

Kitashi turned off the lights in my room and climbed in bed next to me. He stayed on top of the blankets and laid his head down on the pillow next to me. We laid in silence, facing each other, and he started playing with my hair.

"Is that okay?" he asked.

"Yeah, my mom used to play with my hair to help me fall asleep."

"Goodnight, Avery."

"Goodnight, Kitashi."

Although I couldn't see Kitashi, I kept my eyes open for a little bit longer, watched his shadow and hearing his breathing. I was so exhausted and relaxed that I fell asleep right away. When I woke up the next morning, Kitashi was still in bed next to me. He had stayed with me the whole night. I was faced away from him but cuddled up against his body. His arm was wrapped around me and I could feel his warm breath on my hair. I didn't want to risk waking him so I laid as still as possible until he woke up. When I felt him stir, I closed my eyes and pretended to still be asleep. Kitashi moved his arm off of me and moved around a bit more before leaning in and kissing my head. He got off the bed and quietly left the room. I waited a few more minutes before sitting up in bed and I could smell food. Then, the door opened and Kitashi brought in a tray of food.

"Thought you might be hungry when you woke up," he said placing the tray in front of me on the bed.

"Thanks," I said, propping myself up. A jolt of pain hit me suddenly and I grabbed my stomach.

"You okay?"

"Not entirely. My stomach hurts really bad."

"Good thing I brought these too," he said holding out two pills. "It won't make the pain go away but it'll help. These are what Charlie gave me for my stitches."

"Wow, you really know how to take care of a girl in need, huh?"

"I know how to take care of you," he smiled. I blushed.

"Did you stay in here the whole night?" I asked.

"Uh, no. I left after you fell asleep."

"Really?" I raised an eyebrow.

"No. I stayed the whole night. Sorry, I accidentally fell asleep."

"It's okay. You kept me warm last night so that was nice."

"That's good. Yeah I got a little cold too."

My phone started vibrating and I checked the message I had. It was Andrew saying that he was excited about our date and that he had a surprise for me. I caught myself widely smiling and then lost it when I saw Kitashi glaring at me.

"Come on," he said. "The team will be getting here soon and Susanne has something exciting planned for us."

"You already know what it is?" I asked.

"Yeah, I talk to her all the time so I find out about things."

"What are the plans?"

"You'll see," he smiled. "Oh by the way, I'm going to need your costume so I can get the bullets out of the plate and sew up your suit."

"Alright. Thank you."

"So are you looking forward to your date?" Kitashi asked as we walked down to the hideout.

"Kitashi, I don't want to talk about it. Not with you."

"So you're not excited?"

"Yes, I am. Very excited. But I'm not going to talk about it with you."

"Fine."

We walked down to the hideout at the same time as Hayley and Barney. Hayley made a bee line straight for me. I tried acting like I didn't see her coming toward me though.

"Is it true?" Hayley asked.

"Okay, before you freak out, yes. I am having a sort of date with Andrew after practice but all we're doing is watching a movie at my-"

"WHAT!" she yelled in my face.

"About the date Andrew and I have? Wait, isn't that what you're talking about?"

"NO! I didn't even know you two had planned a date! I was talking about seeing you both on the morning news today!"

"What?" I asked.

"You didn't see?" Barney asked. "You and Andrew are local celebrities apparently."

Maddison came in while Barney talked and gave me a mean look.

"Wait, is everyone mad at us about it?" I asked. "Just because we went and helped one of my friends?"

"She didn't ask for help though," Hayley said.

"And neither did you," Maddison added. "This could really mess things up for us. You could jeopardize the whole team by being on the news. What if Belladonna saw? Or Dominic Sloan?"

"I didn't ask to be caught on camera," I explained. "I didn't even know someone caught us on camera! How?"

"One of the guys inside the house took footage of it."

"But I was invisible."

"Yeah but you were still there!" Hayley said. "And they got a ton of footage on Andrew. All because you had to rescue your crack head friend."

I grabbed Hayley by her hair (I know, a very lame move that only girls do) and pushed her up against the wall. Barney and Maddison tried breaking us apart but we weren't budging.

"You don't know shit about my friends!" I said in her face. "At least I have friends."

"And you don't know shit about Andrew!" She said, now pulling my hair. It hurt but there was no way I was going to let her know that.

"Why do you care?" I yelled. "He's not your boyfriend anymore! You have your own boyfriend!"

"I still don't want him dating you!"

"Why!" I let go of her hair and shoved her into the wall. "What the fuck is your problem with me? I've never done anything to you!"

"He'd rather be with you than me! He was crazy about me until you came along! And I know he knows how it makes me feel when he looks at you. You don't notice it but I do. I catch him watching you all the time, like he's mesmerized by you or something. It's not fair! What makes you so much better than me?"

"I'm not better than you, don't you get that!" I yelled, shoving her again. "And you're not better than me!"

"That's bullshit, I am so much better than you! You're only a fraction of what I am! At least I have both of my parents still!"

"Whoa, not cool, Hayley," Maddison shook her head.

"Take that back!" I slapped her in the face.

Hayley grabbed me by the throat with her black glove. I could feel myself getting weaker.

"Hayley, stop it!" Kitashi said, walking towards us.

"None of you come any closer or I'll kill her!" Hayley frantically said. "Don't think I won't do it!"

"Hayley!" Maddison cried. "You can't kill her, she's our friend!"

"No, she's *your* friend, not mine. I hate her. Besides, she's making me awfully strong and powerful."

"Hayley . . ." I gasped. "Don't . . . do . . . this . . . please."

I felt like a carved pumpkin left out a week after Halloween, caved in and dried out. If Hayley hadn't been holding me up, I would have fallen to the ground. The room started spinning and my mouth wasn't working right. I think I was becoming paralyzed; all I knew was that I could hear Susanne shouting and then Hayley let go of me and I fell on the floor. Suddenly, all of my strength was restored and I felt fine again. I growled at Hayley and stood up. By this time the whole team was there and half of them were holding Hayley back while the other half was holding me back.

"Don't," Susanne begged. "Be stronger."

"Don't worry," I sighed, rubbing my throat. "I wouldn't dare to stoop so low."

Susanne looked at Hayley and shook her head. She looked sad.

"Hayley, I am so disappointed in you. I thought I taught you better than that. You two don't have to be friends or even like each other. But you are still on the same team and both believe in the same things. You may have your differences but you still need to respect each other and work together when you are together. Or else both of you will leave this team. Do you understand me?"

We both nodded.

"Alright. Now, about Avery and Andrew being on the news. Well, mostly Andrew since Avery was invisible. There's a good chance that Belladonna, Inferno, Acheron, and whoever else who's against us has seen it. There's nothing we can do about that now. The only thing we can do now is be extra careful about who we talk to, where we go, etc. Never go anywhere alone. Never go anywhere without letting the whole team know. And no more personal rescues or adventures anymore. Avery, I know you were just trying to help a friend out but you could have seriously been hurt. Or Andrew could have been hurt. It's bad enough you were shot."

"But I'm fine. We're both fine."

"Not according to the bruises on your stomach," Kitashi said. "Suanne's right. You both were extremely lucky. And if I may add something. I think the two of them should be left out of the activity today."

"What?" Andrew and I both said.

"Not just as a consequence for their actions but I don't think Avery is physically able to help us right now in her condition. She can't even yawn or cough without doubling over in pain."

"Can't Hayley just make them go away?" I asked.

Hayley shook her head, smiling.

"This is such crap!" I yelled. "This isn't fair! I never signed a contract saying I had to only go out when the group gave me permission!"

"Avery, I'm not going to let you risk the lives of my other students," Susanne said sternly.

"I volunteered to go on my own," Andrew explained. "Avery didn't even know I followed her there."

"End of discussion. If I hear one more word about it, you will not join us today."

"Why is everyone so pissed off about it though?" I screamed.

"Enough!" Susanne yelled. The walls around us quivered, which startled me.

"Fine," I said softly, glaring at Kitashi. "Go without us then. I don't care about the stupid activity anyways."

I walked out of the room, Andrew catching up with me, and we went upstairs to the house. I plopped down on the couch and he slowly sat down next to me. I didn't want to even glance over at him but I could feel him staring at me. I looked at him and he smiled.

"What," I muttered.

"I'm sorry we got in trouble, but at least now I get to spend more time with you."

"Yeah, I guess so. I just don't want to be around any of them for a while. I'm too mad."

"I know. Like I said, I'm sorry that happened. If I tell you something, will you promise you won't be angry with me?"

"What?" I shifted my position.

"I sort of did something, at Sly's house."

"What did you do?" I asked.

"I whispered to one of the guys to videotape us and send it to the news."

"YOU DID WHAT!" I screamed. "WHY WOULD YOU DO THAT?"

"I'm sorry!" he said. "I didn't think we'd get in trouble with Susanne for it. I just thought it'd be cool if people knew about us."

"Susanne wants us to stay a secret though. You knew that."

"Yeah, and why do you think she wants that? Like the bad guys don't already know about us? Think about it, what's the harm in getting noticed? People adoring us, us giving them some hope that there are people in the world willing to risk their lives to save others? That seems like a better payoff than staying secret and only doing missions that Susanne allows us to do."

"I never thought about it that way. I suppose you're sort of right."

"See? So please don't be mad at me. I was only trying to help."

"Okay, I just don't want to talk about anymore super hero stuff anymore. And I certainly don't want to talk about anyone from the group, especially Kitashi."

"What about me?" I heard Kitashi say behind us. We turned around. He was standing there and smiling.

"What are you doing here?" I asked. "I thought you were doing some stupid activity with everyone else."

"Oh, I don't really feel very good so I told Susanne I was just going to stay home and rest some. Don't worry, you won't even know I'm here."

*I highly doubt that*, I thought.

"Okay, well hope you feel better," Andrew said.

What an idiot. I knew Kitashi wasn't really sick. He was just staying home so he could be nosey. I put my arms around Andrew and smiled.

"Yeah, hope you feel better," I said. "Andrew and I will be watching movies and cooking dinner together. When Charlie gets home, I'll see if he can bring you up some soup and medicine."

Kitashi frowned and walked away. I removed my arms and sighed.

"You didn't have to move your arms away," Andrew said. "It felt nice. Besides, it's kind of cold in here."

"Yeah, it is cold, in here. The air conditioning must be up really high. Do you want me to turn it down?"

"No," he smiled. "We can just cuddle under a blanket if we get too cold. So what movie do you want to watch first?"

"Um, how about a comedy?" I asked.

"Do you have any romantic comedies? I know it sounds corny, but I love a good love story."

Barf.

"I think I might have a couple," I said, walking over to the movie selection. "We have one that's about a blind chick who meets this guy who falls in love with her but she's afraid to let him love her because she's blind. So she gets this surgery to make her see only to find out that he's blind too. It sounds pretty lame but it was one of my mom's movies and I never got rid of it."

"That sounds perfect," Andrew grinned. "Although I might need a box of Kleenex for that one."

Double barf.

I opened the movie's box and inside was the wrong movie.

"Oh," I said.

"What's wrong?" Andrew asked. "It's not in there?"

"No, but *Ninjas at Midnight* is. I wonder how that got in there. Well let's check out another movie instead."

However, all of the movies that were remotely close to romantic were replaced with some sort of Asian flick. I told Andrew I'd be right back and went upstairs with the stack of movies. I walked into Kitashi's room to find him shirtless and doing push-ups on the floor.

"So much for not feeling good," I said, tossing the movies onto the bed. "You mind explaining that to me?"

"Oh, I guess my English reading isn't that great," Kitashi stood up and laid down on his bed. "Also, Charlie is off for the night so I don't have anyone to get me soup or medicine."

"Well if you're up here exercising you can go get your own soup and medicine."

"Actually I already checked and we're out of soup," Kitashi said.

"Then I don't know what to tell you."

"I guess I can just wait to eat with you guys. What are we having?"

"*We?* Andrew and I are making pasta."

"Oh, that sounds good."

"Yes, well too bad there's only enough for two people," I said. "So I guess you're going to have to make something else. Now can I please have the right movies?"

Kitashi got up and handed me all of the Asian movie boxes that had the romantic movies in them.

"Have fun tonight," he smiled.

"Yeah, you too," I said sarcastically.

I went back downstairs and sat the movies down on the coffee table.

"Do you want to make dinner before we start the movie?" I asked. "That way we can eat while we watch it?"

"Yeah, that sounds good."

We went into the kitchen and started making the pasta. After the pasta started cooking, Andrew decided to make some garlic bread before we went back into the living room. Kitashi was sitting on the loveseat next to the couch and was watching television. I put my hands on my hips and scoffed.

"Oh hey," Kitashi said. "So did you decide what movie we're watching?"

"Kitashi!" I said. "Go back upstairs! You know we're going to be watching sappy love movies."

"Can I watch it too?"

"Kitashi, maybe you should go upstairs," Andrew said. "We're trying to have a date here. We all know how in love with Avery you are but it doesn't mean you have to ruin our date."

"What did you say?" Kitashi asked.

"Look, you never let anyone else have a chance to fight someone. You're not going to do the same thing with Avery. I like her."

"You don't even know her. You don't like her, you like chasing her. You only want things that aren't yours. That's why you and Hayley never work out. Because you are too similar. You are cocky and irresponsible. I heard what you did at Sly's. You are the one who put our lives in danger. Thank goodness Avery was invisible so no one saw her. You never think before you act. You are childish and foolish and Avery isn't even interested in you. She's only pretending to be for me."

My mouth dropped. I didn't know what to say.

"That's not true!" Andrew said. "She's very interested in me! Right, Avery?"

They both looked at me. I didn't budge.

"Avery?" Andrew asked.

When I didn't say anything again, Andrew shook his head and started walking to the door.

"Andrew, where are you going?" I asked.

"You two enjoy dinner," Andrew said before shutting the door. I looked at Kitashi with watery eyes.

"I hope you're happy!" I cried, walking into the kitchen.

"Avery-"

"No!" I interrupted him, taking the bread out of the oven and the pasta off of the stove. "Sure, I lied and tried to make you think

I liked Andrew so you wouldn't have feelings for me anymore. I lied to both of us because truth is, I liked you too. Keyword is *liked*. But now I see you're just as bad as Andrew, just in different ways."

"Avery, I didn't want to hurt you."

"See, that's your problem. You think everyone is just like you, hard as stone. But we're not! We're squishy, soft, sensitive people. And just because you can't feel anything, doesn't mean I can't either."

"I've bled for you, Avery. I let my guard down and let you into my heart."

"I think you should leave," I sniffled.

"What?"

"Please just go and leave me alone for a while, okay?"

I went up to my room and locked the door behind me. I flopped down on the bed and cried as I heard Kitashi go to his room and then leave the house. When I heard a car door slam shut, I got up and looked out the window. Kitashi's car was driving off as the sun was setting. I crawled into bed and went to sleep.

When I woke up the next day, I was completely under the blankets and my teeth were chattering. My room was freezing cold, literally. The windows were frosted over and the glass of water next to the bed was completely frozen. I knew I had somehow done it in my sleep because of the dream I had. I had learned ice powers and it was making me miserable. I tip-toed with bare feet across my floor and tried opening my door. It was stuck because of the ice but I finally got it opened. The hallway seemed much warmer than my room although I was sure the air conditioner was still on. I went into to Kitashi's room to find it empty. Most of his things were still in there but he was gone and most of his clothes were gone. I sat on the bed and cried quietly, my tears freezing into miniature icicles. I wiped them away went back into my room after turning the heater on. I threw on some clothes and checked my phone for messages. There were a few from Susanne saying that I need to meet with them as soon as possible and there were a couple from Maddison saying the same thing. I called Maddison and told her to have the team meet at my house at once.

I played around with my freezing ability until everyone showed up. Well, everyone except Kitashi and Susanne showed up.

"What happened to you?" Maddison said. "No one could get a hold of you and we were starting to get worried."

"Sorry, I went to sleep fairly early," I explained. "I had a rough night."

Andrew caught my eye and we looked at each other for a moment.

"Where's Kitashi?" Barney asked. "No one knows where he is or where he went."

"I don't know either," I said. "Where's Susanne?"

"She didn't answer her phone," Andrew said. "But we need to catch you up on what's been going on. First off, Susanne wants us to start writing in journals or diaries or whatever. She thinks someday we'll want to publish the stories of our adventures. Just our luck, huh? Summer vacation and we still have homework to do. But that's not the best part."

"We know how to find Acheron," Maddison said. "Barney did a lot of detective work but he finally found where he hides out at."

"Where?" I asked.

"A strip club in downtown Chicago," Barney answered. "It's called The Pink Bunny."

"Cute," I rolled my eyes. "So what's the plan?"

"Well Susanne wants us to wait until the timing is right and we know more about him," explained Barney.

"We're always waiting," Andrew hit his fist on the wall. "I'll bet her and Kitashi are already on their way there to fight Acheron themselves."

"I don't think Susanne would do that to us," Maddison said. "Why would she leave us out?"

"To get more glory? More personal satisfaction? Who knows, but I think we should go ahead and move in on Acheron before we lose our shot."

"Shouldn't we at least let Susanne know about it before we go?" Barney asked.

"No," Hayley chimed in. "Andrew's right. Her and Kitashi get all of the action and we always get left out."

"Because we have no experience," I said.

"And how are we going to get experience if she never lets us try?" Hayley asked, looking around at us. "All of those in favor, raise there hands."

Andrew and Hayley put their hands up instantly. Barney slowly put his up also. I looked at Maddison who shook her head.

"I know you think it's a bad idea," I said to her, raising my hand. "But we've got to at least try."

"Fine," she sighed, raising her hand.

We all got suited up and hopped in my car. It took us awhile to get to Chicago and find the club since the weekend traffic was so bad. By the time we pulled into the parking lot of The Pink Bunny it was night time. I was really nervous because we didn't have a plan and no one knew where we were. All we knew was that we were going to wait until Mr. Sloan, or should I say Acheron, came outside and then we'd jump him together. Hopefully if we caught him by surprise and alone, we'd be able to defeat him easily.

"And now we play the waiting game," Andrew said.

"Well if it's the weekend and we're at a strip club, won't he be in there for a while?" Barney asked. "I mean, I don't know much about strip clubs."

"Well, you are the oldest one, Barney," Andrew said. "You're nineteen now, right?"

"Yeah. Why?"

"Maybe you should go in there and scope out the place."

"Are you crazy? I have my costume on. Besides, I can't go in there! There are nude women in there!"

"Oh my God, it's not a big deal," Hayley rolled her eyes. "It's not like they're completely naked. They're probably just topless. Just don't look at any of them."

"That might be difficult for him," Andrew laughed. "I'm glad I'm not old enough to go in there. I might not ever leave."

"You're such a pig," Hayley scoffed.

"I was kidding. Learn to take a joke."

"Focus!" I said. "Barney, just go in there and look for Sloan. If you see him, come back out and let us know."

"And if I can't find him?" he asked.

"Then, uh, come back out and let us know?"

"Alright, well good thing I have clothes on underneath my suit," Barney said as he started undressing.

"Dude, you where clothes under your costumes?" Andrew asked. "Why?"

"Because when I sweat my costume gets itchy and the basketball shorts and t shirt help. Don't judge me, at least I don't wear spandex underwear as my suit."

"Anyways, we'll be up top," Maddison said. "If you run into any trouble, just come running, and we'll be here."

Barney threw his costume at Andrew and walked up to the door of the club. Meanwhile, the rest of us decided to climb up onto the roof of the building next to the club so we could get a better look of the area.

"So, how was your date last night?" Hayley asked me. I didn't answer.

"Was it that bad?" she laughed. "Or that good? You can tell me."

"She doesn't want to talk about it," Andrew said. "And neither do I. By the way, did you and Kitashi fight after I left? Or did you forgive him?"

"Why do you think he left?" I asked. "Not that it's your business."

"Oh. Well if it helps, I think you two make a better couple than we would have."

"Thank you? I think."

Andrew smiled. We watched as Barney suddenly ran out of the club yelling for help.

"Time to go!" Andrew announced as we all ran down the stairs from the roof and ran over to Barney.

"What happened?" Hayley asked. "Is Sloan in there?"

"Yeah, he's in there alright," Barney said, putting his costume back on. "And he's got a couple of friends with him."

"Who?" asked Maddison.

"Belladonna and Inferno," Barney panted. "We need to get out of here."

"It'll be fine, Barney. You just need to calm down," Andrew explained. "We can take them."

"No we can't," Barney said frantically. "Not without Kitashi and Susanne."

I got my phone out and sent the same message to Kitashi and Susanne. It had the address to the club and a small note that read, "S.O.S." The doors to the club opened and Sloan and Dante came out. We ran over to the car and hid behind it, watching.

"I don't know why but I feel so weird," we heard Dante say. "Like someone hit me in the head with a rock."

"I know what you mean," Sloan said. "I feel like shit."

"Are we just going to hide here until they go back inside?" Hayley whispered.

"I think we should leave," Barney added.

"Fine, then I'll fight them by myself," Andrew said standing up.

"Andrew!" Hayley followed after him.

"Shit," I muttered and got up.

"Well, well," Dante smiled as he saw us. "These are the kids Belladonna and I were telling you about."

"These little runts are what have been causing so much trouble for us?" Sloan looked at us and grinned. "Pleased to meet you all. My name, as some of you may know, is Dominic Sloan."

"Also known as Acheron?" I asked. "You're the man responsible for my parents' deaths."

"Kid, do you know how many people I've killed? You're going to have to be more specific. Besides, I'm not Acheron."

"No time for talkie," Inferno said drawing back his fist. "I think we're in need of a barbeque."

He threw a ball of fire right at us, but I used my ice power to put it out.

"That's cute," Dante snarled. "You learned a new trick. Where's your old lady friend and the Asian kid? Aren't they the ones who usually fight for you?"

"Not this time," I said as I flung ice daggers at him. But he opened his mouth and melted them with his fire.

Barney picked up one of the cars with his mind and threw it at Dante, hitting him and pinning him down. Sloan stood his ground and stared at us.

"What do you mean you're not Acheron?" I asked. "You have to be him."

"No, I work for Acheron too. We all do whatever he tells us to. And in exchange for our work, he rewards us."

"What is he talking about?" Andrew asked.

"So then who is Acheron?" Hayley asked.

"Uh, guys," I said, pointing to Sloan. His hands started glowing.

"Oh crap, that can't be good," Hayley said.

Sloan's hand shot out an energy blast and it flew straight at Barney.

"Look out!" Maddison cried.

Barney shot his hand out straight and made the energy blast shoot right back at Sloan, making him fall backwards. He ran into the building followed by Dante.

"They retreated?" Andrew asked.

"Not hardly," Barney sighed.

Sloan, Dante, Belladonna, and one other figure walked out of the doors. The fourth figure was huge, at least twice the size of Kitashi, and towered over the other three. As they stepped into the light, I could see that Belladonna had a huge grin on her face.

"My I present to you," she laughed. "Acheron."

I gasped and my hands covered my mouth. I couldn't believe it. I didn't want to believe it. Standing in front of me was a monster of someone I recognized, and suddenly everything was fitting into place. My uncle had been gone for a long time, longer than usual for "work." He and Dominic Sloan have known each other for a while and have apparently been working together. Also, my uncle has access to a lab.

I watched as the overgrown version of my uncle moved towards us. I didn't notice everyone else back away from him until Barney grabbed my shoulders and moved me as well. I wasn't going to be able to fight my own uncle; he was the last of my family. I felt like I was going to pass out and I couldn't talk. My uncle charged at us and everyone besides me ran at him but I couldn't focus my vision on anything. The world seemed to be tilting and any second I'd fall over.

"Avery!" I heard Andrew yell. "I'm going after Belladonna. Think you can handle Inferno? Avery?"

"Yeah okay," I muttered. "Don't hurt my uncle."

"Avery?" He shook me. "Come on, focus. We've got to fight or else we'll die."

Everything came into focus as I saw Susanne running up to the fight. She smiled at me and everything seemed to be in balance again. I watched as Andrew ran toward Belladonna, while Maddison and Barney fought Sloan. Susanne was running at Inferno, which left me and Hayley to face my uncle. I knew Hayley would hurt him the first chance she got so I told her to go help Andrew.

"Are you crazy?" she asked. "Look at the size of this guy!"

"It's fine, I can handle it. And I'll call you back over if I need help."

A couple of guys ran out of the club to join the fight. One of them started attacking Barney so Hayley went over to help him. I looked up at my uncle.

"You're Acheron?" I asked.

"Yeah," he growled. "Who are you?"

"Dreamcatcher," I said, fighting the urge to tell him who I really was. "Why are you doing this?"

"Because I'm tired of not having power. I'm tired of taking orders from people. Now they all take orders from me. And I will destroy anyone who gets in my way."

He swung his giant arm down at me and I rolled out of the way.

"It doesn't have to be like this, Ross. You can end this now."

"What did you call me?" he asked. "I am not Ross anymore. That man was weak and a coward. Acheron, he's much stronger. I am Acheron!"

He swung his arm again and I moved out of the way.

"I'm not going to fight you, Ross," I said, sweat dripping down my face.

"Then you will die!" he yelled, swatting his hand at me, hitting me this time.

It felt like a boxing glove the size of a bathtub hit me. The blow sent me flying into a parked car, smashing into the passenger window. *That was definitely a cracked rib*, I thought as I slowly stood up. Ross bent down as if he was going to pick me up. I grabbed a handful of shattered glass and threw it into his face. He let out a yowl and put his hands over his eyes.

I saw out of the corner of my eye that Andrew and Belladonna had each other by the neck. He was telling her something and then she let go of him and walked over to Sloan. She grabbed him from behind and held onto his head. Suddenly, his head burst into pieces, splattering Belladonna and Barney with blood. Everyone stopped momentarily and watched as Belladonna screamed and Sloan's headless body fell to the ground. The sounds of her screams were hideous, like a pig getting slaughtered. She looked down at her red hands and ran off down the street screaming. I noticed Inferno closing in on Maddison behind her back. I created a block of ice in front of him to block her. She turned around as the ice melted and screamed in his face, sending him into the side of the brick building.

Ross roared at me and tried hitting me once more. However, I froze his fist, creating a thick layer of ice over his hand. The extra weight and discomfort only pissed him off even more but at least I was fighting him without having to hurt him. I saw Susanne raise her arms and a few of the manhole covers popped off, huge towers of water shooting out. Inferno opened his mouth to spit out fire but Susanne's water shot him right in his mouth. Then she used the water to pick him up and threw him into one of the manholes. I didn't see anything after that because a huge fist caught me right in the face. If I hadn't known better I would have guessed that I had been hit with a large metal pipe. I landed several feet away from my uncle and I tried to see if he was coming at me but both of my eyes were swollen almost completely shut. Something wet was running down my face and chin.

I barely saw the massive shadow move in front of me and then I felt another blow. This time it was in my stomach and I cried out in pain. Where were my teammates? Had they left me to get beat to death by my mutant uncle? I reached an arm up slowly and tried to talk but all that came out was another scream as I felt my arm snap. My uncle lifted me by my broken arm and dangled me in front of him. A shiny white bone was sticking out of my arm and blood trickled down into my already matted hair.

"This is why children need to mind their own business and stay out of the way," he said.

I tried to say something like, "Please, it's Avery," but my mouth just quivered. I was dropped to the ground, something in both of my ankles cracked, and I tried opening my eyes more. I barely had time to realize that a gust of wind had lifted me into the air and sat me down. My mask came off at some point but I didn't have the strength to get it. Not that I cared anyways since I was probably going to die. I attempted to call out "no" to Susanne but I blacked out. I heard bits of talking around me in and out of consciousness but I recognized all of the voices.

"There's too much damage to both of them!" Hayley cried. "I don't have the power to save both of them!"

"Hayley . . ." Susanne whispered. "Save Avery."

"But if I save her, you'll-"

"It's alright," Susanne breathed. "She's more valuable to the team than I am. Please, save her."

"Nmh," I mumbled, trying to tell Hayley not to save me.

"No, Avery," Susanne said, her weak voice cracking a little. "You let Hayley help you. I'm . . . very . . . proud of all . . . of you. Tell . . . Kitashi . . . goodbye for me."

"Susanne, please don't make me do this!" Hayley sobbed. "Don't make me choose!"

"Everything will be fine," Susanne said smiling. Trust me."

The only thing I could remember after that was Kitashi showing up as Hayley began to transfer Susanne's energy over to me, and about 40 of my uncle's henchmen came running out of the strip club after that everything just went red, and all I could hear were screams until I finally blacked out.

I drifted in and out of consciousness but noticed I was now in a car laying in Kitashi's lap; he was covered in blood and had his eyes closed. I had no idea what had happened but I could hear Maddison talking with everyone and this is what I could hear my teammates saying as they drove me to the hospital.

When Susanne pushed me out of the way, she took a really hard blow in the head from my uncle. He looked over and saw that my mask had come off and freaked out, thinking he had killed me. He ran off yelling, "Kill all of them!" Then, Kitashi showed up just as forty of Acheron's henchmen poured out of the building. He looked over and saw both Susanne and me. As Barney and Andrew carried us out of the way, Kitashi pulled out two swords and began killing all of the henchmen himself.

Maddison said that Kitashi's skin turned a shade of grey, almost like he turned to actual stone, and his eyes became black as onyx. He hacked off heads, sliced bodies in half, impaled people through the heart, and tore off limbs; and that was just with his swords. The last 4 men who were stupid enough to try shooting him were ripped into pieces by Kitashi's bear hands. Kitashi, the most kind and gentle person I had come to know, had slaughtered 40 men, all of them by himself without even thinking twice about what he was doing. Blood dripped off of him and his swords, and not a single drop of it was his own.

# CHAPTER 12

# Where My Mouth Is

*"And now I'm staring at the floor*
*Where my second life just ended*
*Where I lost not one but two friends*
*Yeah, I had it all, sitting on top of the world*
*But I threw it away just to prove that I could*
*I put my money where my mouth is."*

-"Where My Mouth Is" by Taking Back Sunday

I woke up in the hospital a day later. I felt incredibly weak and couldn't move. I saw an IV going into one arm and blood going into the other. I looked over and saw Kitashi sleeping in a chair. I tried moving again and let out a soft, "ow." Kitashi jolted awake and walked over to me.

"Hey," he said with a groggy voice. "How are you feeling?"

"Everything hurts," I gasped, tears running down my face. "Everything hurts."

"I know," he said. "I'm sorry. Do you need anything? Want me to get a nurse?"

"No. Just stay with me."

"I haven't left your side yet."

"I'm sorry," I whispered.

"For what?" he asked.

"For Andrew. And for Susanne. It's all my fault."

"Sh, don't Avery. Everything is alright. You don't need to be sorry for anything."

"I need to tell you something," I said. "Something happened to me when I blacked out."

"What do you mean?" Kitashi sat down on the bed next to me.

"I thought I heard my parents talking to me. They were telling me to turn around and go back."

I started laughing a weak laugh.

"I'm sorry," I said. "I must have lost a lot of blood."

"Avery, you flat-lined."

I looked at him.

"Hayley mended some of your broken bones but we had to bring you to the hospital because there was too much damage and you had lost too much blood. The doctors tried and tried to bring you back, and they almost gave up, but then your heart started faintly beating."

Kitashi started crying.

"They almost called your time of death. Susanne was pronounced dead as soon as we got here but they almost gave up on you. I don't know what I would have done if I had lost both of you."

"I . . . died?" I asked.

"Technically you were dead for two minutes. But you fought, Avery. You were strong enough to fight still."

"No, I didn't fight. That's how I got myself into this mess. I should have fought my uncle. Then Susanne wouldn't be . . . well you know."

"Your uncle?" Kitashi asked.

"Acheron is my uncle Ross. That's why I couldn't fight him. I couldn't hurt the only family member I had left. And then he kept hitting me and hitting me. And by that time it was too late for me to try and fight him. I'm sorry. I'm a coward."

"No, you're not, Avery. In fact, I think it makes you that much stronger that you didn't fight him."

"So where's the rest of the team?" I asked. "In the waiting room?"

Kitashi shook his head.

"Did something happen to them too?" I sat up, grabbing my side.

"No. They just didn't want to be here."

"Oh. I see. Well, that's alright. I understand."

"Um, they want you off the team."

"Really?" I asked. "Wow. Okay. Well, it's not like we can use my house anymore. I can't go home now, can I? My uncle will probably be waiting for me."

"We'll figure something out, don't worry. We have enough money between the two of us that we can find a temporary place to stay until we come out with a plan. It'll all work out."

"Well hello!" said a nurse, walking into my room. "You're awake now! You should have called for me. My name is Sharon. I've been taking care of you. How are you feeling?"

"Hi," I said. "I'm feeling better the more awake I get. I'm really thirsty though. Can I have some water?"

"Sure! I'll be right back."

A minutes later the nurse came back with a cup of water for me. I took a sip through the straw and sighed at how refreshing it felt.

"Also, could I have something for the pain?" I asked.

"Of course," she smiled. "And we threw away all of the clothes you showed up in since they were too covered in blood. But we called your next of kin and he said he'd bring up some things for you."

"Who did you talk to?" My eyes widened.

"Your uncle Ross. He sounded very worried about you but he said he was on his way here."

"How long ago did you call?" I asked.

"When I went to get your water. I wanted to wait until you were awake in case we couldn't get a hold of anyone else."

"Can you please go get some pain medication for her?" Kitashi said. "She's in a lot of pain."

"Alright, I'll be back as soon as possible."

As soon as the nurse walked out of the room Kitashi got up and closed the door.

"We need to get out of here as soon as possible."

"Yeah, but how am I going to get out without someone seeing me?" I asked.

"Too bad you don't have that invisibility power now," Kitashi sighed.

I don't know what made me want to try it out, but I concentrated on becoming invisible.

"Kitashi?" I asked.

"Yeah-" Kitashi looked around. "Avery?"

"I'm here, Kitashi," I said. "So I'm assuming it worked?"

"Yeah, it did. How did you-?"

"No time for that," I said, making myself visible again. "We need to get out of here. Now help me get out of all this crap."

I started unhooking myself from all of the wires and Kitashi stopped me.

"As soon as you unhook yourself, the nurses will come in here thinking something went wrong."

"Then you go ahead and get out of here and I'll meet you downstairs. I'll just turn invisible and they'll just be confused."

"I'll meet you downstairs."

I waited a few moments after Kitashi left and unhooked the rest of my wires and needles. Let me tell you, I hate blood and needles and stuff so it was extremely difficult for me to take a needle out of my arm, let alone *two* needles. I heard my nurse talking to someone down the hall so I quickly got up and moved as fast as I could out the room. I saw her walking with Charlie, coming towards my room. Charlie was carrying a bouquet of flowers. I wanted to badly to become visible and hug him and tell him everything. He told the nurse that my uncle was waiting in the car while he came up to see me. I figured my uncle didn't want to be noticed by everyone since he was now about seven feet tall and weighed over 300 pounds.

I ran down the hall, making sure my feet didn't hit the tile floor too hard and make noise. I thought taking the elevator would be too awkward in case someone else got in it with me so I decided to take the stairs. That worked out a lot better but I was tired once I got down all of the stairs. I saw Kitashi standing by the main entrance so I walked up to him.

"Boo," I whispered next to him. He didn't even budge, which was disappointing because I was hoping to scare him a little.

"Let's go," he muttered.

"Be careful not to let my uncle see you because he's sitting in the parking lot somewhere."

"I thought he was going up to see you."

"No, he sent Charlie."

"You think Charlie said anything to him about how he looks?"

"Probably not. Charlie rarely confronts my uncle about anything. You ready to go?"

Kitashi nodded and walked out the door and I followed. We were both looking around as we made our way to the car. Then, I saw my uncle. He was coming right at us, as if he knew we'd be coming. I grabbed Kitashi and teleported. I wasn't sure where to go so we showed up at the first place that popped into my head. Kitashi and I looked up at the giant Ferris wheel at Navy Pier.

"How did you do that?" Kitashi asked as I became visible again. Luckily, no one was around us.

"Let's find a hotel," I said, ignoring his question.

We walked to the nearest hotel and checked in. The girl at the front desk was staring at me in my hospital gown. I gave her a dirty look and she looked away. When I tried my credit card, the concierge told me that it had been cancelled. I knew my uncle must have cut off any access to money for me so Kitashi paid with his card.

We got into our room and I went into the bathroom. I was startled to see the person in the mirror when I flicked on the light. Both of my eyes were black and my left eye had a broken blood vessel, making the white of my eye red. I had cuts and stitches on my forehead, nose, chin, and lips. I was missing two molars on each side and another tooth was chipped. My arms were cut and bruised badly too. I went back into the main part of the room and Kitashi was sitting on the edge of one of the beds.

"Do you feel okay?" he asked me.

"I feel really weak. I just need a nap."

"I'm going to try and get a hold of Hayley. I'll see if she can come heal you some more."

"It's alright, I just want some sleep for now."

"Alright," he said. "Well I'll be right here if you need anything."

"Don't be stupid," I yawned. "You don't have to stay here and baby sit me while I sleep. Hotel television channels are never that great. Go out and do something fun and I'll call you when I wake up."

"Are you sure?" he asked. I nodded.

I pulled back the blankets, which was always one of my pet peeves. I always felt bad for messing up the bed after the hotel maids made them look so nice. I could feel my body throbbing as I lay still and tried to fall asleep. I wanted to moan in discomfort but I didn't want Kitashi thinking I was still hurting bad. Finally, I fell asleep. I slept extremely hard, nightmare free, for three hours before waking up and hearing Kitashi talking to people in the room. I kept my eyes closed and listened.

"I'm sorry, Kitashi, but I think the team should be done," Andrew said. "After Matt and Susanne both dying, I don't think we need to risk anyone else's lives. Playing super hero and everything was fun for a while but it's too dangerous and none of us are obviously capable of defending the world against evil."

"We haven't been doing this for long though," Maddison said. "Sure, it's going to be kind of rough at first and we may have some losses already but if we quit we'll be letting the bad guys win, giving them what they want. If they scare us away then they'll keep doing bad things."

"That's what the police are for," Hayley said. "Not a bunch of kids."

"But we're not just a bunch of kids!" Barney said. "We have powers and those powers are getting more and more powerful the more we use them. I bend stuff now instead of just move them. I can move certain parts of items without having to move the whole thing. Maddison can control her sonic voice to just one person. It's gotten powerful enough that she can set off every car alarm in the county if she wants. Andrew doesn't even have to touch people to read their emotions or manipulate them."

"That only works sometimes," Andrew said. "Not every time."

"Well, maybe if you keep using it, you'll be able to all the time. But if we just stop using our powers, they'll become weak again, and we might even lose them. And I didn't waste the last year and my brother's life to give up my powers and all of the things I've learned."

"Okay, you've got a point," Hayley said. "What about Avery then?"

"What about her?" Kitashi asked.

"Her powers aren't really improving, she just keeps learning new ones. And if it wasn't for her, Matt and Susanne would be alive still."

"No, if my brother would have just stayed home, he'd still be alive," Barney said. "Avery had nothing to do with that. Or Susanne's death. It was her choice to jump in front of her like that."

"Still, I don't want to have anything to do with her," Hayley said. "And we can all be friends still, but count me out of the team."

"Me too," Andrew said.

As I laid there listening to them all talk, I noticed something. I didn't hurt anymore, at all. In fact, I felt perfectly fine. I sat up and everyone stopped talking and looked at me.

"Avery?" Kitashi said. "What happened?"

"What do you mean?" I asked.

"You look . . . better. In fact, you look better than you did before you got hurt. Did you heal yourself?"

"Yeah, I guess I did," I rubbed my eyes. "Don't mind me, guys. I'm just going to go take a shower and get all of the dirt and blood out of my hair. You can keep talking shit about me behind my back and about quitting the team. Don't let me stop you."

Without making eye contact with anyone, I got off the bed and made my way to the bathroom. It was, without a doubt, the best shower I had ever taken. I felt around in my mouth with my finger and felt that my teeth were back to where they were supposed to be. So I had come to the conclusion that something had happened to me when I flat-lined that made me regain all of my powers at once. I was pretty excited about that until I remembered that I wasn't part of a team anymore. I was my own team. I was going to have to defeat my uncle solo. And I honestly could have cared less if no one wanted to help me. I hadn't had too much help before. This was something I was going to do on my own.

When I got out of the shower, I heard a knock on the door.

"It's me," Kitashi said. "I bought you some clothes from the shop downstairs, sorry if the sizes aren't right. I had Maddison kind of help me out so I hope everything fits."

I wrapped the towel around me and opened the door. Kitashi was standing there trying to not look at me.

"Is everyone gone?" I asked. He nodded.

"Good," I took the clothes from him and shut the door.

"Are you okay?" Kitashi asked through the door.

"Would you quit asking me if I'm okay? Christ! Except for the fact that Susanne died saving me because my uncle was trying to kill me and now my team doesn't want anything to do with me, I'm fine. Fucking peachy."

When I finished getting dressed I walked out of the bathroom and sat down on the bed to put my shoes on. I glanced over at Kitashi who was standing by the window, looking out. He looked slightly hurt and wouldn't look at me.

"Sorry," I sighed. "Really, I'm sorry. I'm . . . scared. And the only way I know how to deal with my fears is with anger. I don't mean to take it out on you, especially you, because you're the person that I'm closest to in the whole world."

"I'm the one who should be saying sorry, Avery," Kitashi looked away from the window. "I shouldn't have walked out on you like that. I just figured you'd be happier without me."

"Kitashi, it's the exact opposite. I'm miserable without you."

"I was pretty miserable without you too," he smiled. "Sorry I tried to sabotage your date."

"Technically it wasn't ever a real date. I didn't want to do it in the first place."

"You did it to protect me."

I nodded.

"Because?" he asked.

"You know why," I rolled my eyes. "Don't play dumb. You can't just say thank you and leave it alone?"

"I want to hear you say it though," he said.

"Sorry," I said, putting my jacket on. "I really don't want this turning into a teen romance story. I think everyone's tired of those. How about a little action and ass kicking instead? A little blood splatter? You seem to know all about that, so I heard."

"What does that mean?" he frowned.

"I overheard what you did to my uncle's men at the club. You killed all of them. Correction—you slaughtered all of them. What was that about? I thought you were all about harmony and trying not to use unnecessary violence?"

"I had just arrived and saw that both you and Susanne were dying. I let my anger get the best of me."

"You let your anger get the best of you?" I scoffed. "When I get angry, I yell or punch a wall. I don't slice grown men in half. And you sliced them down the middle, not just across! And your skin turned to stone? What exactly are you, Kitashi?"

"I don't know. I don't remember."

"You don't remember. Convenient, don't you think? What if you're some government science experiment gone bad or you were made to assassinate someone? What if there's a secret word that sets you off and you start killing everything in sight."

"Avery, this is ridiculous. I'm not a government project. Do you think that about anyone else on the team? Do you think Barney is actually a crazy killer?"

"Barney hasn't ever taken on forty men by himself. Let alone brutally kill forty men. Why don't you remember anything? Was whatever happened to you so bad that you blocked the memories out completely?"

"I don't fucking know, Avery!"

Surprised and hurt, I looked at Kitashi in silence.

"Avery-"

"I'm going after my uncle."

"What? By yourself?"

"Yeah. I don't need help, I can do it by myself. Don't let anyone know."

I put the hood of my jacket over my head and reached for the door handle.

"Avery," I heard Kitashi say. I turned around and looked at him.

"Be careful," he said.

"I know. Don't worry, I won't hold back this time. I'm going to fight him as hard as I can."

I walked out of the room and reached the elevator. The door opened and two men in suits walked out before pausing and looking at me. Everything seemed to slow down a lot as I saw them reach into their pockets for guns. I dodged their shots and rolled onto the floor. While everything around me seemed to be in slow motion, I was moving around at my normal speed. I could see the sparks from the guns as the men fired off more shots. I ran up to one of the men and punched him hard in his face sending him slowly backwards into the trashcan in the hall way. Another two men busted through the staircase entrance. As if it came naturally to me, I screamed as hard as I could at the other man with the gun and made him soar backwards into the wall, knocking him out cold.

Suddenly, everything came back into regular speed and the two men who were left standing ran at me. I shot chunks of ice that looked like golf ball-sized hail, but that just slowed them down a little. They were still coming at me and I had to think of something else fast. I moved my hands up towards the ceiling and both of the men lifted off of the ground. I bounced them off of the ceiling and the floor before making them clash into each other. I looked down the hall at the four unconscious men and heard a door open behind me. Kitashi stuck his head out and when he saw me standing around the men he came over to me.

"What happened?" he asked. "Are you okay?"

"Yeah I'm fine," I answered.

"You took out all four of these guys by yourself?"

"Don't sound so surprised. It's not a big deal. You took on forty by yourself."

"I was just checking to make sure you were okay," he said harshly. "How do you think they found us?"

"Probably because I tried using my card that he cancelled. You need to find a new hotel so more don't come."

"Like I can't fight them if they do?"

"Fine. Then just stay here," I said walking away from him.

"You're not still thinking about going after your uncle? What if he has more men waiting at your house?"

"He's the one who had my parents killed. I have to do something."

I walked away from Kitashi and got in the elevator, looking down at my feet the whole time. I could feel Kitashi watching me still as the elevator door shut. Inside the elevator I concentrated on my house and closed my eyes. There was loud rumbling around me and then I felt outdoor air on my face. I opened my eyes and was standing in my long circle driveway, staring up at my house. I was instantly pissed off. My uncle had been living in my parents' house, the house that they had paid for and worked on themselves, and he was the one who had taken it all away from them. I heard a car in the distance and saw my uncle's car pulling up to the lab. In the heat of the moment, I picked up one of the large rocks that was part of our landscaping and threw it as hard as I could. The small boulder flew the whole mile from my hand and into the car's passenger side window. The car screeched to a halt and as soon as it stopped I started running over to him. The fight was officially on.

My uncle got out of his car and slammed the door hard enough to make the car tilt on its two side wheels briefly before dropping back down. He walked around to the broken window before turning around to face me. I stopped about twenty feet from him and glared.

"I thought I killed you," he growled.

"Sorry to let you down. If it makes you feel any better, you *did* kill my teacher."

"Oh well, now that I have you by yourself without your little buddies, I'm sure it won't be too hard to kill you."

"I just don't understand why you want to kill me. Or why you killed my parents."

"Correction. I did not kill your parents. I would never have killed my own brother."

"So you paid some nut job to do your dirty work for you because you're too big of a coward to do it yourself? And for what? My parents' lab to run your drug project?"

"Avery, none of this was ever any of your business. I left you alone and you left me alone. You didn't want anything to do with the lab so it's not like I was ever worried about having to get rid of you. But now, now you've stuck your nose into my fucking business and we've got a problem. You really think you're going to stop me? Guess again, brat. I've raised you the best that I could and you have never acted grateful for all that I've done for you."

"You haven't done jack shit for me!" I yelled. "Charlie is the one who's always been there for me. He was the one who raised me, not you! People always assumed *he* was my uncle and then would ask me who you were. You've been living in my house all these years, in my parents' house all these years, and you were the one who got them killed."

"I gave them both chance after chance to join me as my partners on this project. Of course your mother didn't want anything to do with me and I almost had your father convinced. But your bitch of a mother saw right through me and tried to keep me away from my own brother. And now you're going to try and keep me away from something that I have spent too much time working on. Unfortunately you're going to end up just like your mother. Although it seems that you've been more like your father this whole time."

"What do you mean?"

"Your father was born with—abilities. So was your grandfather and his father. It runs in our family. Problem is it only happens to one child per generation. Which is why your father has them and not me. And my uncle was born without them since my dad had abilities. You know your parents were going to have a baby before you, right."

"But it didn't survive," I nodded.

"Well since you were born without powers, your parents figured your brother was the one who was born with them. Which is why they did tests and experiments on you. To try and make powers for you. What they didn't know was that you actually *were* the sibling born with powers, they just hadn't kicked in yet."

"But I thought the tests they did on me made me the way I am," I said.

"They just added to what powers you already had. I probably know more about your powers than you do. And I certainly know more about it than your parents. When someone dies for you, like a self-sacrifice—or when you kill someone, you become stronger. And I don't mean you can punch harder or it becomes a lot harder to kill you, but you can actually take powers from other people. It's the same power your father, grandfather, and so on had. When our father passed away, your father became a lot more powerful."

"And when my father died, I became more powerful?" I asked.

"Enough talk now Avery," he smiled. "We need to end this."

"Uncle Ross, I don't want to have to fight you," I sighed. "And not because I'm afraid for losing, because I'm not. But you're the only living family member I have left and a part of me wants to hold on to that."

My uncle smiled slightly and shook his head.

"Well since I'm planning on killing you anyways, I might as well tell you."

"Tell me what?" I asked.

"No, maybe I shouldn't."

"TELL ME WHAT?" I screamed.

"Okay, okay. Calm down, I'll tell you. I'm not the last family member you have left exactly."

"Who else is there?" I asked.

"Your father. He isn't dead."

# CHAPTER 13

# Die by the Drop

*"I never said we was equal, I never wished to be saved.*
*If I'm a problem then preach on. Let's dig a little grave."*

-"Die by the Drop" by The Dead Weather

"What do you mean he isn't dead?" I asked my uncle. "I saw my parents get shot! I was there at the funeral and I saw the bodies!"

"Are you going to shut up and let me explain or are you going to stand there and yell at me?"

I stopped talking and my whole body was shaking at that point.

"I was there the night your parents were shot."

I knew I had seen him there.

"The shooter did kill your mother. And I'm sorry for that. But I couldn't bring myself to kill my own blood so I shot him with a tranquilizer. I had the bodies swapped with a look-alike. I knew no one would pay enough attention at the funeral, and plus the guy was dead anyways and people always look different when they're dead. You didn't notice that it wasn't your own father."

"So where is he then if he's not dead?" I asked, tears filling my eyes.

"I had his memory wiped and sent somewhere."

"Where did you send him?"

"I don't know. I had someone else take care of it for me so I wouldn't go looking for him. You are the only person besides me who knows about this, Avery. Which is why I definitely need to kill you now. Because the secret will die with me and no one else will ever know."

I needed time to process all of the information my uncle had just given me. I had a father roaming the earth who didn't know I existed and didn't know he had powers. I wasn't as alone as I thought but I felt just as alone, if not more alone. And now I had to face my uncle alone. I was scared, more than ever. What if I died, leaving my father without me? He wouldn't know about his super hero daughter who had died fighting his psychotic evil brother.

*No,* I told myself. *I won't let that happen.* My father is going to meet me. And my mother's death would be avenged along with Matt's and Susanne's deaths. I was going to defeat my uncle.

"You ready?" Acheron asked me.

"Whenever you are, big guy," I smiled.

Acheron charged at me like an angry rhino. Imagining my uncle as a rhino made me laugh a little. As he ran towards me, dirt kicked up behind him and I stood my ground, watching him draw nearer.

When Acheron was about two feet away from me, I waved my hand out at him, making him fly up into the air. I jumped up super high and kicked him as hard as I could in the stomach, sending him into his pretty, little car. The car buckled under the sudden weight and Acheron was caught somewhere in the middle of the car. When he stood up slowly, the car seemed to be stuck on his back and butt. This also made me laugh which apparently pissed him off because he then wiggled the car off of his body and threw the flattened vehicle at me.

I dodged out of the way but the car clipped my left heel. I fell awkwardly onto the ground and although I didn't have time to grab my hurt foot, I was in a lot of pain. I lifted my arms up and brought two closed fists down on the ground. The dirt between my uncle and me cracked and rumbled like an earthquake. Acheron fell into the large crevice in the ground and I brought my hands together as the earth sewed itself back together, my uncle trapped underground. I stood up and hobbled on my foot that was fine for a few seconds until the other foot stopped hurting. I heard a grumbling sound coming from beneath my feet and I stepped back to watch my uncle tear through the ground and claw himself to the surface.

"I should have drowned you the moment I set foot in this house!" he spat at me.

"Why didn't you?" I asked, panting.

"I had hoped that you'd grow up to be like me and one day, hopefully, join me. But I see now that you're daft just like your parents."

I ran at him as fast as I could with a fist raised, but he hit me before I could reach him myself. The punch made me crash into the outer wall of the lab. I sat for a moment, seeing doubles of everything from hitting my head on the wall so hard. When I saw a pair of Acheron twins running at me, I ducked out of the way and my uncle ran right through the wall of the lab. I heard a loud crashing sound and stood up, shaking my head clear.

I looked into the hole in the wall and saw a few desks pushed into each other in pieces. Papers and pencils covered the floor but there was no sign of Acheron. I stepped into the lab, surprised to see a couple of workers crouched in a corner cowering. I kept my eyes open for any movement. Then, I saw someone walk out from the back of the building, but it wasn't my uncle. It was Hayley.

"Hayley?" I asked. "What are you doing here?"

"I knew you'd come here," she said.

"Why do you sound like a robot?"

"Shut up. And fight."

"What?" I asked as Hayley kept walking toward me.

She reached out for me but I moved out of the way, making her stumble a little. I looked up and saw my uncle standing at the top of the stairs, smiling.

"What did you do to her?" I yelled.

Hayley came back at me and grabbed me by my throat. I was getting that feeling again, like a balloon getting deflated. All of the energy and power was leaving my body.

"Hayley . . ." I gasped. "Don't . . . do this."

"Shut up you little bitch," she whispered. "I don't have to listen to you. I listen to Acheron now."

I glanced around me for anything at all that would help me at this point. I reached around on the table next to me and felt something that was long and made of glass. I barely had enough strength to grab it and break it. I plunged the broken end of the graduated cylinder into Hayley's stomach. She let out a loud scream and let go of my throat. I instantly regained my energy and kept pushing the sharp glass into Hayley, backing her up against a wall, hot tears and sweat streaming down my face. While she was still leaned up against the wall, I pushed one of the extremely heavy desks up against her to pin her down and away from me. I heard a crashing sound from behind me and turned around to see flames scatter the building. Acheron was throwing beakers of liquid at me, trying to trap me with the fire. Smoke and flames started building up pretty fast and was blocking me from the entrance to the lab and the hole my uncle had made in the wall.

I tried to stay low and wondered why the sprinkler system hadn't come on yet. I heard a couple of people somewhere screaming and running around. I felt a hard blow to the back of my head that knocked me down. I rolled over and saw my uncle coming at my face with his fist again. I turned invisible and moved out the way. My uncle's fist went straight through the floor and we both fell through as the floor crumbled around us. Luckily, Acheron hadn't landed directly on me but my leg was lodged underneath him. I tried wriggling free but couldn't move.

"There you are!" he laughed and smacked me with the back of his giant hand.

I moved out from under him finally and my face was throbbing from the hits I had taken already. I was pretty sure I was bleeding in more than one spot and my side hurt real bad, but I was far from giving up. I stood up and, using my telekinesis, picked up a large piece of flooring and shot it at Acheron, knocking him on his back. More of the level above us was caving in and bits of furniture that was on fire was now setting fire to things around us. Acheron moved the rubble off of him and was bleeding from his forehead. I slowed down time and jumped on him, hitting him in the face as fast as I could. Then, I felt something pull through my body. I looked down and saw a metal threading rod going through the left side of my chest, right under my collar bone. I instantly freaked out and let go of my uncle, falling to the ground. Hitting the ground on my left arm hurt my chest even more and I couldn't breathe. I looked up to see the roof coming down on us and I made myself teleport. However, I didn't make it outside of the building. I was still caught right in front of the doorway.

"Teleport again!" I heard a voice say as someone grabbed me. "Teleport again, damn it!"

I tried with all of my might to teleport out of the building. The next thing I saw above me was a grey sky and I could feel grass underneath me. I looked over and saw Hayley smiling at me.

"I'm pretty sure you have a punctured lung," she said. "I need to pull out the rod, and it's going to hurt like hell but then I'll fix you up."

She held me down and pulled out the rod. I thought the worst pain I'd ever felt was when it went in but I was wrong. Having it pulled out hurt a lot worse. I started feeling cold and couldn't breathe at all. Hayley placed one hand on the ground and one hand on my chest. Oxygen started moving into my lungs and I was feeling better, though still a bit light-headed. I sat up slowly and looked at Hayley.

"Are you okay now?" I asked her. "You're not still—under his control?"

"No, I think the drugs are wearing off. When I came to, I was bleeding out and pinned up to a wall behind a desk. Everything was on fire around me but I realized something earlier. Almost everything has life and energy to it. I used the wood in the desk and the fire to give myself enough strength to get outside. As soon as my body hit the ground, I healed myself. It's a lot faster to use the ground than a tree or a person."

"How did my uncle get to you in the first place?" I asked.

"When we all left the hotel, I was feeling like crap for saying all of that stuff about you so I came here, thinking you would be here. But your uncle was the only person here when I came and he tied me up and gave me a pill. After that, I don't remember anything until I woke up with a hole in my stomach and a building around me on fire."

"Yeah sorry I had to do that to you," I said. "I was planning on coming back for you."

"I know. But I figured I owe you more than you owe me so it was my turn to save your ass."

"I appreciate it," I looked over at the lab. "Do you think he's dead?"

"I think so. I'm sorry, Avery."

"It's okay," I sighed. "I did what I had to."

I brought my knees up to my face and wrapped my arms around them. But then something hit me.

*Avery.*

I stood up.

"Avery?" Hayley asked, standing up with me. "What's wrong?"

"He's not dead," I said before running back to the building.

"Avery!" Hayley called after me.

I ran into the burning building, covering myself with a shield of water. I ran down the stairs to where the floor above had collapsed and ran to the entrance of my parents' secret room. *Come on*, I thought. *Say something again, you bastard. Say something so I know where you are.* I walked through the door that had been busted down and looked around at a trashed room. I saw the tape that my parents had left me and grabbed it. After putting it in my pocket I looked around the room a bit more. I saw the shelf in the back had been toppled over and the freezer was left open.

"Oh no," I whispered.

I looked inside and saw that all of the vials in the tray were empty now. I glanced over and noticed that the doorway down to our lair had been ripped away. I crept carefully through the tunnel down the room where the team had been having our meetings. I didn't see my uncle anywhere, which worried me. I walked over to the curtains that hid away the car exit. As I reached out to touch the curtain, something hit me from the other side, knocking me down on my butt. I looked up to see, not my uncle anymore, but a monster. His skin was an abnormal color and the shirt he had had on was now bits of cloth dangling off of his body. He was twice the size he had just been and looked a lot meaner.

"U-u-uncle Ross?" I asked.

Acheron let out a deafening, blood-curdling roar that blew my hair back a little. I got up quickly and moved around to the other side of the large table in the room. I shot out a few large sparks of electricity and hit him in the face and chest. He barely flinched at my attacks however. He pushed the large table at me like it was nothing and it hit me hard in the stomach, knocking the wind out of me. He tried coming around the other side of the table so I sent another few stronger jolts of electricity at Acheron and one hit him right in the eye. He grabbed his face and backed up a couple of steps and I crouched under the table to move out of his sight. Suddenly, the table flew away from me as he flipped it over and I saw the damage I had done to his eye. Purple, raw tissue was burned around what was an eye just a moment before. Instead there was now a black hole with liquid coming out of it. I could only imagine what the liquid stuff was. His mouth was also hard to look at. I had charred his lips off, revealing an abnormally large, permanent grin, although he was doing anything but smiling.

I felt horrible for doing that to him but I knew that I had no choice. It was either kill or be killed at that point. He was still blocking the car exit so I ran back up to the lab. I heard his loud stomps coming up behind me like an elephant and I moved faster up the stairs. Once I reached the smoke-filled ground floor I spun on my heels and waited for Acheron. I used the smoke around me to camouflage myself so when I heard him through the doorway I crouched down low. He was going to be a lot harder to take out, especially since he used more of the serum my parents had made. I morphed my hand into a sharp, thin knife and reached out to slice through the tendon on Acherons right heel. He roared out in agony and I moved out of the way as he staggered towards me. I morphed my hand back to normal and tried wiping off some of the blood. Then, Acheron grabbed me by my throat and lifted me. I made myself turn into total lead and he had a harder time holding my heavy body up, and wasn't able to squeeze my throat at all. I smiled at him and he threw me through the ceiling that led to the top floor and I fell back down with a loud metal clunking sound. I morphed back to normal and stood up.

I knew that I needed to collapse the whole building on top of Acheron to at least slow him down, if not kill him. The only problem was that I was still in the building and didn't have time to teleport out again. I looked around to find anything that might help me and noticed a bunch of metal beams sticking out of the torn part of the ceiling above us. I reached out with my hands that were glowing white to bring down one of the metal beams, shaping the end into a spike and sent it straight down as Acheron was making his way towards me. The beam pierced right through Acheron's right shoulder and into the floor, bringing him to one knee. He roared and started to stand back up so I brought down another beam into the other shoulder before bringing a third down through one of his legs. Although he was still trying to move, my uncle was slowing down by a lot.

Acheron tried to pull the beam out of his left shoulder and when the beam wouldn't budge, he ripped his arm completely through the beam. He let out a loud bellow and tried moving forward at me, grabbing for my face. Without even hesitating I used one more beam to constrict him from moving and finally taking one deep breath I plunged two final beams straight into his heart and spinal cord. I stood with my eyes closed for a moment not wanting to see what I had just done. I finally built up the courage to open my eyes and there in front of me was my uncle, not Acheron this time but my actual uncle, looking at me with sad, guilty eyes. I stayed where I was and watched him. Blood trickled out of several parts of his body and ran down all of the metal beams that were pinning him down. His body started changing. Shrinking back to what he used to look like. He reached his hand out slowly at me and as I reached my hand out to meet his, he closed his eyes, lowered his head, and his body went limp. I suddenly heard a rumbling sound coming from above me and I looked up to see the building coming down on me fast.

I had never tried using a force shield before and was pretty sure it wasn't going to work. I crouched down and stuck my hand up then lifted off the ground to fly above the wreckage. A bubble formed around my body and all of the debris bounced right off of it. I had never heard anything so loud as the building began falling down around me. I flew carefully through the building, keeping an eye out for anyone who looked injured or trapped. I waited for everything to stop falling as much before I tried walking around on the ground with my force shield. I moved around cautiously until I was clear of anything falling on me.

I let go of the force field and staggered through the front of the building. I heard sirens and then saw three fire trucks pulling up to the building. One of the men got out immediately and ran over to me with a blanket. I looked at my arm and saw that it was on fire, but I wasn't alarmed because I couldn't even feel it. The firefighter with the blanket made me lay down on my side and he covered me with the blanket. I saw a group run past me into the building and then saw a second group run up to me. I smiled up at my friends but they didn't look as enthusiastic as me. Barney and Maddison were crying and Andrew's mouth was gaped open. Kitashi reached for my hand and held onto it tight.

"Move it! Move out of the way!" I heard a familiar voice yelling.

"Ryan?" I asked as the firefighter put an oxygen mask over my mouth.

"We're both here," Kelly said as his face came into view.

"What happened?" Ryan asked. I looked at the team.

"A chemical fire inside the lab," I lied. "I was inside goofing off when it happened."

"Oh my God," Ryan gasped. "Are you okay?"

"She should be fine, guys," said the firefighter. "She has some bad burns but she should recover fairly soon."

"Has anyone found my uncle?" I asked him. "He was inside too when it happened. He's kind of a bigger guy, not hard to miss."

"Hey does anyone see anything of her uncle?" the man asked on his walkie-talkie. "Apparently he's a bigger guy. Any sign yet?"

Another man came on and said there was no sign yet and that they would have to clear out the debris before they could go looking for him. Then, I saw Charlie come over and as an ambulance pulled up by the trucks he kneeled down on the ground next to me.

"Avery, my God, are you alright?" he asked, tears filling his eyes.

"Everyone's going to have to back away now," the firefighter said as two people with a stretcher came over to us. They lifted me up and carried me to the ambulance. Everything was happening so fast I didn't hardly have enough time to register anything. Apparently, it wasn't just my arm that had been on fire. My whole shoulder and upper back had caught on fire and I had second degree burns. I was put on an IV and sent to the hospital. I was also put on pain medication and treated for my burns but I really just wanted to tell the doctors that if they let me go home that I could be healed in no time by Hayley. That, of course, would not go so well and I'd probably get sent to a psych ward.

All of my friends and Charlie stayed with me the whole time and took turns coming into the room to visit me, although Kitashi stayed in the room with me the whole time. He never left my side unless the doctors made him leave every once in a while. At one point, I was awakened by a doctor coming in with another man. Kitashi had fallen asleep with his head on my leg and his hand in mine. He sat up when I moved and we listened as the doctor introduced the man to us. I then realized it was the firefighter who had helped me at the lab.

"How are you feeling?" he asked.

"Bored out of my mind," I smiled. "I can't believe I'm saying this but I'd rather be in school than here."

"I don't blame you," he chuckled slightly before becoming solemn. "Avery, we found your uncle."

"Is he alive?" my eyes widened with slight terror.

"I'm afraid not," the firefighter looked at the floor. "I'm so sorry for your loss. A couple of the steel beams from the ceiling fell on him. There was too much damage from the building falling down on him and . . . . he had already passed by the time we reached him.

"Oh," I said quietly. "Um, thank you for letting me know."

The firefighter nodded and walked out. I looked at Kitashi and started crying.

"I'm sorry," I whimpered. "I know I should be happy that I defeated him and that we don't have to worry about him anymore, but I'm still sad. I've lived with him for most of my life. And now he's gone. And now that I know my father's out there somewhere-"

"Wait, what?" Kitashi asked.

"Yeah. Turns out that my uncle never killed my dad, only my mom. He wiped my dad's memory and sent him away somewhere with a different name and no memory of anything that happened. I feel like my whole world is ending."

"Can I share something with you?" he asked. "It's one of my favorite quotes."

I nodded.

"Just when the caterpillar thought the world would end, it became a butterfly."

"That's kind of pretty," I sniffled. "Where did you hear that from?"

"Susanne used to say it sometimes when things would get a little rough. I'm sure if she was here, she'd say it to you too. Also, I think she'd be really proud of you."

I buried my face into Kitashi's chest and he kissed my forehead. I hoped that he was right. My old life as a caterpillar really had ended. But now it was time to start a new life as a butterfly.

# CHAPTER 14

# Blackbird

*"Blackbird singing in the dead of night*
*Take these broken wings and learn to fly, all your life*
*You were only waiting for this moment to arise."*

-"Blackbird" by The Beatles

I was sent home from the hospital with some pretty gnarly scars. I asked Hayley to heal them but unfortunately, since they were already technically healed, there was nothing she could do about the scarring. Andrew told me that the scars made me look more like a bad ass but I didn't feel much like a bad ass. The week was to be a busy one. Two funerals in two days. One would be a large, crowded one for my uncle. The other, a small, private one for Susanne. I had to attend my uncle's alone, without any of my friends, because I was afraid someone would recognize them even without their costumes. The first week of school and my birthday were the following week although I wasn't really looking forward to it.

Charlie held my hand the whole time as I cried silently at the closed casket. A lot of people I didn't know walked up to me throughout the day to give me envelopes of money and to give their condolences. We all stood outside, listening to the prayers and hymns and watching the casket that was covered with dozens of flowers. The hardest part was when the military salute guns went off. I had always known that my uncle had served in the military but I never thought anything of it until the funeral. The men folded the flag and handed it to me. I felt sick to my stomach. I had secretly been the one who had killed my uncle and here these men were, paying respect to a man they had never even met and handing me this flag that meant so much.

Charlie and I were the last ones to leave the funeral sight since we waited until after the grave was filled with dirt. Even then Charlie couldn't bring himself to leave. After the funeral, I handed Charlie all of the envelopes of money and told him not to tell me how much there was. We went home and I crashed on my bed for the rest of the day. I couldn't sleep and I couldn't eat. I didn't want to talk to anyone and I couldn't cry. I wasn't sad and I wasn't mad. I wasn't anything. I was completely numb. It was the worst I had ever felt in my entire life and I felt like disappearing from everything. I knew Charlie and Kitashi were worried about me along with all of my friends but I just couldn't bring myself out of the feeling that I was in.

The next day was Susanne's funeral. She had wanted to be cremated and taken somewhere beautiful. Kitashi had picked up the urn with her ashes in it and the group met at my house. We all wore our costumes instead of black since she would like that more if she were still with us. No one said much as we gathered in a circle and held hands outside my front door. I looked around at everyone and they all nodded at me. We closed our eyes and I teleported us all to the place Kitashi told me to take us. I opened my eyes and was surrounded by a familiar scene. Fully bloomed cherry blossoms were all around us and a large mountain was in the distance. Hayley was crying and Barney and Andrew were in awe of the sight. Maddison smiled at me before walking over to one of the trees and examining it closely. Kitashi was still holding onto my hand when he pulled the urn out of the messenger bag he was carrying on his shoulder.

We walked over to the large boulder that the two of us had hid behind when we time-traveled and Kitashi opened the urn. The group stood in total silence, apart from the soft sniffling from crying, and watched as Kitashi gently poured out the ashes into the wind. The little cloud rose up away from us and then eventually disappeared. I listened to the creek that was close by. I felt the wind blowing around us, the warm heat from the sun above, and the ground beneath our feet and I knew that the earth was also mourning with us. I faced the boulder and put my finger up to the hot rock. I etched markings into it like a laser and wrote Susanne's name onto it. I looked back at everyone and they seemed to all be giving me a look of appreciation. After returning us back to my house we went inside where Kitashi made us some tea. We sat in silence until finally, Hayley spoke.

"I don't want the team to end," she said quietly. "I want to keep going."

"Yeah," I said. "Me too."

"Me too," Maddison added.

"Yeah," Barney chimed in.

Kitashi nodded. We looked at Andrew.

"Well duh!" he smiled. "Besides, who else would play the handsome front man for the team if I wasn't in it?"

We all chuckled.

"Wait a minute," Barney said. "Not to sound like a nerd or anything, but if we're going to officially become a team than we need a name. You know, like all of the teams in the comic books."

"You're right," Hayley laughed. "You do sound like a nerd."

"No, I agree," Maddison said. "We need a name."

"Okay, let's go with the Y-Men," Andrew smiled. "Because everyone's going to be wondering *why* we're crazy enough to do this."

He looked at Barney.

"You get it?" he asked. "Y? Why?"

"Yeah," Barney said, not smiling. "I got it."

"Anyways," I said. "Let's try and come up with something good. Barney, you know all about this super hero stuff. Got any suggestions?"

"I'm trying to think. I always liked the name Crime Eliminators myself."

"Lame," Andrew rolled his eyes.

"You're an ass," I frowned.

"You're a tease," he said.

"Look!" Kitashi slammed his hand on the table hard. "If we're going to be a team, we need to support each other more. No more fighting or gossiping within the group. We need to all grow up. The only fighting I want to see is against criminals. Understood?"

We all nodded.

"Sorry, Barney," Andrew muttered.

We all sat around with our pens and paper, trying to think of a good team name for a while. Finally, Barney threw his hands up in the air and grunted.

"I give up!" he exclaimed. "Seriously, we're at a dead end. Let's just take a break from this for now and work on it some other time."

My head shot up quickly and I looked at Barney.

"What did you say?" I asked him.

"I said we should take a break and work on it-"

"No, no. The other part. Dead end."

"What?" Barney asked and looked at everyone else.

I got out another piece of paper and wrote down a name before presenting it to everyone. It read, "Dead End Justice."

"I think I like it," Maddison said. I grinned at her.

"I don't get it," Andrew said. "It makes it seem like we're not good at bringing justice."

"No," Hayley explained. "I think it means like no matter what there's always going to be crime and the only way we can stop them is with justice. Like a road sign that says, 'dead end.' We can always bring them to justice."

"Sure," I giggled. "I just liked how it sounded."

"So does everyone agree on it then?" Kitashi asked.

Everyone agreed.

"Okay," he said. "Then from now on, we are to be known as Dead End Justice."

We all raised our tea cups and cheered to our new name. My spirits were a lot higher than they had been in a while. The following Monday was the first day of school and I was going in for the first time as a sophomore. I was excited about some of my classes since I got to pick most of them, unlike my freshman year. Of course I was taking English, Math, History, Physical Education, and Science like everyone else but I was getting to take Acting, Creative Writing, and Introduction to Newspaper. My first day went smoothly since it was mostly just introductions and class itineraries. Kitashi picked Kelly, Ryan, and me up after school and dropped them off before going home. I was happy that things had smoothed over between me and them, especially since we had several classes together.

When I got home Charlie was waiting for me in the living room.

"How was it?" he asked. "You weren't too hard on the new freshman, were you?"

"Nah," I laughed. "I hardly noticed them actually."

"That's good," he smiled before looking at Kitashi. "Do you mind, Kitashi? There's something I need to discuss with Avery."

"Not at all," Kitashi said before picking up my backpack. "I'll put this in your room for you."

Thanks," I said before plopping down on the couch. "What's up?"

"Avery, I've been meaning to ask you this. What would you like me to do?"

"What do you mean?"

"Well, I'm not going to just assume that I'm going to keep living here in your house. I was an assistant to your uncle, but I was never an employee of yours."

"Oh," I muttered. "You want to leave?"

"Of course not!" he put his hand on my shoulder. "You're closest thing I've ever had to having a child of my own. I consider you my family. I just didn't know if you felt the same."

"Well yeah! I want you to stay as long as you want. Besides, I'm going to need someone to help me out on deciding what to do with this huge house and my money and what's left of the lab."

"What are you planning on doing with the lab?" he asked.

"Well I'm going to have to pay someone to tear it down all the way and get rid of the debris and stuff first, right?"

"Yes."

"Okay. And I want to decorate the house, if you don't mind. And I want you to have any room in the house that you want."

"Alright. Thank you."

"And how much was my uncle paying you?"

"Paying me?" he asked.

"Well yeah, for your job."

"He always just said that being able to live in his house without any bills to pay and getting to eat his food was my payment. And that was always alright with me."

"Well what about clothes or movies or whenever you want to go out?" I asked.

"Sometimes, on occasion, your uncle would give me some money."

"God, he treated you like a child with an allowance. Well, I give you full permission to access any money any time you want. Okay?"

"If that's what you want."

"It is. You, me, and Kitashi. We're going to be a family. And when I find my father, we can all be a family together."

"About that, Avery, do you honestly think your father is out there? I mean, I didn't see much of your uncle the last few months he was alive but I don't think he was in a right state of mind. I don't know what all he was dappling in but I don't think it was any good.

I think he was either really sick or tormented or, I hate to say it, under the influence of something."

"Yeah," I said calmly. "I got that too."

"But let's not talk about that right now. Let's talk about your birthday! It's coming up on Friday, isn't it?"

"Yeah."

"You don't sound very excited."

"I'm not really. It's just another day to me."

"But this is a very special birthday. Your sweet sixteen birthday."

"So what?" I'll get to drive, that's about it. My birthdays weren't ever a big deal so why should this one be any different?"

"Well, someone is being a stick in the mud. I guess everyone will just to have a fun time without you."

"Is there already something planned?" I asked.

"Oh, no," Charlie said. "I thought you had something you were doing already."

"Nope," I stood up. "See, this is why I don't even bother getting excited about my birthday. No one else is excited so why should I be?"

"I'll call you guys down when dinner is ready," Charlie said as I walked up the stairs. I went up to my room and opened the door. I closed it behind me and smiled, glancing over at my closed closet door. Using my mind, I swung the door open and Kitashi was standing inside smiling back at me.

"You're getting better," he said.

"You're just not a very good hider," I giggled, laying stomach down on the bed. Kitashi came over and sat on the bed next to me, handing me the remote to the television. I turned it on and watched a show while Kitashi sat beside me and braided my hair for me. It was relaxing enough to put me to sleep but that would throw off my sleep schedule so I fought to stay awake. After the show I was watching was over, I changed the channel to the news so I could find out what the weather for the rest of the week would be. Once the weather was over with, I propped my head up with my hand and looked at Kitashi.

"I wish you hadn't been home-schooled already. I'd really like to see you during the day every day at school."

"I do get bored during the day waiting for your school to get out. No one could know I've already been home-schooled. I could just repeat a couple of years. But because of my age, I'll still be a year ahead of you at the least. They might even make me a senior. Unless you want me to lie about that too."

"No, that would be horrible of me to ask you to repeat high school."

"Well, I've never been to an actual school with other kids. I'd probably enjoy it actually."

"Doubt it," I smirked. "Don't worry about it. Besides, you don't want anyone picking on you because you're the new kid."

"I don't think I would have to worry about that."

"I don't know, some of those high school boys are pretty strong and tough."

"Oh, is that right?" he raised one eyebrow. I started laughing and Kitashi grabbed my sides and started tickling me. We both calmed down and Kitashi wrapped his arms around me.

"I wish-" he started.

"I know," I said. "Me too. But you know we can't. It's too dangerous."

"I know. Thank you for loving me enough to protect me. I just wish you could tell me that you love me."

"You know I can't give into my feelings for you. Just like you can't."

I had never expected to find someone who loved me as much as Kitashi, let alone at my age. He was always full of surprises, so I wasn't exactly shocked to see him walk through the door of my English class the next day at school. He had his schedule made as close to mine as possible. We had English, History, and Acting together. He wanted to take Photography instead of Newspaper and was really excited about it. He also told me that he was planning on trying out for the soccer team. I didn't even know he liked sports, or that he played any. I noticed a couple of girls from classes eyeing him intensely but he acted like the teachers and I were the only other people around him. I loved him and desperately wanted him to be my boyfriend but I also knew that that was not possible for us in our current situation.

"At least you don't have to wait around for me to pick you up from school every day now," he said to me at lunch.

"You were never late picking me up anyways," I said as Kelly and Ryan sat down across the table from us.

"Second fucking day of school and we already have homework!" Ryan said with a mouth full of tater tots. "I mean, it's not like we have lives now or anything."

"So people under the age of sixteen don't have lives?" I asked. "Well good thing Friday is almost here so I can get a life."

Ryan threw one of her tots at me and we both chuckled.

"Are you getting excited?" Kelly asked me.

"Nope. I plan on going to school, coming home, shutting off my phone for the day, and working on homework."

"How lame," Kelly rolled his eyes. "Seriously, you need to do at least one thing for your birthday. And when are you going to make time in your oh-so-busy birthday schedule for your best friends? We'll need to drop off your presents at some point."

"No presents, please," I moaned. "I didn't get either of you anything."

"We were fighting really bad and then you almost died in a collapsed burning building," Kelly said. "I think you're excused this year."

"Speak for yourself," Ryan smiled. "This girl is worth a whopping five hundred million dollars now! She can at least buy me a card."

I looked down at my crappy, over-cooked lasagna and poked at it with my fork before setting the fork down and pushing the tray away.

"Way to go," Kelly said to Ryan.

"Sorry," Ryan said. "I guess we're not at the point of laughing at it yet, huh?"

"It's okay," I sighed. "I guess I'm going to have to get over it at some point. Right?"

I looked up at the three of them and noticed that I was crying. I quickly wiped away my tears and went back to poking my food.

"We need better food," I mumbled.

"High school kids have been saying that for years," Kelly said. "We also need new desks, new books, better computers and dry-erase boards, and a bunch of other crap that the board can't afford to give us."

I stood up and walked out of the cafeteria.

"Avery!" Kelly called after me.

"You mind telling me what you're doing?" Kitashi asked me as he caught up with me.

"I'm going to the principal's office. I'm going to donate money to the school."

"Oh. Well that's very nice of you. How much?"

"However much the school needs. I'm not eating another sloppy joe sandwich with the meat they used for chili the day before. And I don't need all of that money just sitting in my bank account gaining interest. I want to give it to someone who needs it."

"While I admire that, have you ever thought about saving that money for your future? College? Your wedding? Children? Your children's college?"

"If I even make it to see college, Kitashi. I'm first and foremost a super hero. That's my job now, and it's a very dangerous job. I want to make sure my money goes towards something worth fighting for. And while I am stuck in school, I'm not going to sit in front of a crappy computer and wait two minutes for a picture to pop up because it's slow and outdated."

I knocked on the door of the principal's office and it opened. I had never personally spoken with my school's principal one-on-one but he seemed nice. Mr. Matthews invited me in to talk during lunch and I told him what I was wanting to do. Naturally, he was absolutely beside himself and got the school board on the phone with us. I was going to donate five million dollars to my school and in my honor they were going to build a garden in the courtyard and rename it Kendall Garden. They wanted to name it Avery Garden, but I didn't want to seem arrogant and let them name it after only me. Plus, I'm sure my parents would have approved of my decision. The plan was that over the next few months of school, the board would start fixing things one by one. By my junior year, we'd have new and improved everything, including some building renovations that would take place during summer vacation.

On Friday, I was surprised to wake up and find out that Kitashi was too sick to go to school. He didn't mention my birthday at all, which bothered me. Sure, I had told him not to do anything about my birthday but I thought Kitashi would still give me a small present or at least tell me happy birthday. Kelly and Ryan didn't mention my birthday which was really irritating me. Charlie picked me up after school to take me to my driving test, which I nailed except for parallel parking. Charlie let me drive home, which put me in a slightly better mood knowing that I could legally drive anywhere I wanted, but I was in no mood to see Kitashi when I got home. I walked through the front door and all of the lights in the house were off, which I found disturbing. I braced myself when I flipped the light switch.

"SURPRISE!"

I jumped at the room full of people and the loud noise and all of the decorations that were up everywhere. Kitashi came up to me first and hugged me tight.

"Happy birthday, love," he whispered before kissing my temple.

"You're not really sick?" I asked. "But Charlie said you were sick."

Kitashi winked at Charlie, who returned a wink.

"I can't believe you two played me like that!" I laughed, playfully slapping Kitashi's shoulder and hugging him again. Kelly and Ryan came up to me and gave me a hug as well.

"Love you, best friend," Ryan giggled. "Happy birthday."

"Yeah, happy birthday, beautiful," Kelly added. "We didn't get you a card but our present is the black and white polka-dotted wrapped box on the table."

"Oh, okay," I laughed. I looked around and saw the rest of the Dead End Justice team standing behind Kitashi. Maddison and Hayley were both wearing dresses and Barney was wearing nice khaki slacks. Andrew looked nice too and came up to put a hand in front of me.

"Truce?" he asked. "Friends?"

"Friends," I grabbed his hand and pulled him closer to me to hug.

I noticed some people from school and around the neighborhood were also at the party. There was a huge purple cake on the dining room table along with platters and bowls of my favorite foods.

There were bowls of candy, kettle popcorn, marshmallows, and chips. There were plates of pizza, fried chicken, crab rangoon, and macaroni and cheese. Charlie informed me that there were also several different types of ice cream to go along with the cake. And that was just the food.

After we all ate until we couldn't budge anymore, we all went into another room where my presents were. I opened the one from Maddison first. It was a CD of a new band that I really liked. I gave her a hug and opened the wrapped box from Kelly and Ryan. It was a really cool looking jacket.

"Thanks guys, I love it!" I said holding it up for everyone to see.

"Kelly picked it out," Ryan smiled at her twin.

"I know you can't wear it now but you'll be able to soon once the weather cools down," Kelly added.

Hayley and Andrew gave me a lip gloss and nail polish set that had a bunch of crazy colors. Barney gave me a picture frame that said, "friends" on it and had a picture in it already of the team. I smiled at him and said thanks. I opened the rest of my presents until there was nothing left to open. I noticed that there was no present from Charlie or Kitashi.

"Oh wait!" Charlie smiled at me. "I seemed to have forgotten something."

I smiled back at him.

"Close your eyes," he said.

"Why?" I said. "Is it not wrapped?"

"I couldn't wrap it."

I closed my eyes and waited. Then, several people in the room started going, "aw!" and I was getting antsy. I felt something being placed on my lap and it started moving around. I opened my eyes and saw a very small puppy sitting on my thighs. It was a little Yorkshire Terrier with a pink bow in its hair.

"I heard that this breed is hypo-allergenic so I hope it won't make you sick or anything."

"Oh my God, Charlie! She's so cute! I've always wanted a puppy! What should I name her?"

"Whatever you want," Charlie smiled.

"Okay. How about Ziggy. After Ziggy Stardust."

"Isn't that a boy?" Andrew asked.

"True," I said. "Okay. What about Iggy?"

"Again, a boy name," Barney laughed.

"What about Jett?" Kitashi suggested. "Joan Jett is another singer you like so you should do that name."

"I like it," I picked up the puppy and looked at her. "I'll name her Jett."

I let Jett roam around the house and get used to everything while the rest of us played board games and listened to music for the rest of the night. It was all in all kind of a lame party if you think about it, but for not having an actual birthday party since I was four, it was pretty awesome. Several people planned on sleeping over and we were in our pajamas hanging out in the living room when Kitashi pulled me off to the side.

"I'm ready to give you your present now," he said.

I followed him up to his room and he shut the door behind us. The room was filled with white rose petals and lit candles surrounded us.

"Uh, Kitashi," I said. "This isn't what I think it is. Is it?"

"No," he smiled. "Sit down, please."

I sat down on the pillow that was placed in the middle of the floor and crossed my legs. Kitashi kneeled down in front of me, holding a small, jade box. He opened it and inside was a silver, heart-shaped locket. I reached out for it and opened the locket. There was nothing inside.

"I need to tell you something first," he said. "This was a gift from Susanne. She's had it since she was little and it's been in her family for a long time. It's very, very special. It shows you whoever you want it to, as long as they are still alive. Susanne didn't want it anymore after her husband passed away and she gave it to me. I had always hoped to see my family inside that locket but I never did, just like you won't be able to see your mom or uncle. Even before I met you, I would open the locket and see you. I'd always want to see the person who I'd end up falling in love with, and who would do the same with me. And it was always you, Avery. Susanne said she had seen me in the locket before she had found me too. I'm giving you this locket so hopefully you'll be able to find your dad. But on one condition."

"What?" I asked, speechless.

"Wait until after school is out for the summer."

"What? Why?"

"Because you need to focus on school and other things for you. For now, I will hold onto the locket so it doesn't distract you. The day school lets out though, I will give it to you and help you find your father."

"Thank you Kitashi. I really appreciate it."

I leaned forward and kissed him softly. Electricity shot through my body and I felt slightly light-headed. We pulled away and my cheeks felt warm.

"Sorry," I said. "I shouldn't have done that but-"

Kitashi kissed me again before I could finish my sentence. I didn't want him to ever let go.

"Happy birthday, Avery," he said after the kiss. "I hope I get to spend every other birthday with you from now on."

I smiled and we both went back down stairs with everyone. We all stayed up late and watched movies until one by one my friends started passing out from being tired. Surprisingly, Charlie and I were the last two awake.

"How about some coffee?" Charlie asked.

"Sounds good to me," I said, following him into the kitchen.

Charlie and I sat in silence while we drank our coffee. It was now about 5:30 in the morning and I was pretty sure this was the latest I'd ever seen Charlie stay up. Kitashi was asleep on the couch in the other room and I watched as his chest raised and lowered as he breathed. All I really wanted to do was to jump up from my chair and tell Charlie everything. I wanted someone outside the group to know that I was Dreamcatcher. I needed one person to talk to about my double life. I was scared though. I was scared that if one person knew about me, more people would find out and my life would become a living hell. I was also worried that if someone I cared about knew who I was, it'd put their life in danger. I glanced at Charlie and he gave me a kind smile. I smiled back and took a sip of my coffee. Charlie was the only family I had left, and we weren't even related. Charlie was the one person I always counted on no matter what.

"Charlie," I said, sitting my cup down.

"What is it, Avery?" he asked.

"I need to tell you something. Something really, really important. And I'm afraid you won't believe me. Or you will believe me and you'll be pissed. Or you won't be pissed but you won't understand and you'll freak out. But I really, really want to tell you. I just don't want you to be mad. And I know I probably shouldn't tell you because it's a really big secret, but I want you to know."

"Avery," he smiled again. "I've been around you your whole life. I know you pretty well by now. You think you really have that many secrets I don't already know about? Let's just say your secret is safe with me."

I smiled at him as we finished our coffee and watched the sun rise.